Paige + Faith

Hope you had a [?]
today at the confere[nce?]
Enjoy your journey thru

Sharel!

Andrea S   April 2014

MW01103482

Shard

Andreas Zimmermann

iUniverse, Inc.
Bloomington

Shard

Copyright © 2012 by Andreas Zimmermann

*All rights reserved. No part of this book may be used or reproduced by
any means, graphic, electronic, or mechanical, including photocopying,
recording, taping or by any information storage retrieval system
without the written permission of the publisher except in the case
of brief quotations embodied in critical articles and reviews.*

*This is a work of fiction. All of the characters, names, incidents,
organizations, and dialogue in this novel are either the products
of the author's imagination or are used fictitiously.*

iUniverse books may be ordered through booksellers or by contacting:

iUniverse
1663 Liberty Drive
Bloomington, IN 47403
www.iuniverse.com
1-800-Authors (1-800-288-4677)

*Because of the dynamic nature of the Internet, any web addresses or links
contained in this book may have changed since publication and may no longer be
valid. The views expressed in this work are solely those of the author and do not
necessarily reflect the views of the publisher, and the publisher hereby disclaims
any responsibility for them.*

*Any people depicted in stock imagery provided by Thinkstock are models,
and such images are being used for illustrative purposes only.*

Certain stock imagery © Thinkstock.

ISBN: 978-1-4620-8350-3 (sc)
ISBN: 978-1-4620-8352-7 (e)
ISBN: 978-1-4620-8351-0 (dj)

Library of Congress Control Number: 2011962917

Printed in the United States of America

iUniverse rev. date: 3/26/2012

Dedication

To Tracy and the kids,
Adalin, Johnathan, and Maria
for always believing in me.

This is for you.

Acknowledgements

THIS WORK WOULD NOT be complete without taking the time to acknowledge those that have helped me through this journey. It has been a long but enjoyable road. To the following people I give my sincere and deepest thanks for their work, help, support, love, understanding, patience, inspiration and sometimes a good swift kick to get me moving. To all of you, my heart cries with joy in knowing that you cared enough to help me with this. Thank you!

First and foremost, thanks need to be given to God, because He gave me the imagination I have been blessed with, and without Him I know this would not have been possible. Thank you for blessing me with the three children who are at the heart of this story, and for all of the special people in my life that are listed here.

Tracy, my wife and love, who has been and is everything to me: thank you for always being there to help in any way you can, even if it pushed us both out of our comfort zones. Rawr!

Adalin, Johnathan, and Maria, my amazing kids! You bring joy into my life in so many ways, and I look forward to having great adventures with you inside and outside of Shard.

Noel, our Min-Pin Chihuahua! She has given me endless love, puppy dog eyes, and snuggles, always reminding me of great things like joy, compassion and warm sunbeams.

Mike & Su, thank you for....everything! I am not sure how I could ever compile a list of all that you have done, do and continue to do for me. Your generous hearts, open arms and warm smiles have touched many. May you have thousands of blessings returned upon you for being such excellent people.

Mike & Brooke, the dearest of friends, you are absolutely priceless. For a writer, I don't have words to truly express my gratitude for having you in my life. Thank you for letting me lean on your strength in times when I had none, for endless debates that leave us all laughing, and for being a part of the family.

Thom, thank you for teaching me many years ago what I could do with my imagination by involving me in yours. You have been such an influential inspiration to me. Thank you for creating the great art work for this book.

Finally, to you, dear reader, for holding this book in your hands and reading these words; may they take you to another world where you can share in our adventures together. Thank you.

Additional Links

To see a full range of artwork created by Thom Childrey, the artist for this book, please visit www.thomchildrey.ca.

To see more information about the author, please visit the author's page at www.andreaszimmermann.ca.

Table of Contents

1   Awakening

THE FRONT DOOR BURST open and the three siblings crashed into the house. Freedom for the summer holidays was here at last!

"Mom! We're home!" Alex shouted happily, his grin stretching from ear to ear.

Alex and his brother and sister, Jared and Madison, kicked off shoes and tossed their backpacks to one side. The last day of school was finally over, and they were fully prepared to enjoy their summer break! All the way home, the three of them had talked about the movies, video games, bike rides, hiking and other adventures they would experience. What else could a twelve, ten and eight year old do?

"I think I know who just got home!"

They were expecting to hear the voice of their mom responding to them, not this deep baritone. All three kids looked up in time to see a tall man step around the wall from the kitchen, his arms opened wide. His hair and neatly trimmed beard were coloured red, and he had a strong, athletic build. The wide smile on his face beamed at the children.

"Uncle Richard!" All three exclaimed, making a beeline for him. Madison was a step behind the boys – her left shoe had gotten stuck and she was having trouble shaking it off.

Uncle Richard was an affectionate title; he wasn't actually a blood relative. He was a close friend and business partner of his parents and because of his friendly relationship with the whole family, the kids called him 'Uncle'.

Jared and Alex tumbled into Uncle Richard with the force of stampeding rhino's. Uncle Richard stumbled backward in mock agony, dropping to the ground and rolling backward as the boys attacked. The giggles started almost immediately as the tickle war began. Madison made it into the fray an instant later, jumping on top of all three of them with no plan in particular, other than to join the dog pile. Several minutes of guttural grunting, laughing and shouting ensued, and it was some time before Uncle Richard panted for the trio to stop.

"You're getting bigger and bigger all the time! I'm not sure I am going to be able to win next time!"

Jared's face was wild and he sported a large grin, obviously ready for more. His thick, dark and normally straight hair, which was a mirror of his mother's, now looked like a rats nest. His blue eyes twinkled merrily; he was the most physical of the siblings, for certain. "You didn't win this time! We pinned you and you know it!" he exclaimed.

"No, I don't think so. I distinctly remember you shouting for mercy several times." Uncle Richard replied, eyeing Jared carefully. Jared grinned harder and dove into Uncle Richard again. Jared was known to be relentless, a little tank that would never stop. Uncle Richard laughed and tickled Jared more, producing a large fit of laughter, collapsing Jared into a puddle of giggles on the floor.

"Alright kids, that's enough!" Mom called from the other end of the kitchen. "Richard only arrived a few minutes ago and hasn't even had a chance to sit down yet. Go put your things away and wash up before you come back to visit some more. And goodness, please all of you comb your hair! You all look homeless after that little wrestling match!"

All of the kids let out an "Awww" before complying with Mom's orders. Alex and Madison had matching dirty-blonde hair, Alex's cropped short and

Madison's long and flowing. Alex quickly passed a hand over his head and smoothed out the ruffles; Madison would need significantly more time and care to manage hers. The three kids obediently moved to the front door again to grab their belongings then passed through the kitchen to go downstairs to their rooms.

"Great kids, Lynn. I love 'em!" Richard said when the kids were out of sight.

Lynn put the tea down on the table, and the two of them poured and prepared their own cups while they talked.

"Thanks, Richard. Just, please, don't go and spoil them so horribly this time!" Lynn replied.

"Me? Not a chance!"

Lynn rolled her eyes, but stayed quiet.

"Come on, you know I don't spoil the kids!" Richard was doing his best to look innocent, but Lynn wasn't fooled for a moment.

"Yes, spoil the kids! You can't help yourself, I know, but it makes us feel horrible how you dote on them so!"

"Now, come on, buying each of them an iPod for Christmas is nothing special." Richard grinned impishly.

"It wasn't just the iPod's, Richard! You bought them all matching laptops to go with them…"

Richard shrugged. "They need to connect to iTunes as well."

"…*with* a Canada-wide roaming data plan connected…"

"Laptops are mobile! Internet connections should be too!"

"…and *then* a separate iPhone to go with it all?"

"It's annoying listening to music or using an App when the phone rings! Having both allows them to multi-task, that's all!"

Lynn threw her hands in the air and scowled. "Richard! The drum set for Jared, the electric guitar for Alex and the synthesized piano for Madison – it was a little much and you know it, not to mention the noise you created for us in the house, thanks very much. Eddie and I are afraid to buy them anything at all because you already give them so much!"

Richard waved his hands in defence. "I admit the instruments were simply part of a phase I was going through."

Lynn spoke from inside her mug as she sipped tea, her green eyes smiling at Richard. "Watching too much reality TV shows at the time?"

Richard grinned. "Something like that," he admitted. "Bottom line though is they're all just innocent little gifts, Lynn. You know, to be honest, I am surprised that you and Eddie don't do more for yourselves. You do own fifty percent shares in the company, you know. Frankly I'm surprised Eddie is still working at all – he should be retiring!"

Lynn smiled. "He says he's too young to retire fully. Thanks to you, and the gold mine, we've been richly blessed and we are looking at ways to use that money properly."

"I'd just be happy to see you use your money *at all*. I'd expected you to get a bigger house, at least, not to say there is anything wrong with this one of course."

Lynn shrugged. "This works because of how close we are to the schools for the kids. Besides, we live vicariously through you, Richard!"

Richard sipped his tea and looked out the porch screen door. "I just have... healthy spending habits," he conceded. "But I still maintain that I do not spoil the kids."

On cue, all three kids came bounding up the stairs, cheering and yelling for Richard to tell them what gifts he had brought for them. Richard sighed and looked at Lynn, who simply shook her head and glared as if to say, 'I told you so.'

And just as predictably, Uncle Richard did indeed have a present for them all.

"I found the perfect gift for you all while I was visiting in Brazil last month!" Richard's eyes lit up the room as his own excitement mounted. "A section of the mine turned out to have some old architecture buried there, so we have some archaeologists with us now. Our team found these at a dig site, and they gave them to me. Well, there were three of them, and so I thought it would be perfect that each of you rascals should get them!"

Richard got up from the table and grabbed a leather rucksack from the other baggage he had in the hallway. He turned to the three expectant kids and knelt down to be on their level. He had one hand thrust into the bag, and started the description of his gift before Lynn could intervene.

"Now, what I have here for you is something very special. Now I must warn you, they are delicate. That means they are breakable. And they are also very, very old."

All the kids sighed. This meant that whatever they were, they weren't toys and would be something that their mom would store away in a cabinet somewhere where everyone was allowed to look at them, but never allowed to touch.

"However," Richard announced, seeing their faces sink, "they are made partly of gold!"

This lifted their hearts a little – gold was always nice! Uncle Richard had brought some small gold shavings back for them all to look at, and they were incredibly pretty. They had reminded the kids of the shavings they had seen in the Thomas and the Magic Railroad movie.

"And they are also made of a crystal mineral that no one has seen before!" Richard enjoyed the drama that always built up to the unveiling of a present. The kids used to whine and moan, but they had grown used to his way of gift giving, and now stood patiently and expectantly like little soldiers, waiting for their drill sergeant to dismiss them.

"And they sparkle very brilliantly! You should have seen these little babies when we found them – covered in dirt and grime! We had some of our guy's wash them down, and now they practically come alive in the light! I hope you like them!"

He finished this last statement by producing a small bundle of tissue paper, which he handed to Alex. He produced a second and a third bundle, handing one each to Jared and Madison. The trio tore into the tissue, the excitement of opening the gifts consuming them, and soon the floor was littered with bits of paper. Shortly, three small sparkling treasures sat in their hands, and all three of the kids exclaimed their joy with 'oooh's' and 'aaah's'.

Each had a miniature dragon, standing in various poses. They all had a yellow underbelly, which was the main concentration of gold. The tops of each were a different color, Alex's a deep forest green, Jared's a fiery red, and Madison's was beautiful dark lavender. They could not even guess what the backsides were made of, except that it was some type of mineral rock, or crystal, or maybe even a gemstone. And did they ever sparkle! It seemed that each of the small dragons had a way of catching light and making it reflect back twice as bright as before!

The kids all turned their respective gift over and over, staring into the dazzling array of colors. Alex's green dragon was curled around a rock, seeming to be resting, but the eyes were open wide and alert. Jared's red was reared up on its hind legs and kicking the front two, much like a horse and knight in battle. Madison's light purple was simply standing on all fours, looking regal, the wings slightly unfurled. All of the dragon's eyes were a contrasting color to their bodies: the green dragon had orange eyes, the red dragon had light blue, and the lavender's eyes were a shiny yellow.

And the wings! Each had a resplendent pair of wings! They were paper thin, yet they were so hard! The colours all shimmered magically when the figurine was moved around in the light.

Each of the kids gave Uncle Richard a big hug and thanked him for the gifts. They then walked in a solemn procession, carrying their prize before them like royal jewellery. Richard smiled and began cleaning up the discarded tissue paper. He stood to walk to the garbage under the sink, but was stopped short by a furious looking mother.

"What on God's green earth ever possessed you to give the kids golden statues? Those relics were found in some ancient dig in the middle of nowhere, and should probably be overseen by the curator of a museum! Not to mention some unknown ancient curse you could have just cast over the kids by stealing these things from an unknown tomb and then giving it to them! What were you thinking? This isn't some little gift you gave them! The amount of gold and gemstone inlaid in those things is enough to pay for all of their education until the end of college! What were you thinking?"

Richard stumbled with his words, not having even thought of a single possible retaliation. He was saved from needing to reply by the front door bursting open, and Eddie yelling at the top of his lungs, "Honey, I'm home!"

The thunder of children pounding their feet and yelling joyous greetings echoed around the house. All three of the kids dove into their father in much the same way as they had with Uncle Richard. They rolled, twisted and laughed together until Dad gasped for breath and begged for the kids to stop. Richard handed the scraps of tissue to Lynn and feebly excused himself, making his way to the front door and out of harm's way. Lynn tossed the paper into the recycling bin and followed him into the front hall.

"Richard, great to see you!" Eddie cried from under a jumble of arms and legs and giggling bodies. Richard could just make out the spiky brown hair that was his friend in the throng. Eddie was about the same athletic build and height as Richard was, if only a little leaner. Eddie's hand reached out from in between kids to shake Richards hand in greeting. "How are you doing?"

"I'm excellent, Eddie!"

"Oh yes, *excellent*, aren't we?" Lynn added sarcastically.

Eddie widened his hazel eyes, exaggerating his expression. "Hi honey. So what did you get them this time, Rich?"

"You will never guess what *your friend* brought for the kids as a gift!" Hands on her hips, Lynn looked like she could stop a rampaging bull.

Eddie's grin grew larger as he looked to his friend's bearded face. "Whatever it is, it must be a fantastic gift! I haven't seen Lynn turn that sour since you bought all the kids the iPods at Christmas!"

Lynn was obviously upset, but she held it in.

The kids all started babbling about their gifts. Eddie caught snippets of information, something about gold, and green and red and purple colors, and claws and wings. By the jumbled description he assumed they had a pet, or perhaps three. They were talking about how the eyes were different colors, and that you could see your own reflection in them. By the time the descriptions had subsided, Lynn had left the room and was back in the kitchen cleaning up, the kids all making their way to their rooms to retrieve their new stone pets. Richard was suspiciously staying away from the kitchen.

His only hope was to get Eddie on his side, and that would allow the venting steam from Lynn to cool somewhat, or at the very least be transferred to Eddie instead.

The children brought their new treasures upstairs and showed them off. After examining them for only a minute or two, the dragons were returned to their special perches in the kid's rooms: Alex had his facing the sun on his windowsill, where the light could shine off of it, while the other two were on bookshelves.

Eddie agreed with Lynn that the gifts were simply too expensive to accept, but Richard answered honestly that he had never had them appraised, so as far as he was concerned they had no appreciable value. Eddie argued that the term priceless could apply, to which Richard agreed.

"That just means they have no listed price, therefore there is no monetary value. See? They're free!"

Eddie begrudgingly accepted, and Lynn only did so once Richard produced paperwork showing proper authority, claim, and transfer of ownership from the Brazilian Government, where the statues had been found.

Once the dragons were safe on their perches, everyone got ready for dinner. It was a custom with the friends to go out for dinner when Richard was in town, and tonight they had decided to go for BBQ Chicken.

Dinner went by with the usual conversation of where Uncle Richard had been, what he had been doing, and any exciting adventures he had. He always had a way of describing something as a heroic event, even though in reality he was walking across the street to buy a drink. He talked about travel, work and more travel. The kids listened, and were always fascinated by the talk of the caves and mines in Brazil.

When they arrived home everyone was so full there were no complaints at going straight to bed. Richard was especially tired from the long flight that day. He went to the spare room after hugging the kid's goodnight and promptly went to sleep.

After the kids were ready for bed, Mom and Dad appeared on cue to say goodnight and read a story. The children's rooms were situated in such a way that they all shared a bathroom, with Jared's room in the northwest corner of the basement making it central to the other two; Alex's room was the southwest corner of the basement, and Madison's took up a single section along the north wall. Jared's room was where everyone always met every night before bedtime for stories or songs, or sometimes simple conversation. It was Madison's turn to pick the story, and her choice was a short story from the Dragon Tales series. It had been some time since any of them had watched the cartoon on TV, although because of their most recent gifts she thought it was appropriate.

The story finished, they all went to their own respective rooms. There was bright moonlight shinning through the window, dazzling brightly as the dragon hide caught the moon's rays. They all always kept the bedroom and bathroom doors slightly ajar, so that the three of them could speak to each other once Mom and Dad had gone upstairs.

"They are really pretty, aren't they?" Madison called out in the darkness.

"Yup," Alex replied sleepily.

"I like my dragon the best," Jared said.

"Mine is the prettiest!" Madison replied.

"Mine is the strongest!" Jared cried out. There was silence for a moment. "Alex, what about you? What is yours?"

"The sleepiest; be quiet, go to sleep." Alex rolled over and covered his head with a spare pillow. He closed his eyes and relaxed, thankful the pillow would block any further discussion. He was so full from dinner that all his energy seemed to be used for digesting food. In moments he was asleep, not hearing his brother and sister still talking away about their dragons, and also not seeing his small green dragon slowly turn its neck, looking up out the window to stare longingly at the moon.

2   Family

THE FAMILY SPENT THE next day outside at the community park. Lynn packed a great picnic for everyone, with the kids' help. A pick-up game of baseball started just after lunch and lasted all afternoon. They all arrived home exhausted and dirty from running around the field all day.

Uncle Richard was taking them all out to dinner in a couple of hours, so everyone shuffled off to have showers and prepare for the night out. The three siblings went to their rooms, Jared sprinting to be first in the bathroom. He washed, dried off, dressed and made it back up to the kitchen before Madison had even begun her turn in the shower. With a towel around her head and her robe on, she called to Alex through his door that she was finished, and he could have the bathroom now.

Alex, however, was stunned and couldn't move. He had left his window shade open the whole day. He liked both the moonlight and sunlight filtering in, so his room was generally always bright. His intention had been to get clothes and towel, but had not been able to do either. For several minutes already he had been standing in place, staring across the room, completely awestruck.

There was a small green dragon sitting on the window sill, glinting brilliant colors in the sunlight, quietly staring back at Alex. Its little head bobbed a couple of times, and then it blinked. Alex got the distinct impression that it was waiting for him to do something. And Alex just didn't know what to do.

So he stood. And waited.

Alex felt somewhat like he did when he found a bee in the house: stand perfectly still in case the insect came at you. This was supposed to be a miniature statue – statues made of gold and mineral rock were not supposed to move!

Alex realized that he had been holding his breath, so he let it out and forced himself to breath slowly again. Somewhere in the back of his mind he recognized Madison's voice calling out to him. It was several more minutes before Alex snapped out of his stupor, hearing her voice a second time.

"How did you get it to move, Alex?"

Alex looked down to his right and saw his sister. She was wearing a white t-shirt and soft blue jogging pants, and still had her towel around her shoulders. He had no idea how long she had been standing there with him: he had lost all track of time. Slowly he looked back up to the dragon. It made a little squawking noise which sounded somewhat metallic, and echoed a little. It stretched its wings a little to angle them into the light, but didn't move from the window sill.

"Why doesn't it fly off from there?" Madison asked. "It's so pretty!" she added happily.

"I don't know why it doesn't move from there. Maybe it likes the heat from the sun." Alex started scanning around the room for a better heat source – the sun would soon be behind the fence in the back yard, and there would be no light left to filter in. "I think dragons like heat."

"How do you know that?" Madison asked, her eyes completely transfixed on the little green figure before her.

"Come on! I've read *The Hobbit*, and besides Mom and Dad have read us all sorts of stories. Dragons always sleep in caves and the caves are always hot. The poor little guy is probably freezing."

While Alex moved about the room looking for something to warm the dragon with, Madison stepped closer to the window. She started cooing to the little dragon, who's only response was to cock its head to the side in a very curious pose. Alex finally decided upon a thick sweater and moved to the window to place the sweater over top the dragon.

When the shadow passed over it, a great hiss sounded from its mouth, and a little green tongue shot out. Alex backed away immediately. The dragon immediately calmed as the light returned to its hide. Alex and Madison could have sworn it seemed to smile.

Madison shrugged. "Maybe it's allergic to cotton?"

Alex scowled at her. They both watched the amazing creature sparkle in the sunlight, until Alex's curiosity filled him completely and he tenderly reached out with one hand, his pointer finger extended.

"Alex, don't! It'll bite you!" Madison warned.

Alex hushed her, and then carefully extended his finger again. The little dragon snaked its head backwards and hissed lightly. Alex froze with his finger scant centimetres from the dragons head. It perked up and sniffed the finger tip, which was only slightly smaller than the dragon's head. The little tongue flicked out and touched Alex's finger, probing. The dragon apparently did not think the boy was a threat and resumed its sun bath. Alex slowly lowered his finger on the green neck and started to scratch. The little dragon seemed uncertain at first, but soon leaned into the pressure. Alex pressed harder, in longer strokes, careful not to block the sunlight. The dragon started making a fluttering sound that could only be the dragon equivalent to purring.

Madison joined in, rubbing the dragon's sides and belly. It started to growl, a faint purring growl that made both of the kids giggle. The dragon slowly rolled around onto its back, fully enjoying every moment of this massage. An abrupt call from upstairs snapped all three heads around, the dragon's head upside down and twisting to see what the disturbance was.

"Alex, Madison! Hurry up and get ready! Richard is taking us all out to dinner tonight, remember?"

"Ok!" Alex yelled in reply. He spun back to Madison. "Don't let anyone know about the dragon. We need to keep it quiet. And keep the window open for him!"

"Ok!" Madison said simply, and turned back to continue rubbing the little dragon. Alex ran into the bathroom, but was stopped short when Madison asked him a question. "Alex, why isn't my dragon alive?"

Alex blinked, and glanced into his brother's room while flicking on the light. The red dragon was in the same position it always was, completely unmoved. Looking into Madison's room, he saw the purple dragon there, too. It was still a big lump of rock with no sign of life.

"I don't know," he said truthfully. He looked back over at his little green dragon perched on the window sill. "That one is – maybe we can figure out what brought that one to life, and the others will come to life to!" He turned on the heat lamp and started the shower. He left the door partially open to the bathroom, just in case there was a problem with the dragon he would be able to hear. He rushed as quickly as he could through washing up, but there was so much dirt on him from playing baseball that he decided to wash twice to make sure he got all the grime out.

While Alex was washing, Madison got an idea about her own purple dragon. She left the room and went back to her own room. She turned on the lamp near her bed and started to talk with her dragon, just in case it was lonely and would wake up any moment.

The light from the sun faded behind the fence, and the little green dragon clawed a few times at the window pane. It scanned around the room and saw its rock perch it was resting on before. Then it swung its head in the direction of the bathroom. Making up its mind, it spread its wings and beat them a couple of times. Then it launched itself in the air, the wings snapping out to glide.

The descent to the ground was quicker than it thought – apparently the little dragon hadn't flown in a long time or had forgotten how, or it simply needed a lot more practice. It let out a little yelp as it hit the ground and skidded into a pile of toys. It shook a few blocks from the Lego set off and craned its head back up to look at the bathroom light. It rolled over and walked on all fours towards the bathroom. Pushing the door open further with its snout, the dragon entered and slipped a little on the linoleum floor, but managed to keep its footing until it was resting on Alex's shirt that had been tossed in the middle of the bathroom, directly under the heat lamp. It used its clawed feet to push the shirt into a more comfortable lump, and then circled about a few times before settling down.

Alex finished his shower and opened the glass door. He stepped out, narrowly missing the dragon, and retrieved his towel from the top of the toilet where he had placed it. When he turned around, he saw the dragon resting on his shirt and jumped. Recovering from his surprise, he draped the towel around his shoulders and bent down to examine the little creature. He rubbed its head a few more times, but was roused from his playing by another shout from upstairs.

Eddie leaned into the top of the stairway to shout, "Alex! Madison! Let's go!"

Alex ran into his room and hurriedly pulled on some clothes. He quickly combed his hair and brushed his teeth, then looked back down. The dragon hadn't moved, except that it was following Alex's every movement with its eyes. "You're probably hungry, aren't you?"

"What do dragons eat?" Madison asked. She was standing at the bathroom doorway to her bedroom, holding her own dragon in her hands. It was not moving.

"I don't know." Alex replied. He really had no idea at all. There were so many stories about dragons! All of them talked about dragons killing people and destroying towns, but none of them really said too much about the natural science of dragons. Of course, most of the stories mentioned them devouring sheep, cattle, people and anything else that got in there way, but how much of that could possibly be real? There was no definitive guide to the ecology of a dragon that Alex could think of. And this dragon was made out of some kind of rock…what did a rock dragon eat?

The little green dragon rested its head back down and went to sleep. Alex looked up at Madison and shrugged, just as their dad yelled at them from upstairs to hurry up.

Alex leaned out his bedroom door and hollered up the stairs. "Coming!"

"What do we do about your dragon?" Madison asked.

"I guess we can't worry about it now. Let's close the doors to the bathroom so that it doesn't get lost in the house. We can figure it out later."

"Ok," Madison said simply. She walked over and placed her purple dragon beside the green one. The green ones eye opened slightly and it made a little happy squealing sound that the kids could only assume was a greeting. "I'll leave Penelope here to keep him company."

Alex jolted to a stop and blinked. "Penelope?"

Madison stood up from placing her dragon on the ground. "Yup! Penelope the Purple Dragon!" She smiled like a beaming ray of sun and marched back into her room, explaining that she needed to get dressed properly for dinner. No one upstairs would be surprised though – Madison was known for dawdling.

"Where has Jared been all this time? I never saw him come down to get dressed." Alex asked.

"He finished up a long time ago. He ran back upstairs as soon as he was dressed." Madison replied while getting her arms and head lost inside a nice big purple shirt. Alex could see already she was getting a little carried away with the new "purple" theme. He glanced back into the bathroom where the dragon was sleeping. The purple one hadn't moved yet, and didn't look like it was about to anytime soon.

"Come on," he said, closing the bathroom doors. "We'll check on them later."

Madison climbed slowly up the stairs after her brother, fidgeting with her purple belt, her purple socks and purple shirt. She went immediately to Mom and asked if she could have a purple ribbon to put in her hair. Lynn laughed and agreed, finding a few different selections of ribbons, hairclips and other various accessories for Madison to choose from.

"That is a very purple outfit you have there, Madison," Uncle Richard commented when he came around the corner.

"Mmm, hmm!" Madison mumbled her affirmative through the hairclip in her mouth. After a few seconds she pulled it out with a free hand and continued. "Yes! I am going to be purple, just like my dragon!"

Uncle Richard smiled broadly and proudly. "Well, I am certainly glad that you like your present, Madison!"

"Yes! I love it! And maybe one day it will be big enough for me to ride on it!"

Madison was trying to keep still, but in her excitement was bouncing around a little. Lynn held her shoulders in place and warned her not to move unless she wanted to have scary Halloween hair. Madison stood stock still.

Uncle Richard made the suggestion that she should have a yellow belt instead of a purple one, so she could match her dragons golden belly. Madison's eyes went wide and she bolted down to her room again, frantically throwing clothing around looking for a yellow belt.

When Madison came back upstairs she was completely distraught: she didn't own a yellow belt! Lynn gave Richard a shot in the arm then led her daughter upstairs to find one from the parent's closet. Shortly after, a beaming girl and her yellow belt, yellow watch and a mix of yellow and purple glitter on her cheeks, was finally ready to go to dinner.

The group all finished getting coats and shoes on. It was still very warm out, but Calgary weather could change at any moment, so it was always good to be prepared. On their way out the door, Madison started asking Uncle Richard what dragons in Brazil ate, how big they grew, and what they might like to play with. Richard really didn't know how to reply, but said that tomorrow they might go to the library to research it a little bit. Madison certainly didn't seem satisfied with that response, but let it drop.

Richard was taking them to dinner to meet his girlfriend, whom he was picking up on the way to the restaurant. He got into the mini-van and waved before driving off. The rest of the family was driving down in the Jeep.

It was several minutes after they had left the house when Jared finally asked, "Dad, why is Uncle Richard taking the van, and not driving with us?"

"He needed the space in the van for luggage," Eddie replied.

"Dad, why is Uncle Richards's friend going to the restaurant with a bunch of luggage?"

Eddie laughed. "Lilly is getting picked up at the airport, Jared. She is moving to Calgary."

"Ooooh."

"Is she going to live with Uncle Richard?" Alex asked.

"I'm really not sure, Alex. Why don't you ask Uncle Richard when we get to the restaurant?"

"Edward!" Lynn exclaimed, smiling. "Alex you will do no such thing! Richard will introduce us to Lilly when they arrive, and that is that. I don't want any of you asking a bunch of prying questions tonight – and that especially goes for you, Eddie!" Lynn punctuated the last word by poking Eddie in the shoulder.

Eddie responded with a wide, extra-strength grin. "Lynn! I'm shocked! What would make you think I would *ever* do anything to embarrass my best friend?"

The kids all giggled in the back and their mother rolled her eyes.

Eddie looked around, pretending to be shocked. "What? You all laugh at me?" He turned slightly to look at all the kids when the car stopped at a red light. "Come on, kids! When have I ever done anything that was silly or mischievous?"

"Oh, dad, you do it all the time!" Alex laughed.

"You're doing it *now* Dad!" Jared roared.

Madison giggled loudly. "Daddy, you're silly."

The group made their way to dinner, the conversation revolving around whom the mysterious Lilly would be and what she would be like. For the time being, Alex and Madison had forgotten about dragons.

3   Discovery

LILLY, THE WHOLE FAMILY agreed, was a nice lady. Richard had only met her a few months previous, and it had been instant love. She had been working with the government in Toronto for several years, and had started looking for a transfer to Calgary after she had met Richard. The kids thought she was nice, although they didn't have much of a chance to talk with her because the adults were deeply into their conversation.

It was late when everyone got home. The kids said their goodnights and made their way downstairs with orders to brush their teeth and get to bed. Jared pulled his shirt off as he entered the bathroom, dropping it on top of the two dragon figures without noticing. He brushed his teeth and went back to his room to tuck himself into bed. Alex and Madison wandered around the clothing pile on their way to and from the bathroom, unconsciously stepping over or around it.

Shortly afterwards Mom and Dad showed up and tucked all the kids in, making sure they had all brushed their teeth and gotten into their pyjamas. It was a quick goodnight with no stories or songs, as Richard and Lilly were upstairs, and they didn't want to keep the guests waiting.

The kids were all quiet for a few minutes, not a sound coming from any of their rooms. Alex stared at the ceiling and thought about how full he was. Two nights in a row they had all gone out to dinner; tonight he was stuffed with pasta. He looked out his window and wondered what dragons might eat, or what he might eat if he was a dragon. Surely not spaghetti...

Wait! Dragons!

Alex had completely forgotten the little green dragon!

He sat bolt upright in bed and tossed his blankets off. He charged into the bathroom, wondering at his own forgetfulness. He flicked on the light and spied the pile of clothing, Jared's shirt on top. He pinched a corner of it with his fingers and flung it to one side where it thumped against the wall.

"What are you doing?" Jared called from the darkness of his room. The other doors were still closed, so the voice was muffled.

"Nothing," Alex replied unconsciously.

There in the middle of the floor were the little green and purple dragons, neither having moved since he saw them last. He glanced around the room. There was no broken glass, no scorch marks, no sign at all the dragons had even twitched. He stepped up right beside the dragons and started petting the green one, talking to it softly so that it would wake up.

The dragon didn't move. He pushed and poked and prodded. Nothing. The door to Madison's room swung open slowly. She looked in the room before entering, her eyes on her purple dragon. Jared's door opened and he stepped into the bathroom, blinking blearily into the light.

"What's going on?"

"Nothing, Jared," Alex replied, still not taking his eyes off the green dragon.

"Why isn't he moving?" Madison asked.

"Duh," Jared said teasingly, "it's a piece of tin! Of course it doesn't move!"

"It's not tin, it's gold!" Madison exclaimed. She bent over to pick up her purple dragon. "And Penelope didn't move yet, but Alex's did!"

Jared looked down at the little green dragon with new interest. "Really?"

They all waited a few moments as Alex picked up the green dragon and held it up. It was solid, hard as rock, and completely rigid.

Jared smiled. "Yeah, right! You guys are pulling my leg!" Jared stood up and walked back to his bedroom.

"It really *was* moving, Jared!" Madison called after him.

"Uh huh," Jared mumbled as he crawled back into bed.

Alex cradled the green dragon in his arms and walked back to his room, returning the figurine to the window sill. "It's ok, Madison. Jared will just have to see it to believe it."

He tried to place the dragon back on the small rock it had been perched on before, but it didn't fit right. Not only was the dragon curled in a different position than it was before, but the rock it had been resting on was also a different shape now. Alex couldn't figure out why.

Madison put Penelope back on the shelf in her room. "Do you think Penelope will come alive tomorrow?" she asked.

"Oh, yes," Jared laughed from his bed, "it will be swooping loop-de-loops as it flies around, too! We can start a dragon circus!"

Alex propped himself up on his pillow, staring at the silhouette of the dragon against the dim light outside his window. "I don't know. We're not even sure how this one came alive, how are we supposed to know how to make the others move?"

"Maybe we need to give them some sunlight – your dragon liked it in your window," Madison observed.

Alex thought about that, and looked back up at his window. It was dark tonight. The moon was still fairly bright, but there was a lot of cloud cover. There was barely enough light to outline the window, let alone actually shine anything through.

Several minutes passed while Alex stared at the little dragon in the dim light. Did they imagine the movement of the dragon today? He reached his hand up above his head to touch the green dragon again, feeling safety in the assurance that it was still there. Satisfied, he drifted off to sleep.

Mom and Dad were leaving the next morning for most of the day. They were heading out with Richard and Lilly to look at houses. This left Alex in charge at home. He was twelve years old now, and had completed his Babysitters Course a few weeks before school ended. If Alex needed anything, there was a piece of paper with his parent's cell numbers written on them attached to the front of the fridge.

The adults all left immediately after breakfast, saying half a dozen reminders to the kids to be good, brush their teeth after they ate, listen to your older brother, and so on.

As soon as the car pulled out of the driveway, Alex and Madison were racing down the stairs. Jared was still in the living room, the TV blasting loud cartoons while Jared munched on his cereal. He ignored his siblings as they came back upstairs, their dragons in their hands. They each had their shoes on and were heading out the back door.

Madison led the way outside. The two of them walked across the wide back porch and sat down at the table. They placed their dragons on the glass table top and stared. Alex put the green dragon down beside the deformed rock perch and studied the two of them. Madison seemed to notice the rock for the first time and stared at it as well.

"Why isn't the dragon on the rock?" she asked.

Alex shrugged. He didn't like not knowing the answers to all these questions, but he was excited about finding out. "It wouldn't fit. I don't know if it fell asleep in the wrong position, or what. But he doesn't fit on there anymore."

"How do you know it's a 'he'?" Madison asked.

"Uhh....I don't!" he admitted.

They rested their chins down on the table to be eye-level with the dragons, and waited. The budding morning sunshine sparkled on the dragons' backs. The purple hide threw sparkling colors of pinks, purples and blues, while green dragon's hide shone green with dazzling flecks of gold mixed in. The sun slowly came up over the trees and shone brightly down on the back yard. Alex picked up the rock and started examining it more closely in the bright light.

"Looks funny, doesn't it?" Madison asked.

Alex nodded. "Yup." He turned it over in his hands a few times. "It looks like it's smaller than it was before."

Madison scrunched up her face in thought. "How does a rock get smaller?"

"It could have broken, but I didn't see any other pieces of rock around my shelf."

"Maybe it ate some of it." Madison offered. "What kind of rock is it?"

"I think it might be granite," Alex said, peering closely at the rock and rubbing his finger on it. It was a dark coloured rock with flecks of white in it. He put the rock back on the table near his dragon then settled in to wait.

A few minutes later they were both surprised by a little crackling sound. The green dragons neck twisted a little. Slowly, ever so slowly, its head turned from side to side. It looked almost as if it was shaking off an invisible layer of ice. First the head and neck, then the legs and wings, and finally the body moved. It stretched and they could hear more cracking and creaking sounds.

"It sounds like all of its bones are cracking." Alex mused.

"He needs a Chiropractor!" Madison giggled

The two of them got closer to the green dragon and watched. It reared up on its hind legs and stretched its wings out to full span, which was impressive despite its overall small size. They got the impression that it was smiling at them. The green dragon walked forward slightly and nudged the rock with its nose. It started to sniff the stone, and then flicked it with its tongue a few times. It walked around the rock once or twice, examining it with an expert eye. Finally it sauntered up close to the rock and furled its wing around itself slightly, as if giving itself some privacy.

And then it took a big bite out of the rock!

Alex and Madison exchanged puzzled and excited glances as they watched the dragon eat. It was eating stone! They could hardly believe it!

"Told ya!" Madison whispered.

The tiny green dragon used powerful jaws to tear a chunk of the rock off, and sat there happily munching away. After crunching and munching away for a minute or so, it swallowed and then started working at another bite. After its third bite, the dragon pushed the remainder of the stone away. It snorted as it walked around the table top, picking up crumbs of rock dust with its tongue. Satisfied, the dragon sat back on its haunches and spread its wings out low over the tabletop. Alex knew what this was all about – time for a sunbath!

"Why won't Penelope move?" Madison whined.

Alex felt so bad for his sister. "I don't know, Madison. Maybe....maybe this is the only one that was really alive. Maybe the other ones really are just gold and stone."

"It's not fair!" Madison shouted, folding her arms in front of her. "You always get all the fun toys! Why can't I have the live dragon?" Madison's eyes began welling up with tears.

Alex was about to console her, when they both heard a small popping sound. They looked back to the table and saw the little purple head of Penelope slowly pull itself up. The same crackling and creaking sound accompanied the dragon as it, too, looked as if it was shedding an invisible layer of ice from around its body. Penelope was moving very slowly, far slower than the green had moved, and it took several minutes for her to start shaking her body out and fan her wings.

They watched as Penelope stretched. She looked like she had woken up from a very long sleep, her eyes blinking sleepily in the sunlight. She even used a front foot to rub and claw at her eyes. Neither of the kids was sure how long they waited. They would have stayed and watched all day without ever noticing the passing of time, so enchanted were they by the sight of the two wonderful creatures.

Testing the glass surface as she walked about, Penelope was unsure of her footing at first. The green dragon moved closer and hissed at her, but it didn't seem aggressive. More like a greeting. Penelope turned and wandered over to the green dragon, and the two of them bumped their heads together lightly. Alex and Madison both giggled. At the sound of their voices, Penelope looked up. Madison reached out to pet Penelope, but the little dragon suddenly backed away, hiding behind the green. Madison was hurt, and very upset.

"Please, Penelope. It's ok! I won't hurt you!"

Penelope glared at Madison with a short hiss. Madison tried to reach out to her again, but the purple dragon moved further behind the green, keeping an obstacle always between her and the human children. The green dragon made a strange growling sound, then turned back to look at Alex. Alex wasn't sure what to do, so he stuck his hand out to the green dragon and rubbed its neck. The green dragon leaned into the pressure of Alex's finger as it had before, and Alex gave his dragon a good rubbing. Penelope watched this for a few moments, while Madison put her hand out on the table and waited. The green dragon looked at Penelope and made the same growling sound it had done before. Slowly, carefully, Penelope took small steps towards Madison. Madison remained patient despite the growing ache she had inside. Some friends had told her once that when you held a hand out for a dog to sniff you, you should leave your hand there and give the dog the chance to accept you first – move too quickly, and the dog would get scared. She was hoping the same thing applied here, but was biting her lower lip and fighting back tears in her painful anticipation!

At a mid point towards Madison's hand, Penelope turned again and made a hiss. The green dragon replied with a hiss of its own, and fanned its wings out in pleasure. It pushed hard into Alex's hand, demanding a deeper massage. Alex happily obliged, scratching behind the neck and shoulders. Penelope turned back to face Madison and took the last few steps towards her.

"That's right, I won't hurt you, Penelope!" Madison coaxed the dragon ever closer, finally placing her finger on Penelope's head. There were several seconds when Madison began rubbing Penelope's head and neck where Penelope sat unmoving with her eyes wide open. After several good rubs, Madison afraid the dragon didn't like being touched, Penelope suddenly closed her eyes and stepped right to the edge of the table, making the odd little growling purr that the green dragon had started.

"Alex!" Madison cried out in a whisper. "Look! Penelope likes it!" Alex smiled at his sister, while Madison started to cry with joy. She ignored the tears spilling down her cheeks.

"Isn't this great?" Alex exclaimed.

The massage lasted several minutes, when finally the green dragon appeared to have enough. It moved forward and grabbed the stone it had eaten from and dragged it over to Penelope. Penelope opened an eye as the green dragon got near and suddenly pounced on the stone. Penelope tore a big chunk out of the rock and started chewing.

"I suppose I need to give the green dragon a name, don't I?" Alex asked to no one in particular.

"How about Gretchen?" Madison inquired.

"No!" Alex moaned. "That's a girl's name. This dragon is a *boy*!"

"You don't know that for sure. It *could* be a girl dragon. How do you know? Gretchen could work."

"Not happening. I need to find a boy name for him."

Madison shrugged and looked back at Penelope. She was finishing off some of the stone, leaving only a small chunk left over. She sat back after finishing her snack and spread her wings, soaking up the strong rays from the sun.

"I wonder why they like the sun so much," Madison pondered.

Alex thought about that for a moment. "Well, I don't think it is the heat. It's fairly warm in the house, and they didn't start moving around until they were in the sunlight. I think maybe they need the sun for energy."

"Oh, kind of like plants."

"Maybe," Alex said. "Or maybe it is something more than that. I wish they could talk, and then we would know for sure."

"Do you think they are thirsty?" Madison asked. "Plants need the sun *and* water. Maybe dragons need water too."

Alex didn't know if they did or not, but he thought it was worth a shot. He got up from the table and walked into the house. No sooner had he done so then the green dragon started making a sound, a strange sound that was almost like a mix of a puppy whining and a bird chirping. Alex stopped part way through the screen door, and looked back. The green was practically begging now, and leaning over the edge of the table. Alex walked back and sat down again.

"It's ok little guy, I'll be right back...hey!" Alex gave a shout as the dragon suddenly jumped onto his chest, grabbing onto the shirt with its claws. The dragon climbed up onto Alex's right shoulder and waited. Madison laughed.

"You look like a pirate now!" Madison burst into giggles that she could not contain.

Alex stood up and was impressed that his dragon stayed on his shoulder without much difficulty. He walked into the house and found a bowl from the cupboard, then filled it with water from the sink. Then he took the bowl back outside and placed it on the table. He grabbed the dragon from his shoulder and placed it back on the table near the bowl of water. Both dragons eagerly stuck their faces in completely and started drinking.

Alex sat back, tapping his finger on his chin. "I just can't think of a name for him, and no, I am not calling him Polly."

Madison laughed again. "But it was *so* cute, Alex! He sat on your shoulder perfectly! You could get an eye patch and everything!"

"No!" Alex said forcefully, although he couldn't contain his smile and laughter. It was kind of funny having a miniature dragon on the shoulder of a pirate instead of a parrot. He thought about it only briefly but immediately shook his head. No, Polly was definitely not a good name for a dragon.

Some movement from inside the house startled all four of them. It was Jared coming to investigate.

"Hey, loser babysitter brother, what's for lunch? I'm hungry......whoa!" Jared's statement turned into a shout of astonishment. He stared at the table, hands raised instinctively, spying two dragons with their faces fully in the water bowl. The green one pulled his head out right on cue and grinned at Jared.

"What….wha….how…?" Jared stammered. He pointed feebly at the table, Alex and Madison certain Jared was about to pass out.

"We tried to tell you last night, but you didn't believe us!" Madison stated indignantly.

"Yeah," Alex agreed, "told you so."

Jared was quiet for several heartbeats. His voice was barely a whisper when he found it again. "How did you make them come alive?"

Alex looked back at the table. "Well, we think it has something to do with sunlight. Both of them seem to get power or charged from the sun, so…."

He didn't get to finish any more than that. Jared was inside, thundering down the stairs to his room, and they were pretty sure he had tripped at least once in his haste. Alex and Madison could clearly hear the bedroom door fly open and a couple of toys get kicked out of the way. Something fell and hit the drum set, and then there was the pounding of feet as he came sprinting back up the stairs. A few seconds later and the red dragon was sitting proudly on the tabletop, Jared breathless and panting.

"Ok, it's in the sun. Now what?" Jared demanded.

"Uh…I don't know," Alex mumbled.

Jared scowled at him, clearly disappointed. He started poking the red dragon to try and force it to move. "Well what happened to make yours come to life?" Jared yelled.

Madison lurched across the table and grabbed Jared's hand, shoving his arm away from the table. "Stop that! You'll make it angry! You just have to wait like we did. It took a while before they started moving – it wasn't automatic, you know!"

Jared sighed deeply. He focused on the brilliant red statue, once in a while casting a glance at the other two on the table. They had finished their drink of water, which Alex noticed had now left the bowl mostly empty. He grabbed the bowl and was about to go refill it, when he looked down at the green dragon and whistled, pointing to his shoulder. The green dragon happily obliged and hopped up onto Alex again, going for the ride back into the kitchen.

Jared whined out loud after watching the green dragon hop around on Alex's shoulders. He punched his own leg several times in frustration and impatience. He focused intensely on his red dragon and started to murmur under his breath. Madison couldn't hear him, but she was sure that he was probably speaking to his dragon to make it wake up, or praying to God for a miracle, or maybe both.

Alex returned with a fresh bowl of water and placed it on the table. His green dragon didn't take anymore, but Penelope did. Not as much as she had the first time around, but still several good swallows.

"Kishar," Alex announced unexpectedly.

"What?" Madison replied, confused.

"Kishar," Alex repeated. "That will be my dragon's name. I don't remember exactly what it means, but it was a name that I remember from school. We were studying Biblical and Historical Mythology, and the name Kishar was one of the dragons in the stories. I like the name, so his name will be Kishar!"

Madison shrugged. "Ok. Hi Kishar, I'm Madison." She reached out and rubbed Kishar's side.

It was getting hot outside. Alex walked to the doorway and looked inside at the clock. It was ten minutes to noon! They had been out all morning! Where did the time go? He stepped back outside and sat back down at the table. Kishar jumped down into his lap and started nipping at his fingers.

"So, you want to play, do you?" Alex started using his hand to jab at the dragon's side, much like he would with a dog. Kishar responded by biting at his hand, but never hard enough to truly hurt.

Penelope followed suit and crawled down to Madison's lap. She didn't play, however. Both of them were content to sit together and soak up the sun. Madison flipped the bar on the side of the chair so that she could rest back more comfortably. Penelope responded by moving up a little further onto Madison's belly and lying down, eyes already half closed.

Nearly fifteen minutes passed with Jared staring intently at his dragon, Alex playing with Kishar, and Madison sleeping with Penelope. At almost the same moment, as if on cue, Kishar and Penelope suddenly looked back to the tabletop. They both hopped up onto the table, using a slight flap from their wings to aid their jump. Both of them scampered across the glass table and took up positions on either side of the red dragon. Madison set her chair back upright, and all three kids leaned in closer to watch.

Penelope sniffed and then flicked her tongue out to lick the red dragon. Kishar sniffed once and then prodded the red one with his nose. The red dragon shifted its weight slightly, and then suddenly collapsed down on all fours. The sudden movement startled all the kids. It appeared to them that the red dragon had probably been awake for sometime already, but refusing to move until it was safe. The red dragon looked around menacingly, puffing up its chest and trying to look bigger than it was. It jumped back and made a little roar, sounding for all its brave posturing like a miniature lion.

"He's cute," said Madison.

"He's noisy," said Alex.

"He's awesome," breathed Jared. Never in his life had he seen such a cool pet as this one. "I'm gonna call him Rex."

Both Alex and Madison echoed the same puzzled response. "Rex?"

"Yeah!" Jared exclaimed. "Like a T-Rex, you know? Terrible lizard, strongest of all the dinosaurs, a holy terror that can wreak havoc anywhere it goes...?"

Rex seemed to like the title, and stood taller and, if it was possible, more proud then before.

Both purple and green dragons exchanged hisses and growls, which the kids were beginning to understand was them speaking to each other. Rex then boldly walked the few paces over to Jared so they stood nose to nose. Jared dared not move lest he scare Rex away. Rex sniffed a few times, and then head butted Jared in the nose. Jared was startled, but he simply laughed. Rex, having established who his owner was – or maybe whom he owned – turned around and marched straight over to the stone on the table. He chewed noisily at it, leaving crumbs everywhere. Penelope made her way back to Madison, while Kishar stopped and cleaned up the crumbs of stone. Rex, once finished gobbling down the remainder of the rock in several quick, decisive bites, wandered over to the water bowl and dunked his head right in. The kids all watched as the water level dropped rapidly. Rex didn't stop until the entire bowl was empty. Then Rex stomped back to where Jared was still sitting in awe. Rex turned sideways to spread his wings wide in the sunlight, and then looked up at Jared expectantly.

Jared looked confused, and a little worried.

Rex growled.

"I think he wants you to rub him down," Alex offered. Jared looked down at Rex and put his hand on him. He started to rub him down, using his fingers to massage the rough red stone and gold body. Jared continued the massage for a minute or so, and then got an idea. Without a word he bolted into the house, the sounds of his rummaging in the kitchen clearly heard outside.

"What on earth is he doing?"

Madison's only reply to Alex was to shrug. Rex started to stamp the table madly, obviously upset that his massage had ended so soon. Jared finally emerged from the house and scrambled back over to his chair. Rex hissed and growled a couple of times and then stood still, expectantly awaiting more rubbing. Jared complied, but this time he used a small brush. Rex practically glowed with satisfaction.

"Hey, that mom's cleaning brush," Alex said. "It's for silver and all her special metals and jewellery and stuff. You can't use that!"

"Why not?" Jared replied. "He's made of gold, and gems and special metals… it's only fitting that I use it."

Alex was about to respond, but he couldn't refute Jared's logic. The brush he was using was the same one that mom and dad used for cleaning silver, brass, and other delicate items around the house. A small gold and crystal dragon could probably qualify as a small, delicate item, couldn't it?

Rex purred loudly, and they all noticed that he began to shine a little more than before. The brush was certainly helping!

"I've been thinking about how they came alive." Alex said. "It has got to be something with the sun. They collect energy from it."

"Just like plants!" Madison continued.

"That doesn't really make sense," Jared said. "After all, if they got all their energy from the sun, why do they need to eat rocks and drink water?"

"Plants do the same thing, too," Madison said.

"Yeah, I suppose," Jared replied. "But why only now? Why didn't they wake up in Brazil when Uncle Richard found them?"

"They were underground," Alex stated matter-of-factly. "The archaeologists probably cleaned them off and put them into boxes before they ever saw daylight. My guess is that Uncle Richard never took them out again until he gave them to us.

"But these dragons are definitely not plants," Alex said. "They are not really animals, either. They look like they are made of some kind of rock, and I don't know any animal that is made of rock."

"Maybe it isn't actually rock," Jared thought out loud. "Maybe its bone, kind of like a rhinoceros horn."

"There really isn't any way to tell, is there? I mean, it's not like we can turn on the TV and check out the Discovery Channel for a series about dragons."

Madison and Jared silently nodded their heads in agreement. All three of them watched as their respective dragons curled into various resting positions and closed their eyes.

"How come they don't have any ears?" Madison asked suddenly. The boys both looked more closely at their pets.

"They do," Alex said, pointing at Kishar, "see? There is a little bump here, and there is a tiny little hole there. I think these are the ears."

"Cool." Jared said, and he softly rubbed Rex's head. Rex seemed to smile, one tooth on the lower left side poking out over the lip.

"I wonder if there are any books about them?" Madison asked. Both her brothers just laughed. "Uncle Richard said we could go to the library and read up on what dragons eat, don't you remember? Maybe there is a book on how to take care of a dragon."

The brothers both laughed, and Alex responded first. "I don't think so, Madison."

"Yeah, you can find books on puppies, and fish, and cats, and all sorts of pets, but I don't there is any such thing as a book on 'How to Raise a Dragon'."

"Why not?" Madison pressed further.

Jared rolled his eyes. "Be-*cause*," he said, exasperated, "dragons haven't been around for hundreds and hundreds of years!"

"If they were ever really around at all," Alex added.

"Exactly!" Jared finished. "Dragons have never been proven to even exist, so how could there be a book on how to raise them?"

Madison smiled. "Well," she began, "*these* dragons certainly exist, and are very much real. Who's to say that their great great grandparents didn't live hundreds of years ago? *Someone* would have had to take care of them, wouldn't they?"

The boys looked at each other and then back to table. The three dragons certainly were real enough, so Madison had to be right! Someone had to have written something about dragons at some point in time!

"Ok, we're supposed to stay home until mom and dad get back. Maybe we can get Uncle Richard to take us to the library tomorrow. Until then, we can see what we can find on the Internet."

"Good idea!" Jared exclaimed, already hopping up from his chair and dashing for the screen door. Rex glanced up, saw Jared enter the house, and started keening. Jared poked his head back out the door and looked at the red dragon. He stepped back outside a little ways and said, "It's ok, I'll just be in the house, Rex. You stay here and enjoy the sun, ok?" Rex gave one final little grunt, but finally rested his head back down. Alex and Madison both noticed his eyes did not close this time. They were staring intently at the door.

"Interesting," Alex said.

"It's ok; I'll stay out here with them all. You can go look on the Internet with Jared."

"Ok," Alex replied, and started into the house. Kishar immediately stood up on all fours and made the same keening sound Rex had. Rex's head snapped up and started looking at the door.

"It's ok, Kishar, you stay here with the others," Alex said. Kishar growled again, and suddenly his wings snapped out to either side as he leaped off the table. He flapped only twice and landed gracefully on Alex's shoulder.

Madison giggled. "Polly wants to go with the Captain," she laughed.

Alex glared at his sister. "His name is Kishar, not Polly!"

Madison laughed again, and then went back to talking and playing with Penelope. Rex, on the other hand, took Kishar's flight as a sign, and spread his own wings. He launched off the table and soared through the open screen door, calling out in short little growls. Alex called out to Jared, and upon Jared's reply, Rex suddenly banked in the air and made a beeline down the hallway to the computer room. Rex zoomed in the door and landed on the desk beside Jared, curled up, and went back to sleep. Jared was startled to say the least, but accepted the company and continued his search on the Internet. Alex entered the room shortly thereafter and turned on his own computer, Kishar still happily clutching Alex's shoulder.

The afternoon wore on with Madison alternating between playing and napping with Penelope outside, and the boys on their computers, searching for anything they could find about the proper care of dragons.

4   Chores

"**N**OTHING."

Alex and Jared had spent the entire afternoon searching for any information they could on dragons. How to care for them, feed them, bathe them or any tips on dragon care. Sure there were websites, but they all were based on fictional stories, like *The Hobbit*, or the movie *How to Train Your Dragon*, but these didn't offer any solid advice, and none of the dragon descriptions matched those of the three living ones they had with them.

They were stumped.

Madison had spent the entire afternoon outside, playing with Penelope. After Penelope had napped and sun bathed, they moved into a corner of the garden where it was just dirt and started building a miniature town. Madison was using pebbles and rocks she found around the yard as buildings, and was using a small rolling pin to make roads. Penelope wasn't much help – she kept eating little pebbles that seemed to appear appetizing to her, and stomped around in the small dirt town, flattening all the work Madison had done. It took some time for Madison to explain what she was trying to do. Penelope understood eventually, and started hopping around the yard gathering small stones to use in construction.

Kishar and Rex had been asleep all afternoon, and had stubbornly refused to leave the boys' sides. Not that either Jared or Alex had noticed – they were so intent on their Internet research. The boys would look up once in a while and compare the dragons with pictures they saw on the screens, but other than that the dragons both had curled up and slept.

Madison had come inside briefly at one point and grabbed a snack from the kitchen, and then immediately went outside again. The boys had completely forgotten to eat at all.

It was already nearing dinner time when they heard the front door open up. Alex and Jared both yelled out a hello from the computer room and continued staring at their computer screens.

"Hello, boys!" Dad called from the front doorway. They could hear Mom and Dad taking their shoes and coats off and making their way into the house. The boys could hear the sound of grocery bags being placed on counter tops. It was several minutes before Dad appeared in the doorway to the computer room. He leaned against the doorframe and folded his arms, looking stern and mocking at the same time.

"So, too busy playing games to come and say hi to Mom and Dad, huh?"

"We're not playing games," Alex started.

"Yeah, we're researching dragons," Jared finished.

"Oh?" Eddie moved a little closer and peered at the screens. "What are you looking for?"

"Anything we can find – what they eat, their sleeping habits, anything at all. We want to make sure we raise our dragons properly!" Jared beamed up at his father proudly. Eddie smiled and tousled his son's hair.

"Don't dragons eat people?"

"Daaad!" Alex rolled his eyes as he spoke.

"No, they eat rocks!" Jared exclaimed happily.

"Rocks, huh?" Eddie questioned. "Not a very exciting diet."

"Well we haven't seen them eat anything else, just rocks. And they really like the sun." Jared was beaming proudly.

"So what else have you learned from the Internet?"

Jared spun around in his chair. "Oh, that wasn't from the Internet – that was from watching Rex and Kishar and Penelope. They were all sunbathing today, and each of them ate rocks! It was really cool!"

Eddie looked confused, trying to piece together the information. Jared continued to talk as he turned back to the computer and started closing all the search windows he had open.

"And then I rubbed Rex down with the brush – oh, sorry, I used the brush from Mom's silver shining kit on Rex and I forgot to put it away. But Rex really loved it, and then I came in here and Rex flew into the room after me and curled up to sleep! He's really awesome, Dad!"

Jared finished closing up his windows on the computer, and then powered it off.

Eddie laughed. "Sounds like you all had a busy afternoon! And I am glad you like your dragons that much."

"Yeah, they're awesome!" Alex said. He was in the process of shutting his computer off as well. "Maybe we can go to the library tomorrow and find a book on how to care for them. What do you think Dad?"

"I don't think you are going to find any books on dragon care, boys. But maybe we'll pick one up on how to take care of jewellery or antiques or something. That would probably be better."

"Dad, our dragons aren't jewellery – they're real!"

"Yeah, and they fly on their own, Dad!" Jared finished.

Eddie stared at the two boys for several seconds, and then laughed out loud. "Ok, fine. I'll play along." He stepped forward and started rubbing Rex. "Hello, little dragon, how are you today?"

Alex and Jared held their breath. Rex wasn't the easiest-going of the three dragons, and they were certain he was going to bite their father's finger off with all the poking and prodding he was doing.

Nothing happened.

Eddie picked up the red dragon in his hands and turned to Jared. He tossed the dragon in the air a couple of times and smiled. Rex didn't move. "See, boys? Gold. Solid lump of rock or gemstone, or whatever these things are made out of. Not alive. I really appreciate your sense of humour and imagination, though!" Eddie finished off by handing the little red dragon back to Jared. Then he continued talking over his shoulder as he left the room. "Now please come to the kitchen and help us with the groceries. We'd like to start cooking dinner soon. You two can put the groceries away and set the table please."

Jared and Alex both stared at their father's back, then turned to poke Rex. No movement. No movement from Kishar, either.

"What happened?" Jared asked. He was hurt and confused.

Alex put his face in his hands. "Sunlight," Alex said flatly. "We've had them inside with us all day. They haven't had any sunlight to keep them charged!"

Alex paced the room as he worked out the system that the dragons seemed to operate under. "Look. We had them outside this morning, and they started moving around. Around lunchtime, you and I came inside and the dragons followed. They haven't been back in the sunlight since. They work like batteries, solar-powered! The longer they stay in the light, the more of a charge they can keep up!"

Jared looked back down to his little Rex. He was completely crestfallen. Even if they put the dragons outside right now, it was late in the day. They might not have enough sunlight to get them going again – they would have to wait until morning.

"Boys! Come and help! Hurry up!"

"Dad's calling," Alex pouted.

The boys picked up their dragons and carried them to the kitchen. There was a flurry of grocery bags and assorted food all over the kitchen table and counter. Mom was in the fridge making space, and Dad was standing on a chair in the pantry, organizing something on the top shelf. He glanced down as the boys wandered in.

"What's the matter with you two? You look like you're walking a funeral march."

Lynn looked up from her work in the fridge. Jared looked almost in tears, while Alex seemed overcome by a deep melancholy. "Oh, my boys," Lynn opened her arms wide and took them in. "Whatever is the matter? You two look horrible."

Jared couldn't hold it anymore. "We had our dragons with us today and they were alive and then we brought them inside and then forgot that they needed sunlight and even though we gave them water and rocks but then they stopped moving and Dad thinks we're lying about the dragons but we're horrible parents to them 'cause we forgot the sunlight!" He was wobbling back and forth over the verge of tears.

Lynn really didn't understand everything that was said, but she did pick up on one part of the babble. She looked pointedly at her husband. "Eddie, what did you do?"

Eddie stepped down from the chair and gaped. "Me? Wha...I...I didn't do anything!"

"He said that you thought they were lying. What did you think they were lying about?"

Eddie blinked, trying to remember when he had accused either of the boys.

Lynn waved Eddie off. "Oh, Jared, here. Have a tissue to wipe your eyes and take a few deep breaths. When your calm, tell us what happened."

"He did tell you what happened," Alex said. Both parents looked at their son expectantly. There was silence for two breaths before Alex realized they were both waiting for him to continue. "Uh, we had the dragons outside today. But they aren't alive anymore because we only had them outside for a couple hours, and we think they need sunlight like plants or a solar panel does, in order to get energy."

The silence deepened. Lynn and Eddie stared at their sons for a moment, then back at each other. Then they both laughed.

Lynn returned to her work in the fridge. "Sorry, honey. I thought you were being serious at first."

"Great imaginations, kids. Y'know, Lynn, they were even on the computers doing research about the dragons. Pretty convincing."

Eddie put the chair back at the table and returned to the pantry to finish organizing the shelves. Lynn poked her head out and saw that neither son had moved yet.

"Oh, come on, boys, you don't expect us to believe that, do you?"

"I already told you, they are just lumps of rock and gold," Eddie added.

"They're not alive!"

"But we do congratulate you on your great imaginations! You'll have to tell us more of the story later, ok boys?"

Jared exploded. "We didn't lie! They are real!" His scream of anger stopped both parents short.

"Now Jared," Eddie began, "there is no reason to yell like that. And there is no reason to continue making up this story. We'll play with you guys later, and we can make up all sorts of stories about the dragons. Right now, we have some chores to do and dinner to get ready."

"But I'm NOT lying! Rex is REAL!" Jared yelled louder.

Eddie clapped his hands harshly. "That's enough!"

"No! Dad..!" Jared started.

"Not another word!" Eddie boomed. "We've asked you nicely to stop playing make believe, but if you don't want to listen you can go to your room!"

"But..." Jared whined.

"NOW!" Eddie roared, pointing to the stairs. Jared burst into tears and tore down the stairs, howling all the way into his bedroom and slamming his door behind him. Seconds after he left, Eddie felt horribly guilty for yelling as he had, but without anything more to do he turned and continued to work.

Alex looked to his Mom and spoke quietly. "Jared wasn't lying, Mom. They were actually moving today."

"Oh, Alex. I know you want us to discover the excitement of your toys with you, but now really isn't the time, ok? Later." Lynn returned to her work.

Alex was about to protest, but instead quietly said, "Ok."

"Can you call your sister in? You'll all need to wash up for dinner, and I think I saw her in the garden."

Alex nodded and opened the back door. "Madison! Come in for dinner!"

Alex put Kishar on the kitchen table and started helping put groceries away. They worked away in silence, only the occasional question or comment breaking the sound of rustling bags and jars and tins. The sound of the back door opening turned all their heads.

Madison was a wreck. She was covered head to toe in mud, dirt, twigs, grass and other unknown grime. If it wasn't for the gigantic smile plastered on her face, Lynn would have thought Madison had been attacked by a monster.

"Oh my goodness, what have you been doing all day?" Lynn laughed. It was going to be messy cleaning her, to say the least, but at the very least it looked like Madison had fun, whatever she was doing.

"Penelope and I were playing in the dirt! She needs to be cleaned too! She loves rocks and dirt, Mom!"

Lynn smiled and started forward to help her daughter out, then stopped. She was rooted to the spot, staring. Eddie caught the strange expression on his wife's face and followed her gaze. Then he, too, stared and gasped. Both parents were frozen in time and space.

There, climbing from underneath Madison's hair and around her shoulder was a small grime covered dragon. It shook its head like a dog, sending pieces of dirt and grass sailing off to land on the floor.

Madison scratched Penelope under the chin. "Mom, Dad, this is Penelope the Purple Dragon! Penelope, this is my Mom and Dad! She's a live dragon!" Madison exclaimed the last point full of enthusiasm and innocence.

Alex laughed as he looked back and forth from his Mom and Dad's stunned faces. "Told you so."

Penelope hissed a little and bobbed her head up and down. Madison reached up and patted the little dragon on the head. She dared not step any further into the house – she knew Mom would brush her down on the porch first with a broom or something, to get the least amount of filth in the house as was possible. She looked up to her parents and waited. They just stared, flabbergasted.

"What?" Madison asked innocently. She obviously didn't see anything abnormal about a living, breathing dragon, especially one as cute as Penelope.

Eddie finally snapped out of it. "Lynn, call the police!"

Lynn blinked, confused. "The police?"

"Ok, fine, an exterminator then! Madison, stay still. Don't move! I'll help you."

"Eddie," Lynn began, but was immediately cut off.

"I'll handle this, Lynn! Madison, just stay still." Eddie was creeping ever-closer to his daughter. Penelope was looking at Eddie with curious eyes, and her head cocked back and forth as she studied the strange man walking towards her. "A little closer….that's it."

"Dad, what are you doing?" Madison asked sweetly.

"Madison, don't talk! Don't move. I'll get that….thing away from you!"

Madison started doing circles in place. "Oh no! Did I bring a bug inside? Eeeeeeew! Is it a bug, a worm? What is it? Yuck, yuck, yuck!"

Alex and Lynn laughed at Madison's antics. She was skipping up and down, spinning in circles, trying to find the object of her father's concern.

"Dad's talking about Penelope, sis." Alex laughed again and nonchalantly returned to his grocery chores. This, after all, was no big deal to him. Living, breathing dragons had been known to him for two days already!

Madison stopped spinning and looked at her father, who was looming over her like he was ready to swat a wasp or mosquito away. "Ok," Eddie began, "when I count to three I'll knock that beast off and you can run to your mother. Then we'll get rid of this nasty thing."

Madison had never been so confused in her life. "You mean Penelope?"

"Eddie, I don't think your firing with all the right pistons right now."

"Lynn!" Eddie hissed. "Just get ready to get the kids out of here!"

Lynn placed her hands on her hips and struck a very aggressive pose. "Eddie, for goodness sake! Are you a complete idiot?"

Madison struck the identical pose as her mother. She had gotten very good at imitating Lynn's attitudes and postures, and was growing up to be quite a formidable little budding teenager. Eight years old going on twenty is what most people usually described her as.

"You'd better not be thinking of hurting Penelope, Dad!" Madison challenged.

Eddie wasn't about to wait any longer for his hysterical family to realize the graveness of the situation. He lunged forward, striking an open palm directly for the mean beast he saw on his daughter's shoulder, ready to swat the thing to the floor...

...and then Eddie went sailing backwards across the room, landing with a thud in the pantry, a large smudge of dirt staining the centre of his shirt.

Penelope soared through the air above Eddie, circling out and landing neatly on Madison's shoulder. Eddie groaned in pain, and the rest of them roared in laughter. Not even Lynn could help herself. Madison giggled so hard that tears welled up in her eyes.

Eddie slowly lifted his head off the floor. "What...what happened?" he mumbled weakly.

"You just got tackled by a dragon, Dad!" Alex shouted, laughing harder. Penelope hissed at Eddie, and then looked at the others in the room. She seemed to relax a little as she heard the joyous sound, and nuzzled into Madison's neck.

Eddie slowly raised himself up to one elbow. "See? I told you that thing's dangerous."

"Only because you completely freaked out!" Lynn yelled, still managing a laugh. "What is the matter with you anyway?"

"The matter with me?" Eddie said defensively. "Do you even know what that thing is?"

Lynn turned to examine the mud balls that were her daughter and pet dragon standing in the doorway. "Madison and her pet dragon?"

"Exactly! A dragon! A dangerous little fire-breathing….." Eddie stopped short. "What did you say? Her…..her pet?"

Lynn rolled her eyes. "Well obviously she belongs to Madison, and after seeing the way it pummelled you over to protect her, I have no concerns whatsoever!"

"It attacked me!" Eddie yelled.

"You attacked it first."

"But…"

"Oh be quiet!" Lynn spat, and led Madison out onto the porch. She started stripping off what dirt and muck she could from her daughter.

Eddie looked around the kitchen only to see Alex grinning. Quietly, Eddie laid his head back down, still lying down in the pantry, and mulled things over.

"Oh, uh, dad?" Alex called. Eddie grunted a reply. "You'll need to apologize to Jared for saying he was a liar."

Eddie responded by closing the pantry door.

5   Secrets

IT TOOK A FAIR length of time for Eddie to get comfortable with Penelope. The family had sat down to dinner, but Eddie and Penelope both eyed each other constantly.

Eddie had apologized to Jared and Alex, who both had their dragons at the dinner table with them even though they were currently nothing more than statues. Penelope on the other hand was hopping from the table to the back of Madison's chair and back again, excited about all the food that was available. She had tried a little of everything that Madison had on her plate. So far the only thing she didn't seem to like were the green beans.

The transition from chewing on rock to all this other food was interesting to everyone at the table. They could only speculate on the digestion abilities of the dragons, however, having no basis of reference to draw from. It was eventually agreed that the dragons were omnivores of an extreme kind – apparently they could eat anything they chose to!

Both parents listened intently as the kids described their day with the dragons. They were particularly interested in how it all started. They all looked to

Alex, who had been officially pronounced as the first witness to the dragons awakening.

"Kishar came alive yesterday. I'm not sure when. At first we thought it was heat, 'because we had him in the heat lamp in the bathroom. But then he went solid again. Today we had him out on the deck and he came alive, and then he ate some of the rock. Then Penelope did the same thing. And then Rex did too, but that was after we had to prove they were really alive to Jared."

"I knew they were real all along," Jared retorted.

"You did not," Madison countered.

Jared just grumbled to himself and kept eating.

"Tomorrow," Lynn said, "Richard will be coming over to tell us more about where these dragons were found, and hopefully we can get to the bottom of this. It is vitally important, *all* of you, to not mention these dragons to *anyone*, ok?"

"No one at all?" Jared asked.

"That's not fair! They're sooooo cool!" Madison whined.

Lynn shook her head. "No one, friends or family or strangers all included, can know about the dragons, at least for now. We simply don't know enough about them!"

Dinner was finished and the kids got themselves ready for bed. Alex and Jared had long since stopped being upset that their dragons were not moving. They were sleeping, just like all pets do. Tomorrow they would make sure that the dragons stayed in the sunlight all day to charge up. They wanted to be sure the dragons had enough energy to last through the night.

At bedtime Penelope circled on Madison's pillow two or three times, then lay down and pushed herself into the pillow as far as she could. Curled into a ball, she closed one eye and scanned the room with the other. Madison happily snuggled up to her, nuzzling her nose and face into Penelope's back, and draped her arm around the pillow on Penelope's other side. When Eddie came to kiss Madison goodnight, Penelope hissed but did not interfere. The boys had put Kishar and Rex in their windows, hoping to have the very first rays of sunlight as soon as they were available.

Eddie and Lynn made it to Alex's room at the same time. They said their goodnights and had moved to the door when Alex spoke.

"Dad?" There was a short pause. "We're going to keep the dragons, right?"

Eddie really didn't know what to say. He felt like it would have been better if they were all pet snakes instead of dragons. At least then he would know what they were, if they poisonous, could bite, and could call Animal Control if something went wrong. Having dragons in the house was very unnerving – who would they call if something went wrong, or the dragons got out of control? He didn't have the slightest idea what to do with these new pets, let alone what to tell his son.

Compassion won out over concern, and after several moments of silence, during which all the kids collectively held their breath waiting for the answer, Eddie spoke. "Absolutely. Now get some sleep. Goodnight."

Alex rolled over and closed his eyes, content. Jared called out to the darkness that Rex was the best. Madison whispered to Penelope, who purred in reply. They were soon asleep.

Lynn and Eddie made their way to their bedroom and got themselves ready for bed as well. Eddie was sitting on his side ready to crawl in, when Lynn spoke.

"What on earth are we going to do, Eddie?"

He turned at the fearful sound in her voice. She was leaning against the doorway, her eyes wide and thoughtful. Lynn looked like she was about to cry.

"What's the matter, honey?"

"Oh, good lord! Haven't you noticed, we have dragons in our house! OUR house, Eddie!"

"Now wait a minute. Just a couple hours ago you said that anything that could protect your daughter like the way Penelope did was A-OK in your books. Now you changed your mind?"

Lynn put her hands to her temples. "I don't know, hon. I really don't know. I mean, yes, I still feel good that Madison was protected like that. Penelope obviously loves her very much! But…oh, I don't know! Eddie, for crying out loud, what the heck *are* those things anyway?"

Eddie was silent, thinking. As he started to take in a breath to speak, Lynn cut him off.

"If you say they are dragons, I am going to punch you, Captain Obvious."

Eddie closed his mouth, smirking. Shrugging, he replied, "I don't really know what they are, Lynn. Dragons, pets, or figments of all our imaginations…I really don't know. But I do know one thing. Like you said, the kids love them, and they apparently love the kids back. And that, I guess, is that."

"Oh, I know, but is it enough? I mean, what if they get dangerous, or violent? How do you fight a dragon?"

Eddie shrugged. "Let's just hope it never comes to that. We'll be able to think more clearly on this in the morning."

They brushed their teeth and finished their other nightly duties, then snuggled up together in bed.

Christian Woods leaned back in the seat of his BMW Series 7 Sedan. He jotted some notes into his notebook then tapped away at the laptop beside him.

Packages were delivered as noted. Delivery man does not appear to know of the packages potential and nature. Observed all three packages operating as hoped for and expected – secondary marks all observed operation as well in direct contact. Will continue to monitor until further instructions given.

No sign yet of Government agent at scene. Please inform of additional agent details.

Christian verified the encryption before clicking 'send' on his email then closed the laptop. It was time for dinner. Tomorrow would be a big day.

6   Council

THE CRIMSON RED SKY flashed with blue light, while dozens of shapes floated through the clouds. A Grand Council had been called, one of which had not been seen for several hundred years. Gigantic wings beat as dragons of every color and size flew in from the horizon, making their way to the enormous ziggurat that was the grounds for the Council. The ziggurat was large enough for three full-grown adult dragons to perch upon, and it stood in the center of an even larger coliseum. Soon the surrounding coliseum's normally grey stone was covered in red, blue, gold and green, as dragons flew in to sit and wait for the Council to begin.

A few dragons were still in the sky when a massive, lumbering dragon walked in from the opening to the south. The dragon was ancient, far older than its companions surrounding it. The old dragon's scales had once been brown, but with age had turned a dull shade that resembled a greying dry pond. Two younger dragons – though still old themselves – walked on either side of the Master, one as crimson as the sky, the other a rich shade of blue. They could still fly, but ceremony and respect demanded that they follow the oldest of them all in his own way. He still had wings, but lacked the strength to make them beat. So he walked. Several minutes passed as the Master slowly made his way to the ziggurat and climbed the stairs to the top. His escorts followed suit then took positions to either side. Each dragon on the ziggurat faced a different direction, making a triangle so that all members of the coliseum would see and hear them.

The Master lifted his head and looked about. Silence fell in the coliseum like a heavy blanket, coating the entire area. Even the crickets and birds hushed. The last remaining dragons to coast in from the sky landed silently, staring at the Master expectantly. The Master stared about the coliseum a few moments more, than closed his eyes.

A low song began. The sound rumbled deep from within the Master's chest and spread from him like a wave. It sounded somewhere between a beautiful bass voice and a growl. His escorts joined in with their own song, one a deep baritone, the other a high tenor. One by one, in order of rank, the other dragons joined in, and the Song of the Council rose up above the coliseum walls and echoed through the surrounding lands, valleys and mountains. It had been several hundred years since nature had heard a similar song. The trees themselves held their breath to listen to the song and await the meaning behind it.

The song lasted several minutes while each dragon joined into the chorus. Some dragons closed their eyes and wept at the beauty of the sound, others smiled for joy as the Dragon Song continued. Finally, in a crescendo of sound, the Master roared. His roar equalled the sound of the Song in intensity, but where the Song was made of peace and love, the roar was full of fury and power. The two sounds mixed, clashed, and then sang together, and the first Dragon Council in 200 years came to its official opening.

The roar stopped, and the Song slowly faded with it. Silence again swept over the entire region. A bird nearby chirped once, almost questioningly. A green dragon leaned slightly to one side and stared at the bird. The small song bird swallowed, embarrassed, and then nodded apologetically. Satisfied, the green dragon returned its gaze back to the Council.

The Master swept his ancient gaze over the gathering one more time. Then he smiled broadly and spoke. The language was ancient and resonated with power. It was the true language of Dragonkind, soft and harsh simultaneously, with power and truth resounding in every word.

"It is good to see you have all remembered our Song, despite the long years since we last sang it. It is a good sign." The Master finished by resting his head on his front talons. His eyes blinked sleepily. "Taeromondanius will continue, and explain the reason for this Council."

The blue dragon beside the Master raised its long neck to better be heard by the throng. Taeromondanius' voice was soft and lilting, much higher pitched than the deep mountainous sound of the Master. "Greetings to you all, my dragon kin. Thank you for answering the summons of the Song. We are here to discuss what many of you have already felt, and to determine what action needs to be taken."

Somewhere in the crowd a voice drifted up. "The lost children?"

Taeromondanius nodded. "The feelings are true, and have been verified by the Master himself."

The crowd gasped as one, and again a voice drifted in from the surrounding Council. "Surely this is not possible. The Gate was frozen shut many years ago, by magic, and by human and dragon blood. How could there be any left behind?"

"Do you not feel the pull of magic, Distiril?" Taeromondanius replied calmly. He received no reply, proving the point. "The Gate is still sealed by ice, my friends. Yet three of our children have awakened, and the pull of magic through the Gate is growing stronger. We must act."

"What are we to do, Master?"

Taeromondanius lowered his head as the Master rose up once again. "We need to find our children, and bring them home. I do not need to tell you what will happen if they are allowed to grow up on the other side of the Gate, do I?" The Master looked about the coliseum and waited. Every dragon knew the consequences of allowing magic to flow more freely through the Gate, of the possibility of re-establishing contact with humans, and of having their own kind exist in the human world. It was that exact reason why the dragons had fled, had sealed themselves in their own world and closed the Gate behind them.

"One of us must return through the Gate and find the children. Once found, they must be brought here. They must be returned home, before any lasting damage is done."

There was silence after the Master spoke. None of the dragons spoke, or dared twitch, lest they be the one chosen to return to the land of the humans. Long minutes passed and still no one moved. Finally, a stunningly coloured dragon rose to all fours and leaped into the air, landing gracefully in the grounds between the ziggurat and the seats of the coliseum. The scales shimmered like a perfect pearl as he moved, changing iridescent color in the light from faint blue, to white, to faint blue again.

"I will go, Master."

The Master smiled. "Are you so certain, Azurim?"

Azurim nodded. "I know the dangers of crossing the Gate. I know I may not return, and may not even survive the transition from our world to theirs. However the risk of leaving the children on the other side is greater. I know what is at stake, and I will not fail the Council. I will not fail you, Master."

The Council remained quiet while the Master studied the young dragon before him. This dragon was full of spirit, full of life and very wise, but was still so very young! He did not have the experience of many of the dragons in the Council, and for personal reasons would not have been the Master's first choice. However, the Master was confident of the selection nonetheless.

"Very well, Azurim," the Master replied. The Council released its breath as one, thankful the decision had not been overturned and one of them had been chosen instead. "You will return through the Gate. You will find the lost children. And you will return with the children to our land, where we can teach them the Song. You will do this, Azurim. Failure means…"

"I understand what failure would mean, Master. I am not afraid."

The Master smiled sadly. "Very well. Taeromondanius and Vivartalus will take you to the Gate, and see you through it. Remember our Song, Azurim, and return to us soon."

Azurim knelt low on his front legs and bowed his head. "It shall be done, Master." He spread his wings and shot into the air like a blast from a cannon.

The two dragons at the Master's side followed suit, and the trio made their way south, to begin the long journey to the Gate.

The Master watched as they flew away. "Farewell and success to you....my son." A tear welled up in the ancient eye as the Master began singing. The Council all joined in the Song, closing the Council session and speeding Azurim on his way. The Song sped forward a thousand leagues to where the Gate and its Guardians waited. The Song echoed, reverberated and the Gate shimmered in response, acknowledging that a Dragon was coming to attempt the crossing. The runes etched on the Guardians rippled with power, waiting for Azurim to arrive.

7   Research

U NCLE RICHARD PROVED TO be more enthusiastic about the dragons than even the children were. He was completely enamoured with all three of them. Penelope was cautious and protective at first, but when Richard came forward with open arms and big smile Penelope fell in love. She purred and crooned as Richard rubbed her down, with Madison looking on and correcting him in the proper technique of dragon care. Kishar was happy to have another person admire him, while Rex hissed and growled in his typical fashion as he was known to do to just about everything. Richard was concerned at first, but Jared waved it off, saying it was Rex's way of saying 'hi'.

Lynn and Eddie felt that Richard must have known something, for he was so casual with the dragons as if it was a normal everyday kind of pet. He insisted that he knew nothing about them, however, and the mystery of the dragon's origins was as deeply rooted as before.

The kids and Richard spent the afternoon at the main Public Library, doing every kind of research they could about dragons, archaeological digs in South America, and anything that may possibly have been related. Lynn and

Eddie spent the time at home looking after the dragons, which was easier said than done. Kishar settled down fairly quickly, although he would drift from the front to the back window, searching for Alex. Rex simply sat and howled for about half the time, whimpering and stomping around the other half. Penelope, however, was happily sitting on Lynn's shoulder, hissing and raising her wings whenever Eddie would come near (to which Eddie would stick out his tongue, hiss back, or many other retaliations he was getting good at), and quite content to follow Lynn about the house as she went about her business.

Eddie had gone around the entire house, making sure that every window shade had been drawn back and opened wide. Alex and Jared never wanted to have their dragons fall asleep again, and so had insisted that the windows all be opened wide 24/7. Eddie agreed to have the shades all drawn back, but refused to simply open the actual windows…who knew how much trouble they would all get in if the dragons were allowed to simply fly in and out as they pleased.

Rex had decided at one point that he was hungry and started chewing on the tiles in the bathroom. Lynn had screamed, which of course had drawn Eddie into a panic. He charged into the bathroom with a baseball bat, only to be knocked off his feet again as Rex bolted out the door. Lynn couldn't decide whether to laugh at her husband lying on the floor, or to find Rex and wring his little neck for wrecking several tiles in the bathroom. She decided instead to laugh, and have Jared help her fix the tiles later. It was after all his pet, and Jared would need to learn to be responsible for it.

The kids all arrived home in an uproar, Richard grinning gleefully, Alex fuming horridly and Jared and Madison skipping and laughing.

"Alex has a girl dragon, Alex has a girl dragon!" The siblings were relentless. They were briefly interrupted by Kishar coming zooming into the room and landing full force on Alex's chest, knocking him onto his back. Everyone laughed, including Alex, who was overjoyed to have his dragon in his arms again. The two of them hugged happily, Kishar making all manner of strange growling noises.

Penelope had much the same reaction; she leaped off of Lynn's shoulder and promptly landed on Madison's shoulder, immediately making the same strange noises. Madison swatted at Penelope to get her to buzz off; it was nearly impossible to take your shoes off with a dragon hovering and bouncing from shoulder to shoulder, knee to knee, chattering incessantly.

Jared looked around for Rex but didn't see him. Jared quickly tugged off his shoes and went into the house to search. He found Rex slowly marching along the floor in the kitchen, making his way at his own pace to the front door. Once Rex spotted Jared, he roared and then turned to fan his wings out, waiting impatiently for a rub down. Jared complied happily. Rex was a lot of work, but he was worth it and still the best pet anyone could have ever asked for as far as Jared was concerned.

Lynn and Eddie were hoping that some useful information had been found, but not really counting on it. It just didn't seem feasible that a text book would exist somewhere with the "How-To's" of dragon listed inside.

"Did you find anything out today at the library?" Lynn asked the group in general.

Jared yelled hurriedly from the other room. "We found out that Kishar is a girl!"

"He is not!" Alex retorted, his face turning red in anger.

"Is too," Jared teased.

"HE IS NOT!" Alex roared.

His anger was growing so quickly Lynn thought his head might explode. She tried to intervene before it actually happened. "Boys, Jared, that's enough!" Neither of the boys said any more, but Alex's anger continued to boil inside him. "Richard, could you possibly shed some light on this for us, please?"

Richard was still grinning foolishly from earlier. "Not really sure what to say, Lynn. We didn't really find anything useful at the library about caring for dragons, but we did find the name Kishar in a book about mythology."

"Yup," Jared called from the kitchen. "Kishar is a GIRL in the legend. So Alex has a GIRL dragon."

"I do not!"

"Kishar is a girl, Kishar is a girl!" Jared continued with his taunting, while Alex sprang to his feet and charged into the other room. Kishar jumped up as well and flew after Alex, a curious and distraught look in his eye. Jared soon stopped chanting, and the sounds of fighting took over.

Lynn shook her head and sighed. "Eddie, would you please go and take care of your sons."

Eddie boggled. "MY sons? How come whenever they are fighting or being bad they are MY sons?"

Lynn waved him away with her hand. "Oh, please, just go and take care of them will you?"

Eddie stalked into the kitchen and had to yell to be heard over the ruckus being brought up by two dragons and two fighting boys. Lynn turned back to Richard, who had knelt down beside Madison. Both of them were petting Penelope, who beamed brightly under all the attention. Lynn cleared her throat, jolting Richard out of his reverie.

"Uh, yeah. So, like I said. Nothing much to find at the library."

"Nothing at all?" Lynn was upset for she was truly hoping that a miracle would occur, and the kids would have some kind of training manual given to them for the dragons' sake.

"Nope."

"That's not true," Madison said calmly, still petting Penelope. "There was lots about Kishar."

Lynn was puzzled. "How can there be anything about Kishar in a book?"

"The name Kishar shows up in several different mythology books," Richard explained. "Kishar was a daughter of a couple of some Mesopotamian serpent-gods, and in later stories shows up as a sort of dragon, or serpent, or something in between. I'm not really sure. When Jared found out that the Kishar from mythology was a girl, he started to tease Alex, and the two of them have been fighting ever since."

"Oh, I'm so sorry you had to deal with them while they are fighting, Richard."

Richard shook his head. "No worries at all! We had a great time! I made sure to buy them all ice cream as long as they would stop fighting. It worked,"

Richard looked past Lynn and into the kitchen, "well, for a little while, anyway."

Lynn followed his eye and sighed. The fighting hadn't stopped yet, in fact it sounded worse than it was before. Shaking her head again she stepped into the kitchen, Richard, Penelope and Madison trailing behind. The sight before her was laughable if she hadn't already been so tired. Alex and Jared were a tangled ball of arms and legs, rolling around the floor, punching and kicking as they went. Occasionally you could hear Alex telling Jared to 'take it back' or 'stop saying that' while Jared continued to taunt saying 'your dragon's a girl', and other similar things. Eddie was rolling around the ground as well, except he was being tackled by two dragons. One red one was wrapped around Eddie's leg and was making it impossible for Eddie to stand, while the green dragon was clamped firmly around Eddie's left shoulder and part of his neck. Hissing, grunting and groaning were coming from the colourful mound, but not much else.

It was evident that the dragons had attacked Eddie when he had gone in and tried to stop the boys from fighting. Either the dragons thought he was a threat to the boys, or they were simply joining in on what they thought was a lot of fun wrestling. Lynn called once for silence, but no one seemed to hear her. After watching the writhing war on the floor for a minute, Lynn threw up her hands in despair and walked down the hall to the TV Room. She needed a break. Madison followed, Penelope on her shoulder. Richard watched a moment more then followed as well. He had thought of trying to help, but was fairly certain anything he would do would be useless. Stepping in to fight the boys off of one another would only bring the dragons down on him. And stepping in to help Eddie was certain to bring the same result.

So Richard, Madison, Penelope and Lynn watched some TV and chatted about their experience at the library, waiting for the testosterone in the other room to settle down.

Several minutes passed with the boys rolling, arguing and smacking. Finally, after an unplanned and lucky blow caught Jared on the nose, the boys stopped their combat and pulled apart. Jared was not seriously hurt – the sharp pain in his nose was more stunning that it was lethal, just enough to stop the fight. The boys stood up and went their separate ways, Jared angrily stamping outside with Rex to soak up some sun and Alex to the fridge to find a snack.

Kishar happily jumped to Alex's shoulder and stared into the refrigerator with him, searching for a tasty morsel.

Eddie lay on the floor, staring at the ceiling, bruises and scrapes on his neck, shoulders and legs from where the dragons had latched onto him. He had tried fighting back and prying the dragons off of him, but his reluctance to hurt the dragons had held most of his strength in check. They were, after all, pets, and while they could pack a mean wallop, Eddie really didn't know how tough or delicate they were. Their gem-like bodies shone like jewels, but that could mean hard as a diamond, or fragile as a crystal. He didn't know of any veterinarian who would be able to give them advice on dragon care, so the less damage the dragons took the better.

Because of all these thoughts going through Eddie's head, he had spent most of his time grumbling and fuming at the dragons. When the boys had finally left the room, the dragons followed, leaving a still angry Eddie lying on the floor.

That afternoon they made sure to give their dragons a couple hours of sunshine, and then come back inside to wash up for dinner. Eddie had spent the greater part of the time hiding in the study, reading a book. Richard watched some TV with Lynn and Madison and Penelope, then headed home to get his own dinner prepared for him and Lilly. He promised not to say anything to Lilly about the dragons, and that he would call back to the dig site in Brazil tomorrow to see if there was anything else uncovered since he had left.

Lynn had decided it was sandwich night, and so the kitchen table had every possible condiment on it: one loaf of sandwich bread, one package of bagels, one loaf of dark rye bread, jam, honey, three kinds of cheese, butter, peanut butter, honey ham, pepperoni, Hungarian salami, some dark roast beef and some kind of turkey that no one knew the correct name of. Everyone dove into the food with a good mixture of fun and conversation. It was one rare meal where there was no limitation on "playing with your food". The kids would chew holes out of a round piece of pepperoni and then look through them like glasses. The sandwiches were sometimes one layer, and other times a triple-decker. It was a two-hour funfest, with the whole family laughing and enjoying good food.

The dragons surprised everyone by being exceptionally well behaved at dinner time. Lynn had set a place for each of them with small plates, so Kishar swooped out from time to time, snatching a tasty bit of bread or meat and bringing it back to the other two, who split it evenly on their plates. The dragons munched away, enjoying every bite.

When dinner finished, and everyone pitched in to clean the table, Eddie decided it was time to ask the question he had been wondering all day.

"Well, kids, you've had a busy few days with the dragons, and spent some time today researching them at the library. We know you didn't find anything specific about them – no jokes Jared," Eddie added quickly as he saw Jared ready to taunt Alex about Kishar again. "I want to know what we are going to do with the dragons now." The entire family hushed at this point, suddenly serious. None of the kids wanted to lose their pet, and yet they had been wondering the same thing as well. These were no ordinary pets, and they were certainly not educated on how to raise such unique animals – no one was!

"There are so many questions to answer," Eddie continued. "They appear to eat anything including rocks, so there is no shortage of food for them, but have any of you seen them go to the bathroom yet? Will they stay this size or get bigger? How big will they get? How do we measure dragon age? Dogs are about one human year to about five or seven dog years, depending on the breed. What about Kishar, Rex and Penelope? How old are they now?"

Eddie paused to let his questions sink in. He knew there was no answer to any of them, yet he also knew they needed to discuss it anyway. They desperately needed information about them, some insight or some idea of what direction their upbringing should go in.

"While we are thinking about how old they are, let's go back to how big they will get. How long will it be before they get too big to fit in the house? Or will they remain this size forever? And most importantly is the problem of risk. What happens when your friends want to come over to play and they see the dragons? Will they see them as cool creatures, like Uncle Richard did…?"

"Or will they call the police?" Alex finished.

"Exactly." Eddie folded his hands on his chest as he leaned back into the chair and stretched his legs out. "There are so many unknowns and variables right now. We have been fairly carefree about it all for the last few days, simply because we have absolutely no idea what to do, or what to expect! But we have to make a plan at some point."

"Your father's right, kids," Lynn added. "What do we do when school starts, and the dragons are left at home while you are away each day? We had a hard enough time keeping them contained in the house today while you were at the library. I don't think we could keep them locked up every day while you are at school."

Madison suddenly started crying, which caused a wail of sorrow from Penelope. "Oh, Mom, Daddy, please don't take Penelope away!"

Madison sobbed harder, causing Penelope to shoot from the mantle to the table, wrapping her wings around Madison's face and hissing at everyone else.

The scene touched Lynn. She knew, of course, that the boys were thinking the same thing and feeling the same emotions, they just hadn't voiced them yet.

"Oh, Madison, we are not going to take the dragons away! Ever!" Lynn exclaimed. Then she looked over to Eddie. "Are we?"

Eddie paused, lost in thought.

"Dad! You can't be thinking of getting rid of them!" Alex cried.

"I won't let you take Rex away!" Jared proclaimed, calling Rex to him.

"Dear, honestly!" Lynn said.

Eddie snapped out of it. "What? No! We're not getting rid of them! Never. Sorry…I was simply thinking of…." He trailed off, for he had yet to finish his own thoughts and didn't want to start speaking until he had completed the idea in his mind.

They all stared at him, expectantly. A full minute went by without a word, when Lynn finally broke the silence. "Well?"

Eddie snapped out of it again, glancing around the table. "What?"

"Oh I hate it when you do that!"

"Do what?"

"Can you please just let us know what is on your mind and stop with the mystery already?"

"Sorry," Eddie apologized. "I was thinking of moving."

Lynn squinted at her husband. "Moving? Where?"

"I am sure we could find a way to get a second home outside of the city somewhere."

Lynn perked up. "Outside the city?"

"Yes. We can sell this house or keep it if you wish. But I was thinking, what with the three dragons and all, we should find a place out west towards the mountains. A nice big ranch or something, where we don't have to worry about the neighbours accidentally seeing the dragons flying around the backyard."

"But what about school, and everything else we have going on in the city? Gymnastics, events that we are a part of...?" Lynn trailed off, hopeful but still doubtful as well.

"Well, school is something the kids are going to have to decide on. The best option to me seems to be home schooling now, unless the kids want their dragons to be alone all day."

All three of the kids cried out at once, "No!"

Eddie smiled. "We can find a location for a trampoline at the new place. We could make it into a mini-gym and have the teacher come out to the house to do classes with the kids."

Lynn nodded her head, but still seemed troubled. "But what about all our commitments? We have our friends and charities..."

"All of which we can drive into the city for when we need to, and we can have others drive out to us when we don't want to head into town. Besides, there is email and the internet, and even snail-mail if it gets down to it."

Lynn was quickly warming up to the idea. "Ok!" she exclaimed as she jumped to hug her husband.

Their imagination ignited, the kids started talking about what their rooms would look like, and the adventures they would go on with the dragons out on a ranch.

Lynn leaned over to Eddie and whispered, "Do you think Richard and Lilly would want to buy this house?"

Eddie looked at her for a moment to see if she was serious.

"Well," Lynn continued, "Richard always sleeps over here anyway. And he hasn't closed a deal yet from those he's looked at so far."

"You really want to sell our house to our one of our best friends?"

Lynn bit her lip and looked coyly at Eddie. "Actually, I was thinking that if they buy the house from us, then maybe we could still have the house 'in the family', so to speak." She winked, and Eddie laughed.

"My wife, the forever schemer."

"I do not scheme!" Lynn protested.

Eddie simply fixed her in his gaze and held back a laugh.

Lynn bit her lip again. "Ok, ok, fine, I scheme....a little."

The rest of the evening was spent talking about the possibilities of a new house, where they should start looking, and what type of preparations they would need to make for themselves and the dragons.

8   Shock

THE CAPTAIN OF THE Lufthansa jet plane checked his controls and confirmed flight times with his co-pilot. The lights in the cockpit were overpowered by the bright sunlight shining all around the plane. The co-pilot relayed their updated arrival times to the tower in Frankfurt. Once the tower acknowledged, the co-pilot then spoke into the intercom for the plane and announced to the passengers that Lufthansa would be landing about five minutes ahead of schedule, the weather in Frankfurt was partly sunny today and currently twenty degrees Celsius, and they would be making their approach in about ten minutes. He repeated the message to the entire plane in German then reverted back to English to confirm coordinates with the tower in Frankfurt.

A shadow passed by the plane, causing the captain to look up from his chart. He saw nothing but clouds. Assuming a high cloud had blocked the sun momentarily, he returned his gaze back to the charts. The shadow passed again. This time both the captain and co-pilot searched the horizon, trying to find out what was blocking the sunlight. Nothing. Nothing to the horizon in any direction.

The plane shuddered as a massive vibration swept through the steel frame. Instrument panels and warnings lights flashed. The central computer on the plane began lighting up a mayday, querying the captain whether to signal to the tower or not. After a moment the lights stopped flashing, and the turbulence stopped.

"What was that?" the co-pilot asked aloud, not expecting an answer. His voice carried only a slight German accent.

The plane shuddered again, this time more violently. Instrument panels went berserk, and the plane veered slightly off course. Both pilots grabbed the controls as the plane started to dip. The captain searched the sky for the source of the disturbance, but saw none. They checked their instruments again, but were unable to get any specific readings.

This was no ordinary turbulence, and certainly not expected in this region. They had been traveling at thirty thousand feet for the last twenty minutes and had not hit any turbulence at all – to have this amount now was strange to say the least. There were no storms, no weather systems building up.

The plane rocked to the side from what could only have been physical contact with something. The instruments went haywire again, and this time the computer's fail-safes kicked in – the mayday call went out to Frankfurt tower, advising of an impact on the plane.

The captain slammed the emergency seat belts button, and quickly spoke into the intercom for the plane. "Ladies and gentlemen, this is the captain speaking. Please return to your seats and fasten your seatbelts. We have encountered an unexpected severe weather pattern. Please....oh mein Gott!"

The intercom went dead as the captain yelled and turned off the com link. The most recent shock wave had pushed the plane sideways and stalled out the starboard engine. The plane dipped again, this time accelerating as it shot down through the clouds. Lights and buzzers throughout the cockpit blared to life as dozens of warning signals alerted of cabin depressurization, rapid descent, and loss of stability on the starboard side. Both pilots worked frantically to regain control of the plane, the captain feverishly trying to pull the plane out of a nose-dive, and the co-pilot trying to get power back to the stalled engine.

Oxygen masks dropped from the ceiling in the passenger cabin, and the plane was filled with cries of terror as everyone scrambled to get their masks on.

Outside the plane, Azurim looked at the strange white and blue steel dragon. It was apparently very afraid as it was running away from Azurim, and was also unwilling to communicate. Azurim had tried talking, but was ignored, and so he had given the steel beast a gentle nudged with his claw. The sudden blast of air was a shock to Azurim, and he stopped immediately, hovering in mid-air. He had heard screams, voices....*human* voices coming from within the steel dragon! That was why the dragon was not responding. It was no dragon at all!

Azurim looked down at the clouds where the plane had disappeared through. *What have I done? I did not wish ill on them.*

Azurim took only a moment to decide then shot like a bullet in pursuit of the plane. He caught up to it quickly, before they had left the cloud cover. He flew above it and slightly behind, looking at the damage his gentle prodding had done. A small tear in the metal canopy was venting what appeared to be steam. Azurim inhaled and then breathed softly on the spot, his breath causing a thick sheet of ice to form on and around the hole.

Azurim continued pacing the plane, listening. Something did not appear normal as one side of the plane was making more noise than the other. He looked at the two large barrels hanging under the wings, one on the left and one on the right. One was spinning, while the other was stationary. Azurim studied it a moment, attempting to discern how they worked. He was fascinated, but knew he had little time to ponder the technology. He flew low behind the wing and breathed in again, then let out a small, short, contained breath of flame. The thin stream shot forward and instantly melted the ice caked around the engine. It roared to life with the sudden explosion of fuel from the heat, stress fractures appearing around the frame and wing. Azurim used his cooling breath again to stabilize the fractures, even if only temporarily.

Satisfied that the plane would be able to make the rest of the journey on its own, Azurim turned away. He paused when he noticed the small black markings along the planes side. He had mistaken them before for scales or age-rings. He discovered that they were actually windows, as he saw perhaps thirty or more human faces staring in bewildered shock.

Azurim pulled away from the plane and roared. While the plane continued its descent, Azurim banked and climbed, just as the cloud cover stopped.

Azurim roared again in joy – that had been fun! He enjoyed excitement like this! He spread his wings and climbed back into the sky, soaring at levels above the clouds and making his way west.

The captain congratulated his co-pilot on restoring power to the engine. He got no response. He looked over and saw the man staring fixedly out the window. The captain followed his gaze and caught the tail end – literally – of the dragon banking away out of sight as it roared. Several moments passed and neither spoke. They simply stared at the empty cloud where only a moment ago something they both knew didn't exist had just flown.

The co-pilot turned and swallowed hard. "How would you like us to log this in, Captain?"

The captain shook his head and throttled back, bringing the plane back to a safe speed and levelling out. "I don't know, Peter. I don't know. Let's just get safely on the ground, and we'll worry about reports later."

Peter nodded agreement. "We're close enough to Frankfurt to make our landing there. I will radio ahead for an emergency crew to be available, and find our runway."

The captain nodded mutely. He was still too stunned to reply. His logical mind was still wrapping itself around the image burned into his mind.

"We didn't just see….." the captain trailed off.

"Eine Drache? Yes."

The captain shook his head to clear it. "There's no such thing as dragons... is there?"

In the coming hours after they landed, the captain would discover that his co-pilot, and fully thirty-five passengers, would confirm that there indeed *was* at least one dragon that did exist.

9   Country

THE LAND THE ZEDMORE'S eventually chose was a rugged and serene portrait typical of the Alberta Foothills. About two hundred and forty acres of land in total, it was picturesque; tall pine trees mixed with aspen and poplar dotted the countryside alongside open stretches of scrub grassland. The tall white peaks of the Rocky Mountains were ever present on the south, west and north views, while the east opened onto an endless sight of rolling hills that stretched to the horizon. The sunrise each day was captivating and full, instantly bathing the ranch in a fiery orange glory. Sunset each day lasted for hours: the sun would approach the mountains, lighting the underside of the clouds in brilliant purples, reds and yellows, and then twilight would set in afterward, darkness not fully coming until after bedtime.

Richard approved of the land at once, making comments that it was about time they had finally started throwing some of their money around.

"Not only have you been sitting on your wealth," Richard proclaimed when they were showing him the section of land they had purchased, "but you have barely touched a dime from all of the money you're bringing in from your other investments!"

"That's precisely *why* we have plenty now, Rich. We don't spend it all immediately."

"You don't spend it, ever!" Richard laughed. He was pressing the point, but he was truly happy that his friends were starting to live to the higher standards that Richard himself had always known they deserved.

The house already on the land was an old ranch-style, which they lived in temporarily while a newer house was being built. The kids and dragons were confined to the ranch house while construction workers were around, to keep the secret safe. Eddie hired several construction contractors all at once, to the get the work done more quickly. Half way into September, just six weeks from when they purchased the land, the new house was completed!

There had only been one major incident while work was being done. Rex had somehow gotten out of the house and was found in the back of a pickup truck, tossing tools around and sniffing at everything. Thankfully the excuse of a wild lizard causing mischief was enough to dispel any further investigation, although the carpenter who owned the truck was confused as to how one of his hammers was missing a chunk out of one side. Only the family knew that Rex apparently thought the hammer smelled good, only to spit out the metal after tasting and chewing on it for a minute or so.

Richard and Lilly did indeed buy the old house from the Zedmore family, and were very happy with the deal! The house was ready to move into, as far as Richard was concerned, however Lilly felt there were some minor feminine touches required to make it 'hers'. Lynn had at first been worried about too many changes taking place in her old home, and her heart ached temporarily: in week two of construction, Lynn had become so excited about the new house that she lost all concern for the old one!

Lynn and Eddie were impressed at how intelligent the little creatures were becoming. They had figured out how to open doors on their own, knew when to hide when strangers were around, and helped out around the house if they could. Rex was particularly adept at helping light fires in the fire pit in the back yard. Eddie had made a perfect tee-pee style collection of paper and wood one night, and was trying to get a flame to light on the lighter he had. Rex had been perched nearby watching for some time, and as Eddie started lighting edges of the paper Rex let loose with a short blast of flame. The centre of the fire pit erupted with heat and smoke, and within moments the wood was being consumed by hungry, licking flames. The kids all held their laughter as best they could – parts of Eddie's hair had been burned, and he had jumped backward in shock, stumbling and falling on his rump.

The transition from city to country life was accepted quickly by all. The kids all finished their daily school work in the morning, in order to have as much time as possible to play with their dragons, usually outside. The dragons perched around the school work, and seemed to be trying to understand the different topics as well.

It was a hot day near the end of September when the unexpected event occurred.

Lynn was in the kitchen preparing fruit and other snacks for the kids. Eddie and the kids were all out on the back porch playing with the dragons, awaiting the arrival of delicious fruit, crackers, juice and whatever else Mom was bringing out to them. The dragons were playing games of catch: Alex would throw a rock into the air, and each dragon would leap up to try and be the first to grab it. He had a small bag of about fifty or so treats for them, nice looking stones they had all collected the day before. He tossed a stone into the air; all three dragons jumped, spread their wings and soared – just as a blonde haired man wearing khaki shorts and a work shirt with a *Direct Energy* logo on it stepped around the corner and onto the porch.

"Whoa! What on earth...?"

The dragons all seemed stunned, not sure what to do with this stranger around. Lynn heard the commotion and saw the stranger from the window. She quickly ran out to the porch, but it was Eddie who recovered first.

"Pretty impressive, aren't they?" he said with a wide smile.

The stranger looked from Eddie back to the dragons, which were now perched on the table and doing the same thing, looking back from Eddie to the man and back again.

The man pointed, and stumbled over his own feet, leaning against the railing. "Uh...what, uh..."

Eddie stood and wandered over, shaking the other's hand. "Yes, I know, they look real, don't they? Latest thing in robotics! Sorry about that, we're just trying them out for a company that I am working with. Should be coming out next year for Christmas!"

"Next year...?"

"Yes! They'll be the talk of the town...well, that is if the manufacturer can get the radio transmitters to work right. Remote controls don't work one hundred percent of the time."

Eddie looked down and noticed the scanner in the man's hand.

"Here to get a meter read?"

The man shook his head and laughed. They could hear a faint maritime accent when he spoke. "Yeah! Jus' getting a meter read fer the new lines, water and gas."

Eddie looked back at the table. The dragons had all stopped moving. If he hadn't known better, he would have assumed they were statues again.

The meter reader beeped several times as the worker walked off the porch to the wall of the house. When he was finished, he made his way back to the porch, stepped up and looked over at the table.

"Mind if I see one?"

Eddie began to sweat, but he hid it as best he could. "Uh, sure," he sputtered, not knowing what to say.

Alex leaned forward and picked up Kishar. "Here, look at this one. Careful, though, the motors inside are a little scrambled, so it doesn't work all the time like you want it to."

Lynn swallowed hard, and Jared and Madison paled. The stranger held up the little green dragon and examined it from all sides. Kishar didn't move a muscle.

"Well, I'll be. That is one mighty cool remote control toy! My nephew would love one of these! Where are they being manufactured?"

Eddie stammered a moment, but once again Alex saved him. "Japan."

"Issat so?" The stranger looked the dragon over once more then placed it back on the table. "You say they're coming out next Christmas? Cool. Any idea how much they'll be?"

"Uh, well," Eddie ran his finger down Kishar's back, stalling, "there hasn't really been a price point agreed upon yet. We'll just have to see when they come out!"

"Right, well hey, thanks for letting me see 'em! I'll let you all get back to yer dinner. Have a great day!"

Eddie shook the man's hand again. "No problem at all, mister...?"

"Woods," he replied, and then made his way to the stairs of the porch and waved. He walked to the front of the house, where they heard a vehicle door open and close, and the engine come to life as the man drove away.

Eddie let out a long breath and plopped himself back into his chair. The dragons all slowly moved their heads around, scanning the deck. Penelope cradled herself in Madison's lap, while Rex and Kishar flew to the top of the house, presumably looking around the rest of the property for more intruders.

Jared broke the silence with a whistle. "That was close."

Eddie smiled humourlessly but didn't reply.

Jared high-fived his brother. "What made you think of Japan as a manufacturer, and why did you let him hold Kishar?"

Alex shrugged. "Japan is easy – far enough away place that most people here won't know much of, and they tend to be high in technology too. I was just hoping that Kishar knew enough to stay still. They all looked like they were playing along anyway."

Jared looked sidelong at his brother, smiling. "So basically you just guessed?"

Alex nodded.

Lynn stepped up behind Alex and patted his shoulder. "Good work, honey."

Lynn and Eddie exchanged worried glances. Eddie motioned his wife inside and went to the kitchen. He sat on a bar stool around the kitchen island while Lynn went outside with the tray of food and drinks. Moments later she was back, closing the glass door behind her instead of the screen.

"What is it, honey?" she asked, stepping closer and holding a hand out to comfort him.

Eddie thought his words through carefully. "It just strikes me that, well, it is really only a matter of time before more and more people start finding out about them, isn't it?"

"I thought so too. Here I was hoping that with all this space out here we'd be safer than in the city. But..."

"How easy was it for a stranger to drop by and find out about them?'"

Lynn put a hand to her forehead, pursing her lips.

"Exactly."

Lynn slowly made her way around to the counter by the window where she had left her own drink. "So what are you suggesting? Sending them away? Where would they go?"

Eddie was shaking his head. "No, no, I am not suggesting anything like that. I honestly don't know what I am suggesting. Just thinking out loud I guess. But I think this is a problem that is only going to get worse. I had thought the same as you – that having a bigger house with more land around would provide the solution to the problem of the dragons' discovery. The more I think about it, though, the more I believe we are just delaying the inevitable. They will get found out, sooner or later."

Lynn wanted to argue, but she also knew he was right. "It's only a matter of time before everyone knows about them," she replied echoing Eddie's earlier words.

Eddie nodded, but didn't respond. He had tried several times to begin conversation, but stopped because he really had no more to say than before. Lynn pushed herself off from the counter and wandered over to the small TV at the far end. She turned it on and went back to her previous spot, the remote control in her hand. There was an old movie re-run on the current station.

She flipped channels randomly, not really interested in TV but wanting a distraction while the two of them pondered.

A news report on CNN flashed on the screen, the bottom caption riveting them both.

Dragons in Germany? Elaborate hoax, or authentic truth?

Lynn immediately turned the volume up, and Eddie leaned closer. The picture was a city street across from an airport, showing a few planes moving in the background, the city of Frankfurt listed as the reporter's current location, and a man in a trench coat in the foreground holding a microphone.

"...German authorities have told us very little, most likely because they themselves don't have much of an idea of what to make of it. Yet the report stands with twenty-three people so far from Lufthansa Flight 467 having come forward and confirmed that they saw a dragon flying in the skies, attacking the plane and then flying away again. The original counts of eye witnesses was only a handful, but as the days have passed more and more passengers have come forward confirming the story, including the Captain and co-pilot."

The scene changed to show a plane, and then some paper records showing types of damage and repairs required from the post-flight manifest.

"This plane shows signs of damage that one mechanic, who has been repairing airplanes for thirty years, described simply as nothing he had ever seen before. The wing, fuselage and paneling along the right side of the plane showed scorch marks and gashes."

The picture returned back to the reporter again. He was smiling as he continued.

"So is this an elaborate hoax and if so why would Lufthansa want to go through the trouble of it? There would appear to be no upside to it for the company, other than perhaps a publicity stunt, to give people the possible thrill of wanting to ride with the airline that flies with dragons."

"There is no way one of our three dragons could have possibly flown all the way to Germany and back, is there?"

Lynn didn't respond, too stunned by what she was seeing. The program continued with various interviews of people who had been on the plane, all swearing that what they described was true. This was followed by an interview with the Lufthansa flight crew, which now included a stewardess, who were all asked why they hadn't spoken of this earlier, why they were only coming out now, a week after the incident, to affirm what other passengers had reported.

"How do you fill out a report for your company, stating that a dragon attacked your plane?" the Captain replied. "We didn't know what to say, and in fact we still cannot believe it ourselves! But we saw what we saw, and once the passengers started talking, we felt it was our duty to step up and report the truth."

The scene changed to the inside of the studio. Eddie and Lynn leaned in closer.

"We have with us in our remote Frankfurt studio this evening Doctor Alistair Schmeltz, an American born scientist and writer whose parents are both from Gottingen, Germany. Doctor Schmeltz has done research and lived in both countries, and has doctorates in Psychology, Behavioural Studies and Political Science.

"Doctor, you have been in Germany this entire week, helping conduct interviews and assessments for Lufthansa and the German government. What can you tell us of these events?"

"I can tell you that in many cases of human psychology there are a myriad of possibilities. Delusions, hallucinations, factual events being changed by the psyche one or another...in most patients I have talked with the list is endless. And this is before we introduce outside influences such as narcotics, alcohol, stress, and the like. The people we have interviewed this past week have, for the most part, seemed like normal, rational people. I have found no evidence of lying or other deception in any of my examinations.

"So you think the story is real?

"No, no, I do not think it is real. The bottom line is that there are no such things as dragons, except where exist stories such as the Lord of the Rings, and other such fantasy. While I believe that all of the passengers of Flight 467 were telling the truth, I also believe that this truth has been implanted

in their minds: perhaps a toxin in the ventilation of the plane, trick of the light, or some other phenomenon to cause a mass hallucination. Let's face it, the plane was thousands of feet in the air, bright sunlight and cloud formations all around. The plane had been in flight for over five hours, and the computer reports that the cabin had depressurized, which may have caused the passengers to be operating with very little oxygen. All of these conditions could compound together, and create the perfect conditions for a mass hallucination, or mass hypnotic effect. One person starts pointing out the window at what they believe is a dragon, and the rest simply follow suit, their minds in such a state that they would believe any suggestion given to them."

Lynn flicked off the TV. The silence in the kitchen was broken only by the steady ticking of the hall clock. Lynn began to stammer out a few questions but stopped, unsure. Eddie nodded, feeling the same way. The clock ticked another minute, and one of the weights shifted a notch lower.

Lynn shook her head and busied herself by cleaning up in the kitchen. Eddie reached for a bowl of fruit, sprinkled some sugar on it and grabbed a fork.

Lynn took in a deep breath and exhaled loudly, facing away. "Eddie, don't tell the kids about the news report. The last thing we need right now is more questions, when we don't have any answers at all."

Eddie nodded. "Yep."

Lynn massaged her temples, feeling strained. "The only possible explanation is that there is a fourth dragon out there, one that was large enough to attack that plane, and oh my word what on earth am I saying?"

Eddie smiled weakly. "The only thing that actually makes sense."

She turned to face him. "How can that be, Eddie?" she whispered. "How can it be that something the entire planet, us included, would say is absolutely impossible actually be right? I know we have personally witnessed the three dragons playing with the kids, helping us light campfires, and flying around the house helping with chores. I know they exist and are not a figment of my imagination. But even so, how can this possibly all make sense?"

Eddie smiled again, and shrugged.

"Oh please, Eddie, I love you, but I need more than your cute smile and puppy dog eyes right now."

Eddie hopped off the stool and made his way around the island, putting the empty bowl in the sink, and wrapping Lynn in a big hug. Lynn sighed deeply and nuzzled into him, enjoying the warmth and companionship. Eddie said nothing for a long while, collecting his thoughts and rocking his wife slowly in rhythm with the clock.

"Lynn," he began finally, "I have no way of telling you some great insight or truth you don't already know. The fact is, we simply don't know! We're dealing with...no, let me correct that, the *kids* are dealing with something that for all intents and purposes are make believe. I won't lie to you – reports of another dragon, large enough to attack a plane – scare me. If the coming of our three dragons marks the beginning of a return of more of these things, I am not sure I want to be around for it. But I can tell you this much: the kids are truly loved and protected by the dragons. And for that reason alone, I can relax."

"You don't fear something bad happening?"

"Of course I do!" Eddie cried, laughing. "I've been terrified of anything bad happening to the kids since they were born! Heck, we still go check to make sure they are breathing alright when they are sleeping."

"You actually haven't done that in a while, you know," Lynn replied, nudging him in the ribs.

"Exactly. Do you really think that we wouldn't know if something was wrong? I am one hundred percent confident that if anything happened in the night, the dragons would come shrieking into our room, dragging us bodily into the hallway to get our attention."

Lynn smiled, hugging her husband tightly. "I guess you're right."

Eddie pulled away to put his dish in the washer.

"Besides, if those little buggers can knock me flat on my butt so easily, I just dare anyone else to mess with the kids!"

They both laughed.

Lynn put the last of the food back in the fridge and looked through the glass door to the kids outside. They were playing with the dragons again, as the sky began to grow dark. "You think that big dragon will show up here?"

"Well," Eddie began, thinking it through, "for starters we don't actually know it's real, but for argument sake let's say it is. Why would it be coming here? I mean, logically we have three dragons in the house, so it would make sense, but this is a big planet! And it's in Europe! And we also don't know how big it really is, regardless of what the passengers might be saying. What if that dragon is only as big as our three? It becomes three against one!"

Lynn walked over and flicked on the porch light. "Eight against one, actually, when you add the whole family together."

Eddie put an arm around Lynn's shoulders and smiled. "See? We're just one big happy family. I don't have any real answers, honey. I just feel like everything will be okay."

Lynn hugged him again, satisfied with that for now. They stepped outside and enjoyed the company of the family, joining in on games and conversation. When Madison began falling asleep in her chair, they all went inside and tucked in for the night. Lynn finished by turning the house alarm on then laughed silently to herself. What good would a house burglar alarm do against a dragon? And when the police arrived or phoned to check in, what would she say?

"Thank you, Doctor Schmeltz, it is very much appreciated, and very fortunate that as a member of the Order you were in Germany, on hand to provide that report."

"And what about on your end?"

"Yes, I have been monitoring the situation here. No sign of another, just these three."

"Have you been in contact?"

Christian looked down at the scanning unit in his hand. "Yes, I ran the test. Great amount of potential in the whole unit."

"Interesting. So we can assume that the packages may have been fated, or even drawn to that location for a reason? Or on purpose, perhaps?"

Christian shook his head. "If it was, I don't believe the group knew about it. Must have been subconscious, coincidental."

"Ever more interesting...." Doctor Schmeltz trailed off in thought. "I don't suppose you would want to tell me where you are so I can aid in your observations?"

Christian clicked some keys on his laptop, looking for some notes. "You know the rules, Doc."

"Yes of course, and the Order has them in place for good reason. Good night Mr. Woods."

"Good night Doctor."

The line went dead. Christian clicked away on his laptop for several minutes scanning information from the Order's encrypted archives. Two items in particular interested him; one a photograph of an ancient manuscript written in hieroglyphs, and the other a translation of a Gaelic text, the words 'Prophecy' from the former and "Merlin, Royal Court of Arthur" signed on the latter particularly standing out.

Beside the laptop, in the open case file, was a picture of each of the Zedmore family members.

He rapped his fingers against the armrest as he looked from the screen to the family pictures. "Just how did the dragons make it here, to your home, in your hands, if it wasn't planned by you?"

A soft jingle alerted him to incoming email. He switched the appropriate window and checked his roaming encryption status before opening the mail. He read it quickly once, then again more slowly, opening the attached picture when he was done and memorizing every detail.

"So, *you're* the government agent. Well, that's unexpected."

Christian smiled and looked to the heads-up display on his windshield, examining the night-vision image shown from the connected telescope that was positioned outside the vehicle. Everything in the house was dark, as it had been for the last hour or more. He reclined his chair and adjusted the air-compressed cushioning, getting comfortable for a night's rest, mentally making plans for morning.

10 Portals

"I DON'T REALLY HAVE ANY ideas, do you?"

Jared shrugged, shook his head, and then tossed a stone into the pond. The kids were sitting with their backs against the trees, staring out across the water.

"Maybe Penelope will learn how to turn invisible and we won't have to worry about it at all!" Madison exclaimed.

"That's stupid." Alex remarked.

"Besides, that would still leave Rex and Kishar out."

Madison was forever innocent and full of optimism. Her brothers thought she was just naïve. "Maybe they will all learn how to be invisible."

"They won't suddenly learn how to be invisible! There is no such thing!" Alex felt too upset from their talk with Mom and Dad this morning to be wishfully thinking.

"Are you saying there is no such thing as magic?" Madison asked sweetly. "Cause if you are, just remember that we have three dragons as pets!"

"Yeah, and my dragon can breathe fire! Rex is awesome!" Jared cheered. At the sound of his name, Rex came waddling over and crawled up onto Jared's leg. The wings flapped out in an expectant position for a rub down the spine. Jared complied happily. "You are the bestest wittle fire-bweathing menace, awen't you, wittle Wex!"

"Oh please," Alex groaned, rolling his eyes.

"Hey," Jared retorted, "don't be mad just because Kishar doesn't know how to breathe yet."

"He can breathe just fine, dummy."

"But not fire!" Jared taunted.

Alex fished for something to say in retaliation, but found nothing so he settled for throwing another stone into the pond.

It was a hot day, and the kids all found solace from the heat in the shade of the trees. All of the dragons had spent the last hour simply enjoying the sunshine, walking back to their owners for a rub, or getting a snuggle every few minutes. They had all been resting there for a couple of hours, undecided as to what to do. Their parents had given them the task of coming up with solutions to the problem of the dragons being discovered. It had been far too easy for Mr. Woods the meter-reader to arrive unannounced the night before.

All of the kids had suggested putting a fence around the house, building secret passages in the house, building the kids their own house, and several other creative ideas. So far none of them had appealed more than another.

They had all been asked to continue brainstorming ideas and bring them to the dinner table that night. Uncle Richard and Lilly were coming over for dinner, and Lynn and Eddie wanted to have a full discussion with all of them for options of what to do with the dragons. Lilly had been told about the dragons, although she hadn't seen them herself yet, but seemed to take the news without too much shock.

Jared looked about suddenly and thought out loud, "I wonder why the dragons aren't playing their game over the pond today?"

Alex and Madison both looked up across the pond as well. True enough; the dragons had been sitting with the kids without any of their usual games.

"That is kind of odd," Alex noted.

"Maybe they're upset, or sick," Jared added.

"Does the pond look bigger to you?" Madison asked. All three of them stood up to get a better angle on the water level.

"Yeah, I think it is."

"Look," Jared pointed, "there are the rocks where they all usually fly to." The rocks were clumped together on the far side of the pond.

"They look so small today," Madison observed.

"Have the dragons been eating them?" Jared wondered.

Alex took several steps towards the water's edge. "No, wait!" he said excitedly. "Look here! See, this is where the dragons usually perch on this side when they are playing the game." His brother and sister both confirmed his observation. "And see, this is where Penelope usually sits." Again, nods of affirmation. "Don't you get it? Look! Penelope's perch is usually about four or five meters out from the water but we wouldn't be able to walk there now!"

"We'd be wet and muddy if we walked that close," Jared confirmed.

"So the pond _is_ bigger!" Madison finished. After a moment she added, "But how?"

Alex folded his arms and tapped his finger to his chin. "It didn't rain last night as far as I know. Where did the extra water come from?"

"Alex, look." Jared was pointing back behind them to the tree line.

All three of their dragons were standing back near the trees, not coming any closer than they had all day. In fact, now that the kids were standing close – Alex was only two steps from being able to jump right in – the dragons all seemed agitated, anxious even, walking from side to side and seeming concerned. What was bothering them so?

"What's the matter, Kishar?" Alex asked. Kishar hissed a soft reply, his nose pointing to the pond. Alex turned around and regarded the pond, instinctively taking a couple steps back: if Kishar was worried about the water that was more than enough warning for Alex.

"Oh, come on, this is stupid!" Jared yelled. "It's just water!" He threw a stone hard into the centre of the pond, grunting with the effort.

"No wait!" Alex warned, but it was too late. The small rock flew through the air smoothly. Time slowed to their senses, and somewhere deep inside they felt the dragons develop a pure panic. The dragons were all bleating strange warning sounds, and Jared knew instantly he had done something bad.

The stone arced towards the water, and then stopped abruptly. It hit something solid, bouncing off nothing in mid-air before splashing into the water.

The ground shook. A low sound rumbled from the centre of the pond, causing ripples to shimmer across the surface. The sounds jarred the kid's right through into their bones, a deep bass echo that shook them to their knees. Rocks and dirt jostled all around, water splashed. It lasted several seconds and then was silent.

"What was that?" Jared whispered.

Madison scrambled backwards in a crab-walk, eyes darting everywhere.

Alex was afraid they were about to find out what was going on, whether they wanted to know or not.

Eddie stepped into the kitchen, wearing shorts and a golf shirt, but still rubbing his wet hair with a towel. "What's going on?"

Lynn shook her head at him and continued to listen on the phone. "Someone got a picture? A dragon flying by a plane? Of course I don't know anything about it, other than what we've seen on the news! How would I…? Richard! Just because we have a few little ones here doesn't mean….well…yes, I guess that is a very easy assumption to make. But no, these are the only three we know about."

Lynn listened for a long time while Richard read the story out of the paper. "Yes, Eddie and I will certainly need to talk more about this. Email that story to me if you can…Yes, thanks…about 4 o'clock today? That sounds great… Yes, we will make sure to have the kids and dragons prepared for you. Ok. Bye."

Lynn hung up the phone and closed her eyes, saying a quick and silent prayer.

Eddie hung his towel over the back of a chair. "That sounded interesting."

Lynn nodded, leaning onto the counter. "They're coming for dinner tonight. Richard wanted to come over sooner, but Lilly is at work right now, so they'll come over as soon as she is done for the day."

Lynn walked around and sat down on a bar stool, looking exhausted. Eddie stepped behind and gently rubbed her shoulders.

"You ok?"

Lynn smiled weakly. "Not really."

"What was the talk about the pictures of dragons?"

"Just one dragon, and several pictures. Turns out that some people from the Lufthansa plane had cameras or cell phones handy and took some shots – nothing very clear, but photo evidence nonetheless."

"And Richard thought we had something to do with that?"

Lynn nodded. "Apparently it has been on the news all morning."

"Well, maybe they will have experts who will claim the photos are fakes."

Lynn squared her shoulders. "It was in the *Herald*, pictures shown on the CNN news and the Internet, and several German police agencies verifying the pictures were not doctored in any way."

Eddie paused a moment. "I don't think it will be too hard to assume those pictures will go the same way as reported UFO pictures go – into a file and forgotten."

"We need to figure out how to hide the dragons. We can't simply allow them free reign of the house. And we need to have a contingency plan for when they are discovered. Let's face it, even with a six foot high fence around the entire house and property, the dragons fly...they *will* be discovered, eventually."

"Yeah, I suppose you're right. We have to assume that it won't be *if* they are found out, but *when*."

Lynn rubbed some sleep from her eyes, and then looked around the room. "Are the kids around? I have lunch ready for them."

Eddie looked out to the porch. "No, I think they are still over by the pond. You want me to go get them?"

"No," Lynn replied, "I have an idea. Let's bring lunch to them. We can give them a picnic out in the sunshine, and maybe see this game they say the dragons play."

Eddie clapped his hands and immediately started gathering paper plates and utensils. "Sounds like a great idea! And while we are out there, maybe we can put our heads together and come up with some answers to the dragon dilemma. Never mind the contingency problem of ours being discovered. We have to tell the kids about this other sighting, and figure out what we would ever do if that new dragon shows up here."

In a few minutes they were on their way, picnic basket and drink cooler in tow in one of the kids' red wagons.

I believe I have been discovered! Azurim thought.

He sent out a low growl, trying to call the young captive dragons to him. The world shook around him as he did so, yet the dragons did not respond. Instead, they hissed and cowered, staring directly at him.

Interesting, Azurim thought. *They can see me, although these human children cannot. So their powers are waxing, that is encouraging, yet they do not fly to me.* The dragon pondered that for a moment. *They do not know Dragon Law! Perhaps they are too young, and have not been taught?*

Azurim watched as the human children backed away from the pond, and the dragon whelps jumped defensively in front of the children.

Surrogate parents, it seems. I am not impressed. Dragons need other dragons for parents, not humans!

Azurim stood up fully and bellowed again, this time demanding with his Song that the young dragon kin come to him. The first call had been a question, a request, soft and gentle. This one was a command, and the sound blast knocked the human children flat. Azurim did not want to see dragon whelps perverted by human hands, taught by human customs.

The dragon whelps did not respond as he had hoped. The red one shot a spout of flame. The purple blasted some ice out and hissed a warning. The green stood up on its haunches and expanded its chest, the wings unfurled to make it as big as possible, shielding the children as best it could.

Azurim could not believe it. The whelps were protecting the children! Truly a strange sight indeed.

Azurim quickly made a decision, and shimmered into full view.

Madison screamed, terrified yet too scared to move. Jared and Alex sat mutely on the ground, dumbfounded by what they saw. All three of their dragons hissed louder, moving to protect the children.

Eddie and Lynn had heard sounds and had come running, the wagon bouncing and jostling as they ran. Just as they crested the final hill they saw their nightmare from the newscast the night before standing before them in real life.

In the middle of the pond, water cascading down its scales as it stood up and out of the water, was a fully-fledged dragon. The scales shimmered in iridescent colours. His body, wings and tail all gleamed in the sunlight, alternating between blinding white and a smooth light blue. As the dragon moved, the colours changed and flowed, catching the light and shining vibrantly like a perfect pearl.

Eddie dropped the handle of the wagon, frozen in time.

Lynn's mouth worked, trying to form words, but no sound issued forth.

The children still sat in the dirt with the boys staring wildly and Madison curled into a ball, crying.

The four dragons faced off, seeming like an old Western movie with the Sheriff and his Posse standing out in the street ready to draw his pistols against the villain.

Azurim began to shift again, launching all three of the small dragons into action. Penelope leaped into the sky, banking left then right, shooting a blast of ice. Rex jumped skyward as well, but made directly for the giant beast, hurling a fireball and following up with battering-ram speed. The small red dragon bounced off the thick hide of the much larger dragon, landing back with a splash at the edge of the pond.

Kishar flapped his wings to gain some air, but did not move. Instead, he hovered in place above and in front of the children, a living protective shield.

Noble, young green, however futile, thought Azurim. He open his mouth just a little and breathed out, a thin stream of ice darting like lightning out towards the human children.

Kishar open his mouth as well. Alex thought it would be fire, or ice, or acid, or something equally impressive. What happened was not what any of them would have ever expected.

Kishar breathed out a song.

The high-pitched song reverberated quickly, then found its focus and blasted into the jet of ice. It sounded almost like a chime, continuously being struck in a level rhythm. The ice streaming from Azurim vibrated then shattered, showering the children with small ice shards moments before the full blast could hit them.

Azurim stepped back one step, shocked. His step caused a wave to travel across the pond, crashing into the dirt and rocks on the other side.

That Song should not have been possible by one so young! He needed to test the whelps further.

Azurim, ignoring the feeble attacks from the other two dragons, lowered his head and prepared a blast of flame. Thin, short, and aimed directly into the dirt.

Kishar did not react.

Very good, young one.

A second jet of flame shot out, this time aimed directly for the children. Kishar lunged to one side, his mouth open again, a song blasting out. This one sounded like a low reed pipe, haunting and echoing. The flame was sent awry, impacting the dirt and leaving scorch marks.

Azurim was very impressed. A dragon so young could not have mastered the art of the Song – it had never been done before as far as Azurim could recall. This young green was only a whelp, a dozen or so years at most! How had it sung a Song already? Unless....

Kishar still hovered, but was obviously tiring quickly. Penelope was still flying circles, shooting ice when she could, but the ice was coming slower now, her strength waning. Rex was the only one that seemed full of energy, although he had realized his fire was useless and so was now head-butting Azurim in the side in a continuous stream. It was a laughable sight, if it hadn't been such a serious threat.

Azurim saw the older humans nearby and decided that this contest had to end, now. He bellowed a cry, knocking Penelope and Kishar from the air. Rex continued to pound with his head, and was sent reeling when a claw from Azurim flicked Rex away.

"You are coming with me, now!" Azurim ordered. The words were an unintelligible hiss to the humans, however the three young dragon whelps seemed to have heard every word clearly. They cowered and rasped, children begging their parents to stay longer at a party. Azurim heard none of it, and began singing his Song.

The pond churned, water frothing. The ground shook, rocks protesting the magical music. A shimmering wall appeared and began drawing the small dragons into it. Jared, seeing Rex being pulled away, flung himself completely onto the small red dragon and wrapped his arms around him. He screamed, but the sound was not heard in the roar of the Dragon Song. Rex clawed the ground while Jared's feet tried to dig in. Slowly, they were pulled towards the shimmering wall.

The other two children had found similar problems. Penelope had leaped onto Madison in fear, and the two of them held onto each other for dear life. Alex and Kishar defiantly held their ground, Alex grasping a rock and Kishar pinned to Alex's chest.

The safety of her children overcame Lynn's fear and shock. She sprinted down the short hill as fast as she could go, her legs pumping wildly to get her to her children. Eddie was still stunned by the events that had occurred, still processing what he had seen.

Azurim roared louder, knocking Lynn down in a jumble of arms, legs and dirt. Rex and Jared flew into the air and disappeared into the shimmering wall. Kishar and Alex followed shortly after, with Penelope and Madison stubbornly refusing to move. Madison called out for her mother, to which Lynn responded by diving for her daughter. She landed a meter away, straining with outstretched hand to grab Madison, when the purple dragon and her owner tumbled into the air, swallowed up by the shimmering wall.

Eddie finally snapped out of it, and started running as well, abandoning the wagon. He ran, but felt hopelessness in his heart.

Lynn screamed in panic, returning to her feet and running for the portal. Azurim faded into the portal, Lynn only a second behind the tail as it shimmered from view. Lynn dove again to try and follow her beloved children.

She landed squarely on muddy ground; the portal was gone, the pond back to its normal size. Her heart leaped into her throat, her mind scrambling for some secret, some alternative to the reality before her, some way to undo time for the last few precious seconds. But it was no use, and the horrible truth hit her like a knife through her heart: her precious children, her babies and the dragons, were gone.

11 Hiking

THE SENSATION OF FLYING. Wind. Rain. A beautiful song echoed. Silence. Darkness. Light. A strange vertigo and nausea. Reality twisted, then set right again.

The children sat up, feeling very sick. Their dragons were faring no better, stumbling around trying to regain their senses. Slowly the world came into focus.

There was a waterfall nearby, crystal clear waters almost blue in their perfection. The water rushed over a two-meter drop, splashing down into a pool of water teeming with colourful fish of red, blue, yellow, orange and purple. One particular large fish had a full yellow body with white stripes on the underbelly, glowing with light coming from within, shimmering along all its scales. Vibrant green moss and lichen grew from the water's edge, turning into lush fronds further out. Even the grass the children sat in appeared to be a deeper hue than normal, the teal blades swaying in the gentlest breeze and looking like an underwater scene. The grass was very soft, like falling into a set of bed sheets and pillows freshly changed.

The pool of water turned into a stream on the opposite end of the falls, snaking its way down a shallow hill, to fall again several meters over large rocks. All around them, tall trees with black bark and green and purple leaves obscured their view. The thin trunks were made up for by the incredible amount of foliage.

For several minutes they all steadied themselves, as if they had been out to sea and were getting used to solid ground again. The dragons recovered only slightly faster than the children did, walking about their new environment, testing it with their tongues, sniffing the air and listening intently.

Kishar suddenly hissed, and all the others spun at the sound.

The head of a giant dragon, one they were familiar with, was resting on the ground, covered mostly by branches and leaves. Azurim smiled as he saw the reaction, and slowly drew himself up to his full height. He was certain that a normal human could not have made the shift to the dragon realm of Shard without the use of a Gate. Surely, it had been attempted with temporary portals like the one he created today, but usually with failure – death – as a result.

But here was the proof of three human children standing before him. And three dragon whelps standing guard. All of them must have some kind of inherent magical power to have survived the trip. *Or maybe these dragons were able to protect the humans during the crossing,* Azurim thought. He wasn't sure what that might foretell, and dismissed the thought for the present.

"I mean you no harm, whelps. Why do you cower so?" Again the hiss was unintelligible to the humans, however the whelps understood precisely. They did not respond in kind, but simply guarded the children more alertly.

"They cannot be your parents! They are human!" Another hiss. Kishar shook his head and hissed in response.

It was a moment before Azurim responded. "I see." He growled then hissed more. "You have made them a part of your Clutch."

The whelps cocked their heads, remembering with a slight nod of agreement of the name Azurim gave the group. They had never given a title or description to what the human children were to them, only an emotion. They were their friends, their counterparts, and a part of their soul. What happened to one happened to all.

Azurim moved forward, and the human children scampered back. The dragons moved with them to protect them once again. Azurim stopped.

"I will see no harm to you, as you are part of their Clutch." Azurim felt a slight pang of guilt already for having attacked the human children earlier – had he known they were a part of the dragon's Clutch, he would have not fought at all. "I will not break Dragon Law."

The children stopped, as did the whelps, completely stunned. The dragon had spoken…in English!

"You…you can talk?" Alex asked rhetorically.

"As I see you can," Azurim replied in a deep rumble. "Come, we have a long journey ahead of us."

Azurim turned to move away taking several strides before stopping. He looked back and saw the six small figures staring at him, unbelieving.

"We do not have time to waste, young humans. We must move on."

"Where are we going?" Jared asked.

"That is not for you to know. Your place is only to follow." Azurim turned and moved, but once again stopped. None of them had stirred. He returned, suppressing his anger and impatience. Curiosity was winning out over his heated emotions.

"Explain why you are not moving."

"We're not going anywhere until we get some answers," Jared declared loudly. Rex hissed his agreement.

Alex was bolstered by Jared's bravado. "Yeah, like where are we?"

"Why'd you attack us?" Jared added.

"Where are we supposed to go now?" Alex demanded.

"When are you going to take us home?" Jared roared, bolder now.

"And when will our dragons be able to talk to us, too?" Madison asked quietly. She was calmly petting Penelope, stroking her head and wings, imagining what it would be like to have Penelope speak, what her voice would sound like, and what they would talk about.

Azurim sighed deeply. Children. Whelps. This was not going to be easy, and he was no Clutch Mother!

Kishar spread his wings and hissed. The children all listened, and realized with sudden clarity that the dragons had been trying to talk to them all along! They spoke their own language, using hissing, rasping, growling sounds combined with body movement to communicate, exactly as Kishar was doing now.

Azurim listened intently for almost a full minute as Kishar growled on. When Kishar was done, he snorted a matter-of-fact snort that showed he was not taking no for an answer.

The large adult dragon's head snapped forward so quickly that it caught all six of the other's off guard. One moment the dragon was towering above them, and the next they could feel his breath as the head stopped only a few centimetres away from Kishar. Kishar bleated in shock, but quickly regained his composure and stood as proud as he could, albeit with a slight shake in his legs.

"You, young whelp, would be wise not to make such demands of an Elder. Impressed with your bravery though I may be, you have no place to ask me of anything! You must learn and obey Dragon Law."

Kishar seemed to shrink a little after having been scolded, trying to hold his ground. Azurim snorted, moving away to once again tower above the group to be certain they knew their place with him. He was the Elder here, and thus his direction was absolute.

"Excuse me, um, mister dragon, sir," Jared stumbled through his words. He had felt brave a few minutes ago, but seeing the speed at which the dragon had just moved scared the fire out of him. "It would simply be nice to know where we are, and where you want us to go, before we blindly follow."

Jared waited, certain he was about to be squashed into a puddle of human goo any moment. Instead the large dragon studied Jared intently, finally seeming to side with him.

"Perhaps you are correct. It is clear that the whelps have no memory of learning Dragon Law, or are instead choosing to be forgetful, and they have chosen incredibly poor candidates for their Clutch. I assume without a real Dragon Brood present, they simply made the next best decision they could have, although a Unicorn or perhaps a Faun would have been a much better choice.

"I am Azurim," the dragon introduced himself, settling down on his haunches and crossing his front legs in front of him. His wings bent backwards at what seemed an impossible angle before pressing into the sides of his body. Without the wings, he looked like just another lizard. Huge for certain, and the shimmering colours of his scales were spectacular, but still a normal, albeit gigantic, looking lizard.

"I was chosen by the Dragon Council to come and find the whelps," Azurim continued, nodding towards the three small dragons.

"They have names, you know," Jared said, feeling somewhat insulted that his mighty Rex was being referred to as a whelp.

"Indeed?" Azurim inquired.

"Yes! This is Penelope!" Madison enthusiastically called. Her purple dragon purred and spread her wings in what appeared to be a bow.

"I assume then that *you* named the whelps, and they did not choose names for themselves?" It was obvious this was not proper etiquette for dragons, however Azurim still appeared to approve.

"The green one here is Kishar," Alex said eagerly. Kishar was wearily eyeing the greater dragon, but bowed in much the same fashion as Penelope had.

"Interesting choice of name, child, although it is a name typically given to a female."

Jared laughed and poked his brother tauntingly, and Alex swatted him back.

Azurim continued, not acknowledging the brothers fighting. "I find it interesting you would name a male dragon with a female name."

Alex jolted. "He is a boy dragon? For sure?"

"Of course!" Azurim assured him.

"How can you tell?" Madison asked innocently. She looked underneath Kishar, and then Penelope. "I can't see a difference."

Azurim faced Madison squarely. "How does your kind tell the genders apart? It is somewhat difficult at times for dragons to clearly define the genders of humans, but for us recognizing gender in another dragon is simple. I will not waste time describing it here."

Madison was still looking at the underbellies of the dragons, and still not seeing anything truly different to tell them apart. "Why would it be hard to tell a boy from a girl with humans? It's really simple: boys have a...."

"Ahhh! Mr. Azurim!" Alex jumped in quickly. "Can you tell me why Kishar is a female name? How do you know that?"

The large dragon raised an eyebrow at the sudden interruption, turning to face Alex. "The name Kishar is from the Akkadian texts of the dragon goddesses. She was the daughter of Tiamat – you will know all about Tiamat, of course?"

Alex shook his head slowly, somewhat at a loss. "Sorry, no, well, we did some study of legends and that was one of them, but I really don't remember too much about it...."

"Then why would you choose such a name?"

"Um...it...sounded cool?" Alex offered awkwardly.

Madison looked at Penelope a moment, then back at Azurim. "Is Penelope... is she, a she?"

"Of course she is," Azurim concluded quickly. "And Kishar is a fine name from a great legend, gender notwithstanding."

Madison sighed in relief and flung her arms around Penelope's neck, hugging and kissing her precious friend. Alex felt encouraged as well, patting Kishar on the shoulder.

"And you will want to meet Rex! He can breathe fire!" Jared roared proudly. Rex responded by puffing up his chest and unfurling wings, trying to be as impressive as possible.

"Of course she can breathe fire – I felt it on my scales once already," Azurim responded.

"Yeah wasn't it cool...?" Jared trailed off. Had he heard correctly?

Alex could not contain his grin. "Umm...did you just say that Rex is a 'she'?"

"Yes," Azurim replied flatly. "Now that introductions are complete, can I inform you of what you need to know so we can be on our way?"

Jared stared blankly at Rex. "F..f..fe..female?"

"Yes," Azurim said flatly. "Is there a problem?"

Alex laughed out loud, one short blast followed by a full tremor of laughter as he rolled on the ground. When Jared turned to fix Alex with a cold stare of hatred, Alex wisely clamped his mouth shut and focused his own attention on Kishar, pretending to inspect a wing.

"There has to be some mistake!" Jared yelled, wheeling back to face Azurim, feeling like he had been cheated out of the winning point in a game of basketball.

"Why would I speak an untruth, or make a mistake? 'Rex', as you so vulgarly call her, is a female. However she has said she is happy of the name – so be it. She breathes fire, and in the majority of times only females can breathe fire. Penelope breathes frost, and Kishar can sing the Song, albeit at a rudimentary level. He will need much training before he can master the Song."

Jared was crushed, looking like he had just lost a limb. His shock and disappointment were etched on his face.

Azurim raised his chin in a proud stance. "Come, child Jared, there is no reason to be upset. Rex has chosen you for her Clutch-mate, and that is an extreme honour! You should not be saddened by something as ridiculous as gender."

Jared was simply too upset, embarrassed and hurt to respond. He had named the dragon Rex because it was supposed to be a boy! Big, tough, strong, powerful, Rex – a man's dragon, a Tyrannosaurus Rex! Why did it have to be a girl? He felt bad now for teasing Alex about Kishar for so long, and his loss was more to wounded pride than for lack of affection for Rex.

He stood mutely, with Rex at his side feeling his sorrow and trying to persuade him to rub her neck. She cooed and pressed into his hand, attempting to befriend him again.

Alex had picked up on something that Azurim had said, and asked about it now.

"How did you know my brother's name?"

"I know all your names, child Alex," Azurim replied matter-of-factly. "Kishar told me."

Alex looked at Kishar and back to Azurim, confused. Azurim sighed, shaking his head slightly. Humans knew so little, and were so slow to understand!

"During our minor skirmish near your pond, Kishar told me. He told me to leave the child Madison, child Alex and child Jared alone, as well as the parents."

Kishar snorted and shook his neck like a dog shaking off water. Azurim responded with a low, deep growl from far within his chest, and then clicked a couple of times.

"What was that?"

Azurim translated for the children. "Kishar told me that the warning was still in effect about his desire to protect you, and I told him to mind his place and not to talk to an elder in such a common fashion."

Alex's head was starting to hurt from all the new information he was going through. This meant that the dragons had been listening and understanding them all along! They just weren't able to talk back!

"So they will all eventually learn how to talk with us?" Alex was impressed.

Madison's excitement boiled over. "Yay! Oh Penelope! That means you and I will be able to talk, just like sisters! And have sleep over's, and gossip, and everything!" Madison dove headlong into another body hug with her dragon. Alex rolled his eyes, and Azurim matched the expression.

"Now then," Azurim began, "if there are no more interruptions, may I begin the explanation you require?"

Alex shrugged and found a nice patch of grass to sit in. Madison was still rolling on the ground, holding onto Penelope tightly, so intent was her affection. Jared still stood mutely, but his hand had found function again and was slowly stroking Rex's neck.

"We are going to the Dragon Enclave where the Council is awaiting our return. When the whelps awoke from their slumber in the earth, their presence was sensed even here. They were assumed lost forever, since the time when the gates were closed. The Council met to decide what to do, and I was chosen to go to your Earth and find the whelps. I have done so, and now must bring them to the Council so that they may be taught in the proper fashion of Dragon Law.

"It is a long journey. I had expected only the dragons to come through the portal, not human children. We would have flown to the Council however I see that you do not have wings, and therefore we must walk. By Dragon Flight it is only a trip of a few days away – to walk will be much longer, I fear, however I believe we have a solution to even that problem. Time will tell.

"And so, let us be on our way," Azurim concluded, standing up suddenly. The children did not readily move. Neither did their pets.

"Is there a problem?"

Kishar hissed, to which Alex added his own retort. "Of course there's a problem! A few minutes ago you tried to burn us and then freeze us, then you warped us to some unknown place and expect us to simply follow you after that lame explanation?"

"Lame...?" Azurim echoed, irritated, one eye rising up.

Alex cowed down a little, but Kishar hissed and ruffled the scales on his neck. Azurim sighed and settled back down again.

"Very well. What are your questions?"

The children all looked around at each other, no one electing to speak first. They were each bursting with dozens of questions but not knowing where to start, or how much time they had to ask them.

It was Rex who began the questioning. She stomped and bleated, hissing and rasping a few times. Azurim seemed to smile, but the kids couldn't be sure if it was a smile or a sneer with the large fangs showing when the upper lip curled back.

"Yes, Rex, I pulled you here against your will. Dragons do not belong on their Earth any longer. Our time there is past, and you will learn more of this when you begin to study Dragon Law."

"What is Dragon Law?" Madison thought out loud, not really expecting an answer.

"Dragon Law is the history and teachings of all dragons, telling us how to behave, act and interact with others."

Jared plucked out a long piece of grass and chewed on one end of it. "Sounds like a description of the Bible."

"Where exactly is 'here'?" Alex asked.

Azurim glanced around before replying. "We are standing in the forest of Dom'Shar, fourth province of the Tao'Zhendre faction, western edge of Khalndros, Valley of the Master's Chair."

Six pairs of eyes stared unblinking at Azurim, confused. Azurim sighed and shook his head.

"That doesn't sound like any of the maps we've looked at in Social Studies," Jared said.

Madison silently nodded agreement while the dragons simply snorted.

Alex looked up at Azurim with expectation. "Maybe it's in Asia, or India."

The large dragon seemed indifferent. "I cannot tell you any more plainly than that. We are standing in the location where I have just designated for you. Any more embellishment would simply confuse you further."

Penelope hissed and tilted her head, scales at the back of her neck flexing. Azurim turned to her and replied in kind. All three of the small dragons seemed to flinch at the response, becoming agitated and looking scared.

"What did you tell them?" Alex asked, concerned.

"And what did she tell you?" Madison added, petting Penelope to calm her.

"Penelope asked how far away we were from your home, near the body of water where we first met. I told her that we were too far away to return now, if ever."

"What?" all three children exclaimed simultaneously. Upon seeing the children's reaction, the dragon whelps all began cooing in panic, more disconcerted than ever now.

"We can't ever go home?" Jared wailed.

"Why not? That's not fair!" Madison cried.

"Send us back!" Alex demanded.

Azurim took it all in stride. He understood that a lack of knowledge is a right cause for upset and inner turmoil, and so his patience for these children was growing. He was beginning to like them. "I cannot send you back. I have not the power."

"Then who does?" Alex demanded more angrily.

"The Master of the Council. *If* he decrees that it is necessary, and *if* he grants access to the Gate, then it *may* be possible for you to return to your own world."

"So where is this Master?" Jared blurted.

"The Master of the Council is waiting at the ziggurat, with the rest of the Council, for our arrival. Which again, I stress the importance of to you. We must tarry not long and move towards our goal quickly. However I sense many more questions still budding within you all."

"Why is it so important that our dragons get back to the Council so fast?" Alex asked.

"There is a sense of urgency from the Council, for when the presence of the lost children was felt it brought with it a dark omen. The Gates between our worlds have been sealed by a decree from the Master for a great length of time, avowed never to be opened again for fear of the resurgence of the Great War. The Council was successful in sealing the Gate, yet was unable to seal it completely. A fissure has always remained, insignificant though it may be."

"A fissure? You mean a hole?"

"Yes. Infinitesimal, but apparent nonetheless. There was no explanation for the fissure and so a guard was set. The gates were sealed completely, but the last Gateway was never fully closed. If the Master allows it to be used for your travel, there is but this one remaining Gateway to your world."

"Only one?" Alex asked. "If there is only one gate, why didn't we come out through the gateway? Why did we end up here in the middle of a forest? Shouldn't we see a shimmering portal, or doorway, or something?"

"Very astute observation, child Alex. We did not appear at the Gateway because the Gateway is many leagues away. Several thousand of what you call kilometres, I have come to discover. The Gate is the only possible passage to your world from this side; however the limited magic still flowing in your world allowed me to create a portal from your world to ours."

"Magic?" Madison asked.

"Yes. The flow still exists on your side, although fairly weak. Here it is much stronger, but the flow on Earth was beginning to increase, and has been increasing from the very moment that Kishar, Rex and Penelope were awakened. If the flow had increased too much for too long a period of time, it is likely that the Gate would have collapsed completely, opening once again, and we could not allow this to happen, which is why I was sent to retrieve the whelps. Bringing them back here would allow the flow of magic to Earth to cease."

"But that doesn't explain how you were able to magically bring us here, instead of having to use the portal."

"I was given permission by the Master to use a crystal to power a spell, allowing me to create a temporary portal. The crystal stores magical energy, which is released when required."

"Then you could use another one and send us home!"

Azurim shook his head. "Unfortunately, no, I was only given the one crystal, and its power has been spent."

Alex was getting more and more lost by the moment. He looked at his siblings and realized they were feeling the same. Azurim was answering all their questions, but the amount of information to absorb – and how alien it was to them – was something hard to take. Even with all of their video games and movies, this was just too much! Alex shook his head to clear it. He was getting tired and needed to rest before trying to understand more of this, and he noticed his siblings looking tired as well.

Azurim noted the strained look on the children's faces, from both physical and mental fatigue.

"Come," he began as he rose to all fours, "we will travel a short distance, and then take rest and sustenance. There is a camp nearby that will serve us."

"Sustenance?" Madison asked, not sure of the word.

Azurim thought a moment. "Food."

The children hesitated for only a moment: Azurim did not seem to want to harm them, and appeared to be as good as his word. Whatever his underlying intentions he did not appear to be hostile, besides rest and food sounded good to them. They hadn't eaten anything since breakfast!

The children, Rex and Penelope all stood up and stretched their legs, ready to go. Kishar did not. He hissed, rasped, bleated and growled, obviously saying something at length to Azurim. Once Kishar was done, he sat firmly down, refusing to move until his question had been answered.

Azurim glared at Kishar with a penetrating gaze. The impertinence of youth! His hissed a short reprimand, reminding the young dragon to learn his place and not speak to an elder so. Then Azurim turned to translate for the rest.

"Kishar does not trust me, and wants to know more about where we are going before we leave. He also warned me that if harm came to any of the five of you that I would be the one to pay for it. I replied that he should never again question my honour, nor the Word of an elder. You must all understand that dragons speak the truth, or they say nothing at all: honour is everything, and we follow it to the code of Dragon Law."

"*All* dragons *always* speak the truth?" Alex asked.

"Yes," Azurim replied shortly. His eyes wandered to the trees. "Those who follow Dragon Law speak only the truth, and those who reject Dragon Law are banished from our kingdom.

"However, to speed our journey, and to answer Kishar's questions and demands: I will lead you all to the Sylvan Camp. It is an outpost on the edge of Dom'Shar Forest where we will find suitable lodging for you all. We will rest there for the night, perhaps two, and once rested we will resume our journey. The Sylvan Camp is a short distance away.

"And no, Kishar, I will not lower myself as a steed and allow you all to ride me as a common horse!"

Azurim stated the last with finality and a somewhat indignant air. It was obvious that Azurim's pride was in question, and the children snickered quietly.

As they began their walk through the forest, Azurim clearing the way with his bulk, Alex had one last question for him.

"Azurim, Kishar seems to try and be the leader for our dragons all the time, like the big brother. Is he the oldest, or is there something else in the nature of dragons that makes him act that way."

"An excellent question, young Alex. Kishar is the eldest of the three children. He is also the only male, and therefore assumes the role of leader, protector and guide. However, he has not learned or remembered yet that in Dragon Law, I, being the eldest male in this entourage, am now fulfilling that role. He is supposed to step back and let me assume the mantle of authority here."

Alex thought about that, which led to another question.

"Do you know their ages?"

"At first I did not," Azurim admitted, "and am unable to give you an exact number, but after speaking with them I have come to know that Kishar is the eldest, followed by Rex and then Penelope. It is rare for hatchlings such as these to be so close in age, however all three were born very close together. Dragons usually have only one, and sometimes rarely two, in a single hatch. These three were all born close together, that is certain, but specifically how close I do not know. Because of their absence and dormant-state sleep I cannot be completely accurate, however each of them has said they were at least fifty years old when they went into their slumber."

"Fifty!" Jared exclaimed.

"Yes," Azurim continued his teaching without pause. "These dragons appear much smaller and younger – I myself had guessed at only a dozen or so years. I believe that the disconnection from the magic flow, as a result of the sealed Gates, slowed their growth and eventually sent them into a long slumber. Now that they are here, the magic flow should allow them to grow to match their maturity.

"You must understand that for dragons, fifty years is still very young. Dragons do not age much during their first sixty years. On or before the eve of their sixtieth birthday, the dragons must undergo the Ceremony of Stars, in which their age is recognized and the continuance into adulthood begins. Once the ceremony is complete, those that survive are formally invited into the Enclave."

"Those that survive?" Alex asked, worried.

"Yes. The Ceremony proves those of which understand Dragon Law, and those that do not. Those who do not have a vote cast at them from the Council: if they have found favour with the Council, they are allowed 10 more years to prove their knowledge and worth; those who do not have favour are returned to the Weave, as they are not suitable for the responsibility of taking part in the Song."

"Returned to the weave?" Jared wondered out loud.

"Killed," Azurim explained.

"Killed! Why! Just because they don't pass some stupid test!"

Azurim halted abruptly, his head swinging around to stare directly into Jared's face with glaring eyes, hot breath and sharp teeth. Jared turned a pale shade of white while Azurim bellowed.

"They are not stupid tests! The Ceremonies of Dragon Law have held our kind together for thousands of years. They are traditions that hold our society in peace and cooperation. The sanctity of Dragon Law is the basis of our very way of life! I do not ask you to understand it, human children, only that you obey it! Dragon Law is what these young whelps must learn if they are to survive, and is indeed the only reason why any of you are alive now!"

Jared nodded, hoping the big teeth before him didn't change their mind and chomp him in two, as Azurim turned to resume their journey.

Alex grinned in spite of himself, poking Jared in the ribs to get him moving again. Jared swatted Alex's hand away and grumpily moved forward. Alex wanted to tease his brother more, but still had more questions.

"Azurim, you said that Dragon Law is the only reason why any of us are alive. Why is that?"

Azurim continued walking, staying low so he could push his way through the trees to make a clear line for the children to walk on. He called his answer back over his shoulder. "Humans are not allowed here. This world in its entirety is considered sacred ground for Dragon kind. Any human that sets foot here is breaking the Law, and is immediately put to death, with exception for those whom the Council has decreed are allowed to reside here. It was necessary to create this Law after the Great War. You three are spared. Fortunately for you, the whelps have officially claimed each of you as a Clutch Mate, and so the Law is now in debate. As part of their Clutch, you are considered to be blood brothers and sisters to the dragons.

"Any member of a Clutch cannot be harmed, in any way, until they have completed the Ceremony of Stars. Once the Ceremony is complete, rivalries, matters of honour and any other violations may then be taken into account."

"Well, we appear to have plenty of time then," Jared said, smiling and relieved.

"No, child Jared, you do not."

"We don't? I thought you said we were safe until the Ceremony of Stars was complete. Our dragons can't take that test until they are grown up, and they aren't growing very fast – that will take forever!"

"No, child Jared," Azurim repeated. "The Ceremony of Stars is precisely what ushers a young dragon into their life as an adult and it must occur on or before their sixtieth birthday."

"Azurim?" Alex asked, getting the dragons attention. "You said that our dragons were over fifty already. Do you know exactly how old they are?"

Azurim sighed. "Not precisely, young Alex, however with Kishar's help we have been able to come to a very close estimate."

Alex was sure he didn't want to know the answer to his next question, but he asked it anyway. "How old are they, then? When do they need to take the test? The Ceremony of Stars?"

"Kishar was born first, sometime before Rex although the exact amount of time he does not recall. Rex was born five days before Penelope – Kishar does recall that detail. Each of them will be facing their trials in the Ceremony of Stars when they are ready to, and must complete the Ceremony within the next few weeks."

"Weeks?" Madison echoed. She was suddenly feeling very scared and worried for her poor Penelope. The purple dragon sensed Madison's unease and came soaring in close to try and sooth her.

"Yes," Azurim replied. "The dragons are very close to the right age, and Kishar tells me that they have not forgotten all of Dragon Law, they are simply slow in remembering it. It has been, after all, a very long time of sleep for them."

"Ok, wait a minute," Jared began, pieces falling into place, "we're part of the Clutch now, right, and Dragon Law protects us from harm because of that, until the Ceremony of Stars has been completed. Does that mean *we* have to take the Ceremony of Stars challenge too? And whether we do or not, once the Ceremony is complete does that mean we're free to go, or killed because we're human?"

Azurim did not slow his pace as he replied. "Those are all matters that the Council will need to decide."

The group fell into silence, unsettled by what they had learned so far. There was already a lot of knowledge to digest, and the remainder of the travel time was absorbed quickly in silent thoughts. Azurim was thankful that no more questions were forthcoming, although he had to admit the human children had surprised him with their obvious care and concern for their Clutch Mates; he, too, had learned a lot this day.

It was nearly an hour when they arrived at Sylvan Camp. All expectations of what kind of camp they would find were completely wrong. Standing on the hillside looking down into the site made each of the children realize they were definitely not in Canada any more, and they were starting to wonder if they were even anywhere in their own galaxy.

12 Kansas

THE SETTLEMENT WAS NOTHING like anyone would have dreamed of. Nestled on the edge of a great forest, the Sylvan Camp was the size of a small city. The forest to the north and west touched the horizon, a line of craggy rocks filled their view to the distant east, and the vast open grassland to the south appeared endless. As it was nearing dusk, hundreds of lights dotted the landscape in a myriad of colours: red, pink, green, yellow, orange, blue and several other shades that the children were sure they didn't know the proper name for. The sources of light came from lanterns, windows, flying creatures both large and small, and some of the light seemed to just hover in mid-air with no discernable purpose other than to glow.

The buildings came in all shapes and sizes as well. There was very little that seemed familiar to the children. Buildings seemed to spring up right out of the ground, and as they walked closer they found out that they did! One large tree had been shaped as it grew, creating walkways and doorways until it housed several strange looking creatures with goats' legs, horns and a vaguely humanoid looking appearance.

There was also a giant rock that had been carved or sculpted into its shape: several windows and doors at various angles had been cut in at the sides and top, allowing insect creatures to move about easily. One such insect came around the corner as the children entered the city, saw them and immediately backed into the rock. It was a centipede of some kind, except that the hindquarter had a large segmented shell with two great pincers, looking like a cross between a millipede and a crab.

Madison's face was scrunched up in a combination of amazement and confusion. "You call this a camp?"

Azurim snorted, which they assumed passed for a short laugh. "I admit, the name is deceiving, however it stands nonetheless. The Fair Folk had a small outpost here many years ago which at the time was only the size of a camp. The name has never changed, despite the growth.

"Children, stay close to me, step where I step, and follow directly behind me. Stray not! I can protect you, but only if you obey me."

"Protect us...?" Jared trailed off.

Azurim did not answer, but instead forged ahead into the strange city. They all followed closely without another word.

Everywhere they looked there was something bizarre. Azurim seemed unimpressed by any of it and simply marched forward. The children were fascinated, stumbling forward and pointing at many things, while also keeping their mouths shut: they didn't want to attract trouble in such an alien environment. All of their questions would need to wait until they arrived at their destination.

Penelope and her siblings created a protective circle around the three children, flying at close angles to them and hopping from perch to perch as the kids walked. It seemed to be working: no other creature walked within ten paces of the group as Azurim led them through the city.

Azurim passed through an archway made of twisted brambles of wood, grown together from two different trees on either side of a path. He ducked to go through, even though the arch was very high, far above the children's heads. The pathway also widened here immediately after passing through the arch, spacing out so the children and all three dragons, plus maybe a friend or two, could all walk side-by-side and still not touch the edges.

A black, dark, foreboding shape loomed in the shadows, stepping in front of the children as Azurim passed. They were forced to stop, all three dragons instantly hovering forward and hissing. They saw the shape move slightly, and the sound of a long blade being drawn from a sheath could be heard though not seen. It advanced on the human children, smiling, the moonlight glinting on triple rows of razor sharp teeth that formed a triangular mouth. The shadowy form had four legs, and at least two arms, but it blended into the night so effectively it was hard to make out anything more than that.

It spoke in a deep baritone voice, a language not intelligible. The voice chilled the children to their core, and they felt like they may have already died so cold was the grip filling their hearts. Dozens of creatures lined the pathway and climbed up the archway for a better view, waiting to see the outcome of this battle. The children sensed the spectators already knew the outcome, and were just coming to watch the show.

A wreath of flame blasted from ahead, engulfing the dark opponent in a blink. It roared and squirmed in pain, trying to escape the heat. A great clawed arm shot forward, holding the demonic figure in place while the flame continued to press down. Azurim blasted fire over his own paw, holding the figure in place like a glassblower might hold a piece of art in a kiln, making sure it could not escape. Several long seconds passed as the flame continued, not ceasing until the creature went limp and stopped all motion and sound. Azurim shot flame in two more direct arcs, and when he was satisfied the creature was no longer moving he discarded it like a rag doll to the side of the path. He then roared a challenge into the night air, to which the response was a chorus of chitters and squeaks as thousands of beings great and small scampered to safety. In moments the way was clear, every creature giving Azurim and his charges a wide berth.

"Is it...?" Alex asked, unable to finish the question.

"Dead?" Azurim finished for him. "No, this creature regenerates its health quite quickly, but the damage done will leave it incapacitated for some time. It was a warning to it, and all others in this town, that you are in my care and protection."

Azurim look left and right one more time. "I believe they will leave us be now."

"No kidding," Jared murmured.

The others nodded mutely, stunned by what had just happened. Azurim turned and resumed his walk, the rest of the group falling quickly into step, staying close.

No one else dared confront them on their way through the city. Azurim's encounter with the demon – the children were calling it a demon simply because they had no other name for it – and the bellow that followed had indeed cleared a path for them.

Near the center of the city was a large two-story building, somewhat familiar in style. It was a white building with brown wooden crossbeams, looking like an old European inn. The top floor had stained-glass windows, shinning colourfully with some type of light behind them. The main floor had a large barn door to one side, where livestock would be housed, and a small door on the opposite end of the same wall where people entered the tavern.

It was the only building of its kind, and in a city such as this, it stuck out visibly from the rest.

Azurim strode forward, straight to the smaller door and reached out a claw, rapping three times on the wooden panels.

"Come in, it's open!" came a call from inside.

Azurim knocked again.

"I said its open!" the voice called again. The sound of heavy, hard footsteps could be heard clopping on wooden floorboards. The door opened outward, and a small man stepped through. To call him a man was not truly correct, however the children didn't know what other title to use.

He stood about five feet tall, with two strong horse-like legs that seemed to be put on backwards. Above the waistline it turned into a human man's body. His hair was quite different, however, flowing down his back like a long and beautiful golden-blonde horse's mane, tapered at the top in a V, leaving the sides and front of his head bald. He wore a purple and yellow shirt that was open at the back to allow his mane, which ran all the way to the small of the back, room to shake free. He wore circular spectacles, perched on the end of his nose which made him look scholarly and book-wise.

The children were all instantly enchanted by this charismatic man, his beaming smile showing that he had an open-arms policy for anyone! Madison wanted to rush forward and hug him, and the boys felt the same.

Azurim narrowed his focus on the innkeeper, but remained tall in a strong posture. "Ithicar, it is good to see you again."

The horse-man looked up and squinted, then lost the spectacles from his face as his eyes widened. He bowed quickly and shook out his mane.

"Lord Azurim, a pleasure as always," Ithicar replied, guarded and icy.

"I assure you I am not here on any malicious purpose, Ithicar...this time."

"What do you want?" Ithicar asked directly, wanting to get immediately to the point. His eyes squinted in suspicion.

"I have a favour to ask of you, one which I will consider to cancel any debt or remaining ill-blood between us."

Ithicar thought long, obviously not trusting the great dragon.

"What is this favour, Azurim? Word has already spread that a dragon torched a Sentinel tonight. I assume that was you?"

Azurim nodded. "It was necessary," he said unapologetically. "I have some charges that need food, lodging and travel gear. You are the best person I can think of to equip them."

Azurim stepped slightly to the side to open the view of the rest of the group. Ithicar bent down and retrieved his spectacles. When he stood with his spectacles suitably perched on his face, he looked to where Azurim had indicated.

The transformation was like deepest night to brightest day. When he saw human children his face exploded in a supernova smile. The spectacles fell from his face again as he rushed forward incredibly fast, engulfing the children in a great hug, then prancing circles around them as he inspected the children at great length.

"Oh my goodness! We have guests! This is unprecedented – you must tell me all about your journey, and of earth! I assume you are from earth, and not some hidden location in Shard? What has happened? Please, please come in to my humble abode! My home is yours! Oh, look at how precious you all are! A young little girl – oh, no, my apologies! A Princess! And two young Princes! Surely you must be royalty of the highest order to garner a Dragon as a guard! Please, please come in! I will have the beds made ready, and a table for dinner!"

Azurim smiled a toothy grin, confident he had made the right decision.

The children were being ushered into the building without another second glance from Ithicar. Azurim spoke quickly to the dragon whelps, and then called to the children.

"Young ones, I will speak with your Clutch here, as we have much to do. Please, enjoy the hospitality of Master Ithicar Horsemane, master innkeeper of the Sylvan Camp."

"What do we do?" Lynn sobbed, tears flowing down her face in torrents.

Eddie was silent a moment. "What can we do?"

The two of them had sat out by the pond for several hours already, searching and calling for their kids, the dragons, God or anyone else that might hear and help them, and then finally just sitting in the dirt beside the pond crying. Their children had been swallowed whole by something strange that neither of them could fully explain. Everything in life precious to them was gone, and they were powerless to do anything about it.

They had cursed and wished the dragons were never real but then took it back. The kids loved the dragons and they wouldn't want to take that away from them. So they wished that they had been here sooner, or that the portal had stayed open long enough for them to follow, or this, or that, or that.

And so it went all afternoon, throwing curses, prayers and wishes to the wind. They couldn't go to the police. Who would believe them? And what could they do anyway? They couldn't tell family or friends, or gather a search party – only Richard really even knew about the dragons, and to tell anyone else would be pointless right now because they had no proof. The dragons and the children were gone.

Eddie came to his senses as the evening began turning into night. The first stars were coming out in the twilight, and the cool summer night air brought to him the realization that they were cold, hungry, tired and alone, and no matter what had happened they needed to get home.

"Lynn, there is nothing more we can do out here now. I don't think there is anything we can do but wait."

"I can't just sit around doing nothing!" Lynn cried.

"I know, sweetie, I know. I want to act as well. I want to rescue them, or cast a magic spell and follow them. Or just do ... something! Anything is better than nothing, but unfortunately there is no course of action we can take right now."

It took several minutes of coaxing, but Eddie finally managed to gently get Lynn to her feet. He had cleaned up the mess of the food that had spilled from the wagon, and now pulled it behind him as he led his wife back to the house.

"They will be ok, honey, you'll see."

"How do you know?" Lynn asked, hysteria building up inside her.

Eddie put his hand on hers and stopped, gazing into her tired, fearful eyes. "I feel it, Lynn. There is something that tells me they will be just fine. We will see them again. Right now we just need to have faith, and wait, which I know is the hardest thing to do."

Lynn was empty inside, drained. She simply nodded and let Eddie lead her back to the house. She had cried all afternoon until she was exhausted and dehydrated.

Eddie pulled the wagon onto the deck and then led Lynn inside. He sat her down at the kitchen table and brought her something to eat. She refused at first then realized how hungry she was. The two of them ate in silence. Eddie finished first and ran upstairs. Lynn heard a bath being drawn, and smiled briefly despite her sorrow.

Lynn mutely allowed herself to be led upstairs to their room where Eddie got her ready for a bath. There was a robe, nightgown, towel and slippers nearby, the bath was steaming and a laundry basket set for all her dirty clothes. Eddie then led her into the bath, pushing a waterproof pillow behind her head so she could soak and rest. He left to attend to the dishes and a general clean up of the kitchen and deck. About thirty minutes later he returned upstairs to find that Lynn hadn't moved. She was simply soaking in the same place, staring out through the high window to the stars that were appearing.

Eddie washed her down, took the shower handle down and rinsed her clean, then dressed her in a nightgown and led her to bed. Lynn stumbled behind, her mind fixed on the last sight of her children before they disappeared, her body too tired to argue. She settled into bed easily, Eddie kissing each eye to force them to close. In moments Lynn was asleep.

Eddie took his own shower and finally allowed himself to open his heart up. He cried, he prayed, he cursed, but finally just washed it all away in the suds of the shower. He brushed his teeth, made sure the house was turned down for the night, and went to bed. It was a few minutes later when Lynn spoke.

"Eddie," she said softly, "thank you."

Eddie grunted a reply. He was too tired to form a coherent response right now, and wasn't sure he could remain as strong as he had previously if she pressed the conversation.

"Thank you," Lynn repeated. "It must have been hideously difficult for you, but thank you for keeping the level head and getting us moving, otherwise I would probably still be out there by the pond, crying."

Eddie didn't turn to face her, but kept his head buried snugly into his pillow and took a deep breath. "Get some rest, honey. We'll....we'll think better about this in the morning."

Lynn reached out and grasped her husband's hand.

"I feel better, thanks to you. And because of that, I *can* feel hope now. I know we will see our kids again." Lynn pondered that for a moment. To her mind, there was simply no other way. "We *have* to see them again."

Lynn forced her thoughts away, lest she begin crying again. She drifted off to sleep.

Eddie woke the next morning, late. The sun was already very high into the sky when he blinked his eyes open. Lynn was not in bed. He looked over to the clock – almost eleven. His emotional exhaustion had taken its toll, and he was glad for the rest.

He dressed and slowly made his way downstairs. There wasn't a sound in the house, and he was reminded of the disappearance of the kids. His heart instantly sagged, saddened by loss. He swallowed dryly, trying not to cry. Instead, he busied himself with tasks to keep his mind off of negative thoughts: making toast, tea, cutting an orange.

Eddie stepped out onto the porch, noticing that the picnic table wasn't there anymore and it was then he realized he hadn't seen Lynn yet. He wolfed down his food and went to the front of the house. The cars were all still there, and in fact there was a pickup truck there he didn't recognize, and a Jeep. Odd.

Eddie shook his head. *What is she up to now?*

Eddie quickly cleaned up and dressed. His guess – which he knew to be true without a second thought – was that he would find Lynn out by the pond, doing goodness-knew-what.

Sure enough, when he arrived at the pond there were tools, equipment, lumber and a couple Bobcats working away. A larger truck and trailer with a large 'Ace Contracting' printed on the doors was nearby.

A table with plans pinned down by rocks, bracing the papers from the breeze, was covered by a large white tarp suspended on metal poles, giving shade from the hot sun.

Guess I know where the porch table disappeared to, Eddie thought.

Lynn was talking at length to a contractor at the table; Richard was standing with them staring intently at the papers, while Lilly was pouring some lemonade for them all, her wavy strawberry-blonde hair glinting almost as much as the liquid in the glass cups did. She smiled at Eddie as he wandered up, waving a cup in his direction, but he declined the invitation with a shake of his head. Lilly's aqua eyes looked like they had been pulled off the page of a magazine showing the best beaches of the world, so deep was the colour. It was no wonder Richard had fallen for her at first sight.

Eddie noted that they were all wearing jeans, hiking boots and work shirts, which already showed splotches of dirt here and there. He sighed and slowly made his way over to the table. He didn't say anything; he just stood and waited to be noticed, trying not to intrude.

The contractor was nodding and pointing to various sections of the plans.

"We'll build the shelter here, Mrs. Zedmore, and the equipment will be housed inside. We can have the electrical run temporarily this afternoon, and then bury it properly later on in the week."

"The sooner the better: I want it up and running as quickly as possible."

"No problem, Mrs. Zedmore," the contractor continued. "My boys can run the cable lines along with the power supply; however we're not computer experts. You'll need someone else to install the computers, sensors and camera equipment for you."

"I've already called a technician, and he will be here soon."

The contractor nodded then headed off to talk with his workers about more specific plans. Almost as one, Richard, Lilly and Lynn all looked up at Eddie.

"Beautiful day, isn't it?" he quipped.

Richard managed a weak smile, but his eyes were worried. "Good to see you had a good long sleep, apparently you needed it."

Lynn made her way around the table and hugged her husband. "Eddie, I am so sorry for not talking to you about all this. I had the idea when I woke up this morning..."

"At five thirty," Richard put in.

"...and things just progressed so quickly. I didn't want to wake you, because you were sleeping so deeply."

"But waking us up was okay, huh?" Richard tried to joke, but there was no real mirth behind his words. Eddie noticed that Richard's usual joyful grin that always shone through his beard wasn't there. He was trying to be casual and humorous, but didn't seem to be getting the full spirit of it.

Lilly smacked her fiancé on the arm. "Come on, Rich. We've already agreed it's your fault, anyway, so she had every right to wake you up!"

Eddie raised an eyebrow, smiling. "Oh? How did this all become Rich's fault? Not that I am complaining, mind you – better you have the blame than me, buddy."

Richard's only response was to look guilty.

Lynn took Eddie's hand and led him to the table. "Richard feels responsible for the kids' disappearance. We've agreed," she smirked, nodding to Lilly, "but at the same time we're not trying to find fault here. Just solutions."

Eddie moved in closer to Lynn to whisper in her ear. "Have you told them what happened?"

Lynn nodded, whispering back. "Every detail."

Eddie turned back to his friend, hands on his hips and an eyebrow raised. "So you know what happened last night, then how does this fall on his shoulders? You a part-time sorcerer or something that we don't know about?"

Richard shook his red head, looking down at the ground, sighing loudly. "No. But...I did give the statues to the kids. Lynn was right, I brought some terrible curse down on them! Or something. This never would have happened if I hadn't been so dumb."

"Oh stop it!" Lilly scolded. "There's no way you could have ever known they would become real, or that another one would show up." Richard looked ready to respond, to which both Lilly and Lynn hushed him.

Eddie leaned into the plans on the table. "Alright, so what are the big plans here then?"

Lynn showed the entire concept to Eddie, pointing out where a computer system in a small weather proof lodge would be setup with camera's and other sensing equipment. The whole rig could be run from inside the lodge, but could also be connected to the house where a secondary line would be. It was being modeled as a nature study, to record patterns that deer, birds and other wildlife may have in the area, but with a larger scope to monitor the trees, pond and surrounding fields within about thirty meters.

Eddie whistled. "Who came up with all of this?"

Richard sat down on a camping chair, wiping sweat from his forehead. "Lynn came up with the original concept, but it was Lilly that really went to work once we got here."

"Oh?"

Lynn nodded as she took a sip of lemonade. "She's a life saver!"

Lilly busied herself with straightening up the paperwork, blushing slightly. "Oh, it's nothing. Just some people I know at the office that was able to put me in touch with the right crews, that's all."

Richard put a hand on her back then pulled her onto his lap. "It's more than that, and you know it. I'm not sure how any of this would have gotten done so fast without you stepping up like you did."

Lilly blushed more deeply and escaped Richard's embrace to return to the table where she retrieved some work gloves. "Look, you don't need to say any more, please! I'm happy to help, and especially with such tragic news. Anything we can do to help get the kids back is what we'll do!"

She walked out from the tarp and moved over to where the major construction was being done. Richard stood up and started fidgeting with his own gloves.

"Hey, uh, listen Eddie," Richard stuttered. "I know it isn't my fault...well, I guess it is, but...but no matter what nice things you all say, I do feel responsible and I need to help out to ease my own mind and heart."

They shook hands then gave each other a quick hug. Richard wiped at his eyes, making a comment about how dusty it was out here, and then walked over to help out the rest of the crew.

Eddie smiled at Lynn. "Guess I better get some work clothes on, huh?"

Lynn grabbed him by the elbow and started walking him back towards the house. "Actually...I was hoping you could help out by getting lunch for everyone. There's the four of us, and six guys on the construction crew, plus two more that should be showing up in an hour or so. Think you can handle food for the twelve or so of us?"

Eddie hugged his wife and kissed her for several long moments. "Thank you," he breathed when the kiss ended.

"For what?"

Eddie surveyed the grand project going on around them. "For taking charge, for taking action. I don't know, but just by doing *something* I feel better. Logically I know it doesn't change anything, but it does feel better knowing that there is some work getting done."

Lynn put her head on his chest and hugged him close. "I thought that if they disappeared here, then they might reappear here too. Seems silly now when I think about it, but it was a good idea at the time. And now that all the work is already underway..."

"...there's no point in stopping, might as well see it through," Eddie finished for her.

He kissed her on the forehead and then turned to walk back to the house. After three strides he spun around, continuing to walk backwards as he called out to Lynn.

"Just one thing I ask!" he yelled.

Lynn stopped and put a hand to her eyes to block the sun. "What's that?"

"Please, whatever you do, don't tell me how much all this is going to cost! I don't want to know!"

Christian read through the email a second time before composing a reply.

Confirmed, original targets and all three children are missing. Disappearance recorded on video. Requesting full support team is made available on standby at the North West safe house.

Verification received on plates from the Ace Contracting truck: Government agency is now fully involved, and will likely be installing tracking and surveillance equipment inside the house and on the grounds. Contact sleeper operative at Provincial level to enable a tap on the surveillance feed.

He paused, reading his message three times again before coming to a decision.

Please advise: I am requesting permission to make direct contact with the family.

He clicked on the encryption key before sending his email. He reached over to the passenger seat and pulled out the DVD that was in his briefcase.

"All on video," he mumbled to himself. *And I can barely believe it myself.*

He took out a permanent marker and wrote 'Wedding Video, 2007' across the disc. He pulled out a blank second disc and wrote the current date and 'Surveillance' across it. Placing them in unmarked cases, he put the discs back into his briefcase and started the car.

Can't hang around here without being discovered too much longer, he thought.

Christian stepped out of the vehicle and took a last look through the telescope, watching as Lynn, Richard and Lilly helped move some equipment around. Eddie was spreading out boxes of pizza and cans of pop on the table.

He collapsed the telescope and returned it to the case in the trunk of the car, then hopped back into the driver's seat. Before the door closed, he noticed a dot in the sky. Retrieving a pair of binoculars he looked up into the sky, analyzing the dot.

Moments later, Christian Woods was driving away, hoping the High Altitude CSIS Survey Aircraft hadn't noticed the BMW on the hill, nor seen him putting the telescope away. He tensed and scanned wildly for any other vehicle, aircraft or otherwise, following him while making his way back to his hotel room.

13 Inn

M ASTER ITHICAR HORSEMANE PROVED to be a fascinating host and his inn was just as interesting. All of the kids felt as though they had just stepped into a movie, or a time-warp, somewhere in the midst of an Arthurian legend, or Robin Hood classic.

The interior was deceivingly large: it had looked like a big building outside, yet inside it could only be described as massive. The main room held fifteen large circular wooden tables, each large enough to easily hold eight chairs around it. The ceiling of the common room was about six or eight meters up, and a large balcony loomed over the entire length of the east wall, showing rooms for rent beyond on the second floor. A large bar and kitchen lay underneath the second floor, and at the far south end of the room was a large fireplace set beside a raised platform made of stones and mortar, forming a stage. Banners with dozens of styles of medieval heraldry dotted the walls and framed the fireplace, and several dozen swords, axes, bows, pictures, trophies and shields filled in the rest of the space.

"I had it made in a classic human style!" Ithicar announced proudly.

He ushered the children into the tavern, where all sound and motion stopped. All the kids felt the eyes and ears of every person…every *thing*…in the room turn and focus on them. A myriad of plant, insect, lizard and somewhat humanoid creatures filled the room. A large insect, looking very much like a praying mantis, with dozens of striped green and yellow lines running down its body, had abruptly stopped playing some strange kind of string music. The praying mantis was staring unblinking, deep black eyes at the kids.

Ithicar did not seem to notice the disturbed patrons of the tavern: he walked the kid's right in to a table nearest the bar, shooing the occupants away (who were all too eager to flee the scene). He sat the children down all the while beaming the brightest smile the children had ever seen, setting napkins in their laps, one on each place setting and several extras in the center of the table. He bustled back and forth from the bar, bringing mugs, wooden plates, utensils and a hurricane-style lantern, talking the whole time.

"It has been so long since I have been to earth! Why, I think the last time must have been in the late fifteen hundreds – that was when the gates were fully sealed, after all. Nope! No going back now! Oh, it is so exciting to have proper guests again! Oh, sorry you all, not to mean you are not proper, begging your pardon. I am just so happy to have you three here! Of all places! In *my* inn!"

Ithicar let out a satisfied sigh and paused, hands on hips, making sure he had everything on the table.

"Oh! How silly of me!" Ithicar exclaimed as he jumped to the bar once again. "Can't drink from an empty mug! What's your preference: honey mead, wine, or ale?"

The kids all stared at him, still stunned by the goings-on, and not really having any idea what those drinks were.

"Uhhh…." Alex began, speaking for all of them. "What is mead?"

"Well it's a…" Ithicar began then trailed off, eyes going wide. "Oh my! Ithicar, blast yourself to the Fire Pits! What was I thinking? You're only children! You can't have this! Let me see…sorry, been a long time since I've had to look after young ones, you know." He winked as he trundled back into the kitchen, still chattering away. He continued to ramble in the kitchen, despite the fact that no one could hear him anymore.

The patrons of the bar slowly started shuffling one by one out the door, keeping a very wide berth around the humans' table. Within moments, the room had cleared to all but a small handful of guests. One small mean looking shadowy shape that reminded the children of the Sentinel that Azurim had burned earlier went upstairs, presumably to a room. When Ithicar returned with a large jug of milk and one of a sweet smelling juice, there was only a total of seven guests left: the three children, the praying mantis at the far end of the hall, two green skinned females with tiny leaves seeming to grow like hair on their skin, and one small tree perched on a chair, one branch dipping into a jar of what appeared to be a red coloured honey. The tree had several eyes growing out of its trunk and branches, most all of which were looking directly at the human children.

"So, here we are! Fresh goat's milk from earlier this afternoon, so I guess it is not really all that fresh…no matter. And some Star Fruit juice! Which would you prefer?"

Jared glanced about the room. "Master Ithicar, sir…sorry about making all the other people leave. We didn't mean too."

"Nonsense! Idiots! All of them! Scared of a human, how ridiculous! Besides which, they will not get to hear the fabulous stories I am sure you have to tell! Please, begin at any time while I prepare some food. I am all ears!"

The praying mantis stepped down from the slightly raised stage it was on and came forward to a closer table. It sat down and settled itself, obviously intently listening. Alex noticed that all of the other remaining patrons were doing likewise.

"Uh…stories? I'm not sure I know what stories to tell you, or even if we have any."

"Of course you do! You just don't know it yet!" Ithicar cried, winking again. "What is earth like now, my boy? Please, tell us! Remember: it is has been a closed world to us all for over four hundred years, and for some of us even longer! I only left earth when I was one hundred and…well…harumpf….age doesn't matter. But the last gate was sealed many years ago. Only the dragons can operate them now!"

The praying mantis suddenly started chirping wildly, its antennae waving back and forth.

"Oh I am not telling them too much! Hush, you!"

Ithicar placed the jugs on the table and marched back into the kitchen. He called back over his shoulder as he left the room.

"Kikrick, why don't you play them something while they eat, give them time to think of a story or two!"

"I like music!" Madison said cheerfully.

Kikrick didn't seem too happy about it. In fact he seemed far more intent to hear the stories the human's would tell. Ithicar saw the pained look creeping into Kikrick's eyes.

"They cannot tell a good story on an empty stomach!" Ithicar said, beaming another sun-bright smile. "Play them some good dinner music, and perhaps they will repay in kind with news from Earth!"

The children could have sworn they heard the insect sigh, but it dutifully hopped back over to the stage and began to play. The music was hauntingly beautiful, the best they had ever heard! Kikrick proved to be no normal praying mantis: it started playing its two hind legs together, rubbing them to create a low sound like a cello. Several bars into its song, strands of yellow began lifting from its sides, rubbing together to form secondary instruments. The yellow strands on its body danced in the air around Kikrick, creating the effect that the wisp-like strands were floating in water. All the strands were rubbing together at specific intervals, masterfully coordinated into perfect rhythm, pitch and tone.

The music was heavenly: a symphony of what sounded like string and wind instruments all playing at once: fiddle, guitar, cello, bass, reed pipe, flute, and more sounds that couldn't readily be identified, a masterpiece by anyone's standards.

Kikrick continued to strum away, playing a slow sombre tune that brought with it sadness, underlined with a sense of freedom. The children all listened intently, too absorbed by the music to notice the food Ithicar brought out for them. Ithicar politely reminded the children to eat after several minutes of the food remaining untouched.

"He'll continue playing while you eat. Please, dig in!"

The platter in the center of the table was immense, and overflowing with fruits, cheese, bread, wafers and several other items they didn't recognize. The children all dove into the food, suddenly realizing how hungry they were. They had taken a lot in today, seen a lot of new sights, and the pace at which they had walked steadily that afternoon had worn them out. Their appetites awoke with a fury, and soon the music had the slurping and munching sounds of a good meal added to it. The children all started with fruit they knew, but soon ventured to various others: a blue-and-yellow star shaped fruit that tasted similar to honeydew; a green fruit smooth like a plum, but far more bitter in taste; and some dark black berries that were shaped like tear-drops, tasting like a raspberry, but without the tart flavour.

The breads and cheeses were fabulous, and the wafers were somewhere between a slice of bread and a cracker. A couple of items looked like they were meat – the children all avoided them, not having any idea what creature it might have come from. All in all, the children had a wonderful meal.

Kikrick played for them the entire time the children ate, while Ithicar ensured their mugs were filled with juice at all times (the children all silently decided to avoid the goat's milk, for it was warm and had a slight yellow tinge to it, and that didn't seem right for milk).

It had been a good fifteen minutes after the children finished their dinner when Kikrick stopped playing. It had been the same song the entire time, and they got the sense that the song itself had a story behind it, much like listening to a CD Soundtrack of *Les Misérables* back home. The other patrons in the bar seemed to know the story behind it, as at certain points they had bobbed and weaved in time with the music, mouthing words and whispering to each other.

Kikrick stepped down from the stage and hopped back to his previous seat near the children's table. Its eyes were fixed on the group, pleading.

"I guess it is time for our young masters to tell us a story or two!" Ithicar announced. He too had found a chair and sat anxiously awaiting the children to narrate.

"I was actually hoping you could tell us a little about where we are." Alex asked. "I have guessed that we're not on Earth anymore, but I am really curious as to where exactly."

"Oh no!" Ithicar protested. "It's your turn to tell! You've had food, music and rest, and now it is time to hear about your world! We will answer your questions in turn, but everyone is so anxious to hear about Earth!"

Alex doubted that very much – most of 'everyone' had left the tavern a long time ago, and indeed seemed scared of them all.

"Uhh...well...I don't know..." Alex fumbled for words.

"What do you want to hear?" Jared asked. "We know lots of stories from school, although I don't know how interesting those would be."

Ithicar put his drink down and grabbed a large quill pen, ready to write notes in a big leather bound book. "School! Your family is wealthy enough to send you to school? That is fabulous! Tell us what your schools are like!"

Jared furrowed his brow. "Everyone goes to school. You don't have to be rich."

"Really? Hmmm...that is interesting." Ithicar jotted some notes down. "Economics must have changed a lot since I was last there."

"I think I know what you're talking about." Alex offered. "I read that in olden days only rich people went to school, because it cost so much. And also because most people worked all the time, or only studied one thing until they were good enough to do it for a living."

"Daddy also told us about other people in olden times, people like Kikrick!" Madison said suddenly, bursting into the conversation.

"Really?" Ithicar said, surprised. "They have Prancitiil on Earth still? Amazing!"

"Prance-eh-what?" Madison asked.

"Prance-eh-teal!" Ithicar said, pronouncing it slowly. Kikrick responded by a flutter of his wings and several strands of yellow, which hummed.

"Yes, yes, enough showing off," Ithicar rebuked.

"Oh!" Madison exclaimed. "I didn't mean bug-people! I meant musicians. Daddy called them Boards, or something."

"That's *Bards*, Madison," Alex corrected.

"Yeah, that's it!" Madison said, pointing at her brother. "Bards! People who sing and tell stories to other people, like Kikrick!"

"Yes, I know what a bard is," Ithicar chuckled. "A minstrel. A story-teller and poet. That is Kikrick's profession, of course! As a matter of fact, most Prancitiil play music very well and are excellent entertainers, however I must say that Kikrick has a talent unsurpassed by his people!"

Kikrick bowed his head slightly at the compliment then returned his focus to the children. Four antennas on his head vibrated slightly as they spoke.

"So if you are going to school, what apprenticeship will you be starting then, child Alex?" Ithicar enquired.

"Apprenticeship?" Alex replied, confused.

"Yes, of course! From what I remember, human children in school usually are put into an apprenticeship at about ten or twelve years of age. You look about that age, so you should be in an apprenticeship by now, should you not?"

"No way!" Alex shot back. "I still have six or so years of school left to go, plus a few more in University! I won't pick a career until I'm done all that!"

"Six more years! Astounding!" Ithicar was dumbfounded. "And what is a University?"

"University," Jared piped in, "is where grown-ups go after they finish High School to get more learning, but usually only in one area they like. You don't have to take all the bad and boring classes in University – just the ones you want!"

"So you are considered a grown-up once you have finished learning in this… University?"

"I dunno…I guess so. Although Mom is always saying that Dad never really grew up. He just stayed a kid forever and had no plans of changing."

"Really?" Ithicar gasped. "Humans have the ability now to choose their own age and growth? How wonderful! So what age will you all choose?"

"No, ha, ha!" Madison laughed. "That's not how it works!" She giggled again, making everyone smile.

Ithicar scratched out a note with his pen. "Oh?"

"No," Alex continued, "Mom was just being sarcastic because Dad is such a goof all the time."

Jared produced a grand smile. "Yeah, he plays video games all the time or plays tag with us at the park, so Mom always says she really has four children, instead of three and a husband."

"Ahh, I see…." Ithicar continued to write notes in his journal. When he finished he looked up from his book expectantly. The children were suddenly looking very sad, their mood darkened.

"Is something the matter?" Ithicar asked. "I hope it was not the food, or something I said!"

"No, it's just…" Alex started.

"I miss Mom and Dad," Jared said, completing Alex's thoughts.

Madison sniffed. None of them had really thought too much of it today, but now that they were talking about their parents an empty hole began forming in their thoughts and hearts. They wanted to go home, and they suddenly realized they had no idea where home was!

"Master Ithicar, sir," Alex began, "can you tell us where we are, so we can figure out how to get home?"

Ithicar was silent for a moment then pursed his lips. He looked at Kikrick, who in turn looked at the two female figures at the nearby table. They looked away, pretending to be absorbed in their own conversation, but obviously straining to hear every word.

"I am not really sure how to answer that for you, child Alex."

Kikrick began chirping and squeaking. Ithicar listened for a moment, then responded, "I do not think Azurim has told them anything. As a matter of fact, I would wager a guess that the children know nothing of this entire world. The Gates were all sealed, after all, so how would any humans possibly remember any of the Fairy Folk, or Dragons, or anything else about our world? They are generally short-lived, if you remember."

"Please tell us," Alex asked again.

"Please?" Madison repeated. Ithicar looked at her small, beautiful face, and the golden locks of hair framing her eyes. The innkeeper broke down entirely looking into her sweet, pleading blue eyes.

"Oh you sweet little Eyshanp, you!" Ithicar cried, tousling Madison's hair and giving her a quick hug. "Very well, what do you wish to know?"

Alex wiped at tired eyes, stifling a yawn. "I think we all really just want to know where we are, Master Ithicar."

Alex was concerned now. They had been here for an entire day without having any idea of how far they had travelled, in what direction, or how to get back.

"I believe," Ithicar began, "the best way to describe where you are is to have you think of it yourselves. We are on a different realm, true, but still on the same world. Does that make sense?"

The three confused looks staring back at him told Ithicar they did not. He sighed.

"Imagine your Earth, the whole planet, like a doorway. Our world, the place you are visiting right now, is very much like your Earth! Indeed we share the same landscape in general, but one does not necessarily affect the other. Imagine this world as one that your Earth *could* have been, if it had progressed differently."

"You mean," Alex thought out loud, "that this place is like what our home would have looked like, if humans weren't around?"

"Not exactly," Ithicar replied. Then he chuckled again. "Well, actually, yes it is a world without much human influence, as there have been no humans here for a long time. But the worlds are still linked. If one exists, the other exists. They are the same, but one is a shadow of the other."

"You said that they share the same landscape, so does that mean if we had a map of the Earth to look at, it would be the same?"

"Almost exactly, with a couple of minor differences."

"Like?" Alex and Jared both said at the same time.

One of the green skinned women spoke up, leaning forward from her chair. Her voice was definitely feminine, and sounded like a rush of wind. "Firstly, Atlantis never sank here. It was destroyed on Earth because humans were too pompous and arrogant to control the conflux there, thinking they were so superior." Her partner shushed her. They turned their backs and resumed listening.

"Yes, that is one difference," Ithicar agreed. "And there are few others. The area you call the Mediterranean – it is still called that, is it not? Good! The Mediterranean on your world is a sea, whereas here a good portion of it is land. You see, when Atlantis was destroyed, a giant flood engulfed much of the surrounding islands and shoreline of the mainland.

"The Islands of the Aztecs are still here, but were sunken in your world. The Mountains of Frost and Fire are still here. Oh, and the true Pillars of Hercules are here as well! Hercules himself moved them here, as he did not trust mankind to properly take care of them. It was a good thing he did!"

"Wait!" Jared said. "I still don't understand. You said that both worlds were the same! Shouldn't what happens in one happen in the other?"

Ithicar scratched his head. "I am not sure how to describe it in terms you would understand. Have you learned the Runes yet?" The blank stares told him no. "I see. How about the Tablets of Sorcery? Do they still exist?" More blank stares. "So truly magic was completely cut off from your world then?"

"Well, I've seen magicians on TV, but they just do card tricks and stuff. I don't think there is any real magic back home," Alex explained. "Although Azurim did tell us that magic was flowing again on earth."

"Oh, I am sure the magic is still there, just in a very small quantity, unused, forgotten." Ithicar thought more, trying to find a way to explain where they were. "This world is like a second skin."

"A different dimension?" Jared asked.

"Not entirely accurate, no."

"A hidden planet?" Alex tried.

"No. It is more like this world is, well…" Ithicar trailed off.

"A dream?" Madison asked.

"Yes!" Ithicar exclaimed. "You wonderful child! A dream! That is precisely it! Our world was once called the Dream World by humans. A place where the Fairies lived! Humans had it all wrong, though. They thought Fairies lived in dreams of people, but that is untrue. This world – our world – exists as a Dream, set apart from Earth. It is the dream that Earth dreams while Mother Nature sleeps. You can enter the Dream World through certain gates and magic if you know where to look!"

The description almost made sense to the children, and they nodded their acceptance of the explanation. Ithicar continued.

"After all, the entire universe is made up of Thought, that formless substance. And yet when thought focuses long enough, hard enough, real things emerge, reality happens and is created by Thought! The Fairies needed a place, many thousands of years ago, to hide from others, and so they used their magic and thoughts to create this Shard, a place that exists only in Thought – like a dream!

"Most humans could not grasp the combined complexity and simplicity of the explanation of where our world is, and so could not make the cross over to come here. You see, you need to have an open mind to accept the possibility of something like a world dreaming, and entering that world. This is why most people who used to come to visit here were human children, and those adult humans who still had the ability to use their imaginations. It seems easy for human adults to forget the simple truths they learned in childhood."

"Daddy could do it," Madison said, yawning. "He's such a big kid anyway!"

The kids all laughed, but were quickly overcome with yawns and stretches. Ithicar saw the weariness in the children, and decided to call an end to the evening.

"As much as I would like to hear more, I can see you are spent. Please, let us retire upstairs where I will show you to your rooms, and where you may wash if you wish."

Kikrick began to protest, as did the pair of ladies. Ithicar waved them off.

"We can hear more about Earth in the morning when we break our fast," Ithicar announced. "You wouldn't mind that would you?" he asked the children.

The children all sleepily nodded yes.

"Master Ithicar?" Alex interjected. "Can I ask one more question?"

Ithicar nodded. "My pleasure, young master."

"You said before that there were wizards that came through to this world before the gates were sealed. Does that mean they are still here?"

Ithicar pursed his lips again, thinking. "Sadly, no. Humans do not live very long compared to most of our kin, not any more. They have all since passed away, I am afraid."

"That's not entirely true, Ithicar," one of the ladies breathed. Her voice was like a soft breeze gently coming through a window at night. "What about Trevistar?"

"Ah yes, thank you Saebrin. A shame that I should forget the tale that Kikrick so masterfully played for us tonight!"

"Who is Trevistar?" Jared asked.

"A wizard of great power," Ithicar began. Kikrick played a few notes from his previous song, adding to Ithicar's narration.

"Trevistar was a human who believed in what we were trying to accomplish. You see, in those days mankind was rising in technology, knowledge and arrogance. Any human who had any sort of magical talent had been hunted for many years. Wizards were in hiding, living mostly in our world to escape the purging of their kind.

"Wizards for hundreds of years were trusted councilmen, advisers, seers. Soon humans in general began to forget about the Fairy Folk and our domain. Dragons were hunted for sport, mages were killed, and fairies were either destroyed or ignored, or captured for various wicked reasons. Many wizards moved their homes here and came through the portals to escape their own certain death.

"However there were some wizards who were very clever, and disguised their magical talents behind religion, political power or sometimes by fear itself. These villainous wizards hunted fairies, dragons and all our kin relentlessly, always hungering for power, or secrets that we would not reveal.

"Trevistar suggested to the Dragons that we seal the gates forever. He saw no hope for future generations of humans any more. He saw only more destruction, and never a return to the ways of old, when all the races walked and worked together. Mankind had decided there was only room enough for one race on Earth, and so the rest of us fled.

"I believe this would be the reason why so many who reside in Shard fear humans in general – we were once at war with you, and we were losing. It isn't hard to see why fear, anger and hatred may still exist."

"So is Trevistar still alive then?" Madison asked.

Ithicar shuffled from side to side, his feet clip-clopping on the hard wooden floor. "In a manner of speaking, yes. Trevistar was helping the Dragons to channel energy into the Grand Arch, the stone work that provided the nexus for the Gateways to work. The Grand Arch is the last remaining Gate that has an opening, and the Dragons control access to that Gate. An unknown energy surged through the Arch and threatened to destroy it when it was being sealed. Trevistar saw the threat and did the only thing he knew to stop the Arch's destruction: he created a solid block of ice around him and the energy pulse. Both froze in place and have been there ever since. Trevistar sacrificed himself in order to save us.

"After the ice formed, the Dragons were able to determine the source of the unknown energy. It was an evil human named Ryddikine. No one knows his original given name – Ryddikine was a name he gave himself. It roughly means 'Fairy Bane' in our language. Ryddikine was and always has been bent on the destruction of our world, and of all our kind."

"Why would he want to destroy this world?" Madison asked.

"If Ryddikine had succeeded in destroying the Arch, our worlds would have collided. Mother Nature would have woken up, and the dream would end. Well, to tell the truth no one knows for certain, but many theories abound. The most accepted theory is a collision of our worlds.

"Think of what would happen if all your dreams that you have at night were to come true while you are dreaming them, so that when you wake they exist in reality. All of the peoples from Shard and Earth would cease to exist as two places. All of the peoples from both worlds would suddenly exist together, doubling or tripling the population of one Earth. The curtains that separate magic would come down and flood the world, killing many, empowering others. Chaos would reign, truth be told."

"Shard?" Alex interrupted. "I'm sorry, you've said the word several times now, but I'm not sure what you mean."

"Shard is the name given to this world," Ithicar explained quickly. "As I say, it is only a theory. No one knows for certain, but we know that the Arch must be protected at all costs. Trevistar knew this and sacrificed himself to make sure the Arch would survive."

"Does that mean he died?" Madison sniffed.

"Oh, I don't think so," Ithicar replied. "His spell of ice was instant, so many believe there is a good chance that he lives still. Unfortunately there is no known way to save him."

"You mean he can never be taken out of the ice?" Madison asked, upset.

"That's horrible!" Jared exclaimed.

"He might as well be dead," Alex finished.

"Oh, no, no! He *can* be taken out, however no one has been able to figure out how. A Dragon's fire breath would be hot enough to melt the ice, however the flames would kill Trevistar even as the ice melted. Dragon Song has not been effective, either, and there has not been any other source of heat hot enough to even begin melting the ice. Weapons shatter against the thick ice. No, I am afraid the dragon's only choice has been to maintain the ice block that has frozen Trevistar solid, until such time that they find a way to melt all the ice away properly."

Ithicar stood once again, looking very tired. "And now, humans, it is time for rest."

They all agreed wearily, very fatigued from the day. They were still concerned, a little afraid, and not sure what tomorrow would bring. But they needed sleep, and it was coming on them fast no matter what they did to try and stop it.

Ithicar led them upstairs and showed them their shared room. Provided for each of them was a one-piece pullover to wear as pyjamas that reached to their knees, and Ithicar showed them a wash basin to clean themselves in. The kids ignored the wash basin except to quickly splash water on their faces and hands. Their host then gave each of them a small, rough, brown nut to eat.

"It is for your teeth," he explained.

The children bit into the nut wearily, not sure what the item was supposed to be or do. It tasted minty with a very starchy texture. They chewed the nuts, as instructed by Ithicar: twelve times on either side of their mouths, twelve times at the front of the teeth, and then spat the rest of the nut out. After rinsing with water and scrubbing with their fingers, their teeth were clean.

Ithicar had made up three small beds in one room, so the children could all stay together. They were very thankful: being in a strange place, they wanted each other's company. They fell asleep with dozens of bizarre images plaguing their dreams, mixed with thoughts of home, their dragons, and if they would ever see either of them again.

14 Invention

C HRISTIAN SAT IN THE hotel room, hazel eyes staring out the window at the evening sunset, his fingers lightly playing along the edge of his wine glass. He'd lost track of time waiting for a reply, and now that he had it he didn't like it. He closed his eyes and saw the words in his mind, burned there since he read them.

Negative on request for opening contact with the family.

The Aegean Council, Median Magi and Aquila Americus all agree that it is unlikely any of the children will be seen again. The gates are sealed.

Sleeper has been unable to make contact: assume they are no longer an available asset.

Standby team is ready for cleanup, awaiting orders at the safe house. Forty-eight hours, then return home.

It had been a full day since he had received the orders, yet despite his commitment to the Order, he had not acted. He hadn't replied to the email nor taken action on it.

Christian couldn't explain it, but to simply cleanup the whole situation felt wrong. This was the biggest breakthrough in magical studies in hundreds of years! Why was the collective council so easily willing to walk away from this? This was a chance of a lifetime, of many lifetimes, to advance, to touch magic, to feel it and truly begin learning its use.

Something felt wrong, and Christian had learned a long time ago to trust his feelings. It was one of the reasons why he had been recruited. His high aptitude for intuition had been explained to him as a magic condition, and with so little magical energy still running in the world anyone with any magical talent had to be a high-powered natural talent to even access it.

He couldn't believe he himself was thinking this, was feeling this...but the council was wrong. Or blind. Or manipulated. He didn't know what their game was, but for the first time since he was sixteen he had decided to act against the Order's will. He had known from the moment his laptop beeped to indicate the incoming email that he would choose this path, he just had to muster up the courage to do it.

He stood up and walked to the bathroom, downing the remains of his wine glass in one gulp. He quickly showered, dressed, and once he was clean-shaven and feeling refreshed put his suit on. He always packed lightly to be able to move from place to place with speed at a moment's notice: only minutes later he was in the lobby, checking out and heading for his car.

Christian saw them before they saw him, two plainclothes men, possibly government, searching around his rented Chrysler 300. Without slowing or missing a step, Christian put his sunglasses on and walked down the sidewalk that ran through the parking lot.

One of the suits saw him and walked to intercept him.

"Excuse me, sir, is this your vehicle?"

Christian noted the partner had a hand on what looked like a taser.

"Pardon? Je ne parle pas bien l'anglais."

The agent looked at Christian, confused for a brief second, then motioned back to the car. He pointed back and forth between Christian and the Chrysler as he repeated his question.

"Is..this...YOUR...car, sir?"

Christian smiled inwardly. *Why is it when people don't understand a language they assume that talking slowly and loudly will make someone understand? Well, at least I know they aren't Government agents.*

Christian pointed at the car as well, exaggerating a French accent. "Uh... mine?"

The other man nodded.

Christian put on his best performance, shaking his fist and making a scene while he spoke. "Je suis déjà en retard pour une réunion, criss moi patience!!"

The high paid hotel security stepped back and Christian continued on his way. He ranted for a few moments more, turning once to call an insult to the men in French before getting to the main street and turning away. He walked a few blocks to Stephen's Avenue, hopped on a train and took it North West. Passing several stations he finally disembarked at Banff Trail station and walked to his secondary hotel. He didn't bother walking inside. Instead he went to the hotel rear and found his BMW Series 7 waiting for him. Walking around the vehicle twice for inspection, and scanning the building windows for anyone watching, Christian got into the driver's seat and unlocked the security process in one fluid motion, driving away quickly.

He picked up his cell phone and dialled a number, putting a blue tooth device in his ear before connecting the call.

"Hi, this in Mr. Woods. Yes, I will be checking out immediately. No, I apologize I have already left the hotel. Urgent flight out I'm afraid. Could you simply bill the room to my credit card on file? Yes, I can hold."

Christian waited as the desk clerk clicked away on her keyboard. He pulled around a tight corner onto 16th Avenue and headed west. Thirty seconds later she was confirming his room was paid for, the amount and GST.

"Thank you, Cindy. I appreciate it. Have a great day."

Christian drove through the city at random, keying in a text message when at a red light, while trying to think of his next step. He was used to having everything planned, staged. Now he was operating spontaneously, making up rules as he went along. He reviewed his text twice more; adjusting it here and there he sent it off.

"Well, Christian, you bought yourself a few days at most by sending the squad away and lying about having cleansed the family yourself."

He looked around the neighbourhood he was driving through, a nice spot on a hilltop close to the hospital, overlooking a park and another community, ending with a glimpse of the Bow River. A road sign marked the hill and open space around it as *Parkdale Park*. He stopped at the side of the road and stared for a moment of the beautiful view. He breathed deeply to steady himself.

"Now what?"

They all slept soundly, so weary were they from the day before, and comfortable were they in the snug beds. The sun had been up for a couple of hours when Alex finally awoke, blinking wearily and looking around. He had been dreaming of home, playing out in the back by the pond with Kishar, throwing rocks in the water, watching his Dad get knocked over by Penelope. It took him several moments to adjust to his surroundings, and when he saw the wood-paneled walls and stained-glass window, he slumped back into his pillow, sighing loudly.

"Yeah, we're still here," Jared mumbled, equally upset.

Alex looked over to see Jared in his bed, wide-awake, staring at the ceiling. It looked as though he had been up for some time already, as Jared had already changed out of the night clothes he had worn and was back in his regular clothes.

"You ok?"

"Yeah," Jared replied. "I just woke up about half an hour ago. I couldn't sleep – thinking about Mom and Dad, y'know?"

"Yeah, me too," Alex sighed again.

It was silent for a few minutes as they both lay in their cots thinking. Alex got himself out of bed, undressed from his bedclothes and re-dressed in his own. When he was done, Jared was sitting on the edge of the bed waiting, ready to go.

"Breakfast?" Jared asked.

Alex's stomach growled an answer before he could, and they both giggled.

"What about Madison?" Jared asked as they reached the door to the bedroom.

Alex looked back at his sister. She was lying diagonally in the bed, the sheets and comforter a tangled mess, the pillow down by her feet. She really did toss and turn a lot! Of course, she always had, so it was nothing new to the brothers. Madison snored softly, still very deeply in sleep.

"She'll be fine." Alex opened the door and led the way downstairs.

What a sight that beheld them when they entered the common room! There were hundreds of creatures, big and small, gathered in the room, with one table left completely empty. Ithicar saw the boys and rushed into the kitchen, promptly returning with two trays covered with towels.

"Please, sit, sit! Good morning, young ones! Good morning! We have been waiting for you!"

Alex and Jared made their way to the open table, aware that every eye – and some creatures in the room had dozens of them – was fixed on them. The boys noticed that Kikrick was still in the room at the table nearest theirs – they wondered if he had left at all last night.

Ithicar saw the boys' inquiring looks at Kikrick, and nodded in his direction as he spoke, "He doesn't sleep. He's been standing guard since bedtime, waiting for you." Ithicar tilted his head and winked. Alex asked his brother quietly if Ithicar ever realized he winked so often. It seemed to be a favourite habit for him.

The boys sat down as Ithicar placed their plates in front of them. Another creature similar to Ithicar entered the room, although this one was female. She had a jet-black coat of hair covering her lower horse half, light sky blue eyes and a jet-black mane to match her legs. She wore a shirt made of silk, the torso a stylish combination of blue and purple, and the billowy arms a pure white. She seemed to be very young, at least compared to Ithicar, who was at least several hundred years old. Who knew what a young age really was to a half-horse half-human creature?

She made her way to their table, displaying another large tray with more fruits, cheeses and wafers on it. Setting it down on the table, she tugged at the towels covering the boys' plates, removing them with a flourish.

"Good morning, young ones," she remarked as she pulled the towels away.

On each plate was a pair of large biscuits, fresh out of a warm oven, melted butter dripping down the sides. There was also a large assortment of fruits, vegetables, jams and jellies. Alex's stomach growled again, and Jared's followed suit immediately after. They paused to look at each other, not sure what to do.

Ithicar looked from one boy to the other, his impatience finally getting the better of him. "Well go on! Eat up!" he cried. He was obviously very proud of the efforts he and his kitchen staff had put in, and was waiting to see if the breakfast was indeed as good as it looked.

Alex reached up, but Jared caught his arm.

"Grace," Jared said softly.

"Oh, oops."

"We forgot last night. I figured we should remember this morning."

Alex pulled his hand back and lowered his head. They both silently said a quick prayer; Alex then took a large chunk out of the biscuit while Jared grabbed a large star fruit, the same as he had the night before. It was quickly becoming his preferred choice.

Through mouthfuls, Alex asked, "What made you remember to say grace? You always forget it at home."

Jared shrugged. "I don't know. I was thinking about Mom and Dad, and it seemed like the right thing to do. I guess they would make us say it, even here in this place, so we probably should."

Alex accepted that and continued to devour his breakfast. In moments both of them had butter, cheese and fruit juices dripping down their chins.

All the patrons of the bar went quietly about their business, although most of them had an eye (or two, or three) on the boys the whole time. They felt a little out of place and awkward, with so many people clearly observing them. Alex was not sure he wanted to know what all these prying eyes were waiting for. Jared, however, was too hungry to care. Even with the awkwardness in the air he dove headlong into the food.

"Delicious," Jared declared as he finished another bite of star fruit. "Absolutely delicious!"

The horse-lady – who, the boys found out, was Ithicar's daughter Breyelle – kept their table tidy while they ate, and made sure their drinks remained full. When Madison came down stairs bleary eyed and yawning, a plate and drink was set up for her as well. Madison said grace quietly, at Jared's insistence, and then slowly picked at her food. She perked up once some sugar hit her system, and began talking to all the wonderfully strange creatures around her, whether they had wanted to chat or not! They were only too happy to listen to her ramble on.

As Madison talked, the creatures all stilled, drew closer and listened intently. Even Ithicar and his daughter hushed. The boys were happy to have the attention off of them, so they let Madison go free in her speech. She talked about her home, her parents, school, and what life was like in their new house. Her toys, friends she had and movies she had seen – every part of her talk seemed to blur one into the other, Madison herself not really paying much attention to where she was going with any particular anecdote, just happy that she had a captive audience. She then related the story of how they found their dragons in a gold mine in Brazil, how Uncle Richard had brought them home to them, and how the dragons had come alive. There seemed to be a particular murmur through the crowd as she relayed the story of the dragon's discovery and awakening.

Ithicar started asking questions about what Earth was like. In particular, he wanted to know about Spain, but Madison really couldn't help him too much with that.

"We're not from Europe – we live in Canada!"

"Canada?" Ithicar said, the question echoed by several others. It was obvious it was a new word to them.

Madison stuffed a piece of biscuit into her mouth, her legs swinging back and forth from the chair. "Yup! The bestest place in the whole world!"

"Canada is in North America," Jared added, reflecting on his geography classes in school.

"The Americas!" Ithicar exclaimed. "I see! Well, then, that is a far ways from Spain!"

Kikrick made some chittering and squeaking sounds.

"Yes, I agree. That would explain why the young ones, and the dragons, came through a portal here and not closer to the Council. Very interesting!"

"I don't understand," Alex said. "How does that explain anything?"

"Our world parallels your Earth, remember? The axis is the same for both, and so shifting from one phase to the other is also a parallel for the location."

Both boys stared silently, had stopped their chewing and held eyes wide.

Madison simply smiled and nodded in agreement, stuffing some fruit into her mouth. "Yup!"

Alex was incredulous. "What do you mean, 'yup'? You don't know half of what he was talking about!"

"Yes I do!" Madison protested.

"Oh please, you do not!"

"I do so!" Madison answered grumpily. "We're in the dream side of the world. The dream world and home world is the same thing, just one is pretty and the other isn't."

"Pretty?" Jared thought he would gag.

"Yes! Pretty! With all the horse people, and cute insect-guys and stuff...it's much more interesting and pretty than home!"

The boys sighed in unison.

"Ok, fine," Alex continued, "the place is pretty. But you still don't know what this parallel world thing is. You just think it's pretty!"

"No," Madison whined. "I know exactly what Master Ithicar and Pretty Breyelle are talking about!" Breyelle blushed slightly with her new title. "We're in the dream world," Madison began her explanation again.

"Yeah, we heard that already."

"AND," Madison continued, angry at the interruption, "our home is on the same Earth, just on the sleep-side. Remember, Mother Nature is sleeping, and when she sleeps, she dreams. It only makes sense that she has been sleeping – what else has there been to do since the world was created? Everything is carrying on now on its own, so she can sleep! So she dreams about the thing that means the most to her – Earth! And her dream world is this world, so it *has* to be the same planet. Just different, the way she really wants it to be and look, 'cause you can do that in dreams!"

Alex shook his head. He was more confused now than ever. Jared simply brushed the comments aside instead of trying to understand his sister. He focused on another piece of star fruit instead.

Madison huffed and began chewing on another biscuit.

Ithicar and Breyelle, as well as many other patrons, peppered the children with questions all morning, so long in fact that the children had long since finished their breakfast and were starting to get hungry for lunch. During that time, they had told stories of skiing in the winter, playing at the lake in the summer, and many other fun times they had with their parents and friends. They described their school and their city, which got a lot of laughs when they told them that there were buildings in the city made almost all of glass, and taller than the tallest trees, or vehicles like cars and trucks that they could all ride inside of.

"What kind of animal do you ride *inside* of?" one of the audience had asked, laughing. Several others joined in with him.

"The kind that eats you, that's what," came a witty reply from the crowd.

"It's not an animal!" Jared tried to explain the concept of a machine, but didn't get too far. Machines simply were not needed, it seemed, in a world of magic.

The children knew there was a lot that was being lost in translation, and more often than not they would simply have to say, "You need to see it with your own eyes to really know what it's like".

At one point, Alex had an idea. He asked Ithicar if he had some paper. Alex was given a long, thick sheet of parchment, which he really didn't think would work well for what he had in mind. The parchment was not an exact size or shape, and was rough on the edges. He asked for some scissors, and when he received a blank, empty stare in return, he settled on getting a knife. Then Alex set to work trimming the paper down to an approximation of a standard letter-sized page. The paper was still very thick, but he supposed it would have to do.

Alex began making folds in the paper. The room had grown very quiet, as all the onlookers were beyond curious now. Several creatures had climbed on the ceiling to hang down low for a better view. What could this young boy be doing with parchment that could possibly be so precise?

"This," Alex explained as he worked, "will be an example of a machine that people ride inside of. It is called an Air Plane." He emphasized the words to make sure everyone around him heard.

"Do you cast a spell to shrink down to fit in this plane, or to grow the plane bigger?"

"No, no, no! This is just a *model* of what a plane is. Not a real plane!"

Alex finished his last folds in silence, flapped the wings out and made certain he was satisfied with his creation, and then cast the plane out above the crowd. It didn't fly too well because of the heavy parchment, but well enough to get the idea across. Several oo's and aah's filled the room.

"See? Planes are made by people, much larger of course, and with seats inside! You then fly the plane to wherever it is you want to go!"

Ithicar seemed confused. "Much larger, you say? How then, pray tell, does a larger plane made of paper hold people in it?"

The children all laughed. Jared was first to offer an explanation.

"No! Ha ha! They're not made of paper! That would never work!"

"Especially when the engines turned on!" Madison added.

"Exactly! No, planes are made from metal," Jared concluded.

There was silence in the room for just a moment, and then the crowd burst out in a roar.

"Metal? Oh don't be ridiculous. Now I know you young masters are joking with us!" Ithicar slapped his knee and let out a deep laugh.

"I'm serious!" Jared tried, but the laughter continued.

"Oh, I am sure," said one small female fairy who reminded the kids of Tinkerbell, "that you can make metal float through the air!"

"There is no magic left on Earth, so we know you can't make metal fly! Especially with people inside of it!"

The children gave up trying to convince them all of anything, and instead answered more questions of their home and country.

At lunch, Breyelle brought out a large round cake that she said was made from honey. It was the sweetest and most filling thing the children had ever eaten! It was somewhere between a loaf of bread, and a lemon-square.

As they were finishing their lunch, there came a loud pounding at the door. Everyone in the building jumped in shock, and all sound ceased. Several of the insect like creatures in the room disappeared from view, turning invisible in fear, which made Madison applaud and ask them to do it again.

Ithicar opened the door to splash warm yellow sunlight into the hall. It was very bright, and it took several seconds for his eyes to adjust. The voice that rolled into the room from outside was unmistakable.

"Young ones, it is time for us to take our leave," Azurim growled. It was not a request it was an order. "Master Ithicar, I trust you have travel provisions ready for them?"

Master Ithicar bowed, his demeanour instantly changing to the utmost formal. "Yes, Lord Azurim. I have three bags packed for flight, as instructed, as well as three packs of food that are almost complete. Is this satisfactory?"

Azurim must have nodded silently, for it was a moment before Ithicar continued without a reply.

"Good. And I can assume that our debt is now cleared, Lord Azurim?"

"Our debt will be cleared once we are all safely in the sky, Master Ithicar."

Ithicar grumbled, but then nodded an agreement. Ithicar slowly turned to face the crowd.

"Our time with our guests has ended, friends. Say your farewells and let us have them on their way."

There were several upset grunts and whines from various creatures, but they all reluctantly obeyed. Most of them would have continued if it was only Ithicar's word they were going on, however they would dare not cross a dragon such as Azurim, with the Sentinels fight still fresh in their minds.

The children all received a sudden rush of hugs, hair tousles, pats on the back and shoulder squeezes. The room cleared quickly, with many of the insect-folk skittering out the windows or front door, and other fairies flying into the sky once they were clear of the building. Soon the children were left alone with Breyelle, while Ithicar saw to packing their food for them.

Breyelle winked and smiled, pointing at the children. "I believe, young ones, you have all made friends and admirers."

Alex looked to where she pointed, and saw a palm print on his shirt near his left shoulder. The palm print was faint, but almost looked like silver and gold glitter paint had been used to colour it. Madison found herself with several small flower petals in her hair, which seemed to be stuck and would not come out. Jared saw nothing at first, but then saw a large green four-leaf clover tattooed onto his left arm. He rubbed at it in shock and alarm.

"Oh, I don't think you will be able to wipe that charm off, young master," Breyelle laughed. "Besides, they are all temporary, and will fade in time. Minor charms as a way to say thank you, from those who enjoyed your performance."

She hugged Jared and kissed him on the cheek, which made him blush deeply. Alex laughed at first, until his own ears turned red when Breyelle hugged and kissed him as well.

When Breyelle made it to Madison, Madison flung her arms around the barmaid's neck and kissed her on the cheek first. Breyelle was surprised, but recovered quickly and held Madison in a loving embrace. Madison was smiling, but tears were already flowing.

Ithicar returned with packs for each of the children, which they accepted gratefully with thanks, hugging him in farewell. Ithicar helped them shoulder each pack to their backs then stepped to the doorway.

"I'll miss you young ones," Breyelle said. "A short visit it has been, however one I will always remember and cherish."

Madison felt emotion welling up inside her again, and hugged Breyelle once more. Breyelle smiled, and a tear fell down her cheek. Madison wiped it away for her, and beamed.

"Don't worry, Miss Breyelle! We'll come back to visit you someday!"

Breyelle smiled at the young girl and held her hand as the group made their way outside.

The afternoon sunshine was warm, inviting and bright. It took a few moments for the children to adjust their eyes to the early afternoon sunlight. Azurim began speaking to them the moment they were all in attendance.

"Children, we will be leaving shortly. Your clutch mates will be showing themselves soon. They felt it would be best that I explain their new appearance to you before seeing them."

Alex's face paled. "New appearance?"

Jared was instantly angry. "What did you do to Rex?" he demanded.

Azurim seemed very tired, without patience. "Silence! We have very little time remaining for daylight and a long journey ahead of us. I did nothing to your clutch mates. I have simply helped them to become attuned to the magic pulses emanating here in Shard. Using that power, they have grown into their true forms. The dragons have lived in suspension on Earth for several hundred years, still yet aging in spirit while the bodies were frozen in time. When they awoke, the flux of magic had been cut off from them. They were unable to grow, and only able to sustain themselves with the inherent power in sunlight and eating nutrients as you would.

"Here, they have been taught now to feed directly off of the magic Weave, and the difference will be somewhat shocking to you. I personally think this is a dramatic waste of time; however the dragons felt you, as humans, would need a warning to allow you to adjust to their new form."

"I'm really getting worried now," Jared stated.

Alex was fidgeting, rocking from foot to foot. "Yeah, me too. Can we just see them now?"

Azurim nodded. "As you wish." He raised his head skyward and bleated a loud note. The trumpet sound blasted for blocks around.

There was a rushing of wind and wings, and a large red shape shot into view. Rex had been on the back side of the building, waiting for the moment to pounce. She stood about nine feet tall with a wing span twice her height! Jared nearly fell to his knees. Her red colouring had deepened to crimson, the leather of her wings was a fiery orange, and the yellow of her chest shone like bronze. She unfurled her wings and growled once, obviously very proud of what she had become.

It was all Jared could do to stare, his mouth dropping open.

Penelope came into view next. Her chest was now a pure white, her scales a medium purple and her wings fading to pink at the ends. She was much larger as well, roughly the same size as Rex. Penelope flew in, landing gracefully but not demanding the attention that Rex had done. Instead, Penelope gave a moment for Madison to adjust then bowed her head slightly, seeking approval.

Madison ran forward and smothered her purple dragon with hugs and kisses. "Oh Penelope! You're more beautiful than ever!!!"

Jared was still staring in awe, unable to take eyes off of Rex, and also unable to function. All he could mutter out was "wow" as he crawled forward on his knees to touch Rex, and make sure she was real.

There were several moments of silence, and Alex began to fear that Kishar was not coming. Maybe something had happened to Kishar. Maybe he went away. Maybe he didn't like Alex. Maybe…maybe he's dead from some stupid test he had to take, Alex thought. A tear started to well up in Alex's eye at this, and his lower lip started to tremble.

The sound of rustling leaves and snapping branches turned everyone's attention. The tops of trees were being pushed away as something drew near. A large green leg emerged from the tree line, and as the second leg came thundering into view Kishar's head poked out. He paused, glancing around until he spied Alex. Kishar seemed to swallow and then walked forward, revealing himself fully yet staying low to the ground.

Kishar was by far the largest of the three. His body was probably fifteen feet long, not including the tail! The head alone was grand, probably able to swallow any one or two of the kid's whole! He still wasn't Azurim's size, but Kishar was impressive to see! The green of his scales shone an emerald blaze in the sunlight, fading to a teal-blue at the tail. The wings were spectacular, with emerald arms and silver for the webbing, his chest a silver-white.

Kishar walked in close to Alex, hesitant. Alex stumbled forward slowly, lifting his arm as he went. Kishar was obviously shy, and not sure of what his clutch mate would do. Kishar waited for approval, not moving at all.

Alex moved closer until they were only a hand's-breadth away from each other.

"Kishar," Alex breathed, "you're amazing…you're beautiful!"

A large tear shone in Kishar's eye as the dragon bolted forward, wrapping Alex inside his now massive wings. The two held each other for several moments while the others watched in joy and approval, except for Jared who was still standing slack-jawed staring at Rex.

Ithicar held his daughter by the shoulders, smiling. It was a touching scene, and they felt blessed for having been privy to it.

After several long moments, Alex pulled himself away from Kishar, wiping tears. Jared had finally closed his mouth when Rex had started prodding him with her nose, and Madison was already well up onto Penelope's back, hugging the dragon's neck and smiling, ready to fly.

Alex sheepishly wiped tears onto his sleeve and grinned, turning to the others. "Sorry everybody. I didn't mean to…ah, you know."

Kishar lowered his head beside Alex. "I was hoping you would approve of me."

"Ahhhhhhhh!" Alex yelled, tumbling forward. The shock of Kishar speaking to him, in English no less, scared him so that his knees had buckled. The strong tenor voice still resonated with Alex.

"You...you talk!" Alex mumbled.

Kishar looked hurt. "Yes...I am sorry. You are not pleased?"

"Oh, no! No, no!" Alex quickly regained his feet and rushed forward. "I'm sorry, Kishar! I was, well...you've never spoken before, so I wasn't expecting it! It just shocked me, that's all!" Alex touched his hand to Kishar's face, more in awe now than ever before.

Madison slid to the ground and jumped up and down in excitement. "Speak to me! Speak to me, Penelope!"

"The fair two cannot speak your language yet. There is some maturing that is still required before they master speech," Azurim explained. "It appears that Kishar is older than his sisters, and far more so than we originally thought."

"How is that possible?" Alex asked. "All of you were found together in the gold mine. Weren't you trapped together at the same time?"

"Yes," Kishar replied, "we were. The difference appears to be our time of birth – I do not know how much time passed from whence I was born and Rex was born. I imagine it might have been a year or more, but I truthfully can only guess."

Alex was still stunned by his own pet talking back to him. He simply nodded and smiled, hugging Kishar around the neck.

Azurim stepped forward. "I thank you, Ithicar. Remember, our debt is cancelled once we are all safely in the air."

"I remember, Azurim. And have no fear – you will not find misdirection or treachery from me. It has been a pleasure to serve the human children, and to see their joy today. I have never known humans to be so in love with a dragon. It is a sight my heart will always remember."

"As will I," Breyelle added. She smiled and waved goodbye. "I truly hope to see you all again."

"Child Alex, child Jared and child Madison," Ithicar nodded to each child as he spoke. "It was an honour to serve you. I hope to hear more of your stories again. Our door is open and welcome to you!"

Azurim snorted and stretched his wings. "Children. We must go, and go quickly. Please, climb onto your clutch mates back. We will travel much more quickly in the air."

Jared seemed to finally find his voice. "We're going to actually fly? Alright!"

Jared shouted, punching a fist into the sky. He clambered onto Rex's back and made himself comfortable. Rex wasted no time in launching herself into the air, Jared yelling a loud whoop of pure excitement. Rex added her own throaty growls to his shouts, and the two of them circled higher.

Penelope and Madison were not far behind, with Madison yelling down to those below "Goodbye Miss Breyelle! Goodbye Master Ithicar! Thank you for everything!" She finished by blowing a kiss towards the ground, but nearly slipped from Penelope's back in doing so.

Alex turned to his hosts who had taken care of him and his siblings for the last day. "Thank you both. I really can't pretend to know how much trouble my brother and sister and I have probably been for you. We had a great time!"

He shook Ithicar's hand and turned towards Breyelle when Ithicar snatched Alex into an embrace from behind. Alex laughed, and Breyelle joined the two of them.

Stepping back once they were done, Alex climbed onto Kishar's shoulders. "Azurim?" Alex asked. The older dragon looked at him questioningly. "If I forget to tell you again later, I want to thank you, too. Without you, we never would have been on this awesome adventure! And I never would have had a chance to ride a dragon! Thank you!"

Azurim did not respond.

Alex gave a final wave to Ithicar and Breyelle then held onto Kishar's neck. "Let's see what you can do, Kishar! Whoo hoo!"

The green dragon shot into the air, blasting wind all around like a helicopter.

Azurim paused before following. Ithicar seemed to know what had given the adult dragon pause.

"Never been thanked, or spoken to so kindly by a human before, have you, Azurim?" Ithicar asked.

Azurim looked into the sky, his eyes following the three shapes circling above.

"No," Azurim said, "at least not so purely, so genuine, as that. There is another thought that disturbs me, however: I do not know if this bodes well or for ill. In my memory, and in any story I know of our past, I do not ever recall dragons and humans being as close as those six children are up there."

Azurim was silent another moment as he pondered his own ominous speech. He spread his wings while glancing at the pair looking at him. "Thank you."

Azurim was gone, a bolt of silver and mystique shining in the sky. He gained height quickly, turning east and roaring the others to follow. Ithicar went inside, but Breyelle stayed and watched until the dragons and their riders disappeared into the horizon.

15 Camping

THE ZEDMORE KIDS HAD never thought the thrill of flying could be so wonderful! It took several minutes while clutching their dragon's necks to fully comprehend it was *real*. They were actually in the air! No nets, no airplanes, and no seatbelts: just the trust they had between them and their friends. The dragons seemed equally thrilled, and the first half hour was filled with shouts of happiness and growls of pleasure. The dragons dipped down, spiralled in the sky, climbed high and went into a free-fall, all because they were finally able to share something of themselves completely with the children.

Azurim took it all in stride, and even joined in once in a while. Kishar had dropped Alex off his back then dove to catch him again, sliding Alex along his neck back into position. Alex was scared the first time Kishar did it, but by the fifth drop Alex felt like an old pro, throwing his arms out to free fall and enjoy the rush of air. It wasn't until Azurim shot by and snatched Alex into a mighty claw that Alex remembered the severity of his situation. Kishar was concerned at first, but then saw the mirth in Azurim's eyes. Alex was safe: Azurim was simply playing with them. It took Alex several long minutes to relax, however, after Azurim had returned Alex onto Kishar's back.

Rex tried dropping Jared a couple of times, but didn't seem as confident in her ability to catch him again, so she stopped playing that game fairly quickly. Penelope and Madison didn't even try once: Penelope wasn't sure of herself, and Madison was already clinging onto her back for dear life, so it wouldn't have been possible to drop her anyway.

As the sun arced across the sky, the dragons flew on. The playing was tiring, and soon all the children were staring in wonderment around the countryside as it darted by. Small villages in trees, on the plains and one built over a lake all streaked by, too small from this height to make out details, and moving away too quickly to accurately see the peoples inhabiting them. A couple of hours into their flight, a giant wall of ice loomed before them, imposing and stretching as far north and south as the children could see.

Rex made a small roaring sound, which Jared thought sounded like a question.

Azurim swooped in close and made a high-pitched keen, to which the other dragons responded by gathering close and flying in a tight formation. It was obvious that Azurim had coached the dragons on this manoeuvre. The children began to wonder how many other tricks they had been taught over the last day!

"The Great Wall," Azurim began, nodding towards the towering sheets of ice. As they neared it they could see large creatures below, some were dragon and others were completely unidentifiable, breathing onto the wall or casting great magic at it. They seemed to be reinforcing the ice, adding to it.

Azurim confirmed their observation for them. "The Dragons and Wiegeteill below are spread out across the continent, always working to ensure the ice remains standing."

"Why?" Alex asked.

"Why-get-teal," Azurim replied, mistaking Alex's question for an attempt at pronunciation.

Alex blinked, not sure of what to say. It was Kishar who continued for him. "Lord Azurim, I believe Alex was asking as to why they are working at the wall."

Azurim looked at Alex and then looked down. "I see. They work on the ice wall to hold the Behemoth and the Ocean Trolls at bay. We may see them as we cross over the ridge."

The wall was impossibly high, reaching hundreds of meters into the air and running like a jagged bolt the length of the eastern shelf of land. The dragons flew over the massive wall, and saw that it was perhaps two or three hundred meters thick in places, more or less. They skimmed the top by fifty or so meters, careful to keep alert for danger.

"If a troll is hiding in the ice lines, we would be an easy target for them to shoot at. It would be rare to see a troll make it this high up, however, I am not willing to take chances at this time, so we will be clearing this stretch as quickly as possible."

Jared had wanted to land and inspect the wall, but after hearing that trolls might attack he was okay with continuing on with speed.

As they cleared the thick wall, the ocean suddenly spilled out before them, a vast wash of blue to every horizon. A loud yet distant thunder and drumming could now be heard, and the children looked down to see large giants using great mallets, ice or sometimes their fists to pound at the wall. There were hundreds of the giants standing on ice floes, wading through the water or clinging to the side of the ice wall! Large chunks of ice were hammered out and dropped into the sea, where others would gather the ice to be shaped into tools or rafts.

"Those don't look like trolls to me! Those are giants!"

"Alas, no, the giants have long since died away, child Alex. Those are trolls, and a nasty breed of them at that."

"Why are they so grumpy and hammering at the ice like that?" Madison asked.

"There was a war many years ago. The ancient Behemoth of the Deep awakened shortly after the last gates were sealed from your Earth. The Behemoth hungered, and devoured everything in its path. Shortly after a Dragon Flight attacked the Behemoth intent on driving it away, killing it outright, or returning it to its slumber. Unfortunately, the Flight failed, and several dragons were killed, eaten by the Behemoth."

"No way!" Jared exclaimed.

"Yes, it is tragic. The dragons who survived returned to the Council and a Conclave was convened. It was decided that the Behemoth of the Deep was too ancient and powerful a creature to be defeated, and so it instead would need to be contained. A spell was cast to trap it underwater, forcing the Behemoth down into the cold waters. Wiegeteill Magic was used to create a barrier of ice. The Behemoth could not escape out in the open water. The only choice the beast now has is to attempt to break through the wall and get onto land."

"It can walk on land, too?" Alex gulped.

"Yes, the only power it does not possess is flight."

"If it's so powerful and hungry, why isn't it eating all the trolls?"

Azurim took a breath and continued. "The trolls live on the ocean bottom, in the cold arctic regions of the north and south poles. The Behemoth summoned the trolls here, and has forced them to do its bidding. They work to destroy the wall, and the Behemoth slumbers, waiting for the signal that an escape for it has been found. The trolls will not stop until they have broken the ice, or found another way for the Behemoth to pass through onto land."

"Why aren't we cold up here?" Madison asked. All this talk about water and ice had made her shudder with a chill involuntarily, which made her wonder why she had not been cold flying up this high in the sky all afternoon.

"Lord Azurim was kind enough to teach us how to use Dragon Magic to warm the air around us for flight," Kishar explained. "In this way, we not only are more comfortable ourselves and protect you from the cold wind, but we can also travel much faster as well. A second enchantment that Azurim cast allows us to communicate with each other with normal speech, rather than yelling into the wind."

"Enough talk for now, Clutch," Azurim interrupted. "We must push forward if we are to reach the shore before nightfall. We must reach land before the sun falls."

"What happens then?" Alex inquired.

"When the sun falls, the spell holding the heat around us – and the speed for our flight – will fail. It will become instantly cold, and while I believe my sisters and I would survive the temperature change, I do not believe you or your siblings would." Kishar finished by tucking his head down and increasing his speed.

Alex looked behind them to the west – the sun was dipping low already! How long had they been flying? He hugged down lower to Kishar and fell silent, trying to work with Kishar's wing beats as if he was the passenger on a motorbike: lean when the driver leans, hug into the body to reduce wind friction.

It didn't take long for them to see land: a long shoreline stretching north, an inlet of water going east, and another section of land extending south. Azurim led the group to the beach and, looking back at the failing light, angled down sharply. The ground rushed up to meet them, and the air suddenly grew cold. The light which had been clearly in sight above had suddenly become twilight as they neared the ground.

The dragons touched down, the younger ones immediately checking to see if the children were alright. Each of them was chilled to the bone, but was able to walk on their own feet. Azurim walked up the beach a short way and crashed into a tree line, knocking several trees flat. He hauled three trees out to the beach with him and ordered everyone to stand back. Breaking the trees like twigs in several places and then piling them up together, Azurim breathed a shot of fire onto them and an instant bonfire lit the night. When Azurim stepped back, the children rushed forward and absorbed the heat from the flames.

It was several minutes before Jared remembered he was wearing the pack that Master Ithicar had given him. He pulled it off his back and opened it to dig out some food. The others saw what he was doing and followed suit, staying near the great fire and eating a late dinner. The dragons curled up in nearby positions and quickly fell off to sleep: apparently the flying had worn them out more completely than they let on.

"Azurim?" Alex asked. The great dragon sleepily turned his head towards the young human. "Can you tell us where we are now? I thought that if you could relate it to Earth geography, we might have any idea of where we are. The worlds are related, aren't they?"

Azurim thought for a moment and settled his head back down on his paws. He seemed tired as well, though not so exhausted as the other dragons were.

"We began our journey in what you would call Canada, just outside Calgary. If my interpretation of the current world geography is correct, we are now sitting on a beach on the south end of Spain, or Portugal. I am not certain of where the country borders are."

"Spain!" Alex shouted. "That's kind of a long way from home, don't you think?"

Azurim closed his eyes and responded somewhat dreamily. "I suppose that would depend on which home you are referring to. In my case, home is only a short hop away to the east."

"Well that's ok for you, but what about us! We can't cross back over to Earth and pop out in Spain!"

"There was never <yawn> any guarantee that you *would* be able to return to Earth at all. I have already explained that to you. Please, hush for now. Eat and sleep. We will be leaving early."

Alex fumed for a moment more, but decided to bite his tongue. Madison had already finished her snack and had curled up under Penelope's shoulder. Penelope had woken up long enough only to snuggle into Madison, and then fall promptly asleep again.

Jared and Alex ate in silence, staring into the flames still hungrily licking the wood.

"Do you think we'll ever get home again?"

"I don't know, Jared. To be honest, I am kind of scared that we won't. This place is great 'n all, but I really miss mom and dad. I want a shower, I need to brush my teeth, and I would just really like to go home."

"I know what you mean." Jared picked up a branch and used it to play with the fire. "But what if we can't? What if we're stuck here forever?"

Alex tossed a few small shavings of wood into the fire. "We can't do that to mom and dad. We just simply *have* to find a way home."

"Do you think they are ok? Are they even thinking of us?"

"Are you kidding?" Alex smacked Jared in the shoulder. "You know mom and dad! They are probably worried sick!"

"Yeah, you're right," Jared agreed. "What do you think they are doing right now?"

Alex laughed. "Mom's probably drained the pond searching for us, and Dad's inside the house playing video games."

"Dad is not! Why would he be playing video games?"

"Cause it's been two days and they haven't heard from us. I saw mom running to us when we got pulled into that portal. She knows we're here and with the dragons, so I'd bet she's camped out right at that spot. Dad probably wants to camp out as well, but you know how much he hates camping. He's probably given mom a cell phone and told her to call him when she sees something, and gone back to the house!"

Jared laughed. "Yeah, he sure hates camping."

"You remember the time we went to Kananaskis Village and stayed in the Tee Pee's there?"

Jared laughed harder. "Yes! Dad didn't admit it, but he hated that place!"

"No, I don't think he *hated* it. I think he really liked the hiking we did every day, but yeah, sleeping outdoors with no indoor plumbing or electricity just isn't him."

"They had a bathroom at the lodge," Jared offered.

"But that meant dad had to walk five minutes to get to it. Face it, dad just likes hotels and home and room service – cabins, tents and campers he can do without!"

"Mom's way better at camping than he is!"

"Yeah, she is."

"I think Dad would be upset about the campfire smell right now, wishing there was a shower nearby."

Both of them laughed, continuing to poke at the fire. Sparks rose into the night sky, as stars began winking into view. The boys were silent as they packed their food back into their packs, and then sat again staring at the fire. It was a long time before either spoke again.

"I sure miss them," Jared whispered.

Alex held back a sob, but a tear came out despite his efforts. "We'll see them again, Jared. Don't worry."

The boys said their goodnights before walking to their dragons. Jared knelt down and placed his elbows on Rex's arm, like he would at bedtime to say prayers. Alex couldn't hear what his brother prayed for, but he silently added his own as well, wondering if God could hear their prayers in such a weird and distant world as this.

The boys fell asleep quickly, warm and feeling secure in the arms of their dragons.

Azurim's eyes opened once the boys had fallen asleep. He arranged some large rocks around the branches of the fire to maintain some heat and embers for the morning then settled back down again. He looked at the six children in front of him, the most unlikely of clutches he had ever seen. His heart went out to the boys and their longing for home and loved ones. He stared at the humans, amazed by their ability for emotion: compassion, sorrow, hope, joy, anger, friendship. These children seemed to be boundless in their capacity for feeling.

Azurim made a vow to the night wind while the others slept.

"Do not worry, children. Azurim will find you a way home."

Lynn clicked the mouse on the camera links, simultaneously looking at six camera views. She had the computer hooked up to two monitors so there was enough room to have all the windows open at once: six panes for the cameras, one for a surface sensor to detect seismic activity, another surface sensor with infrared scanners, a sound analysis program running continuous logs, and a final array of sensors displaying day/night settings, solar light strength, changes in air density, humidity and barometric pressure. She had several other programs that were downloaded from the Internet, including one that collected satellite information for weather patterns. A lot of the displays she wasn't even sure how to read properly, but they were there anyway.

Lynn's eyes scanned everything again, searching for any sign of disturbance.

She had the new computer set up in the existing Computer Room. It was actually a small library and study, but Eddie and the boys always called it the Computer Room, because that was where they all played their networked and Internet video games. Lynn had pushed aside everything on top of one desk and the technicians had installed everything for her, staying late past midnight at her insistence that it had to be completed before dawn. Lynn herself paced back and forth constantly, asking if she could help and jumping every time she saw a flicker of life from the screens. The technicians had to install software and restart the system several times to test programs, which only increased Lynn's anxiety. Eddie had finally gone to bed without her, while Lynn paced on. Eddie didn't know the exact time the technicians left, but he did know that Lynn had never made it upstairs to bed so intent was she on the project.

Richard and Lilly had gone home once all of the work out at the pond was complete. Lilly had to get to the office the next day, but had promised to call regularly to see if there had been any further progress. Richard announced he was heading back to Brazil for a couple days to speak personally with the archaeologists there, to see if they had uncovered anything more about the dragons, and the underground ruins they were located in.

Once the computer install was complete somewhere in the wee hours of the morning, Lynn had been transfixed. For almost an entire day she sat a vigil at the computer, waiting for any sign that her precious babies had come home. She only left her desk once when Eddie had screamed from the kitchen. Lynn, thinking it was the children returning home, rushed into the room only to find Eddie holding the invoices left on the counter from all of the contractors, his face white and sputtering curses. Lynn recognized the papers as the bill for the construction, computer installation and equipment charges. She had left it on the kitchen table by mistake and Eddie had seen it while making some KD for lunch. He fumed for almost two straight hours about how their blessing of wealth they had been given had just been shot into one payment, how irresponsible women were, and several other exaggerated statements that all came from shock and anger. Lynn had brushed it all off as best she could, knowing he would calm down eventually.

And there Lynn sat, staring at a set of computer screens, jumping as birds would fly into view on the pond and then fly away. Several times the wind would stir the trees, and shadows would make her think that someone was there. She worried for her children's safety, and hopelessness was settling into her. Slowly a feeling of embarrassed lunacy was creeping in, chastising her for spending so much money on this system, of how much a waste of time and effort this all was, and how her children were never coming home despite all her efforts.

She spoke barely a word to Eddie, refused to answer phone calls, and ate only once during the whole time. Eddie had brought her food and drink several times, and then took it away nearly untouched hours later. She had lost all track of time, so was surprised when Eddie told her he was going to bed.

"Pardon?" Lynn blinked away from the monitor, her attention on her husband.

"I said I am going to sleep now. It's almost eleven, and I am pretty tired."

Lynn's eyes didn't seem to focus properly. "Eleven?"

"It's night time, Lynn. Eleven o'clock at night, the day *after* the installation was completed. I am going to sleep. Please wake me if you need anything."

Eddie pulled the covers up and fluffed his pillow just right. Lynn noticed for the first time that there was a bed made up in the study. The hide-a-bed from one of the spare rooms had been moved into the study behind her, folded out and made into a double bed. There were fresh sheets, blankets, and Lynn's PJ's were folded on top of the pillows on the far side of the bed. The entire make-shift bedroom was only a couple of meters away from her computer set up.

"Where did all this come from?" Lynn asked, already knowing the answer but shocked Eddie had done it all himself. She hadn't heard a thing, or at least didn't remember it!

Eddie sighed. "I pulled it all in from the spare room down the hall a couple hours ago, not that you'd noticed. You had your nose so deep into the screen I thought you might fall in!"

Lynn placed her hands on her hips and squared off against Eddie. "Now don't you get mad at me! I am just..."

"...doing what you can to find the children, I know!" Eddie finished for her. "And do you have any more of an idea where they are now as compared to two days ago?"

"Two days...?" she began.

Eddie sat up in bed suddenly. "Yes, Lynn! Two whole days! You have been obsessed for two full days about the cameras and sensors and I'm getting worried about you! Not that I blame you for wanting to be active in looking for the kids, but really, Lynn! You haven't eaten, you don't talk to me even when I ask you direct questions, you're so deeply involved staring into those screens that you didn't even see me pull all this crap in here and set up the beds! And furthermore, you need a shower!"

Lynn was about to reply hotly until he made that last comment. Lynn turned her head to one side and sniffed. She smelled like old sweat. Realizing that he was just telling the truth, Lynn's anger quickly fell, a sudden fatigue setting in. Seeing him already tucked into the bed had made her realize how tired she was.

"I'm sorry, honey."

"It's okay, Lynn. I understand, I really do, believe me! I want the kids back too! But killing yourself like this is not helping! You need food, a shower and some sleep! I moved all this in here to sleep in this room so that I could try to keep an eye on you. That, and I didn't want to spend another night alone in our bed so far away upstairs."

Lynn glanced up at the computer. No movement, no alarms or signals, although she did see that the barometric pressure had dropped some. She sighed, feeling a good portion of stress leave her as her shoulders sagged. Eddie almost smiled, knowing that Lynn was finally beginning to return to some semblance of normalcy, and hoping she would rest.

"Can you watch the computer for a little bit while I have a shower?"

Eddie shook his head. "Lynn, you need sleep more than you need anything else! Get your butt in here!"

"I can't do that, Eddie...you're right! I need sleep, but now that you pointed out that I smell and need a shower, I couldn't possible sleep right knowing I am getting those nice clean sheets all dirty."

"You mean knowing that I would be able to smell you all night."

Lynn threw a pencil at him, hitting him in the shoulder. Eddie didn't flinch, but just grinned.

"Lynn, please. Get some rest. Have a shower if you must, but please get some sleep!"

Lynn sighed again, knowing he was right and hating and loving him at the same time for it. She stood up slowly and stretched, amazed at how stiff and sore her limbs were. Walking awkwardly to Eddie's side of the bed she sat down, leaned over and gave her husband a kiss.

"Can you stay awake long enough for me to have a shower?" she asked sweetly.

"Awwww, Lynn!"

"It will only take a few minutes!" Lynn jumped up, hands on her hips again. "Look, I don't want to miss a single moment on there – the slightest movement could mean the kids are coming back, or need our help, or maybe..."

"Fine!" Eddie roared, roughly tossing the blankets to one side. He stormed across the room and dropped into the chair. "Just hurry up! I'm tired!"

Lynn gave him another kiss on her way out of the room, grabbed her PJ's and made her way upstairs. She hopped into the shower, wanting to make it a fast one so Eddie wouldn't be too upset. The water felt wonderful, however, and she was shocked to see that the room had filled entirely with steam by the time she got out almost thirty minutes later. Scolding herself for taking so long, she pulled her PJ's on and planned on making her way back to the study when her stomach growled mightily. She rolled her eyes at herself and laughed, rushing down the stairs and into the kitchen. She munched on an apple while making a sandwich, then cleaned up her dishes before leaving, noting that Eddie must have scrubbed the kitchen clean today by the looks of it, and would be upset to see dirty dishes lying around.

Lynn walked back into the study with a mouthful of sandwich and almost choked. Eddie was comfortably back in bed sleeping, and the computer monitors were turned off!

"What do you think you're doing?" Lynn cried, her sudden loud outburst waking Eddie up.

Eddie sat up so quickly he fell out of bed.

Lynn's sandwich and plate clattered on the desk top as she frantically pounded on the keyboard, restoring power to monitors as they came out of standby mode. "These can't be turned off Eddie! We have to keep them on all the time! Twenty-four seven, you hear me? What were you thinking? How could you...?"

"Lynn Eleanor Zedmore!" Eddie cut her off, his shout filling the house for a few seconds as it reverberated.

Lynn's eyes were wide, locked onto Eddie's. He was standing now beside the bed, burning anger coursing through him, exasperation taking its toll.

"Lynn, don't you dare touch that computer again or I swear I will toss it out the back window!"

"Eddie..."

"No! Not another word! Get your butt over here! Get into bed and go to sleep!"

"Eddie, I can't..."

"You can, and you will, Lynn! I will not allow my wife to work herself to death fretting over this! You have had your shower and now you need sleep! I swear I will tie you down to the mattress if I have to, Lynn, but one way or the other you are going to sleep!"

Lynn waited, knowing this was the end of her marathon session on the computer, but not wanting to give up on her kids return. She was at a loss for words, knowing any argument she raised would simply be a desperate attempt at best, not good enough to sway Eddie's mind.

"Fine, I will go to sleep. But will you...?"

"No, I will not stay up all night while you sleep and I stare bleary-eyed into the screen!" Eddie answered.

"But what about..."

"Oh good lord, Lynn, don't you know anything about this system you set up?"

Eddie stomped across the room, seeming to glow in his heated anger, jabbing his finger at the screen to point out each icon as he spoke.

"Look! I set an audible alarm for each icon here. If there is any movement on the motion sensor larger than an atom, it can tell us! This program is smart enough to monitor plants swaying in the wind and know what they are, so it won't alert us to that. I have another sound alarm for seismic activity. Another for the infrared and another for all the rest of these bloody gadgets you had installed out there! If a termite so much as sneezes near the pond we'll be woken up so we can inspect it! Besides which this entire system has a constant profile logging all of the information in to text files so we can review it later, not to mention the saved video feeds. And the entire process is backed up remotely every night, so if anything goes down here we can always restore it from the safe remote drive. Ok? Finished! Done! Satisfied? Good! Go to sleep!"

Lynn looked at all the windows open on the monitor, highlighting the mouse over each and seeing the pop-ups telling her of the alarm settings for each one. The speakers had been set on a stand-by mode so there was no static or hum coming through, but with a command to power up as soon as the computer ran an alert. It was a great program, and she was upset that she hadn't known about these features before. Of course, she was previously only looking into features of the program that allowed her to monitor the pond and not worried about going to sleep, otherwise she probably would have noticed it eventually.

Lynn spoke, but continued to look at the monitor. "Well why didn't you set this up yesterday so I could have slept then?" she demanded.

Eddie threw his hands in the air and thundered back to the bed, cursing and grumbling under his breath. Lynn laughed at her own joke while checking the settings one more time to make sure all was ready, wolfing down the last of her sandwich. She went to brush her teeth, leaving Eddie grumbling unintelligible threats of titanic proportions. She put her plate in the dishwasher then wandered over to the far side of the bed and climbed in. Getting herself settled, she wrapped her arms around her husband and kissed him on the cheek.

"Thanks honey," she whispered. Eddie growled sleepily in return, but Lynn saw a faint – *very* faint – grin tug at the corner of his lips. She kissed him again, turned out the light and the two promptly fell asleep.

The cameras recorded all night long, the microphones caught every sound, the sensors sensed what they could, but still there was no sign of the Zedmore children or their dragons. No alarms tripped all night long, allowing a long, peaceful sleep for both Eddie and Lynn.

Lilly arrived home from the office late. She had endless meetings and paperwork to do, and was worried throughout the day about Richard and the rest of the family. She hated sneaking around like this, but being a Government employee and having former military experience on her resume had made her the perfect choice for this assignment. The fact that she had been dating Richard at the time the discovery of the dragons had been made had been too good an opportunity to pass up.

Lilly dropped her purse and briefcase on the kitchen table and grabbed some yogurt from the fridge. She ate slowly, running her hands through her hair and rubbing her eyes from time to time as she thought through the events of the day. As she was putting the empty yogurt container in the garbage, the phone rang.

"Hello?"

"Hi sweetheart."

Lilly found energy where previously there had been none. "Richard! Oh my, it is so amazing to hear your voice, believe me!"

Lilly sat down at the table again, fumbling through her things to find her notepad.

"Great to hear you too," he said flatly.

Her features darkened. "You don't sound so good. What's going on?"

Lilly quickly looked at the phone and caught the number displayed there. It was the hotel in Brazil.

"Uh, we've got some serious problems, actually."

Lilly's heart skipped a beat, and she stopped all motion. "Are you ok? Richard, what's wrong?"

"There's people here...I dunno. Lilly, I won't lie to you, I'm scared. I'm heading to the airport now."

Lilly started to cry. She hated this whole mess she was in, she hated her job, and she hated that the man she was in love with was a continent away where she was powerless to help him.

"Rich, you're scaring me now. What's happened?"

"Lilly, I went to the dig site, and it had been completely destroyed."

"Destroyed?"

"The foreman had no idea what I was talking about when I asked him about it. No one here remembers anything about the figurines, or the archaeology that was supposed to be going on."

Lilly noted that he had used the word 'figurines' instead of 'dragons' like he normally did.

"What do you mean, *supposed* to be?"

"That's what I am telling you! No one here knows anything! It's like it never happened."

"Where are the archaeologists now?"

"They're gone. The two from the US are back in the States, Walter from England touched down back in London a few days ago, and the couple guys that were local here don't even remember having met me before! I'm telling you Lilly, it's like they all have amnesia. When I checked back at the dig site, none of the paper work is there, either. There is no record of the university or government having been involved. And the area of the dig on the maps is gone too. The guys here all said that the entire plant was shut down for a week or more, because of a landslide. A special team was brought in to repair the damage and make it safe for the vehicles to get back to work. Apparently some dynamite was used to level it out. I checked it out myself first hand. The entire area of the dig was destroyed by the dynamite, Lilly. And then the crews began working back over the area again, so any further evidence or clues are gone."

Richard paused, and Lilly stayed silent, concerned and not knowing what to say. Richard sounded like he was pacing back and forth, and she assumed he was in his hotel room packing while he talked.

"Lilly, someone powerful has gone to a lot of trouble to remove any evidence of the figurines ever existing, and to cover their tracks while doing it. I tried to stay calm at first, but the more I have been checking around, the more freaked out I have been getting. I'm coming home tonight; I've already changed my flight.

"Lilly, do you think you could do some digging at work, and see if there is anything you could find out?"

Lilly paled. "Wha...what, uh....Richard, what makes you think that I would know anything? I work in an accounting office."

"I know that, sweetheart. But isn't there someone you could talk to, make some contacts within the team that might know someone, who knows someone maybe....?"

Does he suspect I am doing something else than accounting, or is he just fishing here?

Lilly closed her eyes and steadied her breath. "I'll see what I can do, Rich."

"Thanks. Hey, gorgeous, one more thing, you have to tell Eddie and Lynn for me. I have to run, I'm a little late for my cab already. Call them, please. I love you."

"Rich, I love you too, so much. Be safe, please!"

"Gotta go, Lilly. See you soon."

The line went dead.

Lilly turned off the phone and placed it on the table.

"Well, that call went well."

Lilly yelped at the unexpected voice as a man entered the kitchen from the hallway. He was wearing black gloves, holding the cordless phone from the bedroom in his hand, a voice recorder held up to the receiver.

Lilly stood up and stepped to the side of the table, preparing herself in case this encounter became physical. "Who are you?"

The man smiled, his hazel eyes twinkling. "Lilly, I assure you I mean you no harm. In fact I want to help you."

Lilly's eyes narrowed. "Easy to say, mister, hard to prove. The fact that you obviously broke into my house suggests that I can't trust you."

He laughed. "I expect someone in your line of work would know about the need for secrecy and sticking to the shadows, possibly a little break and enter now and then."

The man dropped a folder full of paper work on the table before walking past Lilly to the counter. He filled the kettle with water and plugged it in, setting the switch so the water would boil. As he searched for a tea pot, he glanced back. Lilly was standing in much the same position as before, but he noticed she now had gun in one hand. He smiled and turned his attention back to preparing tea.

"Let me guess: SIG-Sauer Model P225 non-standard nine millimetre semi-auto pistol, eight shot clip, designed for Canadian Government and Military personnel who use a shoulder holster, or have smaller hands to fit the grip better."

He turned and leaned against the counter, holding up several boxes in his hands. "Earl Grey, Peppermint, Chamomile or this one here that is pretending to be a fruit blend with some strange African leaf?"

Lilly slowly raised the gun, which had up to this point been pointed at the ground. "Who are you, what do you want, and give me a reason not to call the police and have you arrested."

"I'll assume Earl Grey. Let me know if you change your mind."

He turned back to the teapot and prepared a bag for it, talking over his shoulder the whole time. "Lilly, I am on your side. Originally I wasn't, but recent events have made it clear to me that I need to work with you in order to accomplish both our tasks."

He faced her again, noting that her stance with the gun left him no room for error. She was obviously an experienced and practiced shot.

"Lilly, if I had wanted to hurt you, I would have done so already, and not bothered with a conversation."

She didn't move.

The man sighed. "Alright, questions and answers. But after I answer, you have to promise to put the gun away, join me in some tea, and get down to business. We won't have a lot of time.

"Who I am is a member of the Order, and my name is Christian Woods. What I want is to help you and the Zedmore family stay safe and protected, and to get their children back. And a reason to not have me arrested – if you call the police and don't allow me to complete my work here tonight, by dinner tomorrow you won't be able to remember anything that has happened in the last several weeks, just as no one in Brazil has any recollection of dragons begin discovered in a gold mine."

16 Verdict

ALEX AWOKE TO THE early morning view of sunrise. The sky was purple and red, with flashes of orange flaring on the bottom of scattered clouds. It was already fairly warm, even though the sun had not come out of its hiding place fully yet. Alex stood up and stretched, the motion causing Kishar to stir. Alex silently walked down the beach to the water's edge and gazed towards the horizon to the rising sun. He pondered for a moment all the sunrises he had seen before, and although he was in another world, this sunrise was the just same as he had experienced: beautiful. It was simply breathtaking no matter how many times he saw it. There was something of a mystery to the sunrise, something speaking of God's little miracles, yet Alex had never quite fully put his finger on it.

Kishar stepped up beside Alex and gently wrapped a wing protectively around the boy. They spent a few moments in silence, the pair soaking in the sun rays and beauty together.

"It is very beautiful, is it not?" Kishar asked aloud.

"Aaaaaaaaaah!" Alex yelled, jumping slightly.

Kishar leaped back, and the others in the camp awoke, except for Madison, who snored grumpily and rolled away from the sound. A hurt expression flashed across the green dragons face and Kishar bowed slightly.

"I am sorry, child Alex. What did I do wrong?"

Alex laughed, slowly approaching his green friend with an outstretched palm. "I'm so sorry, Kishar! You did nothing wrong, really! I simply...well...forgot that you could speak, and it startled me."

Kishar nodded, smiled, and nuzzled Alex with his head. Alex stroked Kishar above his left eye, while Kishar leaned into the gentle massage.

Azurim shook himself awake and yawned, which sounded like a lion's growl for its depth and intensity. The shimmering dragon stretched its wings and beat them several times, shaking the last vestiges of sleep off. The others slowly began their own morning routine, the children rummaging through their bags for food and the dragons pawing the ground with great claw marks as they loosened stiff muscles. They were not used to flying so long or with passengers, and it was obvious they were still sore from the exertion.

"I wish I could help you, Kishar," Alex said in between mouthfuls of bread, "but I just thought of two problems. One, I don't have my brush here to rub you down with, and two, you're so big now I am not sure I could finish in one day!"

Kishar smiled and nodded again. "Perhaps we shall need to find a larger brush!"

Rex joined the conversation with a series of growls and grunts, flashing her teeth and beating her wings. Kishar snorted at her. Rex responded by narrowing her eyes, and the children felt that the only part missing from the expression was her tongue sticking out.

"What did she say?" Jared asked.

"She said that she is very excited about getting her next rub down, and fully expects you to get a new, larger brush. She expects her hide, scales and wings to be kept clean. I told her that she can do it herself instead of being so selfish."

Jared pouted. "I'm sorry, Rex. I'd do it if I had the stuff here! I really would!"

"Nonsense," Azurim interjected. "She will need to learn how to clean herself. Besides which, I find the idea of a human cleaning a dragon...offensive."

Rex spoke to Azurim, to which Azurim simply shrugged and did not reply.

Kishar translated for the children. "Rex told Lord Azurim that the only reason he finds it repulsive is because he has not experienced it. She wants to say that she very much enjoys the time you spend tending to her, child Jared."

Jared stuffed the last piece of fruit he was eating in his mouth and started scratching Rex's neck, like he would a dog's. Rex stretched her neck out in pleasure, while Azurim huffed in disgust. He stepped away and spread his wings instead.

"I will survey the area before we leave. You should all make yourselves ready for another flight shortly."

The dragon did not wait for a reply. He launched himself into the air, the early morning rays of light shining iridescent patterns from his hide in every direction. His scales beamed every colour of the rainbow, so unique in tone were his scales! He rose up quickly with two mighty beats from his wings, the blasts of air buffeting those below.

The children busied themselves by eating their breakfast and washing up as best they could at the water's edge, which was somewhat hard to do in the salty water. Each of them took another bite of the nut that Ithicar had given them to clean their teeth then packed up their gear into their bags. The dragons stretched, yawned, and did several lazy hops into the air, warming their wings up for the coming flight. Madison offered some of the food in her pack to Penelope, who politely shook her head 'no' in return.

"I forgot! You only like rocks, right?" Madison exclaimed, and immediately began scrounging around the area for large mineral rocks.

Kishar shook his head. "No, child Madison, rocks are not our favoured food." Madison stopped to listen, a question forming on her lips, but Kishar continued before she could ask. "We required food on Earth, because the magical energy was very limited. We were forced to pull energy from the sun, and the minerals of the ground. In truth, we could have eaten anything at all – dragons have the ability to process most anything in their stomachs. Here in Shard, however, the magical energy is very rich, and it alone is enough to sustain us without the need to consume food."

Penelope snorted and ruffled some scales, finishing her display by touching Madison gently on the shoulder with one claw.

"Penelope," Kishar translated, "would like to say thank you, Madison, for your thoughtfulness."

Madison grinned brightly, patting Penelope on the arm. "You're welcome!"

Azurim silently returned a few minutes later. The children were all amazed at how quiet the massive dragon was – they only heard him coming as the final beats of his wings slowed him scant moments before touching down! He paused shortly to ask if everyone was ready then took to the sky again. Each of the children climbed onto their respective dragons back and their journey resumed.

They flew in a northeast direction, the sun beginning its ascent directly east, the sharp light blocking a lot of the landscape from their view. Once the sun had risen high enough, however, the kids had a glorious sight of a land they didn't recognize! From horizon to horizon stretched a vast forest with trees of countless varieties, shapes and sizes creating a canopy of titanic proportions. Some trees were so large, spread over a hundred or more meters across, that they hosted a small community of foliage and fauna in their upper branches, like islands in a sea of green.

The children gaped in awe as they sped above the vegetation. At one point, far to the north, they saw a gigantic tree that rose up through several cloud layers, the canopy easily a mile across! Alex leaned over and asked Kishar about it, but the green dragon could only apologize for his ignorance on the subject, knowing nothing of the tree or the forest below. They called to Azurim, who ignored them, so Alex made a mental note to ask about it later, once they had landed.

Another hour went by, and the kids' stomachs began to growl. They had long since gotten used to seeing the endless leaves swim by below them and were now beginning to focus on their hunger, when suddenly the forest ended. A large, flat plain of red and tan coloured stone ran from the tree line to the extent of their vision, with no apparent reason for the change. Barely any vegetation at all grew in this desert-like land, and just as immense and endless as the forest had been, so too was this new landscape. There were massive blocks of coloured rock everywhere, in various shapes and sizes, ranging from the size of a small car to a couple hundred meters in height!

Azurim banked eastward, heading towards a tall pinnacle of rock. In a few minutes, the group had landed at the crest, Azurim gracefully coming to rest at the uppermost thrust of stone and the others forming a semi-circle around him on a lower plateau. The boys were readying to dismount when Azurim halted them.

"I am stopping here only for a moment, children," Azurim stated flatly. "You will need to remain ready to travel as soon as I summon you."

Alex looked around at the barren top they had perched on. "Why?" he asked as he regained his seat on Kishar's back.

"We are about to enter the sacred lands of the Dragon Council. Only a claw full of humans has ever been to the Ziggurat, and fewer still have been there to witness a conclave of the Dragon Council. I want to impress upon you all how serious these next events will be."

Azurim paused as all six members of his audience nodded silently. Madison especially was wide-eyed, feeling very much out of her element and wishing she was back home, watching this all on TV instead of living it.

Azurim continued. "I will fly ahead and announce the dragons return. The announcement will then be carried forward and the Dragon Council will convene. I will return for you at that time to bring you into the Ziggurat.

"The Council will not know that there are humans on their way to the Ziggurat as well. They will have assumed that I am returning only with the three lost dragons. I do not know how they will react."

"Why don't you just tell them that we're coming, so they're prepared?" Alex asked.

"Yeah. Mom always does that for Dad when she's bringing home a surprise. He doesn't really like surprises, so she usually text messages him or phones before she gets there so he can prepare himself."

Azurim shook his head, the scales on either side sparkling. "I have been thinking of these possibilities during our flight, and I believe this to be the best course of action. Admittedly, dragon kind in general is much like your father – we do not like surprises. I believe this delay tactic is necessary in this instance."

Rex spoke, and Penelope added in her own query. Azurim replied in English so that all of them could hear.

"It is for their safety that I choose this method of revealing the children. We need the approval of the Council to open the gateway to return the children home, and so we must play this out in the right way to earn their favour. If I were to fly ahead and announce that there were human children nearby, some of the Council might simply send a force to kill them. If the children were to remain here, hidden, while we fly ahead to announce and introduce the three returning dragons, how long could we keep the human children's existence here a secret? If even one dragon found out, it would besmirch my honour and once again send a Dragon Flight out to eliminate you. Do you not remember the Sylvan Camp, where the Sentinel tried to attack them? There are many here in this world that do not like humans, indeed hate them. They blame humans for our self-imposed entrapment here, for the death of many of their kin, and blame for countless other crimes as well, some real and some imagined. Most of the fairies, dragons, trolls and others here would attack and kill humans on sight, simply for the memory of pain they caused us." Azurim paused. "Just as I may have as well, until I met you three."

The group was silent, absorbing it all. It was Jared who found his voice first.

"Why do so many people hate us?"

"Don't you remember the history that Ithicar told us?" Alex asked, a little sarcastically.

"Well, yeah," Jared retorted, "but it wasn't *us* that did it! *We* haven't hunted any dragons or fairies down. Those were people who lived hundreds of years before we were even born! Why would they blame us?"

"Indeed," Azurim replied softly. "But please do remember, many of our kind are still alive that were also alive when the portals to and from your earth were open. Dragons and fairies can live hundreds, sometimes thousands of years. They remember first hand humans that hunted, killed and persecuted the Fair Folk, the dragons, and all the other mystical races. In their minds and hearts, the sins of the past are just as real today as they were back then."

Jared huffed, crossing his arms and furrowing his brow. "Well that is just dumb!"

Madison copied her brother's stance. "Yeah! Our parents tell us to forgive and forget! Don't your people know how to forgive?"

Azurim fell silent. His eyes betrayed an inner struggle, but he strengthened his resolve to carry out his plan, still feeling it was best for all. "Yes, child Madison, we do know how to forgive."

He stretched his wings and arched his back, preparing to leap into the sky. "I will return shortly, Clutch. Remain here!"

And Azurim was gone, diving off the shelf of rock, using the speed of free fall to accelerate and gain the lift he needed. In moments he shot above the horizon again, disappearing quickly into the distance of the blue sky. Six sets of eyes watched Azurim soar away until he was a small dot. Once he was too far away to see, an uncomfortable silence filled the pinnacle of rock.

Alex looked around at everyone, expectantly. "So? Now what are we gonna do?"

Rex and Kishar responded by lying down and getting themselves comfortable, apparently ready for a nap. Penelope stretched several times then walked in a circle before following suit, curling into a ball as a dog might before resting.

"I guess that answers that question!" Madison exclaimed gleefully, hopping into Penelope's arms and making herself comfortable. Her brothers smiled and shook their heads – what was it with girls and naps, anyway? Girls seemed to love two things more than any other: chocolate and sleeping. The boys hadn't figured that out yet.

Jared explored the sides of the rock they were on, looking down the drop to the ground below. It was a long way down, with no visible way for him to climb. He looked over to Rex, whose eyes were already closed. No help there, he thought.

Alex was similarly looking around the stone slab for something to do. Finding nothing of interest, he and his brother scrounged together pieces of shale and some small pebbles scattered around, sat down and absently tossed them over the edge. The smaller pebbles didn't make a sound, but once in a while the larger chunks returned an echoing crack from somewhere far below.

Jared broke the silence between them after several long minutes. "What do you think will happen when we get to the Council?"

Alex shrugged. "I don't know, Jared. I haven't really thought about it."

Jared stopped in mid-throw of a stone and glared at Alex. "How can you not think about it? We might get eaten or roasted to a cinder, just for showing up there!"

Alex shrugged again, tossing another pebble over the side. "True. But I also have learned that since we arrived here our journey hasn't been something we can control. Everything here is so...foreign, *and* very powerful. We honestly don't really have a choice of what happens next." Alex was silent for a moment as he thought. He threw a flat piece of rock, imagining there was some water ahead of him to skip it on. "I guess I am just accepting that whatever happens, happens, 'because I can't do anything about it anyway."

Jared was ready to argue, but then snapped his mouth closed. He really didn't have anything to say; he just didn't like feeling so helpless.

Several more minutes passed as the boys continued to throw their pebbles until they ran out. They both silently scanned the panoramic view around them, trying to enjoy the endless rock formations. They both agreed it would be nicer if they were closer to the ground and could actually do something with everything they saw, but also knew it was probably safer up here than anywhere else. Who knew what other strange creatures were lurking down below?

"I wonder what mom and dad are up to right now?"

"I was thinking about them, too," Alex replied. "I miss them."

"I miss home," Jared continued. "I miss everything about it, chores and all."

Alex smiled but said nothing more. The two brothers sat in silence, each thinking their own desires and memories of home and what it meant to each of them. The sun continued its descent in the sky, marking the slow passage of time. The dragons were all rumbling snores. Madison was curled into an impossible position on Penelope's arm, her peaceful slumbering making the awkward pose seem comfortable. Nearly thirty minutes went by before the boys joined the sleeping group. Alex curled up with Kishar, sleep capturing him quickly. Jared tried to sleep, but it would not come. He stared out across the world, thoughts of fairies, dragons, trolls and all the other bizarre creatures they had encountered flashing across his mind's eye, mixing with images of home, of his parents, of food that he could actually identify. Not that he minded the food much, especially the blue star fruit!

Try as he might, Jared could not sleep. Several times he closed his eyes, only to open them twenty seconds later to see if Azurim had yet returned. The sun was about an hour from touching the western horizon when Jared spied a shadow moving towards them, the wing beats unmistakable. He waited for several minutes to be sure, and once he was certain that someone was indeed coming for them he alerted the others. The dragons were awake immediately, standing quickly and stretching their muscles, wings and limbs out.

Together, the six companions, clutch mates and friends, watched as a dark coloured dragon lumbered towards them through the air, not at all characteristic of the graceful movements that were typical of Azurim. This dragon was larger and heavier looking by the way it seemed to force its way through the air, rather than gliding on it. As the figure came closer, the dark green scales became more defined, and a single thought echoed in the minds of the gathered clutch: where was Azurim?

Azurim skimmed the surface of the ground, swooping lazily back and forth, stalling for time. He was in no hurry to return to the Conclave, although he knew he must. By now, the Conclave would have already sensed his return and would be gathering together, if not the whole Conclave then the Elders at least. He had no choice but to move forward, tell the Conclave the young dragons were here, and then return to fetch them. He did not like the deception involved in omitting the detail of having the humans along as well, but Azurim felt it could not be helped. If they were to arrive in the Conclave unannounced, many dragons would be hard-pressed not to simply attack. Giving the Conclave some time to prepare for the young dragons return would hopefully disarm them enough not to make a hasty decision regarding the humans, despite how odd it may seem that Azurim was arriving alone and not bringing the young with him immediately. Seeing the children riding on the dragons back would give them pause enough to allow Azurim to inform the Council members and the Conclave as a whole that the six young ones were all part of one Clutch. That should ensure their safety, Azurim thought, at least for those that honour Dragon Law. There were some in the Conclave that did not....

Azurim changed the angle of his wings, allowing his speed to pull the air in a drag that slowed him down, but also lifted him higher. He then beat his wings to give him additional lift, just as the edge of the Ziggurat came into view. The immense size of the structure always amazed Azurim, however it seemed more ominous somehow now, almost malevolent. Azurim had grown fond of the human children, and had no desire to see them harmed. They were incredibly young, and yet their youthful innocence spoke straight through to the truth. Was it truly right, morally and ethically, for the dragons to condemn humankind after generations of their people had lived and died? There was none left behind that would remember the Dragon Wars, the Mage Wars, the collapse of the portals or the Fairy Folk, was there? Indeed, in the several days that Azurim had been in the other world, there had been no sign of there being any true memory of anything magical or fantastical whatsoever!

In a week of travelling, Azurim had seen humans who by and large had no idea what a dragon was, let alone magic, Runes, mystical rites, power stones, or anything else he remembered from the time before the portals were shut. Certainly, there were many humans who wore necklaces with Runes on them, or crystals, or had tattoos and spoke mystic incantations – but none of them were real. They were practitioners in spirit only. The real magic had truly left their world.

Azurim had spent a full day watching the smaller dragons and their chosen human clutch mates before he revealed himself and led the group here. In that time, he had noted how close the children were to one another, and how close they were to the dragons as well. He had thought it silly at first, perhaps even a trick, that the humans had cast a spell to trap the dragons will, making them servants of the children. But Azurim had been wrong: there was a definite love bond connecting the Clutch. Who was he to try and separate them? Who was the Council or Conclave to decide that?

Azurim shuddered at such thoughts. In over one hundred years of serving with and on the Conclave, he had never once questioned the rule, authority or judgment of the Council, and yet now here he was pondering their wisdom and whether that wisdom could rightly be extended to a race that they had all vowed to hate. The Council was a group voted in for life, the wisest and most intelligent of all dragon kind, having been proven as leaders many times before even being considered as a potential candidate. And because the elected seat was for life, it was not very often that a new dragon was voted in! Azurim himself had never been part of a vote for such an event, as the Council had been ruled by the same group for many years before Azurim joined the Conclave.

The Conclave was made up of all other dragons that had passed the Ceremony of Stars, proven their control of magical skills, and passed each of the six Elemental Tests. There were many dragons in the Conclave, but more often than not only a small percentage of them would ever arrive for a meeting, most being too busy with their own concerns.

Finally there was the Master, a dragon voted from among the Council members to oversee the entire body, who had the privilege of two votes in any given session, in case a dispute ended in a tie. The Master was given the duty to maintain Dragon Law both in interpretation and practice.

Azurim's musings came to an end as he banked over the outer wall of the circling stadium, expecting to see only the twelve members of the Council and perhaps a few members of the Conclave as well. Instead, the stadium and the ziggurat plateau were all full! This was by far the largest number of dragons he had ever seen converging for a Grand Council! There were simply hundreds of them!

Azurim tried to cover his shock with an air of bravado that he really didn't feel. He soared high, stalling for time once again, pretending to look for an appropriate place to land, which was ridiculous as there was only one empty place on the field of the Ziggurat courtyard, obviously left solely for him. He had simply never seen this many dragons in a Council before. It shook him. A thought occurred to him and he cursed himself as a fool for not thinking of this before: they already knew the humans were here. How could they not? The Dragon Council lorded over this world for many centuries, and a rumour as tantalizing as humans returning here would be sure to spread like wildfire from mouth to mouth, even from as far away as Sylvan Camp.

Azurim cursed his short sightedness. For a brief moment he debated returning to the clutch, but he knew it was far too late to rethink his strategy. Everyone here had already seen him, had already guessed, no doubt, his plan. All that was left was to carry it out – Azurim had foolishly seen to it that his course was set, and that he had no other option.

His wing-over dropped him sharply in a tight corkscrew directly above the clearing left for him. He fell like a star and padded lightly to the ground, folding his wings in one fluid motion. It was important in this crowd to maintain some semblance of power and control. Political intrigues were not lost on dragons – in fact, many of the court intrigues humans engaged in were invented by their original dragon counterparts.

Azurim scanned the gathered throng more thoroughly than he had before. Something was wrong, out of place that he hadn't noticed before. The Master was not present. A chill and deep suspicion crept up Azurim's back: this did not bode well. This was not an official Council meeting with the Conclave if the Master was not present.

"Well, finally, the *hero* returns."

It was a voice from within the crowd atop the dais. The stinging sarcasm of the word 'hero' was not lost on Azurim's ears. Azurim waited, thinking to bide his time for the right moment to speak, but wondering also if he would even be given the chance. He decided to go with boldness in the case the latter was true.

"I am no hero, Raiscaryn," Azurim began, but was cut off before he could continue.

"Oh ho! On *that* we certainly agree, Azurim."

The thin orange and rust coloured dragon speaking stepped through the crowded wings and bodies until he was perched on the edge of the dais which led to the higher parts of the Ziggurat. He wore a vicious looking grin filled with malice and mischief.

"You are definitely no hero, Azurim. Betrayer is more like it."

Azurim was not sure where this was headed, but a growing concern for the clutch's and his own welfare was festering in his speeding heart. This direct insult and accusation was against Dragon custom: indeed this entire meeting was highly irregular. Dragon Law was built upon honour, respect and a deep sense of propriety. This current spectacle had none of the above.

"I would be most interested to hear your evidence of claim to betrayal, Raiscaryn, however there is more pressing business to deal with. Where is the Master?"

Raiscaryn stepped to the ground and began walking in a slow, wide circle around Azurim. Azurim noted that a line of green dragons still on the dais had their eyes fixed on him, watching and waiting for aggressive movement. Their stance was unmistakable: they were ready to attack if Azurim stepped out of line.

"Azurim, the Master is unable to join us at this current time. He has fallen ill unexpectedly, and has announced a replacement to head the Council until such time that he recovers." A great black eye swivelled to lock with Azurim's. "Me."

"You?" Azurim coughed the word out in disbelief, stunned.

Raiscaryn ignored the question and implied challenge and instead forged ahead with a question of his own.

"Where are the humans now, and why did you not kill them already?"

So they did know, that at least was confirmed. He took in a breath to respond, but was cut off as Raiscaryn rudely continued.

"Why did you bring them through to our world? You know this is a serious offense as humans are forbidden here!"

Azurim took a steadying breath so as not to lose his temper and maintain his focus. Before he could reply, Raiscaryn cut him off yet again with another scathing question.

"What are you plotting against the Council?"

"What?" Azurim barked. "Nothing of the sort!"

"Ah, so you are plotting something in league with the humans! If not against the Council, then what?"

"There is no plot..." Azurim began.

"A likely story, and yet here you are trying to sneak three humans with obvious magical power into the Council!"

"I am not trying to sneak them anywhere!"

"Oh really? Then why did you not bring them directly? Why are they waiting out in the Pinnacle Forest?"

They knew! They knew exactly where the Clutch was! Oh what a fool Azurim had been!

"They are harmless children, Raiscaryn. Quite innocent and naive – almost as naive as you." Azurim threw the insult loudly, trying to goad him on. As long as Raiscaryn was talking, Azurim could learn and put together the pieces of what had happened in his absence.

"Really, Azurim, insulting me will not win any favours for you."

"It is an insult to have you in this Council Ring, let alone pretending to be a Steward for the Master."

"I pretend at nothing!" Raiscaryn nearly screamed, like a spoiled child having his play toys taken away. "The Master spoke in front of witnesses," he gestured with a claw to five Council members a short distance away, "and proclaimed me as his Steward until his health returns, or as his Successor if his health fails completely."

Azurim's eyes went wide. "A Successor? You?" Azurim laughed loudly, a defiant laugh filled with derision, to cover his shock. "You could not lead a flock of chickens to seed."

There was a muted laughter following Azurim's comment, but Azurim also noted several dragons mixed in the crowd that scowled. He guessed that roughly half of those gathered here were not in agreement with Raiscaryn being in any position of power.

Raiscaryn himself was seething at being insulted publicly. "I have been given the right and authority..."

It was Azurim's turn to interrupt. "If your authority expands beyond wiping the dung from a nursery I would be shocked."

"Silence!" Raiscaryn bellowed, his voice cracking. Two large greens jumped from the dais and landed a wing's length from Azurim. Several in the crowd leaped to readiness. Azurim was not sure what was happening here, but he no longer cared. He knew enough – half the Council was not present and was instead being represented by this oaf. Dragon Law stated very specifically the course of justice and stated also who may be named into the Council. For this charlatan to be named as a Steward was insult enough and Azurim knew his father would never agree to such an atrocity. There had been manipulation and political manoeuvring while Azurim had been away, but he tossed those thoughts aside. All Azurim cared about now was getting out of here quickly and returning to the Clutch.

Perhaps it was safer for the entire Clutch to remain back on Earth after all?

"You will be judged, Azurim! For crimes against the Council and all of Dragon Kind! You are hereby charged with conspiracy against your own blood, consorting with humans willingly for your own ends, and teaching magic to humans for your own personal gain!"

Raiscaryn stepped back onto the dais and turned abruptly to stare at Azurim evilly.

"Do you have any last words before I pass Judgement, traitor?"

Azurim looked from side to side, taking a breath. Instead of speech, he used the moment to draw out a rapid magical incantation. The magical word erupted in a sonic burst, doubling as a distraction and also giving Azurim a blast of swiftness as he shot into the air. The two green dragons nearest him roared in agony as the sonic energy hit them, one of them receiving a long tear in a leathery wing, the other getting buffeted to the ground.

Azurim felt surges of energy lashing towards him, and chaos erupted below. An electrical charge hit him on his side, but had not done any great damage. A second charge of magical energy arced towards him, but another dragon appeared in the way, taking the blast meant for Azurim. Yet another ball of green energy chased Azurim, but this one, too, was turned away, a red dragon below casting its own spell of shielding, causing the shot to deflect away from Azurim into the distance.

Below was a scene unlike any other: nearly two hundred dragons drew magic into themselves and hurled it out at each other. Azurim was still not certain as to what had transpired since he left to find the young ones, but it was clear almost all dragons had chosen a side. He assumed that those who were missing from this gathering had either chosen to remain neutral, or were unable to attend because of fear or threats. Azurim did not stay behind to watch the outcome, even though his heart ached to leap to the aid of many friends he saw fighting below. Azurim cast a spell of speed, another of vision, and another of protection as he rocketed back to the Pinnacle Forest, hoping the Clutch was safe, but fearing the worst.

Several dragons gave chase to Azurim, but were attacked from others still faithful and loyal to the Master. All here knew who the Master's son was, and it was obvious the battle line that had been drawn focused on him. The battle quickly spread from the Ziggurat grounds to the fields, forests and surrounding skies. When magical resources had been depleted, breath weapons of fire, ice, shadow and other types exploded all around, merging with cries of pain as claws and teeth fed into the fray.

Azurim sped on, a tear falling from his eye for his comrades who were risking so much to buy him time, and a second tear as he wondered silently where his father was. Where was the Master?

"Something doesn't look right."

Alex was worried, and agreed with his brother's statement.

"Maybe it's just an escort!" Madison's naivety and innocence were nearly overwhelming.

The dragons could all feel a sense of dread, of impending danger, and the boys certainly felt that something was wrong. Azurim said that he would be back. That spelled out a message of caution at the very least.

The green dragon lurching towards them was very large. So large, that even at the distance remaining, which could be counted in only tens of meters, it was dwarfing the group on the plateau. It was trailing a mist of some kind of green and brackish vapour, hanging in the air where the dragon passed.

As it neared, it became clearer that the mist was trailing from the dragon's mighty maw.

Kishar frantically scanned around at the group. "Clutch mates, mount up, quickly! And hold tight!"

Kishar and the other dragons had already lowered their shoulders, and the children wasted no time in scrambling up onto them. As they did so a great roar bellowed from the green newcomer, which shook the rocks around them, down to the children's very souls. Kishar bellowed as well, but it wasn't a challenge, it was a command.

Rex and Penelope launched into the air, then with great urgency dove downwards, accelerating at phenomenal speed. Kishar waited three heart beats and then vaulted straight up, gaining as much sky as he could. Alex looked below them and saw a blast of black and green mist hit the very spot Alex and his dragon had just been standing on. Large shelves of slivered rock sheared off the plateau, falling the great distance to the ground below, leaving a melted pool in its wake, the liquid congealing there and biting its way through the remaining stone. The hole it was carving would have been enough for Kishar to slip through – that was a mighty breath weapon indeed!

The giant green veered up, startlingly agile for its impressive bulk, but not as elegant as Kishar and the others had been. A nasty green and white smile flashed as it gained height, closing the distance.

"What do we do?" Alex cried out, terrified. It was all he could do to hold onto the scales around Kishar's neck and shoulders.

Kishar did not answer. He did not want to reveal his own fear as well, so stayed silent.

Kishar banked and changed his direction into the sun, climbing high and racing for the light on the horizon. The sun had not quite begun to go down into nightfall, but it wouldn't be long. The great green changed course to pursue Kishar, growling threats in a language that Alex didn't understand, but was sure he could guess their meaning. After Kishar had gone an acceptable distance, he banked in a shallow dive, then folded his wings close and plummeted into a free fall. Alex tightened his grip and was forced to cover his face in his arm, so fast was the wind rushing up to him. Their plight was desperate, and increasing their speed to escape was their only hope.

The great green banked as well, but slowly. It opened its mouth, and spat a large dark cloud of swirling gas and liquid. The gob elongated as it fell towards Kishar, getting closer. Kishar looked back and gasped in awe. The great green had changed course and was returning to the pinnacle in search of the others, while the great green gob was catching up to him!

Kishar opened his wings and strained against the pressure of the wind. Alex was sure he heard the dragon teeth grinding against the stress, but Kishar was able to pull out of the dive. It would have been far easier to do alone, but with a rider on his back the manoeuvrability was not as great as he hoped. Idly, Kishar thought about getting a saddle akin to what he had seen on horses, in order to keep the rider strapped on and freeing up the room to move for the dragon.

The disgusting black gob hurtled down past Kishar, eventually splashing down on the barren ground below. Again, a sizzling smoke drifted from where the acid hit, burning holes.

The great green had begun following Rex and Jared, a roaring laughter escaping from its throat. Kishar's eyes narrowed in anger. He saw Penelope and Madison below him, and an idea came to mind. He roared down to Penelope, who glanced up in time to see Kishar do a barrel roll, dropping Alex off his back to plunge through the dusk red sky. Penelope slowed and glanced quickly back at Madison, whose teary-eyed and fearful expression nodded. Hoping she understood, Penelope climbed, trying to elongate her neck, all the while bumping her back up and down as she shifted Madison's weight further and further down her back until Madison's legs were pinned by the wings, and she could slide no further. Penelope waited until she was only a length above the shouting Alex, then drove down with all the speed she could muster, gently sliding her head under Alex as she tried to match his velocity.

Alex, feeling something prodding him, grabbed onto the back of Penelope's head and pulled himself into a roll to get onto her neck. As soon as he did so, Penelope arched, sliding Alex the length of her neck into her shoulders. He was hanging with his legs on one side of her, his upper torso on the other, but at least he was no longer falling.

Penelope, close to exhaustion, could not handle two riders together. She flapped wings furiously, but continued to descend. In moments, the trio had hit ground. Penelope had given every last bit of her strength to try and land softly, but the impact was still jarring to all of them. Alex rolled off as soon as he could, his legs carrying him into a quick jog to slow him down, then skidding to a halt. Despite her fatigue, Penelope did not stop until she was under an outcropping of stone. There, she rested, with Madison trying her best to comfort her friend.

Alex looked into the sky, trying to see what was happening. From this distance, he could only make out specs, not enough to discern who was who. What he wouldn't give for his Super Spy Telescope he had at home right now!

Back in the air, Kishar, divested of his load, surged forward and began singing a song of protection. The green was closing on Rex, who was trying to fly circles around the lower columns of stone. Rex was having the same difficulty as Kishar had before, with Jared on her back making it hard to move skilfully. The great green was almost near enough to reach out and claw Rex, when Kishar arrived.

Kishar collided full force into his enemy from behind, claws raking and teeth biting, using the speed of flight to enhance the power behind the attack. The great green roared, more out of surprise than pain, although a couple of scales did fall loose, and a minor trickle of blackened dragon blood dripped. A minor wound, but enough to get its full attention.

The two greens rolled in the air, grasping and clawing at each other. Twice Kishar had killing blows landed on him, and twice his Song glanced the attack away. The larger dragon tried a different strategy, and belched out a cloud of vapour. The two dragons released their grips, as Kishar fell away, his Song ended, knowing only now to try and flee once again. He had hoped his surprise attack would have been more effective, but the bulky size and brute strength of this foe was too much for a youngling like Kishar to take on.

Kishar looked around, and spied Rex landing lightly atop the pinnacle again. At least they were safe, for now, and Kishar's hasty attack had not been in vain.

Something large slapped Kishar, sending him reeling into a stone column. With dulled senses, Kishar realized it was the same column that Rex was currently on top of. Before Kishar could fully regain his mobility and sense, a large clawed paw punched roughly into his chest, pinning him against the stone column. Blood seeped from beneath cracked scales, red and flowing.

The great green hovered in place, holding one paw onto Kishar, and slapping the small whelp with the other.

"Stupid wyrmling!" The great green roared. "You fight like an infant! Your puny attacks are no match for me!"

A sneering laugh echoed off the surrounding canyon walls as the large dragon continued a relentless beating on Kishar. The vile green dragon was toying with him now, using his right arm to pin Kishar to the rock, while using a single claw on his left to stab and cut. The great wings beat slowly, holding him in place in the air while he continued his assault on the much smaller dragon. Scales flew loose and fell to the ground. Several fleshy wounds appeared, pulpy and exposed to bone. A tooth was knocked out, and it too clattered to the rocks below.

"And now, stupid wyrmling, Greenfist, as your precious humans used to call me, will destroy you."

Kishar looked up, his vision cloudy. He had been straining with all his might to try and wrestle himself free of the enormous grasp holding him, but to no avail. Instead, Kishar slumped, not afraid of the end, but not wanting it either. There was simply nothing more he could do.

A silver streak blasted into Greenfist so quickly, a gob of spit came out from the winded dragon's mouth. Kishar fell a short distance before absently reaching a claw into the stone column. It slowed his fall so that the collision into the ground was a minor impact, rather than a deathly one. A line on one wing snapped with the crash, and the world around Kishar turned to darkness as he slipped into dreams.

Rex looked on from above, Jared anxiously peering over her head to watch as well. There was nothing they were able to do, and they both knew it, so they could only watch. When Azurim had appeared, seemingly from nowhere, they barely recognized him. The rage in his features and fury in his roar was evident even from their distant vantage point. Alex and the others heard it from the ground as well, and it shook pebbles and dust from the soil. The great silvery dragon had become a beast, features twisted in a snarl of pure anger, unrecognizable as the friendly and fatherly guide he had been to them until now.

Azurim pounded into Greenfist, large chunks of flesh and scale being tossed aside. The green was slightly larger than Azurim, but it was of no matter. Azurim was tougher, and as Greenfist beat on Azurim he realized it too. Greenfist's claws bounced off the shiny scales, and the acidic bile slid off without causing so much as a stain. It was obvious Azurim had placed spells of protection on himself before arriving, but the onlookers wondered if he had really needed it.

As the pair winged in the sky, Greenfist roaring in pain and Azurim roaring in fury, the green scales from its owner's chest sheared off in a single wave, falling in a large pile to the ground. Azurim took his opportunity and belted out a blast of flame that engulfed Greenfist, centered on the now exposed skin of his chest. Greenfist howled in pain and released his grip of Azurim, turning instead to run away. Azurim gave a short chase, blasting alternating streams of fire and ice at the green dragons back. Once he was certain that Greenfist would not be returning, Azurim raced back to where Kishar lay, Alex already weeping and stroking Kishar's face. Azurim called out a single note in Song that the others should join him.

Rex and Jared dove from their perch and arrived in moments, while Penelope loped slowly along with Madison walking beside. They made the distance as quickly as they could, but they were both tired and shaken so the going was slow.

The others all saw tears streaming down Alex's face as he held Kishar, examining all of the various bloody wounds but having no way of treating them.

"He will live, child Alex." Azurim's tone was not compassionate, but stern. It was simply matter-of-fact, and almost anxious as Azurim watched all around them for fear of another attack. "We must leave, and quickly. There will be others, and they will attack us in force once they know our position."

Alex sniffed loudly, the tears still pouring out. "We can't leave Kishar," came out the squeaked words, choked with feeling.

Azurim stared down at the little boy, amazed once again at the incredible depth of emotion humans had.

Azurim looked around at the assembled group. "We will not leave him behind, child Alex. We cannot leave such a brave dragon to an unknown fate. I will carry Kishar. However, we must leave, now. More dragons will be coming, and we do not want to be here when they arrive."

Alex watched in trembling dismay as Azurim hoisted Kishar up onto his shoulders and back, with some help from Rex and Penelope. There would be no possible way to fly now, but perhaps that was best anyway.

The group began their journey through the barren lands, heading towards a sea of green trees in the distance. The sun went down, and in the darkness, they were all sure they could hear the sounds of battle, dragon against dragon, raging into the night, disappearing behind them as they increased their distance from the field.

17 Shelter

LONG INTO THE NIGHT the group walked, the darkness crowding in like a thick blanket. When even the starlight failed them, the dragons walked single file, Penelope in the middle guided by Azurim's swishing tail and Rex at the end. Madison and Jared had begun by walking with the rest, but when the trees had begun to get thick, they hopped onto their respective dragon's shoulders. The sounds of night insects and other distant roars kept their blood pumping in fear and alarm. The tough hides of the dragon's necks kept the snapping branches at bay as they plodded on.

Alex did not leave Kishar's side. Alex held a hand to Kishar the entire time, his eyes wide, straining to see in the forest around them. Azurim had told him to climb aboard the dragon's back, and perch there with Kishar, but Alex refused. He didn't want to risk straining Azurim needlessly, or taking up precious space that Kishar would need to rest comfortably, or any other of a dozen worries that went through his head. So he kept pace with Azurim and the great lumbering walk that he did. There was a moment here and there where a tree, bush, branch or other foliage would get in the way, and Alex was forced to remove his hand from Kishar's scales. In these instances, he stepped backward, keeping his hand solidly placed on Azurim's flank, and then rushing forward again to touch Kishar when the path allowed. For the most part, Alex was at a slow jog for most of the time, but his stubborn refusal to leave Kishar was greater than the fatigue in his lungs or muscles.

Azurim had stopped once, seeing a dragon circling above. He dropped Kishar to the ground and ran a short distance away before leaping into the starry sky. The others saw flashes of light from fire and other mystical energies before all went silent. Several tense moments later, Azurim returned in a rush, scooping Kishar back up onto his back and leading the party quickly away.

"They'll be back, soon. We must hurry," was all Azurim whispered, leaving all other questions unanswered.

Azurim walked quickly for a short time but soon began to tire. He was exhausted and in dire need of rest, yet the urgency and imminent threat of danger kept them all going. He could sense behind him that the other two dragons were asleep on their feet. Azurim's shoulder's, too, were incredibly sore, holding Kishar's body aloft for so long. They needed rest, and needed it now.

But where to stop? Azurim had no idea. He had flown over these woods many times, but never had needed to stop in them before. This was new territory for him. In all his life he couldn't remember a time when he had been confined to land travel such as this.

A whooshing sound above the group made them all stop. Azurim had placed enchantments of concealment on the group, but wasn't sure how long that would stall other search parties. The movement above the trees had been a dragon, that much was certain. Azurim turned suddenly and drew his small band into a tight circle, gently guiding Kishar to the ground. He growled a low rumble to the other dragons, barely audible, who both nodded silently in return. The entire group was wide awake and alert now, fresh adrenaline pumping into their veins and stimulating their senses. Azurim paused a moment and looked around the clutch one last time before vaulting himself into the air. Several branches snapped and fell to the ground around them as he disappeared into the night sky.

Silent minutes passed by. The canopy above was too dense to see more than an inky darkness in between shadow. The clutch huddled together, and with Azurim now gone they could hear much more in the night than they had before. His magic had been suppressing so much noise and movement! They had not realized how much so until he had left. Alone now, they held each other in an embrace, Alex still holding onto Kishar, kneeling beside him while holding a hand to Rex's wing.

A roar of challenge lit up the night with ferocity. Insects became quiet and a general hush fell over the trees. There was a flash of light and an answering roar, this voice a higher pitch and not as guttural as Azurim's. More flashes, more roars, growing distant. Silence fell. Minutes passed, and each member of the silent group realized they were holding their breath. Slowly, the insects of the forest began to chirp their songs again. Here and there something would hiss, or screech, or bleat. The children began to get cold as time slipped by, Madison shivering with Penelope's wing wrapped around her, trying to provide heat.

A sudden crashing of trees nearby made them all jump and Alex yelp in surprise. A few moments more and a great looming dragon pushed its way through the undergrowth to stand above the clutch. They all cowered in fear from this newcomer, except for Rex, who bravely spread her wings in challenge. Still, the unknown dragon was impressed with the display, and lowered its head down. When it spoke, the voice was distinctly female to the children's ears, pleasant and lilting, stern but motherly, with an accent they would never be able to place.

"Young Clutch, Lord Azurim sent me to find you and bring you to him. He is wounded, and could not come himself. Please, let me carry Kishar. Follow to our camp for the night. We must hurry!"

Rex's wings lowered slightly, still unsure of this stranger. She bleated and growled and hissed, only to be cut short by a blast of air from the other dragon, which the kids took for a snort intended to silence children when they talk out of turn. Rex slowly moved out of the way, still warily eyeing the large dragon. Kishar was lifted gently up and onto the shoulders of this large and elegant dragon, in much the same manner as Azurim had before. Without another word, she turned and lurched into the forest, not wasting time to check and see if the others followed.

They did. Alex raced to Kishar's side once again, trying to hold a hand to his best friends hide. The pace was much quicker than Azurim's had been though, and Alex was forced to jog quickly behind the stranger. The others kept up as well, although the going was difficult at the new, quicker speed.

It seemed like an eternity to get to the camp, as it always is on a journey where the destination is unknown. Alex had begun to stumble, his legs getting wobbly. Madison had fallen into a deep slumber on Penelope's back, the latter of which was beginning to see only through nearly closed eyes, so weary was she. Rex and Jared kept up the rear guard both wild and alert.

And suddenly they were in a small clearing. There was a cave off to one side and a thin ribbon of moonlight lit the area. Several dragons stood guard at even points around the glade and two stood guard at the cave mouth, one just inside the gaping maw in the earth, the other perched above it. One other much smaller dragon raced from place to place with blinding speed, a faint trickle of golden sparks shooting behind it as it zoomed about. At least, they assumed it was a dragon: it was moving too quickly to be sure, but it was definitely too big to be a firefly. Or was it? In this world, Jared thought, it would be possible!

Their guide wasted no time and made a direct line to the cave, her crimson scales shimmering in the moonlight. Each of the guards eyed the group, not out of malice or reaction to any threat, but simply pure curiosity. They all wanted to get a look at the strange human children, at what their friend and leader had risked his life for. Their escort moved swiftly past all the staring eyes without a single thought to their gawking, pressing deep into the darkness of the earth. Alex's eyes adjusted quickly to a firelight coming from somewhere deep within, and felt a heat begin to rise from the depths.

Rounding a corner, the group stepped into a large cavern, an enormous fire blazing at the far end in what appeared to be a great oven carved into the stone. Three other dragons were in the chamber: Azurim, asleep near the flames, one blue dragon of equal size near him licking a wounded wing, and a third smaller dragon bent over Azurim, humming a low tune. Its scales were shinning silver, reflecting thousands of beams of red and orange as the firelight danced.

The blue dragon looked up, wincing with the effort, and sounding surprised when it spoke. "You made it, Corash. It is agreeable to see you again." The children were surprised to hear a perfect English baritone voice emanate from the large blue dragon, like they had heard on their visits to England. They assumed this was a male dragon.

"Yes," Corash replied shortly. She moved quickly to the fire and gently deposited Kishar onto the ground close to the heat. Alex was not able to stay near to his friend, for the heat was too intense. Instead, he leaned against the far wall and watched.

Penelope and Rex moved to positions farther away from the rest and settled in for a much needed nap. Madison allowed herself to be guided down into Penelope's embrace, sleeping soundly once again when they were both comfortable.

Jared suddenly yawned and stretched, realizing how tired he was. It had been a very long night, and now that they were in what appeared to be safety, the adrenaline was leaving his system quickly. He began walking to Rex, but then stopped and looked to his brother. Alex's eyes were rimmed red with worry, sleep, tears, exhaustion and concern. He stared at Kishar longingly, his hands wringing over themselves as he imagined the worst. Jared went to his brother and stepped in front of him, blocking his view.

"Alex, we're safe now. You need to sleep."

Alex bobbed back and forth to look around Jared. "But what's going to happen to him?"

Alex sniffed away a choked tear as he talked. He'd only really known Kishar a very short time, but what if he died? Alex wasn't certain his heart would be able to take the strain of living life without his new best friend. Jared stepped into his brother's sightline and placed his hands on his hips.

"Look, they have several dragons here that all obviously care about Kishar, and Azurim. They'll be fine! Besides, there isn't anything we can do now, anyway."

Jared waited, but his words didn't seem to be sinking in.

"Alex," Jared tried again. This time he waited until Alex looked him in the eye. "Kishar would want you to be sleeping right now. Think of it this way – right now they don't need your help, but what if they do need your help later and you're too tired to do it? If you sleep now, you can be ready later when they need you."

Alex mulled it over for a moment more, but then finally nodded and followed Jared over to where the rest were sleeping. Jared curled up with Rex, while

Alex stepped in between the two dragons and leaned against the wall. He kept his eyes on Kishar for a few more minutes, watching as the silvery dragon bent low and sang a soft song, presumably for healing. Small motes of ash drifted from the fire from time to time, coming to rest lightly on the three injured dragons, leaving small smoking embers on the scales and skin.

Alex regarded the sliver dragon as a doctor, and this was his hospital. The doctor continued to sing his low song, calm, tranquil, soothing. The same music eventually held Alex in its sway, and he fell into a very deep sleep.

Corash looked at the human children surrounded by their dragon clutch mates and was in awe, especially of the child Alex's deep compassion and concern. He truly loved his clutch mate, and the emotion was so obvious it was impossible for it to escape notice. She looked at Azurim, and Kishar, and back to the remaining group. Yes, Azurim had chosen well. These humans had already proven their worth, simply by the depth of their conviction for each other.

Corash gave some orders to the silver dragon, then headed out into the night, many errands still yet to be done before she herself could rest.

The doorbell rang loudly through the still house. Lynn looked up from the computer monitor to see Eddie nod.

Eddie waved his hand towards Lynn. "I know, you're busy. I'll get it."

Two gentlemen stood at the door, smiling as Eddie opened it up part way. One older man, standing closest to the door, was wearing a dark suit, tailored to fit his overweight frame, his partly bald head covered here and there with wisps of white. The other man had darker skin, was about thirty years younger than the other, wore a green v-neck shirt with a dark blue Italian made jacket, black jeans and sported a thin moustache. He was two paces behind the older man, at the bottom of the step.

Eddie thought the pair of them looked as unlikely a set of partners as could ever be, but didn't voice his thoughts.

"Can I help you?"

The older man stepped forward, flipping a wallet open to show government ID. His accent was definitely European, but Eddie couldn't place the exact location. "Yes, if you please. I am Everett Marshall and this is my colleague Emilio. We would like to ask you a few questions about your missing children."

"Missing?"

The older man paused, having already assumed that the door should have opened wider for him and his expression showed that he was surprised it was not.

"Yes, your children were reported missing a couple of days ago. I apologize for not getting here sooner. We have been so extremely busy this time of year."

Eddie couldn't possibly think of what he meant by the time of year. "Excuse me?"

Emilio stepped forward and placed a hand on the door. "Look, friend, someone here reported some children missing, and we're here to investigate. Quite frankly, your lack of cooperation is making you look awfully suspicious. Now can we come in and ask you some questions?"

Eddie was certain that this man was a native Calgarian based on his lack of any discernible accent, and doubted that his name was really Emilio. Not wanting to argue, he turned into the house and let the door swing open.

"Suit yourself, come on in gentlemen."

Eddie led the way down the hall and into the main study, where Lynn was still working away on the computer. He stopped inside the doorway and turned to introduce the men he considered intruders more than guests.

"Honey, these men are.....uuuhhhhh...."

Eddie felt something tingle in his arm, like an electrical jolt. His eyes rolled upwards and he collapsed on the ground, sprawled at an odd angle.

Lynn jumped up immediately. "Eddie!" She turned her focus from her fallen husband and onto the strangers before her. "Why you…!"

Lynn began to charge the two of them, but stopped part way and collapsed to the floor in much the same manner as Eddie had.

Emilio stood over them, his hand returning the stone wand to an inner pocket. "She has a tiger spirit in her, wouldn't you say?"

"Oh shut up and hurry about your business."

Everett checked on Eddie briefly then searched the room, and continued into the kitchen. Emilio made his way to the desk and searched through every part of the computer. Finding nothing, he left to search the rest of the house. Twenty minutes later, they both returned to the study and picked the two limp bodies up. They propped them both on the pull-out bed, Eddie against the back and Lynn resting on a pillow on Eddie's lap.

Everett pulled out an ancient looking leather case from inside his jacket and retrieved a black feather mottled with white blotches from it. He murmured unintelligible words while he gently caressed the end of the feather over Eddie's eyes. He repeated the gesture to Lynn, and then used a lighter to burn the feather. Placing a hand on each of their cheeks, Everett spoke out loud as if he was having a normal conversation with them.

"Now then, my friends. You both had a little too much to drink today, because you are saddened by the loss of your children. They were abducted in the last couple of days, and you were waiting for the authorities to return your call. Tonight you were visited by two officers who have told you that your children will likely never be coming back. You will mourn their loss for three more days, and then find the strength to move on again. You will find peace and be happy adjusting to your new life together.

"You do not recall anything about dragons, magic, or portals. Anything regarding those topics or your children from the last three months is now erased from your mind and memory, never to be thought of again."

Everett finished by dipping a finger onto each of the Zedmore's foreheads, and muttering some additional strange words.

"Are you quite done yet?"

Everett stood up and jabbed the younger man in the chest with a thick, stubby finger. "Oh shut up George."

"I prefer Emilio."

"That isn't even a real name. Get over yourself. Besides, George more appropriately suits your intelligence and demeanour."

"Jerk. Why am I stuck working with you? And how come you didn't use a false name for yourself?"

Everett was cleaning up after himself and heading to the door, motioning his associate to follow him. "First, my name is distinguished. Second, no one would ever believe your name is George with that ridiculous get-up you call clothing, and lastly, they have been cleansed and will not remember us or anything about the last few months events, so I could really care a lot less what they heard."

The front door closed and the two men made their way back to their car. The motor started and the car drove away, leaving Eddie and Lynn to slumber peacefully together.

Jared and Madison had woken late into the morning, wandering outside with their Clutch mates to get some food. Alex didn't budge from his place against the wall except to stand, stretch, pace for a few minutes, and then sit again. He slept fitfully for many hours after that, waking for moments at a time to peer over to Kishar, then sleeping once again. Kishar showed no signs of life except for a deep breathing, which still sounded raspy despite the magical healing that had been done for him.

Late in the afternoon, Alex's siblings brought him some food and his stomach growled angrily when he realized how hungry he was. He allowed himself to be led outside for about half an hour to enjoy some late afternoon sunshine and dinner, but as soon as he was done he returned to keep his vigil over Kishar.

Strangely, there had been no attacks that entire day, or through the night. Either the enemy dragons were up to something, or the protective magic that was keeping the camp hidden was working well. Azurim woke late into the second day, sore and stiff. He took only a short time to stretch, then suddenly was fully alert. He nodded thanks to his nurse and after a brief glance at the children he sped out of the cave on urgent errands of his own.

The children had no chance to talk to him, so quick was his sudden recovery and departure.

Later that same evening, Kishar finally stirred. Alex nearly fainted in his excitement, but couldn't get near enough to his beloved dragon because of the heat. The silver doctor wouldn't allow Kishar to leave his care for many long minutes, despite the longing stares from both Alex and the green dragon. When he was finally able to go, Alex wrapped his arms around Kishar's neck in a bear-hug grip, promising to never let go again. Jared, Madison, Penelope and Rex all watched but did not disturb the reunion.

Kishar was doing well, but still very weak, so after a short visit through the camp he went back into the cave to rest. Alex never left the green dragon's side, and slept peacefully for the first time in many days.

Another day passed and Kishar's strength returned more rapidly. Azurim had breezed in once or twice with Corash, long enough to give orders, check in on everyone and dash away again. The children did not do much other than eat and rest, and on the evening of the fourth day they had all caught up on their sleep debt completely. Night found the group sitting just outside the cave mouth, the dragons curled in for sleep, Madison snoring loudly, and the boys leaning against their dragons' forelimbs while staring into the coals.

"It's beautiful here, despite the threat," Jared stated, looking at the stars.

Alex did not reply, but simply poked a long stick into the coals of their campfire, causing flashes of flame and sparks to rise into the night air.

"Glad to see that all the dragons have been healed, and really thankful that we haven't been found yet."

Still no reply. Jared was beginning to wonder if Alex was even listening to him.

"I think this is probably the best camping trip I have ever been on," Jared commented, not really expecting an answer.

"You are the camper in the family, really, so you'd know."

"Yeah," Jared agreed. "Although Cubs and Scouts are cool, they can't beat camping out in a dream world with dragons!"

Alex grunted an agreement, but said nothing. It grew silent again for several long minutes, each brother lost in his own thoughts. Jared was the first to break the silence.

"Do you think the dragons will ever be able to come back with us? And if they can't, will home ever be the same again?" Jared tossed a small wood chip into the glowing embers that were now pulsing with heat in the cool night air.

Alex sat up and blinked, looking dazed.

"What is it?"

"I just never thought of that before," Alex replied.

"Never thought of going home?" Jared pressed.

"No! I know we'll find our way home again. What I didn't think of were the dragons. I just assumed that we would all be going back together."

Jared glanced back into the darkness where the others were sleeping. "Well," he began, "they are a lot bigger now than they were before. It would be near impossible to keep them hidden."

"We have lots of land!"

"C'mon, Alex! You heard mom and dad talking about what to do. They knew the dragons would get bigger, and they were already worried about it. I had no idea they would all get this big! But you have to admit there is really no way they would be able to hide now. They are just too big to come back with us, I think."

"Yeah, but..." Alex let the words trail off. There was really nothing more to say.

A dragon stirred somewhere in the darkness, rustling leaves and snapping some branches from a tree. Moments later it fell quiet again as the large beast fell back into slumber. The boys silently nodded good night to each other and found their own bedrolls. Sleep came quickly and the quality of rest was surprisingly good, given that they were sleeping directly on the ground. They wondered idly if there was magic involved in their comfort and decided to ask about it in the morning.

Christian stepped into the study and quietly walked over to the Zedmore's. He gently nudged Eddie's elbow and whispered to him.

"You can wake up now."

Eddie opened his eyes instantly, but had to blink several times to clear his vision. "Are they gone?"

Lilly was leaning against the door frame, arms folded. "Yes, they just drove off a few minutes ago."

Lynn sat up and started pawing at her nose. "Good riddance! That fat pompous fool was wearing way too much cologne, but that still wasn't enough to fully mask his sweat. Ugh!"

Christian laughed. "Sorry to put you both through that, but I hope you understand it was necessary."

Eddie rubbed his side where he had been struck. "You could have warned us about the little shock."

Christian shrugged. "Sorry, didn't know they were going to pull that one. The charm I gave you prevented it from knocking you out for more than a minute or so. You both put on a good performance!"

Eddie raised an eyebrow. "I don't know if we were actually doing ourselves a favour with that deceptive stunt, or getting ourselves into more trouble."

Lynn had a tissue in hand and was blowing her nose. "Probably both," she replied hotly.

Christian sat in the computer chair and looked at each of them in turn. "Believe me; this whole thing is far more dangerous for me than for any of you."

Eddie stood up and stretched. "I wouldn't trust you at all if Lilly hadn't spoken for you. Her word I can trust, but I still don't know what your real purpose here is."

Lilly shuffled her feet uncomfortably and looked away. It was Christian that responded.

"Hey! I helped you out with Everett and George, didn't I? If it wasn't for me, you'd be a vegetable right now!"

Eddie and Lynn both stared Christian down silently. He waved his hands before him in apology.

"Ok, vegetable isn't the right word, but you know what I mean. Your memories would have been wiped out permanently."

Lynn tilted her head and snorted. "You really expect me to believe that sprinkling cinnamon dust on us, touching us with a feather and mumbling like a monk would erase our memories? Give me a break."

Eddie tidied up the couch while he talked. "I thought you said there wasn't any magic left in the world?"

Christian shook his head. "No, I said there was *very little* left. Totems and natural products, like cinnamon, help to focus the little bit that is still flowing here."

Eddie, Lynn and Lilly all shook their heads, not really understanding or believing any of it. Christian finished on the computer and stepped to the doorway, ignoring Lynn's question. Lilly led the way into the kitchen where they all gathered around the island.

Christian pulled out his cell phone. "Ok, now for phase three."

The boys slept late into the morning, which surprised them both. The sun was high in the sky when they awoke, blinking and looking about in a stupor. Jared's hair was bunched and matted, his eyes bleary, as if he had wrestled all night long. Alex's eyes showed his grogginess, but otherwise he was no worse for wear – he had slept like a stone, falling asleep and waking in the same position.

As their senses came to them, they heard Madison giggling somewhere nearby. Looking the length of the glade they saw their sister and Penelope together, Madison chasing a cluster of butterflies, Penelope curled in a half circle watching. Penelope was puffing her breath from time to time, forcing the butterflies to stay in a group around Madison, who giggled in glee.

All the other dragons around the glade were quietly resting, soaking up some sunshine, or appearing to converse in low tones. Most of them had at least one inquisitive eye on the young human girl and her prancing, and were wondering at the magnificent relationship these children all had.

The boys were about to ask about breakfast when there was an explosion above the trees. A great ball of flame and smoke belched into the sky, probably only a kilometre or so away. It reminded the boys of an oil fire they had seen once, where the smoke was pitch black surrounding flames of deep orange. A moment or two after the explosion a roar was heard followed by a thunderclap. Splinters of trees burst into the air with the blast and filling the sky. Somewhere off in that same direction a great battle began. The thought went through the camp simultaneously: we've been found!

Corash charged into the clearing bellowing orders. A group of gold and bronze coloured dragons were following immediately after her. They stopped, forming a line facing back the way they had come. There were many shouts and orders given in their dragon dialect before Corash arrived in front of the children, who were now standing in a close group, wide eyed and pumped with adrenaline.

"Children, it is time to depart! Make haste, we must leave at once!"

The children ran into the cave and returned as quickly as they could, their backpacks securely fastened. They had been warned all week to be ready to leave at a moment's notice and so they had been prepared for this.

The camp became a buzz of activity as dragons whistled about, the attack arriving sooner than anticipated. The children had a momentary flash of documentaries seen at school about World War 2, The Gulf War and other such events; it seemed explosions of fire and earth erupted all around them as they sprinted back to their Clutch and the waiting Corash. Twice while running the boys flattened themselves on the ground as a blue or green shape shot past them, and once Madison was lifted off the ground by the buffet of wind that slammed into her as a dragons wings beat close to her.

Finally making it back to their waiting group, they launched into the sky, Alex riding on Corash's back as Kishar was not quite strong enough to have any extra weight for him to carry. They flew low above the trees, shooting south and then west.

"What happened?" Alex yelled the question into the rushing wind, his curiosity getting him over the initial surge of panic.

Corash spoke low; Alex was sure the others probably wouldn't be able to hear. "Azurim had finished his scouting and investigation. We had just decided on where to move to next and were in fact on our way back to camp to inform everyone when we were attacked. Azurim and the Golden Guard covered my retreat to collect you and will be joining us later."

Alex was about to shout another question when a blast of heat nearly shook him from Corash's shoulders. The dragons banked left, skimming closer to the trees, watching as a large and nasty looking red dragon came up before the group, ugly looking and mean with several scales missing from extensive fighting in the past. It was one of the largest dragons the children had yet encountered, and grinned wickedly as it was about to charge them, malice clearly in its eyes. Two bolts of bronze shot by on Alex's right side, Jared's left, neatly firing themselves in between Corash and Rex and hurtling themselves bodily into the massive red. Electricity, fire and something of a golden liquid type flashed over the trio as they began a terrifying aerial war. In moments, Corash led the others back towards their initial destination and began chanting a magical spell.

The children had a momentary sensation of stillness, as if time had stopped, or nature had stopped to catch its breath and watch. It was like a Star Trek show, where the ship would stand still for a moment before shooting off into Warp 9 somewhere into space. Corash finished her spell, and the group was suddenly whipped forward without warning. Alex was too startled to do anything other than gasp for air, but there were many other surprised shouts from dragon and human alike.

Azurim looked south to see Corash and the others disappear to the horizon line. Her spell complete, it was unlikely anyone would be able to follow them or track them. He made a mental note to ask Corash to teach him that spell someday.

Azurim returned his attention to the battle raging around him. He deflected an electrical surge with his forelimb, watching the bolt streak up into the clouds. The multicoloured green and red dragon that had shot it charged Azurim. He was obviously a novice and Azurim wasted no time in letting that be known. In moments, the other dragon had been knocked unconscious and was plummeting into the trees below. Azurim hated to harm any of his own kind, for any reason, but he knew that as unfortunate as it was this was necessary. He only hoped that the youngling would land safely enough to not spear himself on a tree trunk on his way down.

A tear fell from Azurim's eyes as he surveyed the scene around him. The last thing he ever wanted, or ever dreamed of being possible, was now occurring: a coup attempt to overthrow the reigning leadership that had existed for thousands of years in peace and harmony. Many dragons, he knew, blamed the children's return for it, but Azurim knew the truth. This power struggle had been coming for many years already; the children were simply a catalyst, an excuse to begin the conflict.

Dragons roared in pain all around him, friend and foe alike, all entwined in the political and physical conflict. How he wished none of this had happened, how his father would be here to mediate and protect them all. How had his father been able to contain and control this massive group for so long without battles ensuing?

A sound pulled Azurim from his melancholy, a low horn sounding a blast from the east. A new group of dragons was arriving – Raiscaryn in the lead of a flight of twenty or so, mostly greens. The horn that was blaring was being sounded by an elf riding on Raiscaryn's back! Azurim felt a growing panic and fear rise in his chest. This did not bode well! The Fairy Folk had never joined forces with dragons like this in his entire memory. The only time he knew that they had was a legend, ancient....

His thoughts trailed off, the desperate fear enveloping him, threatening to choke the air from his lungs. He roared loudly several times to be sure all had heard, and one by one the dragons loyal to The Master – or perhaps loyal to Azurim – began their retreat. Without word or emotion, the remaining six dragons that formed the Golden Guard sped towards the new oncoming dragons, chanting powerful magic given them by the Master himself, the Royal blood in their veins pulsing with energy.

Azurim did not stay to watch the battle. He cried openly. He knew that as of today, the Golden Guard was no more. Their final act of defiance to a traitor Lord was to cover the retreat of the son of The Master, and his followers.

For many long minutes the battle raged behind him, and Azurim prayed a prayer to a God he could only hope was listening, to lift the Golden Guard into heaven and remember their names and the valiant sacrifice they gave.

The dragons fled on many paths to make it impossible for anyone to follow them, but they all had the same destination in mind. Hopefully Corash had the children safely to the Gate already, but the problem of opening it without the Council to remove the seal...Azurim shook his head. One problem at a time, he told himself. Putting on as much speed as possible, doubt crept in as he wondered if he was doing the right thing.

18 Atlantis

CORASH COLLAPSED TO THE ground in an unglamorous landing. Alex managed to stay between her shoulders somehow, but hopped down quickly once he had a safe chance to do so. Her deep red scales were so dark that the edges were nearly black. They heaved now as she panted for breath.

"I am sorry, child Alex, for the rough landing. I can go no further at this time." Corash sounded strained to say the least, exhausted and raspy, possibly dehydrated. "The spell took more energy and concentration than I had anticipated – I have never tried it before with so many at once."

Alex noted that Corash's nose was bleeding.

Corash struggled to stand, but her legs wouldn't respond and her head crashed to the ground. "I am sorry," she repeated, "I must rest." She promptly fell into a deep sleep.

The others landed a few moments later, Kishar first and Rex with Jared bringing up the rear. They stood in silence, taking up positions surrounding Corash's head, no one knowing what to do next.

"What happened?" Jared asked.

Alex rubbed his arm and ribs where he had impacted against Corash. "She collapsed. She mumbled something about the spell taking too much out of her, and then she fell."

"Where are we?" Jared continued, assessing the situation and surroundings. "Did we make it to where we were supposed to go?"

Alex threw his hands up in despair. "We don't even know where she was taking us and we don't even know this land, so how are we supposed to know where here is and if it is the right place?"

Jared looked around the group and posed the same question to the dragons. Rex and Penelope stood mutely.

"I am sorry, child Jared. We were informed of the destination and general plan, but I do not know the way, having never been here before myself."

Jared hopped down from Rex and started looking around. Rex followed closely, inspecting the strange looking trees around them. They were in a dry patch of ground surrounded on all sides by jungle, with trees of sinewy green that looked more like lizard skin than bark. Most of it had red and blue streaks that could only be described as veins running the length of the trunks, and the branches ended in sharp three-headed points. Vines seemed to hang and grow in, around, on top of, under and through practically everything else, and in all directions could be seen flowers of every colour. One flower about thirty paces beyond had to be two meters across! Insects of every size and shape scampered about, while lizards of equal quantity and variety chased them. Some were about the size of a medium dog, and Jared had the impression that if the dragons were not with them, some of the lizards might have seen the humans as a good dinner.

Of everything and every place the children had encountered thus far, this was by far the most alien, the most bizarre. The sun's light was still orange and bright in the west, but quickly turning to the blue of twilight. Night would be falling soon, and they were all scared to be out here alone.

"Well, can you tell us where we are going?" Alex asked.

Rex snorted a reply. Kishar looked at his sister, but said nothing. Rex snorted again, this time stamping impatiently. Kishar argued in his own tongue, not wanting to give in, his stubborn refusal to translate obvious.

"Kishar?" Alex asked. The green dragon looked to his friend with concern in his eyes. "What is it?"

Penelope leaned in closer to listen, with Madison, Rex and Jared moving closer as well.

Kishar broke down and finally spoke. "We are going to the Gateway, the last standing portal that holds our worlds together. There, Azurim hopes to find a way to send the human children back home to your family."

Jared's face lit up like a fire cracker. "We're going home? Yippee!"

Alex thrust his hands into the air. "Wait!" he barked. "What do you mean 'the human children'? Are you saying that we're going back, but alone?"

Jared's emotions ran a complete one-eighty, and he didn't know whether to spout in anger or cry in sorrow. Rex shook her head and growled, matching Jared's expression.

Kishar sighed. "Yes, that is correct."

"Why were you trying to keep this a secret?" Alex demanded.

"It is the only way," Kishar began.

Madison pouted her biggest and saddest pout, burying her face in Penelope's neck. "No! It can't be!"

"There has to be another way!" Jared yelled. Rex stamped a foot, indicating her agreement.

Kishar started again. "Please, let me explain. Sending the children through the Gateway is the only way that Azurim can ensure their safe survival, without bringing the Dragon War back to Earth. Your Earth." Kishar nodded indicating the children. "You must go through and we must remain behind, so that the war does not begin anew."

"Doesn't begin? What war? What do you mean?" Jared asked.

"If it is the fighting going on here, then you *have* to come with us, so that you will be safe!"

Kishar shook his head firmly. "No. Please understand, Clutch Mates, we have no choice. Azurim has been discussing this at great length with scholars and the greatest of practiced magic he has still loyal to him. There are things about magic that you do not understand – that I do not understand – that make it extremely difficult, if not impossible, for all of us to return."

Alex folded his arms across his chest. "Try me," he dared.

"I realize that it is hard to accept, but you must see that there is no other way. I do not yet comprehend all of the workings of magic either, but I do know this: the last remaining Gateway cannot be fully opened, and yet cannot be fully sealed. There was an…error when the Great Mage Trevistar was sealing it. More I do not know."

"So what is so wrong with opening it fully then?" Jared asked. "Would it really be so bad to have it always open to travel back and forth between worlds?"

"I admit, I do not know the full extent of the reason why."

"There are many reasons why, actually," Corash chimed in, startling everyone. The group turned to look at her, curious about her story as much as her fast recovery. "One such reason is this: opening the gateway completely would level off the magic contained here, much like having two large jars of water. Right now, one jar is filled almost completely, the other barely at all. Opening the stopper between them would even out the water level in both jars. The dragons do not want this. Here, in our land, we reign with a mastery of magic on a very high level, and the potency of the magic here toughens our scales, lengthens our life spans, allows us to live without the need for food, and gives us the ability to control magic in a way that is much more difficult when the worlds are even in their flow."

"You mean they were even once, before?" Alex asked.

"Yes, for the most part. While the Dragon Song was strong then, it was nothing compared to what it is now that the magic is contained, concentrated into a more powerful, usable source."

"But the other creatures here are magical," Jared thought out loud. "Didn't their magical abilities increase too?"

"Yes," Corash replied patiently, "but not as completely as ours did. We were not sure what would happen when the Gateways were closed, but we know that Dragons and many of the creatures who live in Shard simply cannot survive without a magical flow to help sustain us. Cut it off, and we die. And we also needed to save ourselves from the inevitable war."

Madison scrunched up her face, confused. "Inevitable war? Who would want to war against dragons?"

"Humans," Alex answered before Corash could. "A war against mankind. That's why you sealed it in the first place, because humans are stronger with magic than dragons are. You escaped to save yourselves, from us."

Corash nodded, her pride hurt and a little annoyed at having to admit that humans could be better at something than a dragon could. "There were a few human magicians that crossed the boundary with us. Only ones trusted enough to live with Dragonkind without hunting us down. Most of your stories show knights in shining armour charging into battle with a dragon, shield and lance in hand, and in a later tapestry the head of the dragon mounted on a wall. In reality, it was the wizards who did battle. They usually had a wall of twenty or more knights in front of them to give them the protection they needed to get their spells off. The knights usually died in the attempt, the wizard killing the dragon, and one or two remaining nobles surviving long enough to take the credit."

Alex was enchanted by the history lesson, and absorbing every detail. "I thought you said the human magic was stronger – so why would they need a wall of soldiers to fight for them?"

"The human magic had not yet reached a point where it had outmatched a dragon's physical strength, or types of breath weapon, at least in speed. Magician's of that day needed time to prepare their spells. But we could see that the human mastery of magic was continually growing. Dragon magic has a limit that we have been unable to breach, until coming to this side of Nature. Dragons cannot increase their own innate aptitude for magic, but humans have a great potential for learning, discovery and advancement, and we could see it was only a matter of time before their power would advance beyond that of the Dragon Songs ability to stop. We did the only thing we knew we could do – flee.

"We came here, and sealed all of the gates. One of the wizards of your world tried to stop us, and very nearly succeeded, if it hadn't been for one of his apprentices messing up the ceremony. If Merlin had been successful, it is likely that none of the dragons would have survived."

"Merlin? He was out to kill dragons too?" Jared didn't believe it. He had many books at home about magic of every kind, and the Merlin he had always read about was nearly a hero! He didn't want to think of him as a villain.

Corash put Jared's fears to rest. "No, Merlin was not out to hunt us down. He was not a friend, and yet not an enemy. Best say, a man with a common taste for magic and power. He refused to come to our world, wanted to stay on his own Earth and live among the people he had grown up with. He did not want to live with the Fairies and Dragons without human contact. But for him to stay behind would also mean that his access to the magical power he craved so much would be gone. So he attempted to keep the portal in Scotland open, even just a fraction, so that he could channel the flow of magic coming through it."

"Scotland?" Alex asked.

"Stonehenge," Jared guessed.

Alex shook his head. "Stonehenge is in England, not Scotland."

Corash smiled. "Many of the Fair Folk would disagree, particularly the Brownies and Pixies. They feel the entire island is Celt land, regardless of anyone else who resides there."

Jared nodded his understanding. "So, Stonehenge is a gate, then?"

Corash nodded. "Yes, it used to be a nexus point where the worlds met, a portal that led to many different areas of Shard and Earth. Many of the stone monoliths at the site were a doorway, each to a different specific target, so through that one location you could literally step across the entire continent in moments."

"Cool!" the boys exclaimed simultaneously.

"Indeed, it would have made our trip thus far a much quicker journey," Kishar said, liking the idea of a magical doorway. Flying was great, but tiring over long distance.

"Wait, wait, wait," Jared blurted out, waving his hands and shaking his head. "Ithicar told us that we were in a Dream World, and that the Grand Arch is where the last gateway was sealed by some great wizard..."

"Trevistar," Alex added in helpfully.

"Trevistar, thanks," Jared nodded. "He said it was sealed by the wizard because there was an attack by another evil and powerful wizard, and that Trevistar encased himself in ice in order to stop the evil wizard from getting through, and to finally seal the gate."

Corash closed her eyes and cursed. "Blast Ithicar and his loose tongue. That satyr needs to be bounced down a mountain side head first."

"You didn't want us to know that part of the story?"

"No, child Jared, that is not the case. Ithicar...well, he knows the story from what we told him. The dragons, I mean. The Fairies do not know the real happening at the Grand Arch. At least, most don't..." Corash trailed off, not sure she should continue. Deciding that this entire Clutch deserved to know the truth, if they were going to be separated soon at the Gateway, she continued.

"There was no evil wizard coming to destroy the Fairies. Dragons told them that were the case so that they would allow us to do our work. You see, the Fairies never wanted to seal the gates. They were in no real danger."

"Why not?" Madison asked curiously. She and Penelope had long since made themselves comfy together, Madison lying across the ground and propping her head on Penelope's arm, while Penelope had curled into a more restful position.

"Fairies are the masters of trickery, disguise, and masters of illusion. Even if the humans had built a city right over top their own, the Fairies would have had no problem blending in. They can hide in plain sight most of the time and humans would walk right past! Fairies could use their illusions to pretend to be human for a while if they wanted. They are generally very small, as well, making it all the easier to disappear.

"Dragons have no such luxury. We cannot hide away as the Fairies can – indeed our pride alone for many did not allow them to. Many dragons stayed behind to prove that they were stronger than humans, so sure and confident in themselves and their superiority over humans. They are all dead now.

"Dragons sealed the gate to save *themselves*, nothing more. It was a very selfish thing to do, but it was our only option left to us. I do not expect you to agree, understand or forgive. What has happened is done, and nothing can change that.

"Our problem occurred when the final gate, the Grand Arch, was being closed. As Trevistar used his magic to seal this final portal, a great earthquake began to shake the very foundations of both Earth and Shard. Something was going wrong – to be honest, I do not know fully what. He sacrificed himself, yes, but not to stop a rogue wizard from getting through. No, he sacrificed himself to stop the final portal from closing. He thrust every last ounce of magic he could summon into himself to create a frozen barrier that would hold the Gateway open, and freeze it in place so that it could never be closed, and controlled only by those in attendance: The Fairy Folk that were present to aid him in closing the portal, and a handful of members of the Dragon Council.

"Trevistar's spell, enhanced by fairy magic, was so effective it created a zone around it of such cold that every plant, every rock, even the air itself seemed to be frozen solid. And he stands at the center of it, encased in a crystal tomb of ice. Trevistar saved not just the dragons and fairies, but everyone, everywhere, on both sides of the portal. Our problem is simply that we do not understand fully what he saved us from, or why the closing of the portal was causing such great earthquakes."

Corash finished by standing up and stretching once again. "We must be off soon. I need some time to absorb more energy and collect our bearings, so I will return shortly."

"Hang on a second! You don't get to run away that easily!" Jared called.

Alex stepped forward beside his brother. "Yeah!" he agreed. "That still doesn't explain why we have to go through the portal alone, and Kishar and the others can't come with us!"

Corash knew she would need to answer these questions sooner or later. Might *as well get this over with*, she thought.

"Two reasons, plain and simple. First, they are dragons and you are human. Dragons belong in Shard with their own kind, and humans belong on Earth with their own kind. And secondly, the dragons cannot go back. The longer they would stay on Earth, the more magic would be pulled through in order to sustain them and their abilities. As soon as the young awoke on Earth, the Dragon Council felt the pull here! It was minor, yes, but tangible nonetheless. When Azurim had crossed the barrier, the pull became stronger, like a leak in a bottle, slowly pulling more magical essence back to earth. If the dragons return with you, that flow would continue, until the pressure on the Gateway would be enough to shatter the ice holding the Atlantean portal, or worse, opening other portals around the world."

Jared cut in. "What would be so wrong with the portal opening again?"

Corash closed her eyes and shook her head. "I will repeat one last time. We escaped here, to Shard, to get away from humans. Most humans cannot control magic, and therefore they cannot understand it. What you do not understand, you fear. And so, humans fear dragons, the Fair Folk, and everything else magical that is strange to them. We sealed ourselves away here so that the war between us and humans would stop. If the portals open again..."

"...the war would continue, and maybe this time one side would actually win." Alex finished for her.

"Precisely. We do not know why Trevistar stopped the binding of the portal. It was a sudden and reckless move, which he could never explain because he froze so quickly." Corash looked about the group, seeing anger, frustration and sorrow in their expressions. She forced her own sympathetic emotions away and turned to leave. "I will return shortly, and we will resume our flight. It is a short hop from here to the Grand Arch."

Corash flew into the air, scanning the horizon to plan their next route and check for any possible pursuers.

The children each went through the problem at hand over and over again, trying to find a way that everything would work out without the dragons being separated from the children, but if there was a loophole they couldn't find it.

Corash returned to the group after twenty minutes. When she arrived most of the fatigue was still around her eyes and sagging shoulders. She wanted to sleep more, but forced herself up and summoned the group into their previous positions: Corash in the lead with Alex riding her, Kishar second, and then Rex and Penelope with their Clutch Mates taking up flanking positions behind Kishar. There was little discussion, but worried expressions all around as they got closer and closer to their impending departure from this world.

The kids all thought back to two summers ago when Mom and Dad had decided to go on a weeklong vacation by themselves. The kids had all stayed home with their Aunt and Uncle, but had gone to the airport to see them off. The closer they got to the airport, the more depressed the children had become, because they knew their parents were leaving. This feeling was much the same, except that two years ago the kids knew they would see their parents again in a single week. Today, they were faced with the prospect of never seeing their beloved dragons again…ever. It was so much more final that they didn't want to think about it. But the more they tried to think on something else, the more their hearts were pulled back to the inevitable 'good-bye' that was coming.

Their flight took them across the jungle to a large hilltop. As they crested the hill and glided down the other side, a vast sea, sparkling in the late sunlight from the horizon, stretched out before them. The coastline ran in jagged zigzags in both directions to the east and west, with hundreds of small islands dotting the entire area. Humanoid creatures of various sizes and types looked up in alarm as the group shot by, mostly farmers, labourers and other people just out for a stroll. They were flying by too quickly for the children to make out any detail to identify who these people were, but they looked human. Every one of them looked slender of build, and fair, with beautiful garments and long flowing hair.

We're in this world's version of Greece, Alex thought to himself with a big smile. He looked back and saw Jared pointing to a large stone temple to what appeared to be Poseidon on an island below them. They had studied Greek Mythology in school and with Dad, who was fascinated with Myths' from all around the world. Greek was one of his favourites, with all the Heroes, Deities and Demigods, Gods and Titans and so much more. Hercules was always Dad's favourite of them all.

They banked to their left sharply as they headed out over golden water, the setting sun painting every wave, leaving shore and island behind them. For a short time they saw nothing other than a distant shoreline, but soon a larger island loomed ahead of them. This one was different however; it was guarded on every side by stone and metal statues, and immediately behind them was a vast expanse of snow!

"Behold!" Corash yelled to them all in the wind. "Atlantis, and last remaining portal in the Grand Arch."

Atlantis was nothing what the children thought it would be from all the movies and stories they had heard. It had a large visible dome of magic surrounding it in a giant sphere, swirling colours of yellow, pink and white. The island itself was not really a single island at all, but many concentric rings of islands, most of which were connected to each other with bridges and aqueducts. Everything was frozen over, and it seemed obvious the statues were guardians, allowing access to only those who had official business, or some other type of permission. The children could only guess as to what that permission would need to be for them to get through.

"The portal is in *there*?" Jared asked, somewhat sceptically.

"Yes." Corash responded curtly as they banked low over the water and turned north, landing on a beach facing a wide marble bridge that spanned the distance across the water to Atlantis. The children all dismounted and stretched their legs while Corash continued.

"The portal is located on the central island of Atlantis. We need to gain permission from the Sentinels in order to gain access to it. This is usually done with the sending of delegates from the Dragon Council. They know the magical incantations to force such permission from the Sentinels."

"How are we supposed to get permission from the Dragon Council?" Jared asked.

"We do not necessarily need the Council's permission – it is the Sentinels that allow passage through the barrier. They erected the barrier when the ice flow began, when the great wizard Trevistar sealed himself in ice. We only need the Sentinels to allow us entry – the Dragon Council delegates force that with magic. Without the Council, I really do not know how we will gain entry."

Alex furrowed his brow. "Do you think we'll actually be able to get permission from the Sentinels to go inside?"

Corash shook her head. "As I said, I do not know." Her response was short and to the point, indicating there was no further discussing the subject.

The group tried to busy themselves with something to do while they waited, but there really wasn't much to do on the stone beach. The boys skipped a couple rocks on the water, but tired of that quickly. Madison simply sat hugging Penelope.

It was about ten more minutes before Azurim and a flight of several dozen dragons appeared from the north-western sky. As they neared, several smaller groups of the dragons veered off, landing at various sections of the beach, while Azurim and 3 other dragons came straight on for Corash and the Clutch. They landed quickly and without ceremony, one of the dragons, a deep blue in colour, running quickly past the group and taking up a guard position at the foot of the bridge, the others remaining on Azurim's flanks and keeping their eyes open in every direction for any sign of danger. One of the guards was pure green with six legs, looking like a sleek salamander so smooth was its body, while the other was a jagged and rough looking light blue dragon, its hide much like an iguana or rock lizard that the children has seen at the zoo. Azurim himself had a dangerous, almost wild look in his eyes, and urgency kept his pace quick.

"I am glad to see you are all safe and well. Corash, you seem to have fared the journey well."

"We rested briefly at the Hangman's Nook, and then came straight here. I am afraid I have not much strength left in me, Azurim."

Azurim nodded. "You have done incredibly well, Corash. Please, tarry here while we continue forward. I am certain we will need your strength again before long."

Corash nodded and looked back upon all six children as she slowly moved away. There was care, concern and a motherly want of protection of her brood etched deeply in her features. She waved a claw to them in farewell.

"Come," Azurim stated flatly. He turned and began the long walk across the huge bridge. The children followed suit, all six members of the clutch gathered together, and the two guarding dragons took up the rear of the party. The blue dragon stepped aside at the foot of the bridge, letting the group pass, then resumed watch.

The bridge was immense. Alex guessed that they could probably fit five cars abreast on the bridge, with room to spare for pedestrian traffic on either side as well. He reported this out loud, and his siblings agreed, however the dragons did not respond. The bridge was incredibly long as well – they had no real way of measuring the distance, except to note that they lost sight of the connection of the beach to the bridge after a few minutes of walking.

"Why are we walking?" Madison asked suddenly. "Wouldn't it be faster to fly?"

"We are walking to appease the Sentinels. They are land-bound Guardians, and we walk to appear as equals, rather than as superiors." Azurim spoke without turning.

"Why do we need their permission, anyway?" Jared asked. "If they are land bound, couldn't we fly in from the top and just avoid them completely?"

Azurim closed his eyes for a moment, tired and not wanting to answer so many curious questions. His mind was preoccupied on greater things.

"Perhaps, Lord Azurim, I can be of assistance?" It was the green salamander-like dragon flanking them.

Azurim nodded. "Thank you, Isu-durin."

Isu-durin moved more like a snake, his body weaving back and forth as he walked. He moved forward only slightly, to be closer to the clutch as he spoke.

"The Guardians are stone creations of the ancient Atlantean people. Their exact method of construction is a mystery to even the dragons. They are land bound, and very powerful. There was only one time when a dragon attacked the dome to gain entry – the Sentinels retaliated, and reduced it to ashes."

"Who was that dragon?" Alex wondered out loud.

"And why did he try to enter without permission?" Jared followed.

"Alas, we do not speak the name any more, as the dragon was considered to be a traitor to our kind. We believe he sought to destroy the gate, or perhaps pass through it to live on Earth. We really do not know. We do know that the Council did not give their permission, and the Sentinels declined his request to pass through the barrier and so he attacked them. I am told it was a short fight, resulting in the dragon being burned horribly until there was nothing left to bury."

Isu-durin continued before the children could ask anything more. "We walk on this bridge to show the Sentinels that we honour them. We are lowering ourselves to become land bound as well, in order to win their favour. We will need every advantage to sway them, without the power of the Council's spells."

The group continued in silence, allowing the children to study the bridge in more detail as they walked. The bridge itself was a long slow curving archway, reaching from the island beach they were just on to a point somewhere ahead that they couldn't see. They walked upwards at a gentle angle, and didn't level out until after about ten minutes. The stone was a lattice work of rock, large smooth grey stones intricately placed together to form the base. There was a middle line of blue stone, about ten centimetres in width, running the entire length of the bridge. For all intents and purposes, it looked like the divider line on a highway, however the dragons seemed to ignore it, as Azurim was walking directly over top of it at the bridge center. The sides of the bridge came up in thick black stone guide rails. Detailed into the black stone were frescos and etchings, seeming to come from a vast array of different cultures and origins. Some were familiar, but most were bizarre. One showed a giant squid like creature attacking a ship at sea, while another depicted the squid beside a dock, being loaded with cargo from the pier as if it was a ship.

Azurim signalled silently as the far end of the bridge came into view. The flanking guards pulled in tighter to the group, and Azurim quickened his pace. The children hustled to keep up, while Kishar, Rex and Penelope loped along with them.

As they plodded down the gentle slope, a pair of statues appeared in view, and the children could only guess that these were the Sentinels. They were absolutely massive! They could probably only walk two at a time on the bridge, so great was their bulk. They stood on a platform of granite about twenty meters across at the end of the bridge, and immediately behind was the shimmering shield surrounding Atlantis.

Every step the group took closer revealed more detail about the titanic statues. They appeared to be made of a living stone, jet black yet laced with blue and white veins that pulsated with arcane energy. Their eyes shone with a dim blue glow. When one of them spoke, the inside of its mouth had veins of red and yellow, like lava tubes, marbling all the way down its throat.

"Lord Azurim," the Sentinel to the left of the group spoke. The sound was a combination of thunder and a waterfall, mixed with a grating of stone on stone. "It has been such a short time since your last visit to Atlantis. What brings you here now?" The voice was completely monotone, no emotion on any word. Even the question sounded more like a statement, so devoid of colour was the speech.

Azurim took several strides closer, while waving the others to remain behind. He knelt on one foreleg, his wings tucked tightly to his sides. "Great Sentinels, I seek to gain access to the Portal once again, on a mission of grave importance."

"Of whose importance: Dragons, or to that of Atlantis?" It was the second Sentinel that spoke now. It could almost be characterized as a female voice compared to the first one, though it was still monotone and grating, the pitch was higher. Physically, however, the two Sentinels were identical.

Azurim was unsure of how to answer. "It…the matters at hand are important to all of those in Shard and Earth as well. These human children must be returned to their home."

"We do not care about the inconsequential lives of three small humans. Why does it matter so that they leave?" It was the first Sentinel speaking again.

"The Dragon Conclave is at war, and will continue to be so…"

"Ah," the female statue interrupted. "So, it is a dragon issue after all. This is not important to Atlantis – it is your own fight, and your own problem."

Azurim kept his head bowed low, despite his emphatic reaction. Everything depended upon them getting through to the Gate. "The lives of these humans are at risk as long as they stay here," he pleaded angrily. "They must be returned to Earth where they will be free from harm!"

Silence. For many, many long moments. The Sentinels turned to face one another, but made no motion. The children got the feeling there was some kind of communication going on there, but the statues made no sound or movement of any kind, simply their glowing marbled bodies pulsating with strange energy in rhythm, like a heartbeat. Finally, they turned once again to Azurim.

"Bring these humans forward, Lord Azurim."

Azurim kept his position, bowing in submission, but waved with one claw for them to come forward. Rex made a motion to move with Jared, but the guardian dragons on either side stopped her. It was clear that the dragons were to remain here.

Alex, Jared and Madison all moved forward until they were standing just before and slightly to the right side of Azurim. Alex tried awkwardly to bow, not know what else to do. Jared simply stared at the amazing moving statues in awe. Madison curtsied, her eyes wide.

The male Sentinel stepped forward with one mighty stride then peered down at the group. Its head alone was about the size of Azurim's entire body, the eyes large hammocks the children could have slept in. It peered at them, turning its face fully towards Azurim after the inspection was complete.

"You? You, Lord Azurim, Slayer, Bane and Shining Nightmare? These are the names the humans gave you, and yet you care what happens to these three?"

Azurim closed his eyes, and the children thought the expression was that of shame or regret.

"Names that no longer pertain to me, Great Sentinel. These humans have been made a part of the clutch of younglings behind us, and … "Azurim paused, swallowed a moment, then continued, " … they have proven their worth. They are…loved."

The Sentinel made no motion, no sound, for perhaps ten seconds, but in the tense situation it seemed as an eternity. Suddenly, the giant rock being took a step back to its perch at the end of the bridge.

"You may pass, Lord Azurim. God speed you on your journey."

Jared had the feeling that the Sentinels had decided long before that Azurim would be allowed to pass. This had simply been some kind of test or hazing even: there was a story here that the children were sure they were not going to here the details of today. Azurim bowed lower, saying a short thank you then turned to look at the rest of the group.

"Isu-durin, Rasmodean, take the younglings with you. Children, you are to follow me."

Isu-durin and Rasmodean nodded to their liege then began ushering Kishar, Rex and Penelope away.

"No, wait!" Alex cried. He ran forward and flung his arms around Kishar's leg. "We can't just leave you! You can't leave us!"

Rex bounded to Jared's side, while Penelope waited for Madison to tearfully make her way to her for a hug. The girls held each other with tears in their eyes, but seemed to have already accepted that there was no other way. Jared had seemed to accept the inevitable as well, but Rex was stubbornly refusing to admit defeat. Alex wrapped his arms around Kishar's leg tightly, burying his face into his best friend's hide and refusing to let go.

Azurim gently pleaded with the group. "Please, children, younglings. We do not have much time. Raiscaryn and the others will be coming soon. We must get you to safety, quickly."

Kishar nudged Alex until he was able to pry him loose. "Child Alex. My friend. We have discussed this at length, and we have no choice. I do not want to end our time together, but there is no other way. As long as you stay here, your lives are in danger."

"I don't care!" Alex shouted.

"And the lives of all the creatures, all dragon and Fair Folk who know you, are in danger as well. Raiscaryn will not stop until you are dead, and will use your existence here as leverage to support his claim as ruler of the Conclave. To save you, you must leave, and to save our kind, we must stay."

"But…" Alex tried, but no arguments were left to him. Kishar wrapped his wings around his clutch-mate, and nuzzled into Alex with his green and gold snout, giant tears welling up in his golden eyes.

"Perhaps we will meet again, child Alex. Perhaps. But even if not, I will always be your friend and clutch-mate."

Alex gripped Kishar tightly, tears streaming his face. Many long moments passed until finally Alex pushed himself away. He wiped the tears from his face, and laid his palm on Kishar's cheek.

"I love you, Kishar."

Kishar smiled, one great tear filling his right eye. "And I you…Alex."

They paused a moment, then Alex abruptly turned away, walking quickly to and then passed Azurim.

Jared was having the opposite problem with Rex, having to explain to the beautiful red dragon through their own tears that they could not stay. It was just as tearful, but Rex didn't make it as easy as Alex had. She pouted, she snorted, she roared, she bellowed fire over the side of the bridge while sobbing. Jared pulled himself away, leaving Rex in the care of the large blue dragon, which held Rex back from charging headlong through the dome. Jared forced himself to stare forward, his jaw working vigorously to contain his emotions.

Penelope and Madison hugged silently. They, too, had tears, but their farewell was silent, mutual. They hugged, gave each other kisses, and then turned their separate ways, tears dripping to the stone of the bridge below. Madison did turn to wave at least six times before she reached the others, but didn't complain or whine.

Five dragons turned and began the long walk back across the bridge, with one red more or less being dragged. One dragon and three human children turned and faced the great barrier before them. As they walked towards it, the two Sentinels lifted their arms and locked hands to create an archway between them, moving their arms into position directly into the shimmering barrier. The energy crackled and turned red, and a hole in the barrier appeared beneath the arch they created together.

"Lord Azurim, humans, pass through to what remains of Atlantis."

Beyond the barrier, snow swirled, winds howled and the cold chill of winter spun out of control. The group passed through, all of them instantly made cold by the freezing conditions. Azurim cast a spell, blanketing him and the others with warmth, but it couldn't remove the freeze of the air around them completely. All of their breaths came out in cloudy steam, and they had to push through the heavy snow that was almost waist deep to Madison.

As the Sentinels lowered their arms, the male voice drifted in to them. "Your green dragon friend entered in some time ago, and has prepared the portal for you in advance."

"Green friend?" Azurim asked, but turned back only to see the barrier seal itself again. "What green friend?" he roared, but to no avail. Either the Sentinels could no longer hear him, or they chose not to.

Azurim looked to the worried expressions of the children. Jared was the first to speak.

"So that means we're not alone in here, are we?" Jared had to yell to get the words out. The winter storm was noisy with wind.

"It would appear not, child Jared. We will proceed with all caution. You will need to ride on my back." Azurim lowered himself as he spoke, and the children climbed aboard, Alex at the back and Madison at the front.

"Azurim, why is the barrier here? I know that this wizard guy cast an ice spell to stop the gate from closing, but why did the Sentinels put up the barrier?"

"If the Sentinels had not erected this shield, our entire world may have been engulfed in this ever-expanding winter."

Madison gasped. "The *entire* world?"

"Yes," Azurim replied. "They put the shield in place, originally on the fourth ring of islands, but it has been slowly expanding. Many years ago, they moved the barrier to the seventh and final ring of islands. It appears that they have succeeded in holding it there without the expansion continuing, although I do not know if that will be a permanent condition."

"But why…" Alex began, but Azurim hushed him.

"Quietly, now! The Sentinels told us there was a green dragon here, and not one that I had knowledge of. No more words, lest we give our position away."

Azurim continued to cast spells of warmth for the children while plodding through the thick, heavy snow. Twice he lurched sideways, thinking he had seen movement or heard a noise. But there was nothing but the imposing blizzard, and the group continued as quickly as they could through the frozen wasteland. They passed over thick ice twice, and it was only on the second go that the children realized the water was the ocean below them. They were walking from island to island, long strands of land making rough circles around each other, leading to a small central island at the core.

The children had many questions, but could not ask any of them as the wind and cold was so biting, despite Azurim's protective magic, that they could barely breathe let alone speak. These chains of islands seemed so perfect! Were they natural, or crafted somehow this way? Was this an exact replica of what Atlantis would have been like on Earth? Were all Atlanteans magic using humans, or from different races?

On the fifth island, Azurim turned right and stalked through rocks, standing stones and long dead trees, heading for an area different than what they had seen thus far. It was a miniature valley, more like a bowl, with high, jagged rocks on every side except one small entry way that was smooth, and only a few meters wide. Azurim scanned the bowl with all his senses, but did not detect anything out of the ordinary. There were no scents or tracks, although in this magical storm he doubted that scents would stay in the air for more than a heartbeat, and tracks in the snow would be covered in seconds. Without any real choice, he plodded down the trail and into the bowl.

The wind immediately died down inside the bowl, and the children didn't feel as cold. The ground was littered with huge boulders, great slabs of stone that at one time had carvings on them but were now worn to a smooth finish so that the runes were faint scratches. Towards the opposite end of the bowl was a set of large boulders, piled in a random formation but for the center columns which created a perfect rectangle. It was obvious the surrounding stone was natural, and the central stone was worked, but by whose hand the children couldn't even guess. The central stone was a slightly purple tinge, with deep runes still running the entire span of each column and across what appeared to be two doors. The inset base of each rune was blue in colour, with a faint yellow light emanating from them. The doors were almost shut, with less than a meter to go on each before being closed completely. Because of the size of the doors, however, that still left a large gap.

Directly in the center of the doors was a massive block of ice, and what seemed like fifty small bluish-white pixies darting around and on it. Even from this distance, the children could faintly make out a shape inside the ice. Azurim took one more look around the great circle then pushed through the snow. All four of them kept looking from side to side, expecting an ambush at any moment, but none came. Azurim circled slowly, examining the area before he would let the children down from his back.

The children moved slowly, trudging through thick snow even after Azurim had trampled it down a little. The group stood near the solid block of ice, watching as the pixies darted back towards the portal, staying a safe distance from the strange group that had just wandered near. They had never seen a dragon escorting humans before!

Azurim moved past the frozen statue and began making a strange, high pitched whistle. The children didn't understand at first, but soon they realized he was talking to the pixies! His whistling was shrill, and the replies were for the most part silent, as far as the children could tell, a faint whisper of high pitched wind and nothing more. Yet Azurim seemed to be able to hear what they were saying, and twice during his short conversation he looked back at the children with a stern look – or maybe that was confusion? They couldn't be sure.

While this was going on, Madison began circling the giant block of ice, tracing her hand along the rough ridges. She suddenly let out a loud sob, and cried something out into the wind, alerting everyone to her distress.

Jared was the first to leap forward. "Madison!"

"What did you say, Madison?" Alex asked.

"It's…" Madison sniffed, "it's Daddy!" Small tears drifted off her cheeks into the light wind, mixing with the snow.

The brothers looked up and slowly scanned the ice she was staring at, until they saw what had given her such a shock. Behind the ice wall, there was a tall man with his arms raised above his head, a mixed look of pain and concentration on his face. The face that, while many years older sporting a grey beard flecked with white, looked exactly like their father.

"There's no way…" Jared began, but with all the crazy magical things they had experienced since they arrived here, he didn't want to finish his sentence. It *was* possible that their father might be here – after all, *they* were here, so why couldn't he have found a way, too?

Azurim stepped forward, lowering his face to the ground to be on a more level, and gentle, speaking term with the children, Madison in particular.

"Child Madison," the dragon spoke softly, "I assure you this is not your father. He was left back near the pond of your home on earth."

"But he looks…I mean…" Alex stumbled on his words.

"It has to be Dad!" Jared finished for his brother. "It looks just like him!"

"Except…I can't be too sure, but it looks like this guy is taller than dad."

Azurim shook his head. "The ice pixies here have assured me that this is Trevistar, the last Great Mage. They have been watching over this region for several hundred years, and Trevistar has never been freed from this ice prison. Not even the pixies seem to know how to free him, and ice is their speciality."

Madison cupped her hand to her mouth, crying. She was trying to control herself, logic telling her that Daddy was safe at home waiting for her, but her emotions kept telling her that this man before her, frozen in ice, was an exact picture of her father! Yes, he was older and had grey and white hair, but she was so sure of his face there was no way it couldn't be him! Her tears fell while she tried wiping them away with her hands, and then with tear-streaked fingers she pressed a hand onto the ice, as if holding it there would allow her to holds hands with her father.

Azurim left the children at the block of ice, several pixies floating down to greet them in high-pitched titters. They seemed especially interested in Madison, who busied herself trying to catch the pixies away while they danced easily out of her reach.

Azurim sighed. His feelings for the children had grown considerably, and he shocked himself to realize his connection to them. He growled at himself and pushed the feelings aside, focusing on his task at hand: how to get the children through the portal, while also protecting them long enough once they were safely on the other side. He knew the dangers on the other side waiting for them: the gateway on earth was under the Mediterranean Sea, with several dragon lengths of water to swim through to get to the surface. Azurim had made the trip simply by holding his breath – it wasn't a difficult swim for him. But the children would need to hold their breath for several seconds, or maybe a minute or more, before breaking the water's surface. How would they survive that?

Azurim turned to explain the situation to the children when a scent caught his attention. The ice pixies shot up high into the air just as Azurim dove forward to block a great ball of fire that was intended to consume the children. Azurim roared, turning to face the challenger, while using one claw to push the children into a huddle together.

Unknown and unseen by any of them, except the pixies, a small hand print impression on the ice mixed with Madison's tears began slowly steaming into the ice.

An enormous green dragon thumped into the ground, causing the land to shake and the children to topple over each other. Azurim stepped forward two paces and shot a blast of ice from his throat. The green dodged aside, taking only a small hit in its hindquarters. Azurim noted that the underbelly of this green was somewhat exposed, and not fully healed from a previous fight, with dark charring still evident like soot from a fire.

"Ah, so it is you again, Greenfist. I could smell your foul stench when we entered here."

"You thought you could beat me before, Azurim, but I have learned new tricks since last we fought!"

"What?" Azurim asked, dripping sarcasm. "You've learned to roll over and fetch now, is that it?"

Greenfist ran forward, bellowing his challenge, and creating a wedge of magical hues in front of him, a battering ram of spectral origin. The ice fairies shot behind Azurim and pushed the children aside, where they landed in a heap before the portal doorway. Azurim was slammed hard by the charging green dragon, his back pinned into the sheer stone wall behind him. Greenfist bellowed laughter as he continued to paw at the ground, slowly crushing Azurim deeper into the rock.

The iridescent dragon called magic to his aid, and a great fist of stone shot with explosive force from the ground under Greenfist, punching the lumbering green lizard hard in his stomach and lower quarters, flipping him sideways into a bank of snow several meters away. The fist then fell back into the ground, leaving no trace behind that it had existed at all except for the disturbed snow.

Greenfist was absolutely shimmering with magic. Azurim wasn't sure how, but this green oaf had definitely become more powerful in the short time since their last encounter. But how?

A gob of acid shot out from Greenfist, Azurim dodging easily to one side. The stone sizzled with smoke, and snow and ice evaporated instantly. Azurim shot back with a blast of fire, and noted that Greenfist took great care to avoid the heat. Ice didn't seem to bother him, Azurim thought, but he flinched from the fire!

Azurim took to alternating shots of fire from the ground and short leaps into the air, trying to catch Greenfist off-guard. His plan was working, until Greenfist grew tired of side-stepping the flames and instead cast another spell.

He disappeared completely.

Azurim blinked, and in that time Greenfist re-appeared a beat beside and above Azurim. Before the prince could react, Greenfist pounded down with both of his broad forelimbs, using his whole body as leverage. Azurim was sent sprawling into the ground, his world spinning. He crumpled and rolled past Trevistar's icy prison, and nearly collided with the children. He sat motionless for a moment, before shaking his head slowly to try and clear it.

That was a stronger hit than I have ever felt before, Azurim thought. Still, he is expending his magic quickly so he won't be able to keep this up much longer. I have to keep defending, and force him to tire himself out!

It was taking too long for Azurim to stand. Greenfist blasted a gob of acid at Azurim directly from above, who stood and took the blow on fully, only to shield the children. His magical protections were fading. Where did that green salamander get his extra magic boost from?

Azurim leaped into the sky, exchanging blows both physical and magical with the green beast, trying to find a weakness but finding none. After several tense moments, Azurim found himself on the ground, beaten down by a powerful fist once again. He simply couldn't seem to get past the magical barriers that Greenfist had up!

Greenfist slammed into the ground scant meters from where Azurim lay, the ground shaking in all directions. No one had noticed that it had stopped snowing. No one yet had noticed the stillness in the air, or the crack that had begun forming on the icy tomb of Trevistar.

The prince of dragons pushed himself up, struggling to get muscle and sinew to obey his commands, opening his wings to protect the terrified children who once again stood behind Azurim, their backs to the open portal.

"And now, young prince. You and your pathetic friends...will die." Greenfist grinned and laughed, a growing sound that ended in an almost maniacal bellow. He was gathering dark magic around him, green and black wisps of shadow swirling around as the ugly green made ready to finish off his enemy.

A blast of flame from his left flank shot into him, catching him unawares.

Azurim looked to his right and saw Corash come charging into the sacred circle. Greenfist saw her too, but chose to ignore her in favour of continuing his focus Azurim, his most hated foe.

The great green bellowed out massive gouts of flaming acid from its mouth. Azurim reinforced his scales with a spell of protection and fanned his wings wide, absorbing the full force of the blast. He toppled backwards, his wings pushing the children headlong into the crack in the ice. The children all tumbled into the portal.

Azurim felt his wings pass through the icy stone gates. He tried to keep himself from falling through, but the pressure was crushing him. If he stayed here, his body would be ripped in two, yet he strained with all his might to stay and continue his fight against Greenfist. He could not leave Corash here alone to face that green monster.

Weakened as he was, Azurim could not resist. The portal had him, like a black hole swallowing a star. He felt water wash over him as he was wrenched through to Earth.

Corash rushed forward and yelled at Azurim, even as he disappeared from view. She paused a moment, then turned to face Greenfist. He had a smirk on his face as large as the moon.

"Ha ha! Azurim is no more!" Greenfist shouted, dancing on the spot. "All hail Greenfist, the mighty conqueror!"

Fury, rage, frustration, sorrow and a symphony of other emotions filled Corash to tears. She had arrived too late! All the emotions she felt pooled into one spot in her heart as she launched herself fully into an attack. She flared fire from her mouth directly into the green dragon, and used magic to fling massive chunks of ice and stone from the ground to hit him on either side.

Greenfist had not anticipated the smaller red to attack so fiercely, and he back peddled to avoid the onslaught, but too late. Fire wrapped itself around him, while he felt stone pound his left side, and ice dig into his right. In moments his back was against the jagged stone wall, so he unfurled his wings to leap skyward. He gained only a short distance, just enough to clear the surrounding rocks, when Corash struck him, jaws first, still blasting fire. She bit deep, tears streaking down her eyes as she thought of losing Azurim and the children. She clawed harder and harder, pummelling the great green into the ground, a shower of snow and ice erupting around them both from the impact. Soon scales had been torn away, and she felt her claws and teeth find purchase on soft meat. She tore into it, yanking pieces up and throwing them aside. Through her tears she saw nothing, but continued her relentless rage until she was exhausted.

She stopped attacking and sobbed. She cried fully, wailing sobs for the love of her life that she had lost, and had never told of her feelings for. The swirling snow around her slowed, and the wind hushed until the only sound that remained was her crying. Minutes passed in the stillness, her sobbing cries mixing with the sound of ice breaking, piece by piece. It was several minutes before Corash knew she was not alone.

"It is true that hell hath no fury like a woman scorned, but it seems the same could be said of a woman in the pain of lost love as well."

Corash looked up quickly, ready to attack her new adversary, but stopped. It was Trevistar. She gasped.

"How...?" she began.

Trevistar smiled then glanced from side to side. Ice pixies, snow fairies and others of the Cold Fair Folk flitted about, dancing in celebration in circles around the wizard's head, body, and feet. A flurry of snow swirled beneath him, carrying him gently up the rise to stand on top of the ridge, and Corash realized it was the pixies giving the wizard the lift. The old wizard held up his hand, and a pixie landed there lightly, the silvery wings sparkling.

"I am curious, Corash, as to how you made it through the barrier after the Sentinels closed it again?"

Corash blinked. "How do you...you can't possibly have known....?"

Trevistar smiled, a fatherly gesture. "I have my tricks, and besides the pixies have been keeping me informed of the events in the world for a long time now. I may have been frozen, but they have kept me alive."

Corash simply stared; she had many thousands of questions instantly burning in her mind, but no voice to know where to start. The shock of seeing the old wizard alive, breathing, and speaking to her was astounding.

"I was...there was an attack, first on us and then directly against the Sentinels." Corash sped up as she recalled recent events. "The Sentinels returned their attack on the dragons, but one of the Sentinels was actually destroyed...the shield dropped as all of the rest of the Sentinels came to meet the Flight." She looked directly into Trevistar's eyes. "You...I thought of you for some reason, and then of Azurim and the children. Did you call me, somehow? I came as quickly as I could, realizing that with the shield down you were all vulnerable. My lord, how is it that you...are alive?"

The wizard looked up into the sky, verifying the dome was no longer in place. "The Cold Ones here can freeze, but they also control that cold and can thaw out again as well."

Corash tilted her head, trying to understand. Trevistar, legend said, had a greater ability to communicate with and understand the Fair Folk than any other. "You mean to say....they could have released you at any time? You are obviously a friend to them – why did they not release you sooner?"

Trevistar smiled a friendly, sagely smile. "They could not fully release me from the ice until another outside source could first begin the process. They required a Channeler to invoke warmth first. Much like a Princess awaiting her Prince to kiss her and break the spell." The red dragon simply looked confused. Trevistar continued without waiting for a reply. "Come Corash, you must be exhausted, but we must be on the move. There will be time to answer your questions. For now, however, we need to prepare for the possibility of your friends return."

"Return?" Corash blinked.

"Did I or did I not hear you give directions to Azurim before he passed through the portal?"

Corash thought for a moment. Rage, it seemed, had dulled her mind. Now that she was able, she remembered everything slowly, as if waking from a dream. "Yes, I had, but only out of a futile wish. It is impossible...the portal will never open! But if it can...oh, we have no time to lose!"

"Yes, yes, child, we do. And besides, I believe you may want to clean yourself up first."

Trevistar pointed down to where she stood.

Corash glanced, and then wished she hadn't. She stood in the centermost point of a macabre scene. Greenfist was dead, and had been rent in twain. Scales, organs, muscle and bone had all been ripped out by a merciless killer, and it was a moment more before Corash realized that the merciless killer had been....her.

Corash turned away from the old wizard and vomited, overcome by the horror of what she had done. Gruesome as it was, she had hated Greenfist for all the torment, murder and terror he had caused; he deserved his fate. But that Corash could have been capable of causing *this* level of death...? She threw up again. Trevistar looked away and allowed time for Corash to finish, wondering at how small and insignificant even the mightiest of creatures can seem when they are in such a vulnerable position, emotionally and physically, as sickness.

When she was through, Trevistar walked slowly to her side and rested a gentle hand on her shoulder. "My dear, do not hold onto thoughts of yourself in such a harsh way."

"How would you know what I think of myself as?" Corash whispered.

Trevistar paused. "Monster?" he offered.

Corash looked sidelong at him. Could he read minds? Trevistar smiled and winked, then turned to cast a spell. A large circle of snow melted into a bubbling, steaming pool of water. Corash let herself be led inside the water, where she bathed. She gulped at the water to rinse her mouth of the foul taste. She felt better after a few minutes. Trevistar sat down on a stone nearby to watch, patiently waiting.

She looked over to the mound of ice, which now lay melting in sunshine that had not covered this land in many years. "How is it you are alive, great wizard?" Corash repeated her earlier question.

"Well, asking how I am alive seems to imply that you thought I was dead already. And seeing as I was never truly dead, simply suspended in ice, I am not sure how to answer your question, except to say that yes, I am alive, thank you!"

The red dragon shook her head. Trevistar may be intelligent, and the greatest wizard spoken of in dragon history, but his eccentricity was unparalleled.

"You don't seem to be in a rush anymore, Corash," Trevistar commented, smiling broadly.

"Trevistar, you astound me. You seem to know what I am thinking before I say it – truly you are a great wizard."

The old man nodded in thanks and continued smiling, but said nothing.

"I am in no rush, because you seem not to be, and you had said earlier that we do have time to waste."

Trevistar pulled out an hourglass from a fold in his dark blue robe and studied it thoughtfully. Returning it to its hidden pocket, he suddenly jumped up. "We must be off! Corash, quickly please, when you are ready!"

Eccentric old fool, she thought again, but the aura about him was unmistakable. He was pure magic, through and through. She knew he had to be several hundred years old, but he appeared to be a human man in the prime of his life, somewhere just passed what she thought would be middle age. She shouldn't be surprised of *anything* he showed that he could do.

Corash made ready to fly, dipping her wing to allow Trevistar onto her back. The old man simply smiled at her, another twinkle in his eye. He shook his head no.

"Are you ready?" he asked, as Corash stood again. She nodded, despite her confusion.

"Good!" Trevistar exclaimed. He raised one arm, and a flurry of the Cold Ones attached themselves to him. With the other hand, he touched Corash with his palm and chanted mystical words. Without a sound, the group disappeared.

19 Shattered

AZURIM LOOKED QUICKLY BEHIND him. The magic of Shard was still trickling through, but waning rapidly. The ice would hold for…how long? He couldn't even guess. He was certain of one thing only – he could not return back through to Shard through this portal any longer.

Movement to his right snapped him out of his daze. The children! The three of them, chilled to the bone, were struggling to swim, but in this dark water they did not even know which way was up. Azurim sped through the water, his wings snapping shut along his sides, his powerful legs propelling him through the water like a torpedo. He snatched up Jared first, then Madison and lastly Alex, who had been underneath his sister, trying to force her to swim in the proper direction. Alex was obviously the most competent swimmer, but this task was simply beyond him.

Azurim made sure he had a secure grasp of each child and made his way to the surface as quickly as he dared: too quickly, and the children would be injured by the rushing water, too slowly and they would drown. Azurim could not risk casting a spell to create an air bubble around them – he could still feel magic pulsing into him, but he had to save it for his last, desperate hope of returning to Shard. Corash had yelled at him just before he had been forced through the portal. One word only – Stonehenge. He had to store up and conserve his magical power to try and reach the portal there. It was his only chance, impossible as it was he believed it to be.

They broke the surface, and the dragon heard all three of his riders gasping and sputtering for air, water spitting out in fitful spurts. Azurim rolled onto his back, using his body as a raft for the children to ride upon. It was night time, with only a faint trace of sunlight on the horizon. The water was dark all around them; the faint light of stars, a waxing moon, and a distant port city their only illumination.

Madison had several large swallows of water in her lungs. Alex apparently knew what to do, as he had spent a great deal of time in the pool back home. He was working towards getting his Life Guard certification, and was glad now that he had started it. As he helped Madison cough up as much water as possible, he began to regret missing out on his last set of instruction because he had been so busy playing with the dragons. He felt emotion welling up within him, but couldn't decide if it was home sickness, his concern for his sister, anger at not finishing his class, or his desire to see Kishar again that was overpowering him.

The children settled for a few moments as Azurim assessed his strength and theirs. It would be easier for him to leave the children here, but he discarded the idea. He knew what he had to do, but just wondered if he had the energy left to do it. If this were his final moments, he would at least want those who know him to be present.

"Azurim, what do we do now?" Jared asked, as Alex continued to help Madison.

"We must try to locate a new portal and open it, before this closes completely. And we must do so quickly, before the weave of magic closes to me."

Jared pointed down into the water. "Can't you simply drop us off on the shore and swim back down to go back through the portal there?"

"No, child Jared, I cannot. This portal, in the remains of Atlantis, is currently a one-way portal. We can only come through to this side, but not back again."

Madison coughed through her words. "Why is it only one-way?"

"When the Atlantis islands on Earth were destroyed and fell into the sea, the portal was permanently changed to a one-way door, otherwise the rushing water would never cease to flow through to Shard. Through the destruction of Atlantis, the portal itself was altered somehow, and couldn't be closed at that time, so the one-way option seemed best. Therefore, we need to locate another portal and attempt to open it."

"I thought you said all the other portals on Earth had been closed?" Alex asked.

"Yes, this is true, however Corash yelled at me a possible destination. I believe she intends to reopen the portal at your Stonehenge."

Jared gasped. "Is that even possible?"

Azurim thought for a moment. "I do not know, however I simply have nowhere else to go."

Azurim felt a shudder from the portal below the waves, and the trickle of magic come through it weaken. The ice was surely cracking now. He feared it would only be moments before it snapped shut completely. Then it would only be a matter of time before....

No! He would succeed. He had to.

"Quickly, we must depart!"

Azurim gathered the children around his back as he flipped over. "Hold tightly to me, children!"

The dragon pushed forward in the water, heading away from the city lights. He would gain speed in the water, and when he had enough would spread his wings to clear the sea.

"Shouldn't we go towards the city? I mean, how do you even know where we are going?"

"The stars, child Jared. They tell many things, and they are one thing that does not change, no matter which side of the portal you are on. And I was here not long ago, when I first came to find Kishar and the others. The city behind is the distant lights of Alexandria, gateway to Egypt from the sea.

We must travel north and west, and with all due speed. Quietly now, I must concentrate!"

Azurim continued to pump his legs as he crashed through the waves. The night air was warm, but to the soaked through children it was freezing. Azurim lurched upward, water cascading down his body. His large body didn't allow for easy movement in the water, but soon, the waves fell away, and Azurim's speed increased. It was only minutes and they were over land again.

"Is this Greece, or Italy?" Jared yelled into the wind. He words came out in a trembling shake, all their lips turning blue from the cold. He did not receive an answer.

Azurim blasted out a jet of flame, and then cast a spell of holding. The ball of fire hovered for a moment then settled behind his neck. The sphere of fire danced and sparkled before the children, allowing the wind to pass through it, turning the air into a drying furnace. Their clothes soon dried and their bodies began to warm up. The ball of fire didn't last, however, and several minutes later the air was beginning to turn cold again.

"I am sorry, children. I cannot risk casting that spell again. Magic is fading from me, and I need every ounce that I have left to get us to our destination. It won't be long now!"

"Azurim," Alex shouted into the wind, "will you have enough magic left to open the portal?"

Azurim was silent for several long wing beats. Finally he shrugged. "I do not know, child Alex."

"What will happen if you run out magic and the portals are all closed?"

Azurim did not answer. He looked ahead as they passed over Europe.

Many kilometres away, the last vestiges of ice cracked and shuddered, and the portal of Atlantis snapped shut.

Azurim dropped from the sky for several tense moments as a stab of pain wracked through him. The children screamed, and Azurim pulled himself out of his fall. He had not realized how strange it would feel to have no connection to magic at all. The portal must have closed! He felt weak, tired, and in pain physically and emotionally. He heaved himself forward, straining to continue his flight before the power left him completely.

Down below, and a little behind them, a boom and a flash lit the sky. The children all jolted in their seats, looking around to see a mountain erupting lava and ash.

"That is not the only terror befalling the planet. Look below, children." The dragon's words were rasping, short and shallow.

All of them looked down and around at Azurim's words. Great earthquakes were shaking the ground in every direction, and in many places rivets of steam, gushing lava, and pillars of rock were exploding outward from the earth's crust. They could see tidal waves beginning to crash into shores, and ships being tossed about like they were in a bath tub.

Azurim pressed on, urging more and more speed as they went. He couldn't afford to worry about the children's comfort any more, but he was worried – what was happening? Why was the earth heaving so?

He had no answers, but knew only one hope, one objective: Stonehenge. He used what magic he could to speed them on, and found himself holding his breath at times to fight through the strain. His nose began to bleed, and his head to pound.

They shot over Paris and soon passed over the English Channel. Azurim couldn't hold their height any longer and began dropping low to the ground. The children all sensed that his rapid descent was not on purpose, but caused by his weakening condition. They held on for dear life, saying prayers and hoping for the best.

Azurim's senses were beginning to dim, and he found it hard to breath. He was dying, he knew it. But if his last act was to see these children safely to ground, he would do so. A small town appeared ahead a short distance, and by the time they were above it Azurim was barely skimming over the roof tops of the taller buildings. There were minor tremors occurring here as well, but nothing compared to what they had witnessed further south in Italy and along the coast.

The dragon was breathing heavily now, gasping for air, but stubbornly refused to quit. He pushed forward, banking low over Amesbury and nearly clipping the uppermost tower of Amesbury Church as they sped out of the western part of the town. The children heard shouts of shock and panic from the streets below, but whether they were because of the earth tremors, or the dragon above, they couldn't tell.

Azurim tried to circle to the north side of the great monument, but his magic and strength had finally failed him. He cast a spell with the last of his power to guide the children to the ground, as he himself crash landed only a dozen or so meters south of the standing stones. The weak spell he cast did prevent the children from major harm, but they still rolled and tumbled in the field grass, and stood up sputtering and disoriented.

A motorist had been pulled off to the side of the road, trying to wait through the tremors, and was standing a few meters away to their north. Alex stopped to look at him sheepishly, glancing to Azurim and back.

"Uh...he's our pet," he offered sheepishly. The onlooker just stared, bewildered. The kids ran back to the great dragon's side.

Azurim looked old to the kids, very old. His eyes were sunken, and his scales seemed dulled by age and wear. They tried to help him, but he pushed them away weakly.

The dragon pointed a claw weakly to the ancient monument. "Stones...." Azurim whispered, his voice a mere rasp.

Madison began to cry, and knelt down beside the great beast. Alex's eyes welled up as well, but Jared simply looked towards Stonehenge. There were lights on near the stones – cars, and some lamps as well. There was a group gathered there, and it seemed like they were astronomers, judging by the various telescopes positioned around the stones. They were all staring loosely in their direction, some with night vision devices for viewing Stonehenge, others just seeing silhouettes.

"Alex, come on," Jared ordered as he grabbed his brother's sleeve. Alex didn't move, so Jared yanked on his arm, hard. "Alex, move it!"

Alex stumbled a little, but stammered as he did. "We can't leave Azurim behind."

Alex was crying, his emotions getting the most of him. He wanted to see Kishar, but was now wondering – if Azurim was this bad off, were the dragons on the other side dying, too, or were they protected?

Jared forced his brother into a trot as they headed into the stones. Several tour guides and bystanders were staring past the boys to the dragon beyond them, and in their amazement didn't bother to stop the brothers from running straight into the heart of the monument. Jared left Alex to stand in the middle while he began searching around frantically.

"What are you looking for, anyway?" Alex sobbed. He felt hopeless, useless. "We don't know how to do magic, and Azurim is dead…"

"He's not dead, Alex, you nimrod! Not yet, anyway, but he will be if you don't help me!"

"Help you do what?" Alex shouted back. "We don't even know what to look for!"

Jared knew his brother was right, but he couldn't sit and do nothing. He refused to believe that this was it, the end of the road with hope in sight but no way to turn the key in the lock that would open the door. He dashed from place to place, looking around for something, anything. Tremors in the ground were making progress difficult. The fear and hopelessness was starting to well up inside him, threatening to overwhelm him in panic, and a tear formed in his eye. In anger, he wiped the tear away and renewed his vigorous search.

Alex cried, and knelt down on a stone.

Jared heard the wailing from both his brother and sister and wanted to punch them both, with daggers. What useless whiners, he thought frantically to himself. They won't even try to help, they just sit and cry!

Jared turned to his brother and punched him hard in the shoulder.

"Hey!"

"Well stop your snivelling! We have to *do* something! Anything…." Jared's voice trailed off, his gaze caught on something. "What's that?"

Alex followed Jared's eyes to where Madison and Azurim were. There was a blue glow coming from them!

"Alex!" Jared shouted excitedly.

The pair ran back to their sister, excitedly hoping that Azurim was casting a spell, but he was completely out, with no sign of life. The blue glow was coming from the ground.

"Alex!" Jared repeated, pointing down. "Look at the stone!"

Alex looked down at a broken piece of stone on the ground. It was glowing dull neon blue. The brothers silently searched around, but were having trouble because Madison was in the way. They shoved her roughly to the side, while Madison continued to sob. The boys continued to search, wondering what was causing the stone to glow, when another one began to shine as well.

Madison was sitting on it.

Jared moved his sister out of the way to examine the stone more thoroughly. As Jared peered intently at the rock, Alex watched the path his sister took as she took a few steps away before plumping onto the ground again in defeat.

"Madison," Alex breathed softly, "it's *you*!"

Jared looked up at the same time Madison did, neither of them knowing what was going on. Madison saw for the first time the glowing blue around her. She shuffled backwards in a crab walk, rocks and pebbles all beginning to glow as she came into contact with them.

"Ahhhh!" Madison shrieked, jumping up. She landed in a heap and scrambled backwards, away from Azurim and towards Stonehenge.

"Madison, you're doing it!" Jared exclaimed.

Alex looked around, mystified. Madison however was terrified. "What's going on?" she cried out. She had backed into a standing stone, and moments after the entire arch began glowing. The tremors underneath them subsided, and Azurim caught a short breath of air, yet he did not rise.

Madison and Alex didn't understand yet, but Jared didn't care. He rushed forward and began shoving his sister into every stone he could see, whether it had been toppled to the ground or not. He dragged and spun his sister in circles until the entire area was a beacon of blue shinning in the night. Soon the blue colour spread out faster and faster, whether Madison was touching it or not, apparently the magic touching the stones having reached a point of capacity where it accelerated by itself. Jared let his sister go, amazed by what was happening.

The brothers started walking in circles, captivated by the spectacle. The night air was being lit with a blue fire that shone all around them.

"This is amazing!" Jared whispered in amazement. "Madison, how are you doing this?"

There was no response.

"Madison?" Alex called.

Still no response. The boys looked around once again to try and find their sister, and saw her standing at the center of the monument. She seemed to be staring at them, but there was no recognition there. Alex was about to call to her again when a tremor started, shaking the ground with such violence it seemed to them like the core of the entire planet. Alex tried to grab Jared's arm, but he was thrown sideways as earth shifted and moved. He rolled a couple of times then steadied himself on a fallen slab of stone directly south of Madison, who was standing stock still at the center. The tremors did not seem to be bothering her. A wind whipped around her, tousling her hair and clothing, and yet that same wind did not seem to be affecting anyone else.

Alex clambered up onto the flat rock then was suddenly thrown off as it pitched upward, standing itself upright! He rolled several times in the dirt again, finally stopping when he bounced into Azurim's side.

Jared was thrown to the ground, rolling south and west, away from the monument. He thought they were too late! The world seemed like it was ripping itself open, coming to an end. He tried to rush forward to get Madison to safety before the earthquake toppled a stone on top of her, but he lost his footing as stones hurtled through the earth and into the air.

Jared scrambled away from the stones, realizing it wasn't an earthquake. The night tour guides, astronomers and sightseers alike started shrieking and running away in fear, while a handful of others stared in wonder.

The entire field around them was glowing blue, stretching far out into the grounds around them, and Madison was in the midpoint of them all, standing on a stone that was rising from the earth. Her pedestal was glowing a bright green, a sharp contrast to the soft blue all around her. Her eyes had disappeared. In their place was only a bright green glow, like coloured headlights on a car. The pebbles and rocks strewn about the fields all began racing through the air or rolling along the ground, merging with others to create new sets of stones. Stonehenge was being rebuilt, as if by unseen giant hands! Jared watched as the new stones filled in the gaps where they had been missing before, completing a second ring, and then a third. Seven massive stones, larger than the rest, made up a fourth ring, far out past the roadway. People, cars, and anything else that did not belong with the circles were pushed away like a tornado picking them up and dumping them unceremoniously in a field. Jared ran to Azurim as best he could while the tremors continued, where Alex lay clutching onto the dragon so as not to be blown away.

The wind increased with Madison standing like a statue at the focal point of a column of rock, the square plinth crowned by a dome, atop which Madison shone with green and white light, seeming to emanate from every pore. The column was three or four storey's high, towering over the rest of the field. The stones around the circle all glowed and pulsed, getting brighter every second. The boys swore they saw images of people in the wind, like ghosts, following the circular motion of the gusts.

The wind grew in intensity, and flashes of lightning streaked down from a cloudless sky, lighting the column that Madison stood on with crackling energy. Several stars seemed to shine brighter, and the column cracked into two halves. Madison hovered in mid air, still standing on the domed piece of stone, separated now from the column, while the two pieces moved outwards from each other, and a rushing thunder wave rolled out from the opening in between them. The wave travelled like a sonic boom from a bomb, knocking those who had still managed to remain standing to the ground, and flattening grass around the entire countryside.

Azurim breathed in a deep breath, shocking both Alex and Jared. His eyes snapped open, alert and strong. Magic had been restored!

Azurim stood and looked about the field. He, Jared and Alex were the only beings still remaining within the fourth circle of stones. The dragons bulk had not been moved by the tremors or the shockwave, and the boys had used him as a shield against it as well. Everyone, and every*thing*, else had been shunted away. Cars had been pushed together in the parking lot nearby, and people were toppled to the ground, their telescopes all knocked over and tangled in with the group of onlookers.

A bright flash appeared as something moved through the portal. A second flash accompanied the first, and against the brightness of the stones they appeared only as silhouettes: one tall man, and the second a dragon.

Azurim took a cautious step forward. He roared a low challenge as the other dragon came closer, and heard a soft purring in return.

"Corash?" Azurim queried.

"Azurim, you're alive!" Corash exclaimed, bursting forward and wrapping her neck around his. She lovingly embraced him, then caught hold of herself and backed away. She lowered her eyes and returned to her stern soldier's stance.

"Oh come now, you've been swooning about him for the last several minutes, just kiss him already and tell him how you really feel!" The man behind Corash came forward as well, and revealed himself in the light.

"Great wizard!" Azurim exclaimed.

"Trevistar!" both Jared and Alex cried out at once.

The tall man looked about the stones, sniffed the air then huffed. "So this is Earth," he said with another sniff as if trying to identify a scent. His hands waved through the air as if it was water and he was testing the temperature. "Feels about the same," he commented.

Trevistar looked about, peering into the night. When he spoke, it was as if he had just finished wrapping up another conversation that no one else could hear. "Yes, exactly. But for now we will ignore that!"

The wizard raised one hand, and a swirl of ice fairies and pixies flew through the portal and settled on his arms and shoulders. "Lord Azurim, I will return shortly and yes, I will answer all of your questions." He whispered something and disappeared.

Azurim and the children all looked confused. Corash assumed a reporting stance of a junior officer and filled in the gaps for them.

"Trevistar teleported us to the portal at Stonehenge in Shard, and then disappeared again. He returned a few minutes later to announce that two other portals had been made ready to open. I asked why he would do such a thing, and he explained much. The portals between Shard and Earth have to remain open. He said that when he was sealing the portals in Shard, he noticed the pull of magic was growing stronger and stronger there. He assumed that if he were to seal them all, magic would simply cease to exist on Earth, and the two worlds would exist as individual worlds from then on.

"When he started to close the final portal in Atlantis, he felt the very fabric of reality beginning to tear apart. It was then that he realized, too late almost, that the two worlds need each other. Magic ebbs and flows, like wind or water. Here on earth, the very existence of life is a magical gift: plants grow, seasons change, and everything is in balance. By closing all of the portals, that balance is lost, like tipping one side of a scale completely with nothing on the other.

"Without the balance of nature, both worlds would be destroyed, or at the very least cataclysmically altered. One world with all magic would eventually explode, as it cannot contain it all, and the other world without any would implode, as it cannot exist without the fabric of magic that allows life to flow."

Jared and Alex both echoed understanding by saying, "Ooooh!"

Azurim was concentrating hard. "So, as I understand it," Azurim began slowly, "you have feelings for me that you told Trevistar about, but not to me. Is this correct?"

If a red dragon could blush and make her features even more deep crimson, Corash pulled it off nicely, even in the evening gloom. She blinked and shuffled her feet, tried to speak twice, fluttered her wings, stopping to think while her jaw worked soundlessly, trying to find the right words. Both boys smirked.

"Dragons and humans are more alike than I thought," Jared commented quietly to Alex. He had assumed that no one else would hear, but Azurim perked up at his words.

"Why do you think that, child Jared?"

"Well," Jared started, a little off guard for having been overheard, "I was just noticing that dragons and humans have a lot of the same emotions, and Corash seems to be blushing, and.... Well, before today, I would never have assumed that a dragon could do that."

Corash looked away, more embarrassed than before. She was saved from having to respond, however. For there was a whooshing sound of air as Trevistar reappeared, brushing snow from his robes. "There! That is taken care of! What is next on the agenda?"

"Where were you?" Jared asked. Alex giggled at the clump of snow on the old wizard's head, piled like a pyramid. He pointed at his head, and mimicked the motion of cleaning off his own. Trevistar looked up then knocked the snow off his scalp, brushing his hair out fully.

"Silly pixies..." he muttered as he continued about the business of cleaning himself. The showers of snow and ice coming out of the folds in his robes seemed endless.

The group waited several moments before Azurim loudly cleared his throat. Trevistar looked up and smiled.

"Yes, of course, my apologies. We must be off!"

"But...where were you?" Jared asked again.

Trevistar looked at Jared then at the snow he had brushed to the ground, and back to Jared again. "Oh. You mean the snow! Of course, again, my apologies. Antarctica."

Trevistar made his way hurriedly back towards the portal, assuming his answer was more than enough to appease everyone's curiosity. "We'll need to get moving quickly – it appears we have already drawn far too much attention to ourselves. And I have remaining only the reagents required left on me to teleport one more time."

Jared was very persistent. "Wait! Antarctica? What were you doing there?"

Trevistar looked around again, a twinkle in his eye as he looked down on Jared. "Antarctica? Blustery, cold place, really. I wouldn't want to be there at all, if I could help it. Needed a place for the pixies and fairies to be, however, to guard the open gates. That seemed to be the best place for them, and besides, they absolutely loved the penguins!

"However, we have a gate here to close, as I don't think this will be a very inconspicuous location to maintain."

"Open? You mean the portals in Antarctica are open now? Why is that?"

"Silly boy!" Trevistar replied, tousling Jared's hair. "We can't close *all* the portals, now can we? Yet we needed to find a remote place to keep at least one portal open, and the two at the southern pole seemed the most inaccessible place to do so. And very easy to hide!"

Jared was about to ask something more, but his question was waved off. "Ah, tut tut! No time for questions now, young man. There is a war to wage in Shard, and Lord Azurim is needed there. Corash, will you please take your love through?"

Corash blushed deeply again and gasped. Azurim grinned. "We will continue this discussion at a later, more appropriate, time," he said quietly to her. Azurim led the way towards the yawning portal, Corash following closely behind.

The shimmering dragon stopped at the portal threshold and turned to face the children.

"Fare thee well, children. It was...an *honour* to meet you, travel with you and get to know you." Azurim bowed. "I wish we had more time, but the wizard is right, we must go. Perhaps, another day."

Azurim partially turned, but stopped as he thought of one thing more. He fixed his gaze to each of the boys' eyes, one at a time, before speaking again.

"Thank you."

Corash nodded at the children as she followed Azurim through to Shard. The two dragons disappeared from sight, leaving the boys to plead with the tall wizard.

Trevistar raised his hand up to the boys' protests. "I understand, but you simply cannot return to Shard at this time. Now then, will you be able to find your way home from here?"

Alex gaped, and Jared blinked. "Find our way home? We're in England! We don't live in England! We live in Canada!"

Trevistar mumbled something about needing to invest in a current map to orient his geography. Where on earth was this Canada?

"I am afraid that I cannot teleport you all at this time. I need my last spell to return me to those delightful penguins…er, to Antarctica!"

"Why not go through the portal here?" Alex asked.

Trevistar looked about at the other people, who were now overcoming their fear and daring to step closer. This was too much attention, and time was against him.

"I *will* be going through this portal, however I must return to the now-open portals in Shard to oversee their protection. Children, please understand. This portal must now be closed, and I can only do so properly from the other side. We have no choice now, and I suggest you leave as quickly as possible, too. There is no telling how many other people will come raining down upon this area, with all the recent events. You'll want to be far away at that point. Even by closing the portal, the stones here have been restored, including the ones previously destroyed. Your sister is quite a Channeler!"

"Channeler?" Jared repeated.

"I am sorry, I do not have time to explain in more detail. The three of you must leave once the portal is shut, and find your way home. I truly wish I could do more. Now listen carefully, before I enter the portal, I will say the incantation to shut Stonehenge once again. It will take a minute or two for the stones to revert and the portal to close. Once it is closed, your sister will be quite exhausted. You will need to help her. Remember, the three of you will need to leave this area as quickly as possible, and find your way home."

Alex burst. "No! You can't just leave us here and expect us to find a way when we are thousands of kilometres from home! How can you do that to us?"

Trevistar smiled broadly, a mischievous glint in his eye. "Think of it as an adventure, a great chance for learning!"

There was no humour echoed from the boys. Trevistar put a hand to each boy's shoulder. "The only solace and comfort I can give you is the knowledge that the portals will never be fully closed. So there is a chance that we will meet again. Take care of each other!"

Trevistar turned abruptly and walked towards the portal, whispering words and waving one hand in the air. Immediately the stone column pieces that had been split before began moving back towards each other. Trevistar stopped at the threshold of the portal, ensuring that no one followed, and waited until the doorway was just large enough to allow him through. He raised a hand in farewell then stepped backwards into the shimmering line. Jared and Alex rushed forward, but the stone column collided together, sealing the doorway. The domed piece Madison stood on returned to its place on top of the column, and the entire piece slowly slid back into the ground. Once it clicked into place, the glowing all around them stopped, and Madison, who had been looking like a marionette on strings until that moment, collapsed in a heap. Jared and Alex helped their sister up, but it required all their combined strength to get her moving.

The darkness was sudden. Without the glow from the stones, and with all the previous lamps and torches having been extinguished, it was near impossible to see. People from their right began shouting as Jared tried to lead his siblings in what he thought was a southern direction. If he remembered correctly from what he saw on their flight, there was a road just south of them, and following that east would then lead them back to the town they had flown over. He wasn't sure if that was the smartest place for them to go, but he really had no other choice.

"Come on," he urged, and the two brothers each threw one of Madison's arms over their shoulders. Her legs barely worked, the feet really not holding any of her weight at all. She felt like a sack of bricks on their shoulders, but they pressed on. Madison stumbled several times in her delirious state, and whined about how tired she was, Alex nodding his agreement, but Jared pushed them faster. He was worried – Trevistar was right about them not wanting to be seen in this area. There were dozens of witnesses to what had happened. The best thing they could do was get home as quickly as possible. Jared has seen enough movies to know that when strange things occurred, the people involved were usually locked up in some government jail. They needed to get out of here.

"One thing is for sure," Alex commented as they stumbled along.

"What's that?" Jared asked, grunting as he shifted Madison's weight.

Alex grinned while he stumbled with effort. "Trevistar looks like Dad, and has the same *really* annoying way of explaining something by saying nothing at all, and leaving us to figure it out for ourselves."

"Maybe," Jared panted, "but Dad would never dump us in another country and tell us to find our own way home."

They found the road, crossed over it and turned left, following it in the direction that Jared hoped was the town. Behind them, several lights had flared up, whether from vehicle headlights or some other source was unknown. A hundred meters further on, Jared saw a fork in the road, one sign post showing the direction left and behind them back to Stonehenge, and another smaller one showing the town Amesbury up ahead. Several cars were racing down the road ahead of them, so Jared steered his siblings to his right, entering the ditch and moving into a farmer's field. Alex didn't complain and was more than happy to let his younger brother lead.

The field had recently been run over with a combine, as large long lines of yet to be harvested wheat or barley, or whatever it was, ran the length of the field. Thankfully, the crop lines went in the direction they were going, and the divots in the earth and crop made it easier for them to walk. Another hundred meters or so brought them to a small clump of trees, only four of them in fact, near the road where Jared and Alex dropped Madison down so they could all rest.

After several minutes of panting, Jared and Alex regained their breath and silence came upon them.

"Where do we go from here, Jared?"

Jared had been thinking of that. Looking further east, he could see a pink glow in the sky, so he knew the town must be in that direction. The problem was choosing the best possible route to get there, and what to do once they arrived.

Jared pointed ahead. "There," he hissed. He wasn't sure why, but he felt the need to whisper. "That looks like a nice set of trees for us to rest in a little longer. We'll need to carry Madison there. Once we get there, we'll plan the rest of the route."

"But where are we going?" Alex whispered back.

Jared shook his head. "I don't know, Alex. We need to find a safe place to rest, and a phone to call Mom and Dad. To be honest, I am just guessing at our direction here, ok?" Jared's voice betrayed his frustration.

Alex sighed, feeling uneasy, but not having a better plan of his own. "Ok."

They waited another minute then headed out again, carrying Madison between them. They had almost made it across the field and to the next stand of trees when they heard the sirens coming. Three police cars zoomed down the road, and although there was really no chance at all that the officers would be able to see the children in the dark field, Jared felt a sense of urgency anyway and pushed them to a quick hustle. The trees were thick here, and the group continued until they were deep within. Madison was dropped onto the ground again while the others collapsed, catching their breath. Madison groaned and stirred, not alert enough to do anything actively, but at least beginning to move on her own.

Jared put his head down in his hands and closed his eyes. "Finally, she wakes."

They panted for several long minutes, Alex drifting into a light sleep, Madison grunting from time to time.

Jared rested for only a few moments and then stood up to pace. He once again felt a welling up inside him of frustration and anger. Why had the dragons and that stupid wizard left them alone like this? It wasn't fair, and it wasn't right! How could they expect them to get home? Didn't they understand how far away their home was? Didn't they understand anything?

Jared kicked a low branch then kicked the trunk of the same tree. He just wanted to fight something now, or scream and punch his pillow like he used to do back home. He sank down to his knees – none of that would help, he knew, but he wanted to do it anyway. It may not help, but maybe he would feel better.

Madison stirred, looking about in the darkness and swatting her hands around like she was shooing something away. Jared moved to his sister's side and caught her arm.

"Madison, it's me."

Madison relaxed and calmed. "What happened? Where are we?"

"We dragged you away and we're now hiding in some trees. The dragons and the wizard are gone now, and the portal of Stonehenge is sealed."

"Wait," Madison exclaimed, "there's a portal at Stonehenge?"

Jared blinked. "You...you don't remember?"

Madison looked at the ground, her eyes adjusting. "No, all I remember is touching stones and watching them glow, and getting mad at you for pushing me around."

"Yeah, well, you didn't seem like you were doing anything useful on your own, so I helped you along."

Madison chose to ignore the sarcasm. "The next thing I can remember is seeing a bright green light – and now I am here. What did I miss?"

Jared sighed then slowly described everything that happened. Madison's eyes went wide, but she didn't question whether Jared was telling the truth or not. She was simply upset that she couldn't remember it. Jared concluded the story right up to where they were now, and what his plan had been of going to Amesbury.

"The wizard called you a Channeler...do you know what that means?"

Madison thought about it for a moment. "Not really. Maybe there is something about it in your Wizardology book at home."

"Yeah, I'll have to look it up, if we can ever get back there."

"Well, I am feeling good enough to get moving now. We need to wake up Alex."

"It's all gone?" Lilly asked.

Christian nodded his head. "I'm sorry. They got to him before we did. Probably down in Brazil before he even left, actually."

Richard threw another pillow into the sofa. "For the last time, what in blazes are you all talking about?"

Eddie and Lynn were sitting in office chairs near the computer set up, full of sorrow. They hadn't believed Christian in the first place about a magical way to erase memories, but having picked up Richard from the airport a couple hours ago, they believed it now.

Christian looked at the Zedmore's. "Aren't you glad I gave you the charms, now?"

Richard was fuming still. "Are you two in on this horrible joke, too?"

Lilly walked over to her fiancé and coaxed him to sit down. "I'm sorry Rich, I wish I could change it all, but you just have to listen."

Richard exploded again, leaving Lilly to wring her hands in her lap while he paced around. He started by looking behind some books on the shelf.

"I don't believe this! Where is the hidden camera, huh? You guys have all gone all-out to punk me on this one!"

Eddie raised a hand. "Rich, please, we're telling the truth."

Richard spun around and pointed an accusing finger. "Don't start on me Eddie! This is the worst. You're trying to tell me that you have three kids that you have been hiding on me for years? I was at your wedding, for crying out loud, and we've been partners in practically everything we've ever done since! If you had kids, I would have known about it! This is a sick joke, and I want you all to stop it right now!"

Richard looked around at the group, but wasn't receiving any support for his case. He looked back at the coffee table, where several scrapbooks with hundreds of pictures of his best friend and three children were sprawled out for them to see. He pawed at them again, shuffling them around to glance through them all.

He shook his head and laughed to himself. This was impossible. The story they were trying to feed him, about dragons and magic, and a secret society that went around brainwashing people into forgetting their memories...pure insanity.

Richard picked up a large photo that was loose in the pile, of three smiling kids, and him kneeling in between all of them, every one of them wearing a Mickey Mouse hat, the Disney castle in the distance behind them. It could have been digitally altered...but why?

He tossed the picture down again as he slumped into the la-z-boy behind him, one hand on his temple to try and massage the panic and headache out.

"Look, all I remember is going down to Brazil to check on the mine. There was a collapse, and the government was out to make sure that we followed proper procedures to clean everything up. Once it was all settled, I came back."

He pointed at Lilly. "I told you this before I left! The mine had stopped operations until a senior executive – that's me or Eddie – went down to settle the paperwork and make the decisions. I know how much you are trying to make me believe this, but...Ed, I've never met your kids."

Lilly shifted forward and picked up the Disney picture again. "Honey..."

Richard swatted it away. "I know that's me in the picture! But who the heck are those kids?"

Lynn sighed deeply. "That's Alex, and Madison behind you, and Jared on the right. We all went last summer." She sighed again and turned to Christian. "He's never going to remember, is he?"

Christian shook his head. "Sorry, I don't think so. I've never known anyone who was capable of lifting the erasure charm. I...well....I'm sorry."

The room was quiet for several long minutes. Lilly placed a hand on Richard's knee, concern and worry in her eyes. Lynn played idly with the mouse, clicking things here and there on the computer. Eddie just stared into a point in space, not really seeing anything.

Christian pushed himself up from the wall where he had been leaning by the doorway.

"Well, he's safe now from any more memory manipulation, just keep the charms on you at all times. I apologize there is nothing more I can do, and that I really do have to get going."

Eddie nodded, standing up to shake the man's hand. "Thanks, Christian. You know I really appreciate all you and your group is trying to do, but all this secrecy crap really sets me off."

Lynn smiled. "Yes, you certainly don't like surprises, do you dear?"

Christian waved the Zedmore's over, and the trio walked into the kitchen, leaving Lilly and Richard to talk alone. They walked to the kitchen counter where Christian sat at a bar stool. Eddie joined him, while Lynn made her way to the other side, absently cleaning up in the sink.

"I didn't have a chance to help Richard out, and I feel terribly about that. But I am glad that Lilly and I were able to get to you both in time. Don't let those charms out of your sight. Keep them in a pocket or something, at all times. You may even want to try something like this," he finished, holding his arm up. The bracelet he wore had ten or so small charms attached, and they were pretty sure these weren't bought in a novelty store.

"Where are you going to go now?" Eddie asked.

The other man shrugged, and smiled. "Actually, I don't know! I have officially disobeyed the last sets of instructions given to me by the Order. The only thing I can think of to do is make contact with some friends I know and see from there where fate takes me."

"That doesn't sound exactly well planned out."

"True. The one thing I know for certain is that I need to get away from this household. Nothing against you! You have been more understanding and gracious to me than I think anyone else would have, and that I would deserve. But the Order is going to be searching for me, and if I stay here I just put you all in even greater danger."

He stood up and made his way to the patio door. "Thanks for everything, Eddie, Lynn. Remember, the Order thinks you have no memory of these occurrences, and they seem absolutely positive that neither the dragons nor your kids will ever be back."

Lynn slipped at that and dropped a pot into the sink. Christian was quick to recover.

"I have a strong hunch that they will be back! You'll see them again, soon if I am feeling right about it. But just remember that the Order thinks otherwise. I would bet they will be back to check on you again, and if you suddenly have the kids in the house, or worse dragons flying around….well, honestly I don't know what they would do, but it wouldn't be pretty."

"Can't you tell us more about the Order? What do they want, and why would they be out to erase memories of anyone who appeared to have even the slightest magic talent or involvement?"

Christian looked out the glass door. "I really wish I could."

Lynn felt that he could have told them everything, had he wanted to, but suspected that years of him being a magical secret agent wouldn't let him. The training and experience of keeping secrets from the world wouldn't come out in one night. She walked to the pantry and grabbed some protein bars, drink boxes and other snack foods, stuffing them into a plastic grocery bag.

"Here," she said, forcing the bag into Christian's hand, "you'll be hungry out on the road all by yourself."

Christian smiled and held out his hand. "Thanks, Mrs. Zedmore."

Lynn smiled and shook his hand, stepping back to the kitchen as Eddie came up. He was looking hesitant, and took a moment to collect his words properly.

"Look, I still don't really know you or trust you, but you did coach us on what to do to fool those guys, and gave us the chance to keep our memories. Thank you. I wish you the best, and hope that if we meet again it will be under better circumstances."

Christian put his hand out again. "That fatherly speech….do I call you Eddie, Mr. Zedmore, or Dad?"

Eddie shook his hand and gave him a shot in the shoulder with his other hand. "See ya, kid."

Christian smiled and waved one more goodbye to Lynn, then opened the door and stepped out into the night air. He walked to the back of the house into the darkness and made his way to his car, hidden a fair ways back to escape notice of any other agents that might have come to call. Eddie watched the car's headlights turn on, and waved at Christian again as he drove to the front, and away into the night.

"So," Lynn began, "what do you think we should do about Richard?"

Just then the house began to shake, glasses and dishes rattling in the cupboards. Several items on shelves crashed to the ground, and the lights flickered. The earthquake continued for nearly a minute, and then stopped. The Zedmore's looked at each other with the same thought in mind... coincidence, or connected to all the magical craziness going on?

Something metal fell on the ground in the distance, and Richard cursed loudly from the other room.

Eddie let out a slow breath. This might be a long night.

It took several tries from both siblings to finally get Alex on his feet. They stumbled out of the tree line, further south than they had originally thought they had gone, but the darkness inside the copse had made it difficult to judge direction and distance. They continued toward the pink glow of the horizon, cutting across another field, a narrow band of trees, then another field. They could see a farm house to their right, a group of buildings on their left, and a paved country road connecting them. They crossed the road to the south side and scanned the area around them, hiding behind some trees just off the ditch.

"Does this road lead to the town?" Madison asked. Both brothers shrugged, but decided to follow it anyway. They had only made their way a short distance when the light of police cars appeared up ahead. Madison wanted to go directly to the police and ask for help, but Jared and Alex both agreed, without even knowing why, that they should avoid being seen at all costs, especially by the authorities.

They abandoned the road and made their way instead across some open grassland to another thick clump of trees. They could hear water somewhere ahead, and soon they were standing on a river bank. Moonlight reflected dimly off the babbling brook, and further ahead they could see a bridge. Making their way to it, they decided to cross the bridge and continue on the south side. Before they could move, however, a police car rumbled up suddenly, and stopped in the center of the bridge.

A police officer stepped out of the vehicle while a powerful lamp hummed to life in his hand. It was connected by a power supply to the inside of the car. The children pressed themselves into the foliage against the river bank, holding their breath.

"You see anythin', mate?"

The voice had come from inside the car, a heavy accent rolling from Irish to British and back again. It was a moment before the reply came, as the officer with the lamp was searching the river up and down, and on both sides. The light paused here and there, one time of which was directly on Jared who thought he was caught for sure, but the light continued on.

"No, mate. Can't make anything out at all with all the weeds 'n such. What are we looking for again?" His accent was definitely British, but not nearly as thick.

There was some paper rustling inside the car. "Coupla kids. No, three of 'em. I dunno. We 'ave eye witness reports, sayin' that two, or three, or five kids ran off inna fields afta tha disturbance."

The other officer snorted. "Some reliable reports, those are. At least they all agree that those running off were children."

"Dun get me started on the reports o' giant flyin' lizards, mate."

The other officer turned off the lamp. "There's nothing here, Jake. Let's move on."

In moments, the car had sped away, following the road south. The children all sat motionless until the sound of the engine was gone.

"Told ya they were looking for us."

"Yeah, but, Jared, what if they just want to help us?"

Jared shook his head. "You heard them, Madison! I bet their eye witnesses told them what you did at Stonehenge, and they are going to want to know how all of that happened! If they catch us, you can bet we're not going home any time soon."

Alex nodded his agreement. "Let's keep moving."

The trio made their way to the bridge and crossed the road quickly, diving into the trees on the other side, just in case any cars came down the road. They abandoned the idea of crossing the bridge, as they didn't want to follow where the police had gone, and instead continued their journey through the trees, following the river. Fifteen minutes of hiking brought them to the back side of a line houses, lights on in almost every one of them. The river turned south here, but the lights of the town were east. They followed the river a short distance anyway, trying to decide what to do. Enter a dark house and try to use a phone? Knock on a door and ask for help? No, more than likely everyone in this neighbourhood had already been told of the events at Stonehenge. Three strange children asking for help would certainly be suspicious. They decided to continue on their own, and try to find a different phone they could use.

The children stumbled out of the trees onto a dark tennis court. This estate had a lot of trees surrounding it, and the majority of the lights in both buildings were out. Without knowing where to go, they felt that any path was as good as the next one, so they decided to try looking into this house. Maybe the owners were out on vacation? Maybe they could find a way inside to use a phone, or the Internet?

They made their way up the long yard and to the rear of the house, which was a fair size. The patio was open and all the lights were dim. Alex made a gesture for the other two to stay hidden while he checked it out. He had stepped only a few paces when the patio light came on, the glass door sliding open. Alex yelped and dove to his right, hiding against the edge of the garage.

"Alright, out with you, you mangy cat!"

A woman shooed a large tabby cat out the door and shut it quickly behind. The feline obviously did not want to be outside, as it mewed incessantly at the door, rubbing back and forth on it waiting for the owners to open the door up again. The light turned off, and through a window somewhere the woman's voice came back again, telling the cat to shut up and let her sleep.

Alex hadn't realized he was holding his breath, and let it out with a blast. Jared and Madison rushed over to him, worry and surprise still in their eyes. Silently, the three of them moved around the far side of the garage, away from the house, and into the front yard. There was a large driveway and some parking space out front, mostly empty except for a Range Rover and a Mercedes. The children left the cars alone and ran to the roadway, staying behind the trees. When the road was clear, they crossed it at a slow run, crashing through the trees on the other side, wanting to put distance between the road and themselves in case another police car happened by.

They were facing another large field, but this time the other side of it was brightly lit.

"We made it!" Jared whispered excitedly.

"Yeah, we made it to town, but now what?"

They all scanned the lights of the town ahead, looking for a sign as to where to go. Madison found it.

"How about there?" she asked, pointing. The boys looked at each other then shrugged.

"Sure, why not?"

"Good idea, Maddie," Alex added, "I guess a church is as good a place as any."

The children kept to the trees that surrounded the open field. It looked like some kind of park, and was probably pretty in the daylight but the kids had no time to enjoy it.

The road they had just crossed curved and went to a bridge spanning a slow moving but deep river. The bridge and area beyond it were busy. They had no other way to get across the river, and didn't feel like getting wet. They decided to make the trip in two – Alex and Madison would walk together first, and then Jared would follow twenty seconds later, just in case another Police officer was nearby and wanted to question them. The Police were looking for a group of children, so if they split up they should be safer, shouldn't they?

The boys had originally wanted all of them to walk individually, but Madison was too scared to walk by herself.

They continued across the bridge without incident, but felt justified for their caution anyway. The church was only another block or so away, but as they neared their hearts sank – it was so crowded! There had to be a hundred people gathered around in front of the church, holding lighted candles. A man was making his way through the group, praying with some, and guiding others to places to sit or get a candle of their own. Apparently the events of tonight had shaken a lot of people up, and they were coming together here to pray and feel safe. Even from the block or so distance away, the children could hear loud cries of worry about the Apocalypse, earthquakes being a sign of the end.

Jared wanted to leave immediately, but Alex smiled and led them on instead. "Don't you see? This is perfect! No one will be looking for us in a group of people all praying together. We just need to join up with the group, and make our way into the church when we can!"

"Just try not to say anything," Jared cautioned.

"Why not?" Madison asked, and Alex was echoing her query.

"Because," Jared replied, "we don't have an English accent. Might be a dead giveaway, dontcha think?"

"This is the nearest town to Stonehenge," Alex countered. "Don't you think they would be used to tourists?"

"Oh, well, probably still a good idea to not say too much, I think," Jared cautioned.

Alex let a sarcastic reply die away, and instead focused on leading his siblings into the crowd. Twice the children were hugged by unknown women, who were crying about the end of all things and worried about these precious children who would not see tomorrow. Each of them was handed a candle at some point, and Jared had a Hymn book shoved into his hands after someone had asked if he could read.

Gravestones seemed to litter the yard around the church, and Alex felt uncomfortable walking through them. He wouldn't have been so eager to come here if he had known of all these gravestones. Alex continued to lead the group around the building, a beautiful stone church in the shape of a cross, with a couple of out buildings attached to it. When he did see an open doorway into the church, Alex's shoulders sagged – the church was full too!

"That explains why the grounds are full of people," Alex muttered.

"Why?" Madison was staring around, not really knowing what their plans was, and just following her brothers blindly.

"Because the church is already full of people, so all these people are left to walk around out here," Jared stated.

"Oh."

Alex spied a clock on the inside wall of the entryway to the church.

"It's almost midnight! Why aren't all of these people at home?"

"Scared out of their minds right now, I'd say," Jared replied to his brother.

"I guess, but then why were most of those other houses, by the river that we passed, loaded with people still? Why aren't they all down here?"

Madison shrugged. "They don't go to church?"

Alex pulled Jared's arm to the right, and Jared motioned for Madison to keep up. Alex led them to a set of buildings across a small parking lot. They appeared to be some type of office, or caretakers building for the church. Every light was on, except for a small building at the far end of the lot. All but the front light was out. Alex raced to the door and tried it – it was unlocked. Not giving himself time to think about the consequences, he opened the door and burst inside, ushering his brother and sister in after him. He closed the door as soon as he was able, while Jared fumbled on the wall for a light switch.

It was a simple dwelling, and smelled of dirt. The front doorway had two pairs of boots, covered with dried mud, sitting on a rack waiting to be cleaned. Several jackets were tucked into a closet that was too small to hold everything, the hangers shoved in at odd angles to make them fit. Immediately beyond the doorway was a small room that served as a living room: two plush chairs and a lamp stand between them. To the right of that was a simple kitchen all in yellow, with an open doorway to a staircase that led down to a basement and a side door to the outside. Attached to the kitchen at the back side of the house was a small office and a computer, with piles and piles of paperwork stored in every possible corner. On the wall of the kitchen, before entering the office, was a corkboard, loaded with receipts, reminder notices and a map.

Jared saw the telephone in the kitchen first and immediately picked it up. He dialled his home number, but received a message telling him that in order to dial a long distance call he needed to add the prefix or country code first. Jared shook his head and scolded himself, realizing he couldn't simply dial Calgary from England. He tried again, following the directions the automatic operator gave him for International dialling, but received a message telling him that all circuits were busy. His second and third attempts had the same response.

"I guess that makes sense right now," Alex reasoned after Jared hung up the last time. "Everyone in the world would probably have felt the tremors once the magic flow was cut off. So everyone in the world is probably trying to make phone calls to family, just like we are."

Jared threw his hands in the air, flopping into one of the plush chairs. He had been strong quite long enough, he thought, and it was just about time for him to break down and cry. He felt hopelessness again seeping into him, and his lower lip started trembling.

"Does this computer have Internet?" Madison was standing in the doorway to the office.

Alex jumped up and ran into the office. He fumbled around, moving paper out of the way until he had found the power switch and turned it on. The computer hummed and beeped several times, and the fan sounded more like an airplane taking off than a computer component. Jared hadn't moved from the plush chair – he was feeling comfortable in his moment of despair, and didn't want to rush back to a positive mood just in case his hopes were dashed again. The computer powered up, showing a Windows 2000 logo.

"This ought to be good," Alex groaned.

"No Internet?" Madison was starting to get worried, too.

Alex glanced around the table top. Under some papers he found a modem which had green lights flickering and a yellow light for the PC Connection. "It has an Internet connection, but what I am worried about is how old this computer is. It's going to be a pain trying to use it, that's all."

After two more slow minutes, the computer finally booted up. Thankfully there was no password required. Alex searched for Internet Explorer, as it was not displayed on the desktop. He finally found it and began loading the program, which again took several minutes. Madison watched from the doorway, while Jared closed his eyes and did his best to fight off tears of frustration and fatigue.

Alex cracked his knuckles and began surfing the web. It was, as predicted, hideously slow going, but he managed to find what he was looking for.

20 Stealth

RICHARD AND LILLY WERE busy in the kitchen, scooping plates of spaghetti, sauce and meatballs onto plates for themselves, Eddie and Lynn. They had tried to talk to Richard again, but he simply wanted to have a good meal and stop with the nonsense. His flight had been long, and now he had a big headache. Food was his solution to feeling comfortable again.

They had all converged on the kitchen, getting the table set and food cooking to keep their minds off of other things. Dinner was quiet and awkward, Richard still upset and trying to figure out this cruel game, and the others wishing they could do something about it.

A bleep on the computer speakers caught all their attention.

"Was that movement from your magical portal at the pond?" Richard asked excitedly, dripping with sarcasm.

Lynn smiled weakly. "No, it's just an instant text-message from our business site. It activates automatically whenever we're online, so business partners and associates can chat at any time when they know we're on."

It beeped again. Everyone at the table waited.

"Lynn, aren't you going to check it?" Lilly asked.

"No." Lynn was far more interested in her dinner than in chatting online.

The computer beeped again.

"Ok, seriously, what is that?" Richard asked.

Lynn slurped in a long noodle. "I told you, it's our instant-messaging service. It beeps when we receive a message. Probably someone wanting a price for something."

The computer beeped again, twice in a row.

"Sure sounds like someone is trying to get a hold of you in an awful hurry," Lilly commented.

"Mmm hmm," Lynn mumbled, digging into a meatball.

The computer beeped one more time. Eddie stood up, sipping his drink and bringing it with him.

"Sounds urgent, whoever it is. I'll check it out, you just keep eating," Eddie said as he patted Lynn on the shoulder and began walking over to the station. "I'm sure Lynn's right it's probably just..."

There was moment of silence, followed closely by a crash as Eddie's glass shattered on the ground. Pink lemonade splashed everywhere.

"Lynn, it's Alex!" Eddie kicked the chair hurriedly out of the way and madly began hacking away at the keyboard.

Lynn swallowed a mighty gulp of milk. "So what's the good news? He make another major sale like he always does?"

Eddie blinked twice before figuring out her misunderstanding. "No! Not Alex from Toronto – Alex, your son, Alex!"

Lynn's eyes bugged out. She jumped up from the table, her chair toppling backwards behind her and the remains of her spaghetti scattering across the table and onto the floor. She ran to the computer and violently shoved her husband out of the way, still trying to swallow the last meatball she had in her mouth as she talked. Eddie tripped backwards and sprawled on the ground, soaking his leg in the spilled lemonade.

"Alex! Where? Where is he, how did he get a computer wherever he is, are his brother and sister with him? What's happening?" Lynn shrieked it all in one quick burst.

"How am I supposed to know now? You nearly killed me!" Eddie angrily retorted. "I didn't even get a chance to reply to him!"

Lynn ignored him and instead read the message window as fast as she could.

Mom, dad, are you there?

Guys, hellooooo? I can see your status says online. Answer please?

Hey, it's Alex!

And Madison and Jared.

Mom, Dad, please, we need some help. We're stuck in Britain.

HELLOOOOOOOOOOOOOOO?!?!?!?

The last entry was obviously desperate, and impatient. Lynn frantically entered a reply while Eddie picked himself up off the floor.

Alex! Its Mom here – you're where? How can we help?

Lynn jabbed at the enter key like it was a bug waiting to be squashed. It was a full minute before the next reply came, by which time everyone else had crowded around her, staring at the screen in anticipation, collectively holding their breath.

Mom! We're ok! We just got back from a weird place. The dragons aren't with us anymore. We'll explain later. Right now we need some help. We need a place to sleep, rest, and hide. Again, I'll explain later. We're in a caretakers house near the Amesbury Church. Amesbury, England. We don't know what to do, or how to get home.

Alex! Call the police and tell them to call us too. We'll be on the first flight to come and get you!

Mom, no! You can't call the police.

Lynn paused for a moment, despite her sense of urgency.

Why not? What did you do?

Nothing Right now, we'd really just like somewhere safe to go and rest. Any ideas? This computer is too slow to look anything up online.

"That young man is going to get a swift kick in the pants if he's done anything illegal!" Lynn grumbled.

Alex, give me a minute to look at where you are and come up with a plan.

We're near Stonehenge, in a town called Amesbury, at a church. The caretaker will be back any minute, so please hurry!

"I don't like the sound of that," Eddie said.

"No kidding," Lilly replied.

Lynn opened a new window to browse the Internet, searching for Amesbury church. After finding it, she entered a search for hotels and motels nearby, all of which were showing no vacancy. She switched instead to 'Bed & Breakfasts' and a minute later had a reservation for a four-bed room at the Amesbury B&B, pre-paid by credit card for immediate occupancy for 1 week.

"Why one week?" Eddie asked.

"It was for a week?" Lynn echoed, blinking. "Oh, sorry, wasn't paying that much attention."

Eddie just shrugged. "No problem. Book our tickets as soon as possible – I'll go pack a bag for us." Eddie ran out of the room into the downstairs closet. Moments later he whooshed by carrying two small pieces of luggage and ran up the stairs.

Alex, get you and your brother and sister up the street to the Amesbury B&B. It's a bed and breakfast.

Ok, thanks Mom!

Alex, it is at 36 High Street, with a reservation under Eddie Zedmore.

Ok. Thanks, Mom!

It should only be about 2 or 3 blocks up the street, based on this map.

Mom, someone's here, gotta go!

Alex?

Lynn searched the screen, but the remote user had logged off.

"Alex!" she shouted at the monitor. She waited several moments but snapped out of it when Lilly tapped her shoulder.

"I think you will need some plane tickets to England, don't you?"

Lynn thanked Lilly and returned her attention to the computer to find the next possible plane out of Calgary and into London.

Lilly took Richard's arm and headed back to the kitchen to finish their meals. As Lilly scooped another forkful into her mouth, she noted Richard was staring at her.

"They really have kids, don't they?"

Lilly nodded, swallowing. "Yes, what made you change your mind and believe us?"

Richard put his fork down. "Because even on *Candid Camera* they didn't book rooms and a flight to England just to pass off a joke."

Lilly was about to respond when her cell phoned beeped with a text message.

I think your Government contact was hit by the Order too. I have some leads to show you, though. Keep it quiet. And I think you and Rich should take a vacation to the coast.

Lilly put her phone away. Lynn had just finished booking their flight and was rushing upstairs to help pack.

Richard nodded to Lilly's pocket. "Who was that?"

Lilly glanced down and then back to Richard. "Oh, that? Just work. No worries."

Richard and Lilly promised to clean up and lock the house before they left, allowing the Zedmore's a quick escape to the airport.

The kids all heard someone stomping their feet on the small wooden approach to the front door at the same time. Alex hurriedly typed his farewell and closed all the windows. The computer was painfully slow, so instead of waiting for everything to close he simply powered off the system.

As Alex stood up, Jared grabbed his brother's elbow and yanked hard, pulling Alex into the kitchen and down the back stairs.

"Who's there?" called an old man, now standing just inside the front doorway.

Jared yelped, shoving Madison out the side door, and dragging Alex behind him. The old wooden screen door creaked and made a loud THUMP behind them. The trio ran as fast as they could, shouts for a constable and tyranny against the elderly and the church coming cascading behind them. None of them dared look back to see what was happening. Instead they drove each other onward in their sudden panic and fear, racing between some trees and a low hedge, turning left a few paces around another close building, and into a small parking lot. They slowed for a moment, when they heard a whistle being blown somewhere on the church side of the hedge. They jumped a low fence on the other side of the parking lot, turned left again while staying in the shadows of the fence until they got to a large cluster of trees, then turned right, passing through house yards and car parks until they returned to a street. They collapsed as one against a shed hidden by a large clump of bushes for only a moment, when a dog began barking at them only a scant two meters away, straining against a metal chain and collar. Their terror heightened, they were off like streaking bullets, passing four more buildings before coming out in an open field. Alex ushered his siblings into a line of trees on their left, getting out of the open air and back into shadow. Madison burst into tears while Jared started punching and kicking at a tree trunk. His frustration and anger, as well as the successive fright they had all just received, coming out in physical combat against the defenceless tree.

Alex watched the two of them, too tired now to protest or stop them. He knew they were both being too loud, and knew that Jared would only end up hurting himself, but Alex for the moment didn't care. He simply stood, mute as a mime, staring, catching his breath and letting the adrenaline even out in his system.

Jared stopped kicking and punching at the tree after several minutes. His knuckles, especially on his right hand, were raw and bleeding. But it had felt good to let out some steam, and there was enough bottled emotions within him still that the pain wasn't registering fully. He didn't clean his wounds, but instead let the sting of the night air come on them.

Madison continued to sob for many long minutes, getting slowly quieter and quieter, until she had no voice left to even whisper.

It was a full quarter of an hour before Alex was able to stabilize himself and gather his wits. He turned slowly and peered into the night to get his bearings, but couldn't possibly figure out where they had gone. *Alright, Alex,* he told himself mentally, his internal voice sounding to him just like his father, *you're in charge here, whether you want to be or not. You need to find the place mom booked, and get your brother and sister there. Hang in there until then! Once you are there, you can relax or break down all you want, but until then you don't deserve a break! Get moving, soldier!*

Alex stepped out into the field a short ways and scanned the nearby buildings. Nothing familiar and no signs. All the signage was on the roadside, which were two parking lots away from his current position. He made his decision and sucked in some air to steady him.

"Alright, you two stay here for a minute," Alex began.

"No," Madison cried out, jumping to her feet.

"You can't ditch us right now!" Jared flared.

"I'm not ditching you!" Alex hissed back. "Just stay here and be quiet. I need to find the place Mom booked for us to go. It'll be easier if I can run out on my own and then come back and get you."

"Oh come on…" Jared began, but Alex cast a sidelong glance at his brother, and Jared stopped, understanding the logic. It would be far easier for Alex to move around on his own, get his bearings and then come back for them, and walking alone he wasn't anywhere near as suspicious as all three of them would be together.

Madison continued to argue, but Jared held her firmly in place as Alex walked away across the field. Jared was finally able to get her to calm down enough to have her sit again against the tree. Jared helped her down, scraping his hand against the soft cloth of her shirt as he did so. Ouch! He yanked his hand back in pain.

OK, so, busting up my hands wasn't the greatest idea.

Jared sighed at his own foolishness, cradled his hands in his lap and crouched down beside his sister to wait.

Alex returned only minutes later, which was far too long for them. Silently Alex nodded to them and waved them forward. It was a short walk across the field and between a narrow opening of two buildings before they were on the street. Alex didn't wait to guide them to the corner, but instead pressed forward across the street, turned right and led them to the next intersection. Directly across the street from them was their destination, a welcome looking sign hanging over a doorway reading *Amesbury B&B*.

"That's where Mom booked us," Alex whispered, not sure why he was trying to be so quiet. The streets were deserted, and standing on the corner of this four way intersection they could see no other living person in any direction. Still, with everything that had been going on, he felt it was best to play the spy role for now.

A thousand questions entered their minds as they crossed the street and made it ever closer to the bed & breakfast: is this the right place? Do they know who we are from the police already and are looking for us? When will Dad and Mom get here? What if they ask to speak to our parents, or see a credit card?

When they made it to the doorway, Alex tried the door but it was locked. Swallowing hard and praying, he pressed the button for the doorbell. A pleasant chime sounded inside, and moments later a lovely looking woman arrived to open the door for them.

"Yes, may I help you?" she asked sweetly. Her voice was melodic, with a rich British accent.

"Uh..yeah…we're supposed to have a room here. Um…our parents, well, uh, our mom booked a room, I think…actually I don't even know if this is the right place or not."

To all of the kids relief, the lady answered with a great smile by opening the door wide and exclaiming, "Of course, dearies! You must be the Zedmore children your mother was talking about! I was on the telly with her, just now! Please come in! She mentioned that you were with friends, but with all the craziness with the ground shaking and all, you'd best be served here."

The bed and breakfast was a beautiful place, and the children would have enjoyed more of it if they could have. As it was, once their hostess had showed them to their rooms and explained where all the amenities were, each of them collapsed on a bed and slept for many hours, only waking to the smothering hugs and kisses of their mother, ten hours later.

Epilogue

A LEX AND JARED RACED each other to the back porch, sprinting hard but laughing all the way.

"I win!" Jared shouted gleefully.

"No, I touched the porch first!" Alex challenged.

"Maybe," Jared panted, "but I made it up to the back door first!"

The two of them continued to rationalize their own victory, Alex stating that the original parameters of their agreed race was to be the first one to the porch, while Jared maintained that even though Alex may have technically touched the porch first, Jared had continued on further, pointing out that by going the extra distance he was in fact achieving above and beyond the original task, and so he therefore got more points. Alex retorted that there were no points here, simply first and second.

The argument continued as Madison and her parents walked to catch up, Madison holding a fresh bouquet of freshly picked flowers, and Eddie and Lynn holding hands.

At the house, Eddie stayed outside to light up the barbeque, Lynn and Madison busied themselves in the kitchen, and Jared and Alex continued arguing, eventually replacing their argument with more tests of speed and strength, culminating in a wrestle match on the living room floor.

It had been almost a year since the dragons had been in their lives. Lynn had moved the computer monstrosity she had built into a spare room, just a door down from the kitchen. Eddie had insisted they didn't need all of the equipment set up any more because the kids were home, but Lynn had insisted. They were here before, they may come back again, and if they ever did Lynn wanted a warning of it.

Life had returned more or less back to normal, with the exception that Lynn had become an obsessive mother, protecting the children greedily from anything and anyone else. Now that she had her kids back she wasn't about to let them go flying off to another dimension again. In fact, she hadn't let the kids out of her sight for the last ten months, refusing even for Alex to have a sleep over at his cousin's place in town – she had instead insisted that the cousins came over to the Zedmore house; otherwise there was no chance for a sleep over, period.

Lynn had also kept the family busy. No more school – the kids were home schooled by private teachers. Any trip that Lynn needed to go on, whether for business or vacation or anything in between, the kids were all packed up and came with, teachers and all, and no questions asked. And Lynn had ensured that anyone in the family was always in contact, because she had immediately run out and purchased a new cell phone and data plan for herself, Eddie and all the kids, as well as for the teachers and Richard and Lilly as well.

The family had taken some time adjusting to life without the dragons. Alex was the hardest hit, not able to let go of his feelings or memories of Kishar for several months, and while he was never going to forget his best friend, he also realized that life had to go on.

Poor Richard had been mobbed by the kids when they saw him again, but the kids were hurt when he didn't recognize any of them. Richard spent a lot of time researching Amnesia, Alzheimer's, and any other memory-loss condition he could find, trying to put the pieces together of the great kids he didn't know. They eventually fell into a friendship of sorts, but it wasn't the same: there was always hesitancy there, a feeling of being unsure, and not at all like the Uncle Richard they used to know.

Trying to get Richard to remember, or believe in, the dragons was another task altogether. Lilly and Richard had both taken time off to try and help him sort out his memories, and his feelings, and went on vacation in Prince Edward Island.

Lunch was prepared, but the Zedmore family ate inside to get out of the heat of the day. They had already had a long Saturday morning hike and had more than enough sun. The cool shade in the kitchen was a welcome respite from the heat. Summer was here in full strength.

They talked about their walk and what animals or scenes they had seen that morning. The conversation drifted from topic to topic, until Alex spoke his thoughts out loud.

"I really wish we could have shared the morning with Kishar."

Lynn felt a pang of hurt in her heart, and Eddie looked at his son, worried that Alex's depression might suddenly return. Alex looked up and smiled.

"Don't worry, Dad, I'm not getting a mood or anything. I was just thinking of how good a morning we all had, and that made me think it would be really nice to share that with our cousins and friends...and then I thought of Kishar."

Lynn smiled, but it was Jared who responded first. "I think Rex would have liked it, too. *And* Rex would have agreed with me that I won the race." Jared finished by fixing his eye on his brother. Alex stuck his tongue out but didn't say anything.

"Penelope would have loved the sunshine," Madison agreed.

Eddie sighed heavily, out loud so all could hear. "I'm really sorry that it didn't work out, kids. I miss them too, but obviously not as much as you do. Who knows, maybe we'll see them again someday!"

Lynn put a hand to her temple. "Lord I hope not...."

She looked around the table to see four sets of eyes staring at her with a mix of emotions, causing some guilt to rise up in her heart. "Well, no...what I mean is that I don't want to have to be without you kids again. It was very hard on me the first time around, I am not sure that I could handle that again!"

Eddie put a hand on her shoulder in encouragement.

"We understand, Mom," Alex offered.

Jared nodded his agreement. "It'd just be really nice to see the dragons again. We miss them."

Madison agreed by nodding, but her mouth was full of her last bite of hot dog so she said nothing.

Eddie cleared the table and began washing dishes. Lynn sat and relaxed in her chair, chatting with Jared and planning a card game for the group of them to play. Alex stood up and stretched, not sure of what he wanted to do. Madison made her way out to the porch, dancing to her own spontaneous song of summer.

"Madison, sweetie, don't wander off! We're going to play a game soon, and have dessert too!"

"Ok, Mom!" Madison called back over her shoulder, prancing about in the late afternoon sunshine. She continued to dance and sing, wandering off the porch and out of sight.

As they were settling down sometime later to start their card game, a computer in the next room began bleeping loudly. Alex went to see what it was while Eddie and Jared prepared the decks, and Lynn called out the back door for Madison to come in. There had been several false alarms from the computer over the last year, so more than likely it was nothing but deer drinking at the pond, or some birds flying in, but Alex had never given up hope.

"Dad! Come quick!" Alex shouted.

Everyone felt their hair stand up on end. The room was still.

Alex was yelling as he flew through the kitchen and out the patio door. "Dad! There's something happening at the pond!"

A lump formed in Lynn's throat. "Where's Madison?"

With a mix of sudden panic and excitement, the family raced outside.

About the Author

Andreas resides in Calgary, Alberta, with his wife and children. He has been writing fiction for a number of years, and has been previously published online and in role-playing supplements for the RPGA Network. *Shard* is his first solo-authored published work.

Andreas has studied and worked in a variety of fields, truly being a jack-of-all-trades. He draws upon his wide and varied experiences to create as real a portrait as possible of the people and scenes described. Andreas is currently involved in a number of ventures, including online business and IT support work, but his real passion is being the Storyteller.

Look for more printed, online, and video work from Andreas in the years ahead!

CPSIA information can be obtained at www.ICGtesting.com
Printed in the USA
LVOW130337230513

335086LV00001B/5/P